Praise for *On Ravyn's Wing:*

"…great role reversal with (heroine) Ravyn taking the
powerful and violent alpha role with gusto
…characters exceedingly well-drawn…motivations and emotions
expertly put forth through dialogue and narration
…fully realized story with tales of vengeance, acceptance,
secrets, and of course romance.

Overall, *On Ravyn's Wing* offers something quite unique in the
romance reading experience…highly recommended for fans of
historical crossovers, strong female heroines and
thrilling revenge stories."

"…characterization and settings are solid and highly imaginable
with Cordero's clear and engaging narrative…gripping…
All in all, fans of the genre will find this a fine read."

"…well-executed and cohesive …time travel grabs the reader's
interest in the first few chapters. …streamlined journey back
to the 1800s that, although mysterious, is highly effective.
The settings are evocative, as are the characters…and sense of
authenticity aboard the *Retribution*."

- Readers' Favorite Reviews

On Ravyn's Wing

Mary-Lynn Cordero

Book One of
Sidesteps In Time

Free Spirit Press   *Barrie, Ontario*
Canada

ON RAVYN'S WING

Print Edition
ISBN 978-0-9784619-8-0

Copyright © 2018 by Marilyn Lamb

Cover Art Copyright © SelfPubBookCovers.com/ FrinaArt
Cover Fonts provided by Katie Sweet

Book Design: Marilyn Lamb/Free Spirit Press

This is a work of fiction. The use of historical locales, events and/ or characters are included as a part of the plot and character development, and are not a reflection of actual events. Those remain a product of the author's imagination or are used only as fictitious enhancement. Any errors in historical accuracy are purely the responsibility of the author.

Free Spirit Press
102 Shakespeare Crescent
Barrie, Ontario L4N 6B6
Canada
Free.Spirit.Press@hotmail.com

This work is dedicated to those intrepid readers who enjoy an epic story with complex characters and plot. Your support makes the time and effort of writing a longer novel well worth it.

Also, to my wonderful husband, who stands behind me in my pursuit of the often elusive muse and listens with quiet tolerance to my long conversations about the writing life. You know I love what I do.

"We must be willing to let go of the life we planned so as to have the life that is waiting for us."

JOSEPH CAMPBELL

"Revenge is an act of passion; vengeance of justice."

SAMUEL JOHNSON

Prologue

Nova Scotia—June 8, 2013

*R*ain lashed against the window, the strong winds of post-tropical storm Andrea setting trees swaying under leaden skies. Streams of rainwater swirled along the streets.

Rowena watched from her upper floor bedroom window, twisting the emerald ring on her finger. Her lips moved in silent, fervent prayer. If the storm grounded his flight and he didn't get here...

She shivered, hugging herself against the chill that rippled down her spine.

Crouching, she opened the old blanket chest under her window. She passed a palm over the heirloom journals it held, their leather covers cracked with age. So far, nothing had changed.

She glanced at the ring, its usual bright sparkle dimmed in the sullen light. This was the key to everything, past, present, and future.

Across the street, a gust of wind sent an old elm into a precarious lean. With a loud crack, an upper branch broke away. It spun down and landed with a thud. Rowena shuddered again.

The butterfly effect—her greatest fear—that one small change, even as insignificant as a falling branch, would have dire, far-reaching consequences. He had mentioned it in the journals. She believed his warning.

On her desk lay a newspaper, the article about his upcoming bookstore appearance circled in pen. Beside it lay a manila envelope with an old sketch on top. Rowena touched light fingertips to her high cheekbones. Save for the differing shades of their hair, the woman the drawing depicted could be Rowena's twin. More importantly, she would be the genesis of all their destinies. But first, he had to meet her.

All three were connected by more than blood. Their paths needed to converge as threads crossing in a precisely woven tapestry. And Rowena herself had to be the catalyst. Without her participation, none of it would happen. The irony—and immense responsibility—of her role sent another tremor through her.

She had been born to this task. The fascinating family stories told in her childhood had not prepared her for that revelation. When she turned eighteen, almost four years ago, she had finally been allowed to read the journals from the beginning. Then her father had given her the emerald ring.

"You have to see this gets into his hands." His jovial features creased in serious intent. "It's the ticket for his journey. Too many lives, past and present, are at stake for you to fail. If a single event falls out of place..."

Her heart stuttered in terror and she began to shake.

He had to make it. Timing was crucial. Nothing could change.

Not if any of them were to continue living.

Chapter 1

Nova Scotia, June 10, 2013

"Professor McQuaid, sorry it took so long to greet you. A minor employee crisis kept me in my office."

Farrel set his briefcase on the polished parquet floor. Maureen O'Halloran, the bookstore manager, strode into the alcove where he had been set up for the reading and signing. A petite woman in her late forties, she regarded him from twinkling hazel eyes under a cap of short-cropped, mahogany-dyed hair. They shook hands.

"Good to see you again, Maureen." A few patrons drifted over, eyeing him with mild curiosity. "I'm surprised anyone's attending after the storm."

"We were lucky in this end of the city. No major power outages and only a few reports of water damage." Maureen looked him over, a slow grin creasing her mouth and eyes. "I'm surprised you aren't wearing a pirate costume. It would suit your subject."

Farrel chuckled. "Bad enough my colleagues call me Professor Pirate. I'd rather not give them any encouragement."

The release of his book, *Swashbucklers and Sea Captains of the Atlantic Coast*, had coincided with the end of spring semester, launching him on a whirlwind cross-country tour. Several chapters touched on the War of 1812. Nova Scotia was his last stop before heading home to Toronto. He looked forward to getting back to routine after the last hectic six weeks.

"Oh, I don't know." Maureen tilted her head. "I think it suits you with your rugged good looks. You should get some knee breeches and one of those billowy shirts, maybe an eye patch."

"And a cutlass," he added, grinning. "Mustn't forget that."

Maureen laughed. "I think Security would have something to say there." She glanced over her shoulder at the growing audience. "All set?"

"I think so." He closed the book he'd marked for reading and gestured her to take center stage.

After a brief intro, she stepped back and let him take over. More customers wandered over while he spoke. He'd chosen passages relevant to the Nova Scotia area and read a few paragraphs before wrapping up.

"In conclusion, it can only be stated that our modern depiction of pirates and privateers has been highly romanticized, rendering the reality unbelievable, or perhaps, more accurately, unappealing to the modern mind in its constant search for entertainment."

Farrel scanned his audience, noting they listened with detached interest. He paused, arrested by an intent pair of cerulean blue eyes. They belonged to a young woman in the front row. She leaned forward, a tote bag clutched against her chest. Though she couldn't be much older than his grad students, her rapt focus set her apart.

A cough from an older man startled him. Breaking eye contact, Farrel cleared his throat.

"It cannot be overemphasized that the life of a buccaneer or the militarily supported prize seeker was far from easy and generally not long, even by the lifespan expectations of the era."

He closed the volume, lifting a hand to brush back a strand of hair that had escaped the leather strip tying it. Then he opened the floor to questions.

"How would being a buccaneer back then compare to *Pirates of the Caribbean?*"

The question from a bearded young man in the back row sent a ripple of amusement through the group.

"I'll assume most of you have seen the modern movies." Nods and murmurs of agreement met Farrel's query. "Outside of the obvious fact that they're the stuff of Hollywood fantasies, the realities of a pirate's or privateer's life were nothing like those romantic depictions. They faced violence from enemies, other raiders, or the authorities of the era. Not to mention storms at sea. Most of the historical focus of the War of 1812 centers on Upper Canada, but our East Coast played a crucial role as well. I've covered the key players and those incidents in my book."

He looked for the striking young woman, but she had vanished. Strangely disappointed, he sat down at the table to start signing books.

"Enjoy." Smiling, he handed a book to the last person in line. He glanced at his watch. The signings had taken over an hour, and the store's closing time neared. Rising, he lifted his denim jacket from the back of the chair and pulled it on, then bent to retrieve his briefcase.

"Professor McQuaid?"

He straightened and turned at the husky feminine voice.

The woman had come back. She was even more attractive up close with her animated smile and shining eyes. Her long ash-blonde hair was pulled back in a ponytail.

"Hello." He set his briefcase on the chair and offered his hand. The contact with her warm, soft grip gave him an odd sense of connection. In her other arm she held a copy of his book. "You seem familiar. Have we met before?"

"No, but it's a thrill to meet you now." She held the volume out. "I was afraid you wouldn't make it, with the storm."

"I'm just glad Ms. O'Halloran could reschedule. I enjoy visiting Nova Scotia, whatever the weather. It's like coming home." He'd lived in Nova Scotia until he was twelve, when his father had left, and his mother uprooted him and his sister to Ontario. He pulled a pen from his jacket pocket. "Who should I make this out to?"

"Rowena."

"Pretty name." He signed the flyleaf with a flourish. When he handed it back, she tucked it into the tote bag. "It's a pleasure to meet you, Rowena. Enjoy the book."

"I will. Your work is inspiring. I would've been so disappointed if you hadn't made it."

Farrel smiled at her breathless enthusiasm. "Are you studying history?"

"Yes, at Dalhousie." Her ponytail bounced as she nodded. "I have something for you." She dug around in the tote and withdrew her hand, balled into a fist. Farrel let her drop what she held onto his palm. The bright light of the overhead halogens caught a brilliant green glitter.

A ring. Gold, with a large, square-cut emerald. It appeared old and, if the stone was authentic, valuable.

"I want you to have it. To add to your artifact collection."

Brow furrowing, he looked up. "I usually collect marine artifacts. Not jewelry. It's pretty, but I don't think—"

"It's been in my family for two hundred years. My ancestors back then were...sailors, during the war." Anxiety creased her features. "I'd really like you to keep it."

Farrel brought the ring closer and squinted at engraved lettering inside the band. He made out a date—August 1813—and an inscription too faded to distinguish.

"This piece should be in a museum. I really couldn't accept—" He looked up.

Rowena had disappeared.

Stepping away from the table, he scanned the customers heading for the exit. She was nowhere in sight. "What the hell—?"

A blank business card lay with a manila envelope on the table. He picked them up. Where had they come from? He turned the card over.

Consider this my contribution to our posterity. R.

Our posterity? Mystified, he opened the envelope and drew the contents out part-way. A sketch. It too appeared old.

A woman with long, dark hair tied at her nape, delicate features and wide, expressive eyes gazed up at him. Farrel stared at her, bemused, then ran his fingertips over her face. Who was she? The ancestor Rowena said the ring belonged to? They did bear a resemblance. The artist had depicted an air of sensual vulnerability in her life-like expression, generous lips curved in a soft smile. He looked for a signature, but application of a protective film had smudged it into an indecipherable blur. He set the envelope down and looked back at the card with its cryptic message.

"You collecting phone numbers now?" Maureen's voice startled Farrel. "I saw the young lady leave them while you were distracted." She leaned closer to inspect the sketch. "Lovely. Who is she?"

Farrel slipped the card into his breast pocket then slid the sketch into the envelope and put it in his briefcase. "I have no idea." Unzipping the inner pocket of his jacket, he dropped the ring inside with his digital camera.

"Careful. You might find your pretty admirer following you back to your hotel." She chuckled. "Or maybe you'd like that...Professor Pirate."

Farrel shook his head. "Not quite the adventure I had in mind. How did sales go?"

"Great. It's too bad you have to cut your trip short."

"I couldn't reschedule the return flight any later than Wednesday. Guess I'll have to cram all my exploring in tomorrow."

"Exploring?"

"Yes, a couple of recently discovered coastline landing spots. I'm hoping to find some relevant artifacts."

"Like buried treasure?" They both laughed.

"You never know." He picked up his briefcase and stuck out his hand.

"Always a pleasure, Maureen."

Out on the street he searched the passersby for Rowena. If the ring was a family heirloom, why would she part with it? And who was the woman in the sketch? None of it made sense. Yet, the odd exchange left him with a feeling of déjà vu.

He'd have to try to find Rowena. But not tonight. A dinner speaking engagement with a local historical society would take up most of the evening. In the morning he would explore, wanting to return before too late in the day. Then he'd attempt to locate Rowena. Granted, he had little to go on but her first name. Maybe he'd contact an acquaintance in the history department of the university. Failing all else, he could hire a private detective on his return to Toronto.

He smiled at Maureen's comment about Rowena following him to his hotel. A little young for his tastes. Her blonde prettiness and vivacious manner reminded him of Julia, before—

He bit off the thought. Too much useless anger in those memories.

The past was dead and gone, with no hope of resurrection or restitution

Chapter 2

Farrel inhaled the clean, salt-laden air laced with underlying scents of fish and seaweed. The rush of waves brought familiar peace, a connection to the restless ocean tides. The nickname, 'Professor Pirate' crossed his mind, and he smiled.

Maybe he was the reincarnation of a buccaneer who died in battle, a storm, or at the end of a rope.

He wandered along the shoreline, unmindful to time in his search for an unexplored cave or landing spot. A low rumble sounded in the east. The waves rolled higher in the strengthening wind, slamming into frothing spray against the rocks. Dark clouds loomed on the eastern horizon, and lightning arced toward the roiling ocean. Its formerly deep blue turned gray and murky.

He would have to find shelter, soon. These storms blew in fast.

Glancing around, he spied a building on a bluff above. He backtracked to a path leading up.

The dilapidated structure appeared to be a long-abandoned storage shed or boathouse. It would have to do. Farrel ducked inside as the rain started in a gentle patter, quickly becoming a downpour. The wind drove the rain against the tumbledown walls, setting them shaking. Pelting through holes in the roof, it forced him into the one dry corner, praying the walls didn't collapse. He settled onto a crate and watched lightning, accompanied by booming thunder, streak across the sky in a spectacular display.

He pulled his camera from his jacket pocket. Something bounced onto the wooden floor with a metallic ting. Rowena's ring. He dropped to his knees, searching frantically. A wave of relief flooded him when his fingertips contacted the gold band. He slid it onto his pinky finger, wondering again why she had left it with him.

Settling back onto the crate, he snapped shots of the lightning through the sheeting rain. Flickering bolts of electricity cut through the liquid darkness, assaulting water and land alike.

Outside the window, a jagged fork struck a tree with blinding fury. The instant thunderclap and crack of splintering wood nearly deafened Farrel. He dropped the camera onto his lap.

"Damn. That was close." Smoke drifted up from the split tree as rain doused tiny flames.

His ears rang, and disorientation washed over him. He shook his head and tried to rise, but a stronger wave of dizziness overcame him. He sank back onto the crate. Resting his elbows on his knees, he lowered his head into his hands.

He swallowed bile. It must be electromagnetic fallout from the lightning. His head ached as the strange sensation wracked him. His chest tightened in a painful spasm. Was he having a heart attack? Close lightning could adversely affect the heart. Thirty-four was too young to die.

Mind reeling, he monitored his pulse while the storm abated. As the vertigo passed, his pulse settling into a normal rhythm encouraged him. He bent to retrieve his camera from the floor. Straightening, he waited for momentary wooziness to ebb and eased to his feet. A quick check of his camera showed no damage, and he tucked it back into his pocket.

He felt steadier, invigorated even, as he stepped outside. Sunlight emerged from the dispersing clouds, setting raindrops glittering on leaves and ground cover.

He breathed in the air, fresh with ozone and the scents of damp earth and greenery. Tipping his head back, he stretched his arms wide. The last of the ache leeched from his muscles, leaving only a light tingling in his fingertips.

At the path, he stopped, perplexed. Something had changed. The trees and other foliage looked...different. Not just fresher after the rain, but... altered. Thickened forestation surrounded the lightning-struck tree. Had he found the right path? He hadn't seen another. He glanced back at the building, startled to realize the wood looked less distressed by weather and time.

Giving his head a baffled shake, he headed down to the beach with its rolling dunes, rocks and driftwood. He took one last look over the ocean and halted in surprise.

A three-masted tall ship drifted in the deeper waters, its sails furled. A smaller boat rowed toward shore. Shading his eyes, he counted five occupants.

Three manned the oars, while the other two scanned the shoreline. He could discern little at that distance but their headgear; a tricorne hat, bandanas and tight woolen caps.

Farrel knew most of the sites that put on re-enactment displays. This cove wasn't one of them. Had the storm pushed the ship off course?

He ducked behind a dune to watch the approaching boat.

It slid from the rolling surf, and two of the men jumped out to pull it free of the water's grasp. The other three disembarked and tugged the craft further onto the beach.

They wore costumes of high boots, loose knee-length sailors' pants, baggy shirts and vests. One was smooth-faced and shorter than the others, who sported moustaches or beards. Two bore scars, one from his ear across a stubbly cheek to his jaw, another from nose to lip. The third wore an eye patch. The fourth appeared younger, his narrow moustache neatly trimmed.

Farrel rose and slogged over the dune toward them.

"Hey, great costumes." He skidded to a halt when three pulled vintage pistols from baldrics strapped across their chests. The others drew cutlasses. He put a hand up. "Didn't mean to startle you."

"Who are ye?" The smooth-faced sailor spoke in a husky tone laced with a distinct Celtic inflection. "What are ye doin' on this shore?"

"Farrel McQuaid. I got caught in the storm." He lowered his hand. "Mind pointing those weapons somewhere else?" None altered their defensive stance.

The slender lad stepped closer. Farrel gazed into pale cerulean-blue eyes fringed by thick, dark lashes in a tanned, oval face. Under the black tricorne fluttered a tail of black hair fastened by a tattered ribbon. "Again, sir, who are ye, and what be your business here?"

"Farrel McQuaid, as I said. Professor of historical studies at York University." Impatience sharpened his voice.

"York, ye say. Ye be from Upper Canada, then?" The lad lowered the cutlass slightly. The others maintained their aim at Farrel's chest.

"Yes. Upper Canada." He grinned. "You guys are good."

The four behind the leader gave Farrel stony looks.

"Good, ye say." The young sailor laughed, the sound more mocking than reassuring. "But, sir, I must inquire, what are guys?"

"Oh, I get it. You only speak the lingo of the day." He eyed the guns nervously. "Guys are men. Or boys. Or generic, either male or female, referring to a group."

The leader exchanged a look with the other men. They shrugged, shaking

10

their heads.

"'E's daft in the 'ead, Cap'n," growled a short, stocky brick of a man.

Ignoring this, the lad—Captain? Now there was a revelation—returned an icy gaze to Farrel. "And what would bring ye, a man of learnin', to this place?"

"Exploration. I heard a rumor this location was a pirate landing spot at one time. Being a historian, I wanted to follow up on it."

The captain scowled. "So ye heard a rumor, did ye?" He stepped closer, raising the cutlass until the sharp tip rested against the hollow of Farrel's throat. "I think ye be tryin' to lead us astray, Mr. McQuaid. I never been to York myself, but I know there be no university in the settlement. So, who are ye, truly? Mayhap ye be one of those Yankee spies they keep trying to insinuate amongst us."

"Yankee...spies?" Farrel shifted back to lessen the blade's sting. "Aren't you taking the re-enactment thing a little over the top?"

"Re-enactment?" Narrow brows arched. "There be no re-enactment here. Only the crew of the *Retribution* coming ashore to retrieve wood and hunt game." He glanced over his shoulder without lowering the cutlass. "Tie him up, lads. We best be moving on."

"No!" Farrel swept his arm up, knocking the weapon aside. His knuckles struck the tricorne in the wide swing, sending it flying. Lifted and caught by a gust of wind, it tumbled away. A long plait of black hair uncoiled down the captain's back.

Farrel froze, mouth dropping open.

The captain was a woman.

Her free hand flew to her head, and astonishment altered her harsh expression. Unshadowed by the hat, her face transformed to unexpected beauty. Then her features shifted back into hard lines, her mouth thinning and eyes narrowing. She swung the cutlass back to Farrel's throat.

"That was a mistake, sir." The furious glare from her light eyes skewered him. "Secure him."

Hands gripped his arms from behind. He jerked away, pivoting and aiming a punch at one of his captors. His fist stopped short at a piercing stab against the base of his spine, felt even through his jacket and shirt.

"Belay, else I finish this straightway."

Lifting his hands in surrender, he eased away from the point of her blade and turned. He met and held her irritated gaze. "I'm not a spy, so you have no right to hold me." He hoped she'd give in and relinquish the playacting.

"Aye, well, I've the right to detain strangers." The corner of her mouth quirked up. "Especially when they've no business in these parts." She lowered the cutlass as one of the men dashed to the boat. He returned, carrying a length of rope.

With pistols and cutlasses trained on him, Farrel saw no way out without getting hurt. But it galled when two of the toughs yanked his arms behind him and wrapped his wrists in the cording.

"This is ridiculous." He fixed a steady, offended gaze on the captain. Her expression remained cool and unmoved.

"Cor, Cap'n, lookee this." One of the ruffians unbuckled the leather strap of Farrel's digital watch and passed it to the woman. She gave it a cursory glance and shoved it into a pouch at her waist.

"I'll be keepin' this, if ye've no mind. And don't worry yourself, Mr. McQuaid." She leveled her cutlass point at his chest. "When we return, I'll see to your dispatching myself."

"Dispatching?" Farrel struggled with the binding, but found himself pushed to the damp sand. They pulled the rope to secure his ankles as well. "Good God, woman, you can't mean to kill me!"

"Can't I, now?" She leaned down, setting the flat of her blade against his neck. Her mouth curled into a smirk and her eyes glittered. "I'll make it quick. Ye'll hardly feel a thing."

Straightening, she jerked her head toward the boat. One of the men ran to lift out a pair of flintlock rifles. The captain strode to retrieve her tricorne from where it had caught on a piece of driftwood. Darting Farrel a sardonic grin, she dusted it off and clapped it back on her head. The five headed up the path.

Fuming in immobilized rage, Farrel watched them ascend to the woodland above.

What kind of craziness had he stumbled into?

Chapter 3

Ravyn Flynt paused at the top of the bluff and glanced down to the shore. The strange man laughed, a harsh, half-choking sound. He labored to loosen the rope at his wrists. She smiled in grim satisfaction. He would not succeed.

"Cap'n?" Mr. Fisher's question brought her attention to the hulking man. The others stood with him, awaiting her order.

"Go on." She waved them off with an air of impatience. "I'll gather kindling hereabouts."

They headed off, twigs snapping under their boots. Only Mr. Fisher glanced back, his long, deeply forged scar pulling his weathered features into formidable lines. She shrugged, and he turned away.

She resumed watching Mr. McQuaid fight against his restraints.

This man proved an unexpected and unwelcome complication. She had hoped to resume a southward course, but it might be necessary to return the prisoner to Halifax. She drew her lower lip between her teeth. Though she could dispose of him, something rankled over such a measure. Death need not be the sole option.

She chuckled, recalling his shock when she made that suggestion. He would not be the first man she had killed nor, God willing, the last.

Her mirth ended in a huff of exasperation. His discovery of her identity as a woman created an even more bothersome obstacle. Should he bandy it about that Captain Flynt was not the man she pretended to be...

Pivoting, she headed into the underbrush. She must think on the matter. Hopefully, the men would return with enough catch to replenish their dwindling food supplies. If not, they might be compelled to make port anywise.

As for Mr. McQuaid...

She paused in bending to gather twigs. She needed to restore her crew's numbers. How better to meet that end and protect her interests than by keeping the captive?

His odd manner of speech and dress piqued her curiosity. He seemed a cultured man, one likely not accustomed to the rigors of ship labor. She would have to test his worth.

Farrel struggled. His wrists chafed, fingers straining to the point of pain. Sailors, even re-enactors, knew how to tie knots. The rope didn't feel like nylon, either. It was rougher, more densely woven, probably hemp. As rigging, it would be tarred to strengthen and waterproof it, but this length was untreated. Under other circumstances, the attention to detail might have impressed him. But not now.

Gunshots reverberated from above. Would they take time to clean their kills before returning? He shuddered. Would he be another kill to deal with? Then reason reasserted itself. They were playing a prank, this whole tasteless artifice some bizarre gag. Maybe they weren't even hunting, just making him sweat.

A strident screeching and the whir of a multitude of wings diverted Farrel's attention. A flock of birds, scared up by the gunshots, darkened the sky as they fled en masse to the northeast.

Farrel frowned, squinting into the dense swarm. Wings flickered in panicked flight. Hundreds of them, maybe thousands, judging by the sky they filled, nearly blocking the sun. Feces dropped like foul white rain, splattering onto the rocks. Luckily for him, the flock didn't fly directly overhead.

One separated from its companions, drifting down at an odd angle. It landed on a piece of driftwood not far from where he lay. Farrel stilled, staring at the bird.

It had injured a wing and let it droop rather than fold it against its body. Larger than a mourning dove, it had a slate-blue head and rump, a gray back, mottled tail, and a wine-red breast. It regarded Farrel with as much curiosity as he did it, blinking a crimson eye and tipping its head.

Crimson eye? And a red breast? Though no ornithologist, he knew enough about birds from a historical perspective to recognize this one. A passenger pigeon. But it couldn't be. The last one had died in captivity in 1914. No, it had to be some other kind of shore bird.

A muscle in his arm cramped, and he shifted, drawing a quick, hissing breath. Squawking, the bird shook out its wing, careening drunkenly as it took flight.

Weary, Farrel let his head drop to the sand. The birds disappeared, their loud complaining calls fading. The sun blazed down, a burning wash on his skin. Something stung his neck. A blackfly. So much for the repellent he'd applied.

"Dammit." He tried pulling into a sitting position, only able to stretch the rope enough to allow a hunched curl as the bugs swarmed around him. Again, he strove to loosen the knots at his wrists. They didn't give a fraction. He couldn't tell if the moisture trickling along his hands was sweat or blood.

He raised his head on hearing voices. The sailors descended, the woman carrying kindling. The four men held two deer between them, tied upside down on heavy branches. One was a doe, judging by the lack of horns, the other a buck with a full rack of antlers.

Casting a grin Farrel's way, the captain led her companions to the boat to deposit their catch. Three of the men headed back up the incline.

"So, Mr. McQuaid." She stood over him, hands on her hips, mockery curling her full lips. "I've given some thought to your predicament." She crouched and extended a hand to wave away the miniscule pests harassing him. He met those icy eyes, hoping this was the moment she'd admit the ruse and release him. "Consider it your good fortune we be in need of crew members to replace those lost in a skirmish with your Yankee compatriots. Every pair of able hands can be put to good use aboard ship. Willing or nay." Straightening, she turned and strode to the remaining man by the rowboat, the tallest, most muscular, the one with the longest scar. He glared at Farrel, mouth twisted in a fierce scowl under his drooping moustache.

Farrel couldn't hear their conversation, but her sharp voice rose above the man's gravelly growl. With an abrupt slash of her hand in Farrel's direction, she pivoted away, ending the dispute. The brawny man crossed his arms over his barrel chest, baring yellowed teeth at Farrel.

Farrel met the baleful sneer with one of his own. "This isn't hunting season. You shot those deer illegally."

"Hunting season?" The Captain laughed. "I've no inkling where ye acquire your information, but all seasons are hunting season here. And who is there to argue the legalities of the catch?" She glanced around, sweeping one arm out. "Does ye see any of the King's men hereabouts?"

"You scared up some birds. What were they?"

A slender black brow arched. "Ye didn't recognize them? They're more plentiful than the trees hereabouts."

"But what are they?" He had to hear her say it.

One corner of her mouth twitched. "They're easily caught and make a fine pigeon pie. Had we more time, we'd snare a few for your dining pleasure."

"Pigeon pie? But..." Aghast at the notion of eating a bird that would be extinct—was extinct?—he let the protest hang. This situation became stranger by the moment. He changed tack. "So, you know my name. What's yours?"

"Ye may call me Captain." She smiled, and this time it reached her eyes, making them sparkle in the sunlight. "As to my name, 'tis Ravyn Flynt. Captain Flynt to ye, sir."

"You made that up. Creative, but it sounds like something from a romance novel."

"That may be, but 'tis my name nonetheless." She turned away as the other men descended, carrying more branches and kindling. When she strode back to the rowboat, Farrel wondered how they would fit with all that cargo. That speculation resolved itself when he saw another skiff lowering from the ship, two sailors scuttling down a rope ladder to take the oars. He transferred his attention to Captain Flynt.

A lady pirate. Not unheard of, but that she held the position of captain surprised him. It seemed more reasonable that one of the men would be in charge. Yet, as he listened to her issue orders, he couldn't deny her air of authority.

She returned and sat beside him in the sand, drawing up her knees and wrapping her arms around them. "So, Mr. McQuaid, are your sea legs steady enough for a voyage?"

He squinted at the distant vessel, unable to tell its class. Ignoring the question, he looked back at Captain Flynt. "I'm sure you'll all have a good laugh about this later, but I really have to get back to Toronto. Let's end the game so I can catch my flight tomorrow."

"Toronto? Flight?" Her brows lowered. "Now ye're speaking in riddles. Or tongues. Which be it, Mr. McQuaid?"

"Actually, it's Professor." He shifted in discomfort. "I've been tied up long enough. These ropes are bloody tight."

"Ye'll be staying as ye are till the lads fetch us. But don't ye worry." She pushed to her feet. "I'll be keeping ye company, along with Mr. Fisher here." She nodded toward the man standing a few feet away.

She left him, barking orders to the crew. They pushed the rowboat into the water and jumped in.

Ravyn Flynt trudged back and took her place beside him again. "What is this Toronto ye spoke of?"

"I meant York. Toronto is what the Natives call it." A fine sweat broke out under his jacket and shirt. "What year are you depicting, anyway?"

She appeared nonplused by his question. "'Tis the year of our Lord, 1813."

"Not 1812?" That would have seemed the natural answer.

"Has ye been asleep for a time, Mr. McQuaid? Or did ye mayhap bump your head?" She leaned in and lifted her hand, then hesitated. Seeming to come to a hard-won decision, she gave a negligible shrug of one shoulder before reaching to run cool fingertips behind his ear and over the back of his skull. Her touch generated an odd tingling and ignited something far more startling—desire for her caress, to move his head the tiny distance separating them and kiss those inviting lips. Unnerved by the notion, he jerked his head away. She straightened, frowning. "'Tis June of 1813."

The date engraved on the ring Rowena had left him; August 1813. A couple of months away. Coincidence? Or something more significant? Could Rowena have played some part in this?

Impossible. It seemed too complex a masquerade for a university student to pull off. He had to be the victim of a deluded—but very convincing, elaborately trained, and maybe delusional—troupe of actors. Or some weird cult.

"Come on. I've had enough." He projected anger into his voice. "Untie me, and we'll call it a day."

"And what day would that be, Mr. McQuaid?" She shrugged at his frown. "'Tis no need ye'll have of your lofty title when ye're swabbing the decks or scouring the holds." She returned her attention to the ship. The rowboat had reached the vessel, and a canvas sling lowered to load the deer carcasses. The other skiff was nearly at the shoreline. "Or mayhap your skills will be better served gutting yonder venison."

"I don't gut animals." A note of asperity hardened his voice.

"Ye'll be doing as ye're bid, sir. And bear in mind that 'Aye, aye, Captain' is the proper response."

Her sarcastic tone raised his hackles. "What makes you think I'll do anything you tell me to?"

She touched the grip of the cutlass tucked into a sash around her waist. "My sharp companion here can be most persuasive." Her chin lifted. "If ye're not wanting to become better acquainted, ye'd best do as I command."

Farrel glanced at the weapon and, remembering how the blade's tip had felt pricking his throat, bit back a snide retort. When he didn't respond, she rose and walked away. Farrel stared after her, shaking with anger, frustration, and discomfort.

He had to get away. Maybe some would pay for this kind of adventure, but it wasn't his idea of fun.

Yet, as he watched Ravyn Flynt in profile, her hard beauty struck him anew, along with an impression of familiarity. Was she an actress he'd seen on a television program or documentary? She had a flair for the dramatic, no denying that.

As though sensing his intense study, she turned her head, and their eyes locked. Her stark sensuality stirred an unanticipated reaction in his body.

She was gorgeous. Crazy or not, she personified a fantasy he'd harbored for years, of a beautiful, fiery-natured lady pirate. He almost laughed out loud at the ridiculous whimsy.

What the hell was he thinking? Once that rowboat reached shore, his chances of escaping stood somewhere between slim and nil.

Chapter 4

*W*hen they untied his feet, he stood, legs wobbling like half-set gelatin. Jaw set, he let them conduct him to the skiff, cutlasses and pistols discouraging any notion of running. They settled him on a middle bench of the boat, Ravyn Flynt and the burly Mr. Fisher across from him.

Farrel's thoughts turned to the historical timeline of the war. In June of 1813, the American naval forces suffered a defeat east of Boston Harbor in the taking of the frigate *Chesapeake* by the *Shannon*. The British had hauled the *Chesapeake* to Halifax.

"What day is it in June?" He studied the austere face of his lovely captor.

"'Tis the tenth day of the month." Curiosity sparked in her eyes.

"You know about the defeat of the *Chesapeake*?"

"Aye. 'Twas the talk 'tween the vessels we encountered in the past sennight." She leaned forward. "Be ye one of her crew escaped and fled up the coast?"

He didn't recall any of the *Chesapeake*'s crew escaping custody. Didn't mean it couldn't have happened, though.

"What if I am?" He lifted his chin in challenge.

"Then ye be captured again, Mr. McQuaid." She laughed in her soft, husky tone. It sent an odd shiver down his spine. "'Tis simply a change of loyalties ye be experiencing."

He repressed a grin. Maybe if he played along, she'd be satisfied and let him go.

"But I thought ye said your home is York."

Farrel met her frown with a slow curl of his mouth. Her lips thinned, but she said no more.

He twisted to look at the ship. Closer, he identified it as a battle class frigate with gun ports below and cannons on the gun deck above. Bow chasers on their swivels guarded the upper decks. Masts towered overhead, loose ends of rigging, the swinging ratlines, and shrouds creaking and snapping in the wind. A Privateer Jack flag flew from the mizzenmast. The Union Jack appeared in the upper left corner of a red background, distinguishing privateer vessels from naval ships.

Several hands stood at the rope ladder dangling over the open side of the lower deck. The mate at the skiff's bow caught the ladder and pulled it taut.

Captain Flynt and Mr. Fisher each took Farrel by an arm to pull him upright and help him step over the seats.

"How am I supposed to climb with my arms tied?" He looked down at the captain. Compared to his six foot two, she barely reached his chin.

"Mr. Fisher, if ye'd be so good as to render Mr. McQuaid assistance." Her bright eyes twinkled.

He found himself lifted off his feet and slung over a brawny shoulder like a sack of flour.

Great. All we need is green make-up, and I'm being hauled around by the Incredible Hulk.

Mr. Fisher mounted the swinging rope one-handed, and with a grunt hoisted Farrel onto the deck.

Some twenty or more men hung suspended in the rigging and along the yards, ready to loose the sails on Flynt's command. Others stood at the capstan on the quarterdeck, prepared to reel in the anchor. A quick count gave him a figure of about forty, likely more if any were below deck. Activity ceased as they regarded Farrel with varied expressions—some curious, more suspicious, while yet others took in his appearance with shrugs of dismissal.

"Back to yer stations, ye lazy buggers. Make ready to set sail at the Cap'n's order."

Farrel jumped at Fisher's roar behind him. The men scrambled to resume their duties.

He lifted his gaze to the masts and yards, awed at the raw beauty of the vessel. Momentarily, he forgot his situation in absorption with the environs. When he lowered his eyes from a study of the uppermost yards, Captain Flynt stood before him.

"She be a lovely prize, doesn't ye think?"

"Prize? It's not your ship?"

She laughed. "She be mine now. Renamed and outfitted for the service of the Crown. When it so pleases me." She pivoted and strode up to the forecastle deck. "Anchors aweigh, lads." At her shout, the deck hands turned the creaking arm of the winch that lifted the anchor. "Make all sail."

The men released the bunt and clew lines securing the sails to the yards, hauling the ropes to pull them up. The unfurled canvas caught the wind with a resounding flap, billowing to the limits of the lines as the hands adjusted and secured them while others adjusted the halyards below.

"Hands to braces. Hard about."

Several men hauled on the lines controlling the yards. With loud, protesting creaks, the long wooden beams swung around. The ship began a slow arc, generating a sick feeling in the pit of Farrel's stomach. He stumbled and would have fallen but for Captain Flynt's return to his side and her steadying hand on his arm.

"Ye be a wee bit under the weather, I see." She gifted him with a crooked grin and a spark of humor in her eyes. "We'll retire to the great cabin for a spell. Mr. Fisher." At her call, the man appeared by her side. "'Twould be appreciated if ye'd come and set him loose."

"Ye think it be wise, Cap'n?" The man's low growl accompanied a contemptuous curl of his lip as his glare rested on Farrel.

"This one's too busy regaining his sea legs. I doesn't believe he'll be trying to run." She laughed softly then headed toward the stern end of the ship.

Fisher gripped Farrel's arm in a hard, callused hand to hurry him along.

Sunlight poured through multi-paned windows angled along the stern of the large cabin they entered. A long table surrounded by chairs graced the center of the room. On the wall by the door hung a navigational chart that appeared authentic for the period.

Fisher untied Farrel's bonds. He winced as the painful return of blood flow tingled in his fingers. He rubbed his wrists. Red streaks stained his hands and the sleeves of his jacket. He stared at his fingers. Rowena's ring was gone. A shame.

Captain Flynt tossed her tricorne onto the table and retrieved a pitcher from a side cabinet along with three pewter tankards.

"Sit ye down, Mr. McQuaid." She nodded at a chair.

The ship tilted, and Farrel staggered. Captain Flynt set the pitcher and tankards down and ushered him into a nearby chair. Then she took his wrists to examine his injuries.

"I'll be tending these then we'll be finding ye suitable rigs." She put her hands to his shoulders to remove his denim jacket. He leaned forward to let her draw the garment off. She poured what appeared to be water into the tankards and extended one to him.

He took a long, refreshing swallow. The water eased the dry rawness in his throat. He'd brought bottled water in the car, but not intending to be long away, had left it behind.

Ravyn Flynt sat down and took a sip from her own cup. Mr. Fisher joined them after setting the rope by the door.

"I'm not a cruel captain," she said, though her face assumed a stern expression. "Not when my crew obeys and treats me as they ought." She studied him for a moment. "When did ye join up with the *Chesapeake*?"

He decided to carry on with his ruse. "Not long ago."

"And ye wasn't injured in the battle?"

"It didn't last long. No more than fifteen minutes."

"Your crewmates were easily defeated, then."

"It would seem so." He kept his response vague. Often re-enactment actors underwent intensive training to acquaint them with the events of the eras they portrayed. As deeply immersed as this troupe seemed to be, Farrel despaired they would never drop the pretense. It was well past time to call a halt. He drew a steadying breath.

"This has been entertaining, but it's time for a reality check. I'd appreciate it if you would convey me back to shore." He stood, ready to exit with what dignity he could.

"Sit down, Mr. McQuaid." The captain's voice held a sharp edge. She made as if to rise. Farrel fixed her with a glare.

"No. I need to get home. I'm done playing games." He lifted his jacket from the back of the chair. On turning, he found himself confronted by the formidable Mr. Fisher.

"Sit." The man gripped his arms and pushed him forcibly onto the chair. "Ye'll do as the Cap'n says, or ye'll be feelin' the sting o' the lash. Or mebbe we'll clap ye in irons till ye're ready to do as ye're bid."

"What the hell?" Farrel attempted without success to shake off the constraining hands. It was like trying to throw off a brick house. "You're nuts! All of you! When I get back to shore, I'll be contacting the authorities. And I will press charges."

"Will ye now?" Captain Flynt spoke from behind him, her voice low and silky. Metallic coldness glided along his neck.

He glanced down. A thin stiletto blade rested against his jugular.

"Then we may be obliged to detain ye for some time. And that, sir, is no game. As to your going home... " Her breath whispered along his ear, cheek and jaw as she bent over him. "The *Retribution* is your home now." She straightened. "I must apologize for Mr. Fisher." She gave the man a look, and he released Farrel's arms. "I see ye doesn't yet understand the way of

things on the *Retribution*. My men are loyal or they suffer the consequences."
She lifted the blade and moved to stand before him. "I thought we had that
established on the shore. No matter your previous circumstances, I be your
captain now. Or, if ye prefer, I can be the means of your death." She slid a
finger under his chin, at the same time once more setting the blade to his
neck. A frisson of static danced over his skin. "What say ye to that?"

The look in the captain's blue eyes was colder than ice, her jaw set in a
way that invited no argument. The razor-sharp knife sent a prickle of alarm
skittering down his spine.

Her grim expression left no doubt that if his answer wasn't the right
one, she would carry through with her threat.

Chapter 5

"Well, Mr. McQuaid?" Her finger moved in a deceptive caress under his jaw, leaving lingering warmth in its wake. With her other hand, she skimmed the stiletto knife over his neck. "Will ye die, or will ye submit?"

Several inappropriate responses leapt into his mind, but he bit them back. He flicked a glance at Mr. Fisher. The man's steely blue glare speared him with almost physical menace. What Ravyn Flynt lacked in sanity, that tough monolithic ape made up for in muscle.

Farrel swallowed and looked back at her. "Aye, aye, Captain." He put hard emphasis on her rank. "You win."

She smiled and eased the blade away. He jerked his chin from her gentle hold, not bothering to mask his contempt.

"Much better." Straightening, she tucked the knife into the sash at her waist and strode back to the cupboard.

Farrel ran exploratory fingers over his neck. No wetness of blood. Not even a scratch. Maybe it hadn't been as sharp as it seemed.

Captain Flynt returned with a cloth and bowl, into which she poured a small amount of water. Turning her chair to face him, she sat down and picked up his hand. She dipped the cloth in the water and brushed at the crusted blood on his hand and wrist. She looked up at him from under her long lashes.

"'Tis not so severe as it first appeared. I've seen worse on the lads when they slide down the rigging." She repeated the ministration with his other hand and wrist. Rising, she fetched a glass apothecary bottle from the cupboard and uncapped it. The light scent of lavender wafted from the container. She poured a little of the oily fluid onto her fingers and rubbed it over the abrasions. Farrel frowned.

"'Tis a combination of lavender and oil from the aloe plant. A healing mixture for mild injuries and burns."

Her long fingers encircled his arm and stroked his skin. Her touch, warm and soft despite visible calluses on fingers and palms, rasped over his skin. It incited that strange frisson along his arm which had swept over him earlier. He studied her bent head, unsettled.

Upon straightening, she considered him thoughtfully. "So, what are your skills, Mr. McQuaid? What position did ye hold on the *Chesapeake?*"

He almost said 'Captain,' but she must know the name of Captain James Lawrence. He had died from injuries, so that wouldn't work.

"Look, I don't have any seafaring skills." He spoke quietly, feeling defeated. "I know a bit about ships, but I've never done manual labor on one."

"So what did ye do on the *Chesapeake*, then?"

Farrel met her steady, quizzical gaze. Why wouldn't she give up the playacting?

"Mr. Fisher." The captain shifted her attention to the other man. "Take Mr. McQuaid and see what use ye can put him to."

"Aye, aye, Cap'n."

Farrel didn't trust the anticipation edging Fisher's voice. He risked a glance over his shoulder, almost recoiling from the grin pulling that ugly mug into an evil mask.

"Wait a minute. I—"

"Come along." A meaty hand clamped around Farrel's arm and yanked him up, nearly toppling him off his feet. "We'll soon see what's what with ye."

"Captain..." Farrel cast a desperate look her way. She shook her head, folding her arms. A smile tugged at her lips.

At the cabin door, Fisher shoved and released him. Farrel stumbled, barely keeping his balance. The men crowded along the decks glanced over.

Fisher strode onto the main deck. "Clew up the mains'l." His shout sent the deck hands scrambling to haul on the ropes that led up to the lowest sail on the middle mast. They released the canvas to fall into uneven folds against the yard below. "Ready about. Haul up the spanker."

Men at the stern pulled on the boom of the triangular sail and turned it inward.

"Get out here, ye lazy cockerel." Fisher stomped back and grabbed Farrel's arm. "Get to the lines." He pushed Farrel to where rigging ropes lay coiled on the deck. One of the hands indicated he should catch and hold an unmanned line.

Farrel turned back to Fisher. "Shouldn't I watch a video on how to do this first? Or read a manual?"

Fisher scowled, deep creases furrowing his brow. "Whate'er it is ye're wantin' to do, 'tain't done here. Ye learns by doin'. Now, get to it." Once more he strode away. "Slack off the heads'l sheets."

Hands at the bowsprit clambered into position, loosening the sails until they flapped in a thunderous vibration. The ship turned in a slow arc. Farrel braced his feet, gripping the line in front of him for balance.

"Aft let go!"

The line jerked in Farrel's hand, ripping over his already tender palms. He released it with a muttered curse and opened his hands. Rope burns flared red and throbbing on his skin. The man beside him snorted, making no effort to hide his grin.

Farrel tried to step away, but the swiftly uncoiling line caught his foot and sent him reeling backwards. He landed with a thud on his butt, pain knifing up his tailbone. The line tightened around his ankle, dragging him onto his back across the deck. His laughing companion caught the rope, arresting its release until Farrel sat up and pulled free of the snake-like cord.

"Ye'll get the way of it in time. If ye doesn't hang yerself first." The sailor's young but weathered features crinkled in amusement as he slackened the line and guided it until it tightened on the braces.

Farrel ignored his pulsing ankle. He pushed to his feet, gritting his teeth.

"Brace round forward."

This command had men hauling lines on one side and slacking them off on the other. Farrel lost track of who was doing what, noting only that a few hands took positions at the capstan and walked around it to pull straining sheet lines taut.

"Ease out the spanker."

Farrel watched, hands curled to alleviate their throbbing, as the boom swung out to its original place. The wind caught the repositioned sails and the ship lurched into a forward heading. Farrel swayed, feeling the movement as a rolling in the pit of his stomach.

"What're ye doin' standin' round, ye blasted sluggard?"

Fisher's growl raised the hackles on Farrel's neck. He met the man's denigrating glare with one of his own. He held out his abraded hands.

"I told you, I'm no sailor. At least, not to the caliber of these men." The last thing he needed to do was insult the listening hands.

"Aye, well, ye will be soon enough." Fisher gave the injuries a cursory glance, one side of his scarred face twisting in sardonic amusement. "Or mayhap ye'll be shark bait if ye doesn't mind the riggin' proper."

"No." Farrel let his hands fall. "I'm done." He set off, limping, toward the great cabin.

"Get back to yer station!"

Farrel ignored Fisher, pushing the cabin door open with his knuckles and stepping inside.

Captain Flynt looked up, a quill pen poised over the page of a book. Her brows lowered as Fisher stomped in behind Farrel.

"'E's nay more use than fagots in a rainstorm." Fisher folded his muscled arms and fixed Farrel with a scornful glare. "Ye should ha' let me end 'im." His scowl twitched into a grimace, "Mind, 'e may well end 'isself, as feckless as 'e is. The wee lad 'as more knack than this one."

"In my defense, I've never done this before and didn't know what to expect. You really should keep some instructional material at hand. I could've been badly hurt. If not for my jeans and hiking boots, my ankle would've probably snapped."

Captain Flynt settled back in her chair and set the quill on a blotting pad.

Farrel held out his hands. "This is bad enough."

She glanced at them then up at his face. "I've no inkling what ye mean, Mr. McQuaid. But it seems ye require more ointment for your hands." Rising, she retrieved the bottle of aloe and lavender. She uncapped it and poured some onto his flaming palm. "Rub it in. 'Twill ease the burning."

To his surprise, the raw stinging lessened as the oil penetrated.

Fisher cleared his throat. "Cap'n, if I be sayin' so—"

"Ye may return to your station, Mr. Fisher. And mayhap see to fetching our dinner in a bit."

Fisher's face darkened with anger. "Aye, aye, Cap'n." His harsh tone contradicted the acquiescence of the words. He stalked from the cabin, the door thumping shut behind him.

Still massaging his hands, Farrel sat down at the table. He stopped to look at his palms, still red but less painful. Inwardly fuming at Fisher, he listened to the rasp of the captain's quill. It stopped and she gave a huffing sigh.

Farrel glanced up. She sat with pen poised over the page, features creased in concentration. She exhaled in a gust of exasperation and dropped the quill back to the blotter. Muttering under her breath, she pinched the bridge of her nose between thumb and forefinger.

"Something wrong?"

She started, as though having forgotten he was there. "If there be one task that confounds me, 'tis the keeping of the logs."

"May I see?" He rose and stepped closer to her.

She lifted her eyes, seeming about to refuse. But then, she turned the page she had been working on to an earlier entry. Farrel leaned over her shoulder.

2nd June, 1813

Fare saling this morn. Rashuns running lo. Must mak landfall soon to replenish. Too lads doun with fever. No indicashun of rash or postyules. Mae be heet and lac of fresh fruts.

He looked up. "Did you write it this way on purpose?" At her perplexed look he elaborated. "I mean the spelling mistakes and choppy sentence structure."

"I know not what ye mean, sir. That is how I write."

"Oh." He thought for a moment. "I could help with that."

"Could ye, now?" Her brows lifted and interest sparked in her eyes. "I've ne'er been much for keeping proper records. My education was...negligible at best. Was that your position on the *Chesapeake*, then? Ship's clerk?"

Farrel stared at her, mouth opening then closing again. Should he resume his argument or play along? A shaft of sunlight through the window glinted off the hilt of her dagger. "Yes. You guessed it."

"Then mayhap we can come to some agreement as to your duties." She indicated the ledger with a small gesture. "Since it seems ye lack a sailor's skills, mayhap ye could keep the records for me."

"How will I know what to write?" The notion of tracking the daily happenings aboard intrigued him.

"I can tell ye. I've no way with words, but I'm thinking ye can compensate for that."

"You'll dictate, then. I can do that." It might even provide background research for his next book. The thought sparked an irrepressible grin.

Nodding in evident satisfaction, she gestured to the chair beside her. "Ship's clerk it is."

Farrel sat down, expecting to look over more of the entries.

Instead, she settled back in the chair. "Has ye family ashore? A wife? Children?"

"No. I'm single. No ties."

"Ah." She canted her head. "A widower, then?"

"I've never been married." He cast a sidelong look her way. "What about you? A husband hidden away somewhere?"

Wariness flickered in her eyes, then another emotion—incredibly like pain—that she hid by springing to her feet and striding to the window. For a moment, she stood with her rigid back to him. When she turned, her expression assumed its cold remoteness.

"That be no concern of yours." She met his stare with severity.

"I'm just curious. You do hold an unusual position, after all." Farrel rose. Her body tensed even more, hand gliding to her dagger. "If you're going to hold me against my will and dig into my private life, I think I have the right to know something about you."

Her chin went up a notch. "Your only interest need be your duties, sir, naught else."

"But—" Heavy footsteps behind Farrel arrested his protest. He turned.

Mr. Fisher entered, accompanied by a boy Farrel estimated to be about seven. Under a cap of tousled golden hair, wide gray eyes raked over Farrel as he and Fisher carried trays to the table. Captain Flynt resumed her chair.

"Hi there." Farrel too sat, smiling at the child. "And who might you be?"

"They calls me Liam, sir." The boy's gaze shifted from Farrel to Captain Flynt. "Cook says as 'e'll see to the guttin' of the venison tonight, so ye'll be 'avin' some on the morrow, Cap'n."

"Very good, Liam." She ruffled the boy's hair with an indulgent grin. "This is Mr. McQuaid. He'll be keeping the ship's records."

"Ye knows how to read an' write?" Liam bent his head, abashed. "Sorry, Cap'n. I be forgettin' meself."

"That's all right." Farrel spoke before Captain Flynt could respond. "Don't you?"

"Nay, sir." The boy lifted his head, eyes widening in awe. "But 'tis sure it must be a wondrous thing."

"Liam." Ravyn Flynt's gentle tone brought Farrel's surprised glance her way. Her eyes held the boy's, the tenderness of her smile pure beauty to behold. "Would ye be liking to learn?"

"Aye, aye, Cap'n." Delight shone from the child's eyes. "Does ye think I might?"

Captain Flynt turned to Farrel, assessing and thoughtful as she studied him. "Would it be something ye could do, Mr. McQuaid?"

Farrel remained silent for a moment under their expectant stares. How willing was he to acquiesce to the fantasy? Obviously, they wouldn't be returning him to shore any time soon, so what choice did he have? His gaze shifted from the waiting captain to Mr. Fisher, whose glower pinned him like an insect tacked to a backing board. Farrel's fight-or-flight instinct shot up on high alert, but he wasn't a total fool.

"Teach?" He shrugged. "Why not?" It seemed a reasonable request and certainly within his skill set. He returned his attention to Liam. "We'll start tomorrow. How does that sound?" He flicked a glance at the captain. She nodded her approval.

"Right fine, sir." Liam could barely keep still in his excitement. "Ye hears that, Mr. Fisher? I be learnin' to read an' write." He whirled back to Farrel and the captain. "Oh, thank ye, both o' ye."

Then the most astounding thing happened. The crusty, domineering captain held her arms out to the boy, and he lunged into them for a hug. Captain Flynt looked at Farrel over Liam's head, a full-on smile lighting her face. It chased her usual harshness, transforming it into a vision of true loveliness.

The unexpected sight sent a wave of heat spiking through Farrel, arousing a startling surge of desire. Ravyn Flynt did indeed personify his erotic imaginings. Despite his untenable situation, he easily saw her as the woman of those foolish daydreams.

He traded in his former fantasy for the tangible wonder of the reality before him.

Chapter 6

*R*avyn kept a watchful eye on Mr. McQuaid over their dinner of stew, hardtack biscuits and grog.

"I hope Cook spared us his usual measure of weevils in the biscuit batter." Gabriel Hennessey, the first lieutenant, flicked a twinkling glance at Mr. McQuaid. "If ye sees any bits o' black, they're not raisins, sir."

A look of revulsion crossed Mr. McQuaid's features, and he set the biscuit back on his plate.

Ravyn couldn't resist a small chuckle. "'Tis not often we find the vermin in our food, but Mr. Hennessey's advice is worth heeding."

"Thank you. I'll pass on the biscuit for now."

"Aw, they does no harm, sir. Oftentimes more meaty than the stew." The officers laughed.

"Has ye been at sea long, Mr. McQuaid?" asked Alec Morrissey, Ravyn's second lieutenant.

"Ah...no, not long."

Ravyn's men exchanged curious glances. They tried drawing Mr. McQuaid out, but he remained reticent.

He struck her as a man of inconsistency, claiming to a position on the *Chesapeake*, yet saying his home was York. Had he been pressed aboard the American vessel as well?

Still, the skills he offered were not often found in the common ranks. She would not waste such an opportunity for Liam. Nor let the chance pass to relieve herself of the onerous task of record-keeping.

She did not realize how intently she studied Mr. McQuaid until his reciprocal stare and a raised eyebrow brought her back to herself. Lifting her cup of grog, she smiled and joined in the men's laughter over some banter she had not heard.

At the meal's conclusion, she sent Mr. Fisher to fetch clothes for Mr. McQuaid. The bo'sun returned with shirt, waistcoat, breeches, stockings and boots.

"They belonged to one of the men we lost."

At Ravyn's explanation, Mr. McQuaid's expression shifted from curiosity to mild distaste. "I hope they've been washed and mended."

Mr. Fisher gave the other man a cutting glare. "They be good enough for the likes o' ye." He tossed the garments onto a chair. "Anything more ye be needin', Cap'n?"

"Nay. Ye may go about your duties." She waited for him to depart then turned to Mr. McQuaid. "We can afford to waste nothing at sea. We have no fancy laundering facilities on board, but a good boiling with lye soap should have cleaned any blood, and a few of the hands know how to wield a needle when 'tis needed." She rose. "I'll grant ye privacy to change."

Exiting, she found Mr. Fisher standing outside the door.

She fisted her hands on her hips. "I told ye to go about your duties."

"Aye, well, ye be me duty, Cap'n. I gave me word to yer da."

Ravyn sighed, letting her hands fall. "Aye, and ye'll ne'er let me forget it." She regarded the gruff sailor with tolerant affection. "Ye shouldn't have said what ye did about me keeping Mr. McQuaid alive. My reasons have naught to do with the looks of the man or his story."

"Aye, well, I sees the way he looks at ye, Cap'n, and I's not likin' it one jot."

She shook her head, smiling. "'Tis more likely he's occupied with plotting a way to escape than presuming on my virtue." Her levity dwindled to a pensive frown. "Not that there be virtue left to presume upon."

"Ye're a fine woman, Cap'n." Then he scowled. "I be speakin' too plain, beggin' yer pardon."

She gave a dismissive wave of her hand. "Ye've no cause to ask pardon. We go back too long a way for that."

"Yer da was a good man. He wanted ye kept safe."

"Aye, well, keeping me safe is a tall order, doesn't ye think?"

The door opened behind them. Turning, her heart gave an odd lurch as she looked Mr. McQuaid over. The billowy shirt and waistcoat suited him, along with the breeches and high boots.

"Ye look every bit the buccaneer." She could not refrain from teasing. "Had we any ladies aboard, 'tis sure they'd be falling at your feet."

A slow grin curled his mouth. "And will ye be falling at my feet?" His imitation of her accent amused her, the lilt so altered from the flat way he spoke.

She laughed. "Go on with ye, sir. Ask my crew. They'd say I'm no lady, just their captain."

A cough from Mr. Fisher brought her gaze to him and she sobered.

Mr. McQuaid folded his arms, fixing an irritated glare on the bo'sun. "There's something you forgot."

Ravyn precluded Mr. Fisher's response. "And what might that be?"

His gaze turned to her, altering to discomfort. She tilted her head, matching his stance, her brows arched in query.

"I'm not used to...going commando." He shifted in a way that indicated embarrassment.

"Ye'll have to explain, sir."

He flicked a glance from her to Mr. Fisher.

"Well?" Though she tried to keep her tone even, she heard the impatience in her voice.

"Without...underwear. Drawers. Do you have any?"

A snort from Mr. Fisher brought her attention to him. She recognized the twisting of his long scar as he grinned. A deliberate oversight, then.

"Ah." She chuckled, shaking her head. "Now ye be askin' for luxuries. What ye have is all we provide, outside of coats, rain gear and caps."

"Oh." He glanced down, not meeting her eyes. "Hazing the new guy, huh? Interesting twist. I'll put my own back on, then."

Ravyn smiled. "Ye're a puzzlement, Mr. McQuaid."

"Will ye be settin' 'im to deck duty, Cap'n?"

"Nay. The morrow will be soon enough to acquaint him with the ship. After the lessons, of course." She turned to Mr. McQuaid. "Would that be suiting ye, sir?"

He extended his arms in a gesture of grudging submission. "Whatever you say, Captain. You're the team leader."

"Team leader. An odd term, but I like it." She gestured to the door of the great cabin. "Mayhap we should further discuss your duties."

He preceded her inside, waiting until she seated herself before assuming a chair.

"We'll start with the ship's logs. They be in a sorry state." She leaned forward, folding her hands on the table. "As to the lessons, I'm thinking more than Liam might benefit." She gave a small smile. "Myself being one. I know the rudiments of reading and writing, but far from enough to keep proper records. And it may be some of the lads would like to learn as well."

He appeared surprised, but nodded. "Okay. At least two students, then."

He settled back in the chair. "Is it possible I might keep my own accounts? A journal or some such?"

She thought for a moment, then rose and moved to a lower cabinet against the far wall. Opening the door, she pulled out a brown leather-bound book. She carried it back to the table. "Would this suit your purpose?"

He flipped through the blank pages and nodded. "Perfect. I'll need a pen...quill, I suppose, if we're keeping everything authentic, and ink."

"There's plenty of those in the cabinets here." She felt surprisingly pleased that she could meet his requests. "I keep the log books in my quarters. It might be best to bring them here. Ye may consider this your study and schoolroom."

"Wonderful." He gifted her with an open smile. Again her heart lurched like a restless bird in her chest. One with a broken wing, she mused, unable to repress a reciprocating smile.

They spoke for a while about the logbooks and the lessons. The clang of the watch bell reminded her of the hour. She braced her hands on the table and rose.

"'Tis eight bells. I have watch duty four hours hence, so I'd best be getting some sleep."

"Watch duty?" Mr. McQuaid stood as well. "I thought the captain didn't have to do that."

"Aye, well, I enjoy the quiet of the night." She shrugged. "'Tis not as if ours is a navy vessel bound to official regulations."

"True." The corner of his mouth quirked up. "Pirates can do whatever they want."

"Pirates?" Her back stiffened, outrage churning in her gut. "I am no pirate, Mr. McQuaid. Merely a privateer, carrying out the duty of the King."

"Oh. Right." His amusement remained evident.

Drawing a slow breath, she tamped down her irritation. He could have no inkling the measure of insult his appellation sparked. "Need I show ye my Letter of Marque?"

His expression sobered at her sarcastic delivery. "No, of course not. Privateer it is, then."

A moment of tense silence hung between them.

"Ye might want to examine the older logs and try to make sense of my notes. I'll have Mr. Fisher take ye to your hammock when ye're ready for rest."

"Okay." He followed her out to the upper deck, to her stateroom located below the forecastle. He hesitated when she opened the door.

"Come in." She motioned with her head.

He stood in the doorway, gazing about while she fetched the logbooks from her desk. The room was nothing special; a bunk, the desk and a chair, banks of cabinets for storage, the sea chest containing her clothes and few personal belongings. But the way his eyes drank it in turned it to a wonderment.

She transferred the books to his arms. "I'll take ye back to the great cabin then bid ye good-night. Cook serves breakfast early, so ye might want to retire afore much longer."

"I can get there myself." He shook his head when she opened her mouth to protest. "I'll see you in the morning."

She let him go. If she were going to trust him, now would be a good time to start. Standing at the door, she watched his departure for the great cabin. The crew members on duty spared him brief glances, returning to their tasks as if he were not worth undue notice.

Though low in the sky, the sun cast enough light to admire the fine figure he cut, back straight, long legs moving with swift dispatch over the worn planking. The sun's rays caught his dark blond hair, setting it shining like burnished gold. Pleasing to look upon, but she must never forget the danger a man could pose.

Returning inside, she walked to the trunk and pulled out a brush. Uncoiling her braid, she smoothed the silky locks reaching nearly to her backside. Though tempted to cut it many times, she had promised Da not to. He had often told her it reminded him of the mother she'd never known. Even after his passing, the thought of shearing it off felt like a betrayal of his memory.

She rose to answer a tap at the door.

"Liam." She smiled down at him. With one fist, he rubbed his eyes and yawned. Over the other arm, an orange tabby cat lolled like a small sack of meal. "Ah, ye found Sammy." She took the cat, closing the door as Liam moved into the room. She held the feline up, looking into his furry face. "How many rats did ye catch today?"

"I found three, Cap'n," Liam supplied in the midst of another yawn. "I tossed what 'e left of 'em overboard."

"Only three?" She gazed into the cat's yellow eyes, her expression stern. "Are ye falling short on your duty, kitty? I know there be more than three makin' themselves at home below decks."

"Mebbe he's got most of 'em." Liam pulled a pallet and pillow from the cabinet under the bunk and placed them on the far side of the room, near the sea chest.

"Mayhap." She draped the unperturbed cat over her arm, stroking him as she watched Liam. The little boy pulled off his shoes, stockings and vest and plopped down on the pallet. "Are ye looking forward to learning with Mr. McQuaid on the morrow?"

"Oh, aye." He nodded, his eyes alight. "He seems a nice sort, Cap'n."

"Aye, so he does." Despite his oddities. "Ye'd best be getting a good night's rest, lad." She set the cat down, and he ambled over to the child to curl against him, purring and kneading Liam's tummy.

Ravyn smiled, her heart warming. If she never had children of her own to raise, at least she had Liam. Once he slept, she would evict Sammy to continue his rat hunting. But the little boy adored the cat, and when it came to Liam, no indulgence was too great. Especially after the hard life he had been forced to live when his parents died, left alone on the streets of Dublin at the tender age of five. Thankfully, she had rescued him from what would likely have been a short, tragic existence.

Ravyn sat down on the bunk and resumed brushing her hair. She braided it then removed her own boots and stockings to settle on the bed. Her thoughts drifted back over the day's events and the unexpected acquisition of Farrel McQuaid.

He seemed determined they were playacting, which baffled her. Or mayhap it was part of the ruse he tried to portray as an escaped crew member of the ill-fated *Chesapeake*. No matter, so long as he settled into his role as teacher and record keeper, she would let his oddities pass. Her own education had been gained in sporadic sessions with her father, but he'd had little time to devote to tutoring a girl. Only men needed to read and write, or so he believed, but she found herself eager to acquire more knowledge.

Especially about Farrel McQuaid. Where did he come from? He had an odd, flat accent—except when he imitated her. She stifled a chuckle. So he thought she might fall at his feet. Though not an entirely unpleasant notion, she would never be made vulnerable to the charms of any man.

He thought her a pirate. But he could have no inkling of what it meant to be in the unsavory clutches of a true pirate.

She did, and that ruinous experience shaped the very nature of her existence.

Chapter 7

$\mathcal{F}$arrel stared at the disjointed notes in the log. Dear God, she was worse than the least competent of his students. Had she been pulled out of the backwoods to play her role? Her lack—or supposed lack—of education stood out like a missing limb.

His hand shifted to the blank leather book. Maybe now would be a good time to start his own notes. He'd taken flint and tinder and lit a lantern hanging over the table. Though dim, it cast enough light.

Ravyn Flynt. His lips twitched. A little hokey, but it suited her. That black hair, those icy blue eyes and her tough nature. Except with the boy, Liam. Then she softened, her hard beauty irresistible. He shifted, the memory of her smiling at him over the child's head sparking an instant physical response.

Great. I'm getting a hard-on for the captain. Won't sit well with old Fisher.

He tugged at the breeches, irritated in more ways than one. When he'd returned alone, intending to put his briefs back on, his clothes had been gone. Damn Fisher. He'd probably carted them away while Farrel was with the captain. He needed to find them. His camera, solar charger and cell phone were still in the jacket along with his keys.

Far from soft, the material of the breeches chafed. Much more, and he'd be walking around bow-legged.

"God." He leaned his elbows on the table and laid his head in his hands. Authenticity was great, but did they have to play it so close? If he didn't know better, he'd almost think he'd fallen back in time. Whatever, he'd play along for now. The idea of keeping a journal and turning it into a book later intrigued him. Anything that translated into book sales was a plus.

Outside of missing his flight home, he had no urgent obligations. Though he preferred settling the next semester's curriculum early, he still had a couple of months. He'd also planned on completing outlines for another book, but that could be put on hold for this adventure.

He exhaled a huffing breath. Adventure? He'd been abducted and threatened with bodily harm. Several times. But in the era Captain Flynt and her sailors represented, pressing unskilled men into service was common. Even though they took the playacting too seriously on the one hand, on the other, he would likely not have the same research opportunity again.

He found the quill, a capped bottle of ink and a pouch of sand in a cabinet. Setting to work, he discovered using the archaic writing implement was not one of his finer talents.

The lantern sputtered. Laying the quill aside, he leaned back in the chair and yawned. He should get some sleep but didn't want to trouble the irascible bo'sun without the captain's tempering presence. He pushed the book away and folded his arms on the table to rest his head on them. Just for a few minutes...

"Mr. McQuaid?" A hand fell onto his shoulder. The captain's breath brushed past his ear.

"What time is it?" He straightened and rotated his aching shoulders.

"Past four bells. I was returning to my quarters when one of the lads said ye'd not left the great cabin. Here, I'll replenish the lantern."

The room had gone almost pitch black, the pale light of the moon casting minimal illumination through the windows.

"Sorry. I didn't mean to fall asleep." He rolled his head. It did little to relieve the ache.

"'Tis no bother." She stretched up to detach the lantern from its beam hook. In doing so, she swayed, and the soft curve of a vest and linen-covered breast brushed Farrel's cheek. Her scent was remarkably clean—soap and fresh air underlain by only a hint of body odor. Not an unpleasant smell, more a suggestion of musk that played lightly over his senses...and went straight to his manhood.

Embarrassed, he tugged at the front of the breeches then lifted his hand quickly away when she glanced down at him. Warmth rose into his face.

"And what occupation has kept ye from bed?" She carried the lantern to one of the cabinets.

"Writing. And checking your notes." He remained seated, willing the heat to recede. "Whether or not you've written that way on purpose, it makes your education appear..." He searched for a polite way to say it.

"Sadly lacking?" she supplied with one of those husky, damnably stirring chuckles. "'Tis something of which I am aware, and why I wish to avail myself of your teaching." The lantern flared to life, and she carried it back, stretching once again to hang it.

Farrel jumped up. "Let me." He took it and placed it on the hook.

"Ye've a fine hand, sir." She leaned over the table and pulled the open journal closer. "I hope ye doesn't mind me looking."

"Not at all." Thankfully, he hadn't noted any of his less honorable thoughts about the captain, and the page she examined contained only a few lines. He bent past her and flipped to the first page. "Mind you, I did have some blotting issues." He shrugged. "First time using a quill pen. Fascinating."

"If ye've ne'er used a quill afore, how did ye keep records on the *Chesapeake*?"

"Right." He scratched his ear with a rueful grin. "Never mind."

She turned and leaned her hips against the table, folding her arms. "Ye're a puzzlement, Mr. McQuaid. Ye've a way of speaking I'm not familiar with. What part of the Americas does ye hail from?"

"York." Then he shook his head. "Right. You think I'm an escapee from the *Chesapeake*."

"Did ye not admit it?" Her expression flowed into stern lines.

"Not in so many words. You came to your own conclusion. I just played along."

She unfolded her arms to grip the edge of the table. "Ye like being a man of mystery."

"That's it." He grinned. "Isn't it your job to figure out the truth?"

She straightened and laid an unexpectedly heavy hand on his shoulder. "My job, Mr. McQuaid, is to captain my vessel and ensure no spies or contraband gets past the Crown."

He winced as she increased pressure before withdrawing her hand. Reaching up, he rubbed the ache, rolling his head as he grimaced and tried to shrug away some of the stiffness.

"Sit. I can see ye're in pain." She indicated the chair. He obeyed, astonished when she stepped behind him and pushed aside the loose collar of his shirt to knead his shoulders. "Ye've been too long hunched over the books and sleeping in the same pose." She bent closer, exerting more pressure. He swallowed a groan.

Those hands might appear delicate, but he bet they'd be the envy of his masseuse back home. A shudder of pure pleasure vibrated through him. He leaned his head back as her kneading shifted to his neck then down to his collarbone. If he weren't careful, she'd have him all hot and bothered again.

"You have magic hands, Captain Flynt. Why the sudden kindness?"

She laughed, her breath warm against his ear and cheek. "Thank ye, sir. Why should I not be kind to my ship's clerk? 'Tis something I used to do for Da after a long day. But bear in mind these hands can kill as quick as cure." She wrapped them around his neck, exerting gentle force against his windpipe.

"Okay," he rasped. "Point taken." He lifted his hands to loosen her hold. They both froze when he enfolded her hands in his.

A heated, tingling pulse rippled up his arms, feeling like a static-charged breath. She must have felt it as well, for she uttered a soft sound of surprise. But she didn't pull away. Rather, her fingers twined with his. Farrel, with his head tipped back, stared into her pale blue eyes. Then he realized the sensation had spread, making a swift southward trek. *Damn.*

Her gaze shifted as if she sensed his awareness. She pulled free, taking a few quick, backward steps. He didn't blame her. They were alone, most of the crew asleep below deck.

She moved further away, making a pretense of looking at one of the open logs. Neither spoke, the captain focusing on the log while Farrel gazed in confusion at her bent profile.

What had that been? He couldn't deny a spontaneous attraction to the woman. But what in hell had that tingle meant? He'd experienced it after the lightning strike and in those brief contacts earlier, but not to this extent. The involuntary arousal hadn't been part of it.

"Sorry, Captain. It's been a...weird day."

"I'll show ye below." A tremor edged her low voice.

She extinguished the lantern, and Farrel followed at a tactful distance onto the main deck. She stopped at a hatch and lifted it.

"The hammocks are along the companionway here. I instructed one of the lads to hang one for ye."

"Thanks." Farrel stood studying her face, ethereal in the moon's pale light. "Captain..." He paused, not sure what he intended to say.

"Aye?" Her dark brows arched.

He ran a hand over his hair then swallowed hard. "Nothing. Sorry. Good-night."

"Good-night, Mr. McQuaid."

He descended the ladder, and the hatch thumped shut. His thoughts remained wrapped in confusion. Hell, he was exhausted, bone tired, ready to drop into the first hammock he saw. His mouth twisted in a grimace. Sleep likely wouldn't come easy between his situation and the stench permeating the hold.

But when one of the half-awake mates indicated where he should sleep, he rolled into the swinging canvas bed, his head barely settling before weariness claimed him in dark oblivion.

Ravyn stood on the deck, the light ocean breeze caressing her face.

What an odd, unpredictable man.

She stared down at her hands, remnants of the eerie warm tingle lingering on her fingers. She had never felt anything like the disquieting impulse to bend closer and touch her lips to his.

What manner of power did the man possess? How could he have tempted her to something she'd had no urge to do before that moment? At least, not since—

She arrested the thought before it fully formed. Dredging up grief best forgotten served no purpose. Even being aware of...that, Mr. McQuaid's physical response, had failed to quell the desire to experience...what?

A kiss? She shook her head with a shiver.

Whatever it had been, it could not happen again.

She must never forget the violence of which a man was capable.

Chapter 8

Sleeping in the hammock was more comfortable than Farrel anticipated.

However, he had little appreciation for the smells combined in the air, of unwashed, flatulent bodies, and stinks of unknown origin trapped in the air below decks.

When the watch bell rang, the men tumbled, groaning, from their hammocks. Farrel followed them to the galley, where Cook, a little rotund man with a limp, served up fresh baked bread, boiled fish and cheese along with a cup of watered-down wine.

Seeing the others crowded into the tiny mess cabin, Farrel decided to take his meal to the great cabin. When he entered, Captain Flynt, Liam and the ever-present Fisher were already there.

"Good morn, Mr. McQuaid." The captain's cheerful welcome eased his worry that their shared experience of the night before might cause constraint between them.

"Good morning, Captain. Liam. Mr. Fisher." He took a seat across from the captain.

"Mr. McQuaid?" Liam's piping voice caught Farrel's attention. He looked, still smiling, to the little boy. "When will we be havin' the lesson, sir?" Liam fidgeted in his seat, his eyes sparkling.

"Now, Liam, let Mr. McQuaid break his fast in peace." The captain patted the boy's hand. "'Twill be soon enough then for the learning. Finish your meal and go play till Mr. McQuaid is ready."

The little boy shoved a last chunk of fish into his mouth and darted out, still chewing.

"Do you have slates and chalk? I think we'll start with the alphabet. Return to the basics." After inspecting the heavy, grainy bread for 'little black bits' and finding none, Farrel broke off a piece.

"Aye, there be slates and chalk in the cupboard." Captain Flynt took a sip of wine. "Since I am already familiar with my letters, I'll leave ye and the lad to it."

Farrel met her eyes with a grin. "A refresher course never hurts. I'd like to find out how much you know."

A growl from the end of the table directed his glance to Fisher. The man's scowl deepened, and his eyes narrowed. "Ye'll be addressin' the Cap'n with proper respect, or I'll be takin' ye to task."

"Mr. Fisher, ye needn't be so surly. I'm thinking he meant no impertinence." She turned to Farrel.

"Not me, Captain." He lifted his hands in mock denial. "Maybe Mr. Fisher needs to learn a sense of humor."

She chuckled, and Fisher's cheeks turned a blotchy red. Uttering a grunt, the bo'sun rose, gathering his eating utensils, and stomped out of the cabin.

"I'd be cautious about upsetting Mr. Fisher." Despite the warning, the captain's lips remained curved in a smile. "He tends toward being a wee bit protective when it comes to myself."

"Yeah. Like an unmuzzled pit bull." Farrel returned his attention to breakfast, shaking his head when Captain Flynt stared at him. "By the way, where did my clothes go? I have to retrieve some things."

"They've been taken for cleaning. As to the things ye need to retrieve..." She rose and at one of the cabinets, pulled out a drawer. His camera, charger, cell phone, keys and watch lay inside. She fixed a penetrating gaze on Farrel, standing behind her. "Mr. Fisher thought they should be tossed o'erboard. I brought them here for safekeeping."

"Thanks." He felt around the breeches, realizing he had no pockets. "Guess I'll leave them there. But I'll take this." He lifted the watch and buckled it around his wrist.

"What is that, sir?"

"It's a watch...timepiece." He pointed at the digital readout. "These tell the time of day, the month and date, and the day of the week. It has a built-in alarm as well."

Captain Flynt touched the dial face with a tentative finger then looked back up at him. "So, what day of the week is it?"

Farrel looked at the letters. 'WED.' "Wednesday."

Captain Flynt's brow creased. "'Tis Saturday."

"Saturday? But..." That wasn't possible. She had to be playing head games with him.

"I've ne'er seen such a timepiece afore. Da had a pocket watch, but it had hands and only showed the time." She looked back at the dial. "This seems a more sensible way of displaying it. Though 'tis a pity the day is wrong." She ran a finger over the camera with its retracted lens. "'Tis another odd device. This as well." She shifted her finger to the cell phone with its screen and sliding keypad. "I'm curious as to their purpose, but we can discuss them later."

"Right." His lips twitched. Maybe part of their act involved pretending ignorance about modern devices. "About my clothes, though."

She closed the drawer and straightened. "'Tis likely they're on the boil as we speak."

"Okay." How would his garments fare if they used authentic lye soap?

"If ye be wanting the drawers, we'll return them once they've dried. Mr. Fisher mentioned the odd fastening on your trousers. It caused some stir among the hands who look to the washing."

"You mean the zipper."

"Zip...per?" She frowned. "I've ne'er heard of such a thing afore."

"Never? It's a convenient way of fastening all types of clothing. Other things, too."

"A recent invention?"

Farrel thought about what answer would go along with her act. The zipper's original forerunner hadn't been patented until 1851, a primitive parent of the modern version.

"I guess you could say that. It's not in common use yet."

Her look altered to curiosity. "Are ye an inventor as well as a professor?"

Farrel laughed. "I can't take credit for that. I'm just a teacher and author."

She didn't respond, but her study of him deepened before she turned away.

The lesson turned out to be more enjoyment than work. By morning's end, Liam mastered the alphabet with little difficulty. Farrel suspected he knew more than he let on. The boy's adherence to his role impressed Farrel but left him with questions. Whose child was Liam? The captain's? One of the other crewmen?

Many times Farrel's attention shifted from Liam hunched over his slate, chalk rasping as he printed his letters, to the captain at the end of the table. She appeared relaxed, her lovely face attentive, returning his glances with smiles. Though Farrel tried to stay focused, he couldn't help recalling their mysterious exchange the previous night. What could it have meant?

At the noon bell, they stopped for lunch.

"I think we'll conclude for today." He gathered up the slates and chalk. "You've done a fine job, Liam."

"Thank ye, sir." The boy's face glowed. "Mebbe on the morrow we can put words together?"

Farrel smiled at the child's hopeful expression and ruffled his hair. "Don't be in too big a hurry. Learning takes time. We'll see how it goes tomorrow."

"Aye, sir. Thank ye." Liam darted from the room.

Farrel stretched and arched his back, glancing toward the captain. "If you like, we can go over the logbooks this afternoon."

"Ye're certain it won't be too much sitting for one day?" She neared him along the table. "Or would ye be liking a change of scenery?"

"What did you have in mind?"

"Mayhap a tour of the ship."

The prospect intrigued him. "Could we confine the tour to above decks, then? It's such a lovely day." He hoped they would come across the communications room. If he knew its location, he could sneak back later.

The afternoon sun beamed down from a cloudless sky. Farrel, growing accustomed to the undulating decks, kept easier balance. He gazed up at the billowing square-rigged sails, seized again by wonder. Wanted or not, this was an adventure he'd likely experience once in his lifetime.

Captain Flynt led him from the forecastle to the gun deck, where the cannons pointed seaward in their secured mountings. Mr. Hennessey, the first lieutenant, joined them, adding to the captain's narrative with amusing anecdotes.

They took him to the helm on the quarterdeck and let him take the wheel. Mr. Lancaster, the helmsman, directed him in maintaining course, while the captain and Mr. Hennessey stood by. With the waters tranquil and their heading true, Farrel experienced the thrill of holding control of the huge, lofty ship in his hands. For a few exhilarating moments, he assimilated the experience—the salty tang of the ocean air in his nostrils, the wind at his back, the slow, rhythmic rocking of the deck. Each slight turn of the wheel exerted new pull as the rudder adjusted. The yards and spars creaked under the draw of the ballooning sails. Waves slapped against the hull, the bow plowing a steady path through the calm waters.

"Ye'd make a fine ship's master, with training." Teasing humor twinkled in Mr. Hennessey's hazel eyes as they left the quarterdeck.

"You think so?" Farrel floated on a euphoric high.

The captain let him look through the spyglass from the forecastle. He scanned the distant shoreline, noting little other than rocky beaches and forests. They headed south, so it seemed odd to sight no cottages, marinas or communities. No other vessels either—no sailboats or motorboats on such a fine day. He lowered the scope, pondering the lack of modern civilization. He had also heard no roar of aircraft overhead. That in itself was highly irregular.

"Where are we headed?" He relinquished the spyglass to the captain.

She gave him a sidelong look. "That is not your concern. Suffice it to say I have a course to follow in my duty to the Crown."

He exchanged a questioning look with Mr. Hennessey, but the lieutenant merely shrugged with a crooked grin.

Farrel's main disappointment came in finding no communication room. Not above deck anyway, which seemed the logical place. The chart room by the great cabin came closest. It only held charts and the navigation instruments, authentic for the era. Captain Flynt demonstrated how they worked, and the next hour passed in discussion of the constellational applications.

"Ye're a quick study, sir."

Farrel accepted Mr. Hennessey's unexpected compliment with a nod and smile. "Thank you. Maybe I can help with navigation some night."

Mr. Hennessey snorted. "I think ye be avoidin' the sweet smells of the holds."

Captain Flynt's chuckle ran along his spine like tingly fingers, the sensation new and not unpleasant. "Did ye not spend a comfortable night?"

"Comfortable enough, but the stink down there is overpowering. You're away from it where your quarters are."

She nodded. "'Tis true. There's little can be done to ease it."

Mr. Hennessey faced them, hands clasped behind his back. "If I might offer a suggestion, Cap'n, Mr. Eccleston's quarters remain vacant. Mayhap Mr. McQuaid would be more comfortable above deck."

The captain's return of his steady gaze was sharp. "They ought to be yours, Mr. Hennessey. As ye well know."

He shrugged. "I'm content in my space below, close to the men."

Farrel had noted the "space," barely bigger than a closet with its small, cramped bunk and cabinets. "Are you sure?"

"Ye're certain?" They spoke simultaneously, and Mr. Hennessey chuckled.

"Aye. Mr. McQuaid is more than welcome. I've accustomed myself to the reek." He bowed. "Now, I'd best be returnin' to my duties. 'Twas a great pleasure, sir." He strode away, calling an order to one of the younger hands.

46

The captain led Farrel to a door near her cabin. She threw it open and gestured him inside. It was smaller than hers, with a casement window and desk along with the bunk and cabinets. A trunk stood under the window.

"Did that belong to the previous lieutenant?" He nodded at it.

"Aye. Ye be wearin' his rigs, so ye're welcome to use what ye need."

"Thanks." He turned to her. "We should get to the logbooks. It might be necessary to start over in fresh ledgers."

"We're heading for port in a few days. I can procure more, if necessary."

That caught his curiosity—and hope—but he held his peace.

He followed her back to the great cabin. They sat side-by-side, the logbooks spread along the table. She translated her sketchy accounts from earlier in the year while he wrote in a new ledger. Coming across the accounting of the skirmish with the Americans, he looked up. Fabricated or not, it raised some interesting questions.

"That was a few weeks ago." He tapped the date with his finger. "You've had no opportunity since then to recruit?"

"'Tis oftentimes impossible to make port for months at a stretch, and not always easy procuring suitable men." She shifted closer, fingers skimming his on the page.

Their shoulders touched, but neither moved away. Instead, they gazed into each other's eyes as a warm stirring of air surrounded them. Prickles danced up Farrel's arm, accompanied by mild dizziness. Captain Flynt swayed closer, luscious lips parting. Farrel couldn't take his eyes from them, battling the temptation to test their softness. Yielding, he bent until his mouth hovered over hers, their shared breath inviting completion.

Her eyelids fluttered shut. Farrel lowered his lips to brush hers, their silkiness everything he had imagined. She tasted of fresh air and salt spray. The faint, musky scent of roses teased his nostrils

Time seemed suspended for a breathless moment before the warm tingling faded.

Captain Flynt jerked back, her eyes flying open. She sprang from the chair and moved around the table, arms wrapped around herself as though chilled. "'Twill take some days to make headway, but 'tis a start." She flicked a glance filled with uncertainty his way.

Farrel pulled sand from a pouch and sprinkled it over the writing to set the ink. It disconcerted him that his hand trembled. Captain Flynt gathered the books and stacked them at the far end of the table.

"'Tis nearing the dinner hour. I'll be seeing to reports from Mr. Fisher and Mr. Lancaster."

She left, her stride brisk, long braid swinging and head held high.

Did she experience the enticement he did when they touched? That kiss, ephemeral as it was, had reached soul-deep. At least, for him.

He grinned in wry amusement. Talk about opposites attracting.

Ravyn spent little time with the men, having spoken to Mr. Lancaster earlier. She saw no reason to question Mr. Fisher. Under his stewardship, the vessel stayed in tip-top order. He was harsh, but the men obeyed him without question. For that, she was grateful.

As for Mr. McQuaid...

What force linked them when they touched? It stirred something deep in her, and evidently in him as well. It felt like she'd always imagined St. Elmo's fire would if it swept over a body. But sweet, so sweet. She would never have anticipated succumbing to the impulse to kiss Farrel McQuaid. That moment with his lips brushing hers had been akin to a hint of heaven. A fleeting pleasure she knew could transform quickly into hell.

And what had she done but move him into closer quarters? How long afore he yielded to a man's primal urges?

"God's teeth." She gripped the rail with shaking hands. The sun danced off the waves, glittering like diamonds tossed on the sea. "This cannot happen to me again."

Mayhap she should have left him on the beach. But the way he'd spoken, making her think him a spy, had left her no alternative than to take him prisoner.

Prisoner? He was no more prisoner than any other hand. Truly, he held a freer and more advantaged role than many. She had granted him a position of privilege, both in task and accommodations. But what else could she do with the man? Lock him in the prison hold? Feed him bread and water until that fine physique dwindled to skin and bone? And where could he go at sea? No one would help him. At least she had found a use for him.

What was the truth of his situation? A man of mystery. Aye, that was Farrel McQuaid.

Even thinking his name set her shivering in some strange anticipation. Of what, she had no inkling. His every look and touch awakened something beyond bearing. Yet she couldn't deny instinctive trust in him. That baffled her. She had good reason to trust no individual man. Her crew was a different matter, charged to obey and protect their captain, in the role of a single entity.

Mr. McQuaid, on the other hand...

She closed her eyes, drawing a slow breath. Mayhap if she pretended that brief caress had not occurred, it could be forgotten. His presence mustn't become more than a minor distraction. Her reason for living could never be forgotten. Not until she achieved her final goal.

She had made a vow she intended to keep, no matter what or how long it took.

In no measure would she divert from her course.

Even if it meant the forfeit of her life.

Chapter 9

The dinner of roast venison and vegetables boiled in the drippings made Farrel feel like a king. The ocean air whetted his appetite so he ate with abandon, complimenting Cook's culinary skills and the prowess of the hunters. Even Fisher's dark looks couldn't dampen Farrel's enthusiasm.

"Almost worth missing my flight." He lifted his tankard of grog and saluted his hostess, dismissing her puzzled frown with a shrug. "To your health, Captain Flynt." He drained his cup.

She laughed at the toast, soft color flooding her face as the other officers at the table echoed him.

"So, ye enjoyed the day, did ye?" She proffered the pitcher to pour more drink into his tankard.

"Immensely. Liam's a smart kid. Given the proper guidance, I think he'll go a long way."

"That would please me." She settled back in her chair. "He's more treasure to me than all the gold on earth."

The little boy, tired after the day's excitement, had been packed off to bed. Farrel felt fatigued himself. Or maybe it was lassitude from the meal and the third cup of grog. The rum seemed stronger than he was used to, despite being diluted.

"Everything is so authentic. I really feel like I've traveled back in time. All we need is another ship and a battle to make the story complete."

Looks of puzzlement passed among the men. Fisher grimaced, shaking his head.

"I'm in no mood for more battles, Mr. McQuaid." Captain Flynt's tone turned icy, and Farrel peered at her. "Men die in battles, sir, and I've no wish to lose any others of my crew."

Farrel realized he had spoken without thinking. "Sorry. I got carried away. Of course you don't want any more battles. It would just be the icing on the cake."

Fisher rose, growling. "Ye be needin' me any longer, Cap'n?"

"Nay." She waved a hand without taking her eyes from Farrel. "Mr. McQuaid and I will be sharing some private conversation." She waited until Fisher exited with the other officers.

When they were gone, she stood and strode easily across the room. Farrel attempted to follow, staggering at a roll of the ship. The intoxication of the grog had hit his legs. The captain seemed unaffected. She returned with his camera, cell phone and solar charger and set them on the table. "Tell me what these are and how they are used."

Was this a challenge? Farrel collapsed back into his seat, squinting.

"This." She touched the phone. "It has letters and numbers on the little sliding ledge. How does ye use them?"

Should he play along or call her on the game? Farrel sighed.

"This is a cell phone. It's used for communication." He pressed the button to start the phone. "It has a series of numbers assigned to it. If you activate the communication, you can contact others with similar devices anywhere in the world." He glanced at the screen. The message "NO SIGNAL AVAILABLE" appeared. "Damn. I hoped there'd be some reception out here." That also nixed calling shore for help.

He glanced at Captain Flynt, gauging her expression. Interest mixed with skepticism in the arch of her brows.

"The letters on the keypad are for texting. You can print a message on the screen and send it to another phone. And you can use it to enter information, such as other people's numbers." Farrel pulled up a menu to show her a list of his contacts. The screen went blank, and the device beeped as it shut down. "Shit. The battery's dead." Frustrated, he shoved the keypad in and pushed the phone away. "So much for modern technology."

"And this?" Captain Flynt pulled the camera forward.

"This does something wonderful." He picked it up and pressed the power button. Musical chimes announced the start-up as the lens slid out. Captain Flynt drew back, her brows arching. Grinning, Farrel aimed the camera and pressed the shutter button. The flash lit the cabin for an instant.

Captain Flynt jumped from her chair to stand behind it. She blinked rapidly at the brilliant light, her hands gripping the chair back so hard her knuckles went white.

"Sweet Jesus," she breathed. "What was that?"

"Here. See?" Farrel turned the display screen to her.

She squinted at the image then uttered a low cry, recoiling. "What has ye done? Has ye stolen my soul?"

Farrel laughed until tears filled his eyes. She gaped at him, the color draining from her face.

"God, you're good." He wiped his eyes then turned the camera and pressed the review button. The photo revealed the shock on her beautiful face. He looked up to see her shaking.

"Ye've hexed me. Mr. Fisher had it aright. Give me that thing of the devil. I'll consign it to the sea." She made a grab for the camera.

Farrel jumped up, holding it out of reach. "No, it's okay. I just took your picture. It's like a painting, only done with light."

She withdrew her trembling hand and took another backward step.

"It's all right. Yes, it's your image but nothing to do with stealing your soul. Take my picture. Hold it like this." He demonstrated. "When you see me on the screen, push this button. My soul will be fine." He held the camera out, repressing a chuckle.

For a heartbeat, she stared at it then snatched it and headed at a near run toward the casement window.

"No! Don't." Farrel charged after her. He grabbed her hand and wrenched the camera from her grasp. "It won't hurt you. I swear it."

She whirled on him, features taut with shock and anger. Her eyes widened, her pupils so dilated little of the blue irises showed around them.

"Ye're a sorcerer." She continued to retreat. "No spy. A disciple of Lucifer."

Farrel set the camera on the table and edged closer to her. She backed away, bumping into chairs, without taking her gaze from him.

"You really think that?" Her terror seemed too extreme to be pretense. He extended a hand, and she nearly fell over another chair evading him. "Come on, Ravyn, cut the act."

But staring at her blanched face, he wondered.

In that moment, his belief that he'd fallen into the hands of an overzealous re-enactment company faltered. He remembered his dizziness and disorientation after the lightning strike. Then the birds—passenger pigeons—extinct in his time. The outmoded rifles the crew used for hunting, the lack of modern civilization visible on land or water. A vessel with no method of ship-to-shore communication—in fact, nothing fitting to modern standards.

Maybe something other than electromagnetic energy had enfolded him. Had the lightning opened a time rift that caught him like a fish in a net and dragged him through?

"Am I really in 1813?" He let his hand fall, trembling as an icy wave of incredulity swept over him. "Good God, how is that possible?" He touched his temple, lightheaded with disbelief.

A whisper of sound brought his attention back to the captain. She gripped her stiletto, mouth thinned in grim determination.

"Ravyn, what—" He took a backward step, hands lifted in repudiation, as she advanced on him. "I'm sorry if I upset you. The camera isn't dangerous. Neither am I." He backed off another step. "Put the knife away. You don't need it."

"Doesn't I?" Her eyes glittered as she followed his retreat. "It may be that Mr. Fisher had it aright. Ye're a deceitful devil, Farrel McQuaid. I'll be having no more of your tricks."

She lunged and pulled her arm back, aiming for his gut.

A rush of adrenaline supplanted his calm rationale. He grabbed her wrist as she made the forward thrust. The blade missed his midsection by a hairsbreadth.

She growled low in her throat, trying to wrench her arm free. He forced it back, squeezing to make her drop the dagger. Her other hand flew at his face, fingers curled.

He caught that hand as well. "Ravyn, stop."

A swift glance down caught the upward thrust of her knee toward his groin. It missed the mark when he pulled his hips back.

This was getting down and dirty.

He swept a leg behind hers, knocking her feet from under her. As she started to go down, she clutched at his waistcoat, pulling him with her. His weight drove the air in a whoosh from her lungs. He wrenched the hand holding the knife, loosening her fingers to release the deadly blade. It spun away. He pinned her legs with his and secured her arms on the floor over her head.

"Stop this," he hissed. Her arms and legs strained to escape, her breaths issuing in short, panting gasps. He tightened his hold on her wrists. "I'm not going to hurt you."

She stared up at him, going still. "Release me. Now."

The glint in her eyes entrapped him. His hold softened, and his thumbs rubbed in a caress. The softness of her sun-bronzed skin carried the musky scent of roses. "God, you're beautiful."

Her eyes widened. "Mr. McQuaid...Farrel." His name sighed from her lips. "Ye must let me go." She sounded tremulous, fearful. She shrank away from his touch.

Dumbfounded, he tried to discern what had changed. Then her eyes glimmered with a shattered, haunted look he recognized.

Julia. The thought lanced through his mind, painful and illuminating.

"God, no." Releasing Ravyn, he scrambled up and away, putting the table between them. He expected her to go for the dagger again. "I wouldn't hurt you." He stood poised to face her or run.

She tucked up her legs, gaze darting to the stiletto, then sidled away until her back rested against the cupboard. She stared at him, breathing hard.

"I'd never hurt a woman like that." He ventured around the end of the table, extending a hand.

She flicked a look at his hand then sprang up, her own flying down to pull another knife from her boot. Expression fierce, she advanced toward him.

Farrel shifted his hand, palm out. "Can we talk about this?"

She raised her arm. "Ye should ne'er have touched me. Were I to dispatch ye here and now, there'd be no questioning my reasons." She moved forward another menacing step.

Adrenaline surged through him. He seized her arm before she could start the thrust.

A light, warm ribbon of static-like energy flowed up his wrist. Surprise flashed in her eyes. The sensation expanded, winding around his entire body, binding them together. It stole his breath for a stuttering heartbeat, and drew them closer. Farrel lifted his other hand. It tingled when he cradled her cheek His fear faded, submerged by an overwhelming impression of familiarity. This woman—his fantasy—was real.

Yielding to the irresistible pull, he lowered his head, brushing his lips across hers. Then he kissed her, softly. The clatter of the knife hitting the floor registered as a vague aside.

Ravyn's thoughts whirled in confusion. She should be fighting this, taking Farrel McQuaid to task for his audacity. But her rebellious body rejected the notion.

When his lips touched hers and came to rest lightly over them, the strange feeling enfolding them left her breathless and hungry, longing for... something...more. She let her lips part ever so slightly, fascinated by the stirring that rushed from her mouth to make her breasts tighten and ache, her belly clench and that place at the juncture of her thighs suddenly throb with damp heat.

Dear Lord, she had never experienced such sensations afore! She wanted to lean into Farrel, feel his arms surround her in the same arousing manner the odd, warm current did.

Her grip on the hilt of the dagger loosened, and it slipped from her nerveless fingers. Farrel lowered her arm but retained his hold. His fingers caressing there sent frissons of pleasure up her arm.

This was unacceptable! She must stop this. Now.

But as much as her mind balked, her body succumbed. She angled into the hard line of his form without volition, his heart vibrating under the hand she lifted to his chest. She should push him away. Instead, her fingers curled against him, the brocade of his waistcoat rough under her fingertips. His scent invaded her senses—clean, musky male, far removed from the odors of her crewmen.

As Farrel gave a stifled groan, angling his mouth more possessively over hers, she became aware of the solid ridge of his manhood pressed to her belly.

That was danger. And unbearable pain and grief.

A sound of protest gurgled in her throat. She had to pull away from the threat, prove he held no power over her. But still, her body betrayed her, refusing to obey her silent command.

Rather, her arm slid around him. His hand in turn curled at her waist, then glided to her back, drawing her even closer as her eyelids fluttered shut.

The strangeness binding them had dissipated, but she did not know when. Though her mind continued to reel with disbelief and warning, she could not tear herself from the man's embrace. Pleasure engulfed her senses, ignoring every silent cry of outrage urging her to recoil. As her lips warmed under his, shivers, not of fear, rippled over her back beneath his caressing hand.

When the great cabin door crashed to the wall, her eyes flew open. Farrel released her, looking as flummoxed as she felt. For an instant, their gazes locked in mutual shock. He took a quick backward step.

Recovering, she swooped to grab the knife and straightened in one fluid motion. She aimed for Farrel's throat. He put up his arms in defense and retreated. She followed, preparing to deliver the blow.

Beyond her, Mr. Fisher stood with cutlass in hand, his expression fierce.

"Ye wicked, lustin' blighter. I knowed ye was settin' yer lecherin' sights on the Cap'n."

Caught between them, Farrel had nowhere to run. His gaze flicked from the stiletto to the cutlass. Which of them would deal the death blow first?

"Let me explain." He backed up, only to be stopped by the table.

"Ye ought to be flogged for e'en darin' lay hand to the Cap'n." Fisher's furious gaze turned to Ravyn. "Ye can give 'im the lashes yerself."

"Nay." Her glacial eyes pinned Farrel. "I think this merits a stay in the brig until he understands that touching the captain without permission is a grievous offense."

"Okay. I get it." Farrel lifted his hands in placation. "I didn't mean any harm."

"Aye, well, ye can think on the truth of that while ye're below." She lowered her weapon.

There was no point to further argument. The bo'sun snagged Farrel's arm in a crushing grip, dragging him out the cabin door.

"Mr. Morrissey." Farrel flinched at Fisher's roar by his ear. The stocky lieutenant hastened to answer the call. "We'll be takin' Mr. McQuaid here down to the brig and puttin' 'im in irons at the Cap'n's order."

"She didn't—"

"Silence. Ye has no say." The bo'sun shook Farrel as though he were a disobedient pup. He grinned, yellowed teeth appearing in the slash of mouth under his drooping mustache. "Yer fate be in my 'ands now."

He pushed Farrel down the steep steps into the lowermost bowels of the ship. Farrel grimaced at the noxious smells assaulting him. At the end of a narrow companionway, Fisher shoved him into a dark area with a wooden, steel-barred door.

The sailors secured his wrists and ankles in iron shackles. When Fisher saw Farrel's watch, he unbuckled it with a growl.

"I'll be tossin' this piece o' witchery o'er the side. Ye can retrieve it at yer leisure later." He chuckled, daring Farrel with glittering eyes to oppose him.

The chains attaching the manacles to the hull allowed little free movement. Farrel didn't rise to Fisher's bait. It was just a watch. Not worth arguing over.

Fisher sniggered as the door thumped shut.

"Keep close guard on 'im, Mr. Morrissey. 'E's a wily one." Fisher touched a fist to the bars, glaring at Farrel. "If I 'as me say, 'e won't be a bother much longer." He stomped away, laughing to himself.

Shaking, Farrel sank onto a plank suspended by chains from the hull. With a groan, he leaned his elbows on his knees and laid his head in his hands.

Was this where his life would end? In a distant past and a cold, pitiless ocean?

He ran his fingers over his hair, shuddering.

Chapter 10

*R*avyn lifted quivering fingertips to her lips. They still tingled with the reverberations of the kiss. She drew a tremulous breath, shocked by her body's lingering response. Her breasts still ached, and her femininity continued a gentle, insistent throbbing.

God's teeth! Was that how it felt to be aroused? Terrifying, and yet...

She toyed with the hilt of the knife, watching the play of lamplight across the blade as she turned it. Then she set it on the table. Her gaze fell on the device he had used to... What had he called it? Take her image? She picked it up. The cylindrical protrusion had retracted into the machine. It seemed harmless enough, but doubt nibbled at her. She should toss it into the sea, let its sorcery be swallowed by the ocean. Halfway to the window, she stopped.

What would happen if she threw it away with her image...her soul...still trapped inside? Would she die? Shivering, she set it back on the table. Logic told her such fear was foolish. She should get him to explain more about it. But would he tell her falsehoods to save himself?

She sank onto a chair, willing her trembling to stop. But the memory of their kiss, their physical closeness, her awareness of...that, the hard swell of his arousal, set her quivering even more.

Memories flickered through her mind. Terrible, fleeting visions brought her to her feet, uttering a cry.

"Nay. I will not think of it." 'Twas bad enough the memories haunted her slumber. She would not let them have her waking mind.

"Cap'n?"

She whirled. Mr. Fisher filled the doorway, his usually fierce expression tempered by concern.

"Aye?"

"Are ye aright?" He stepped inside. "Did 'e hurt ye?"

"Nay." She remained standing, at last bringing her tremors under control. "Is he secured?"

"Oh, aye." He grinned, the twisting of his long scar restoring his brutal expression. "I thinks ye should order 'im flogged, or, better still, sent o'er the side." He chuckled, a low, grating sound. "With 'is 'ands tied, so 'e don't give the sharks no trouble."

She lifted her chin. "I think the grog made him unmindful of his manners. A night in the brig should bring him to his senses."

"Ye wants to keep 'im?" Mr. Fisher's face creased in disapproval.

Ravyn thought on that. Mr. McQuaid seemed a skilled and patient tutor, and his talents could be valuable. Most importantly, Liam liked him. She just had to ensure that he understood the protocols. If not...

It felt strange to even consider keeping him. But it would be a shame to waste a life that could be put to good use. As for his devices...

Her gaze flicked to them.

"Let me toss those things o'erboard," Mr. Fisher offered.

Ravyn shook her head. "Nay. I'll see to them myself."

"Aye, aye." He appeared doubtful. "Ye're certain ye're aright?"

She didn't meet his eyes. "Aye."

Mr. Fisher left, shutting the door. Ravyn sat, fingers straying back to the image device. Had Farrel's capturing her within it caused that odd sensation linking them? Had it granted him the power to make her body respond? The notion was unsettling. She needed him to set her free.

That determined, she snatched up the contraption and strode from the cabin. She would make him release her from its spell. She would not be the victim of any man's lecherous designs.

Farrel lay on the narrow plank, staring into the near darkness. Dim light from a lamp on the companionway wall shivered across the ceiling.

Kissing Ravyn had been a mistake. Yet, he couldn't deny the deep pleasure of how she had responded. But had it been influenced by the strange...current enfolding them? He wanted to believe she had reacted on her own—his had been real enough—but it felt out of character for her. Not that it mattered now. He gave a huffing laugh. She had made their respective positions clear.

"Idiot," he muttered, lifting an arm to cover his eyes. The chain clanked and fell to rest cold against his face.

Ravyn Flynt had been sexually assaulted at some time. He was sure of it.

That look in her eyes had revealed more than words. He had seen that same shattered look too many times to discount its significance. And what had he done but hold her down the way any rapist would?

Julia. The pain twisted in his heart like a knife. Self-directed anger warred with guilt over making a woman feel that threatened.

"Mr. McQuaid."

Farrel started at Captain Flynt's voice. He lowered his arm and sat up.

She stood silhouetted at the barred door so he could not see her face.

"Captain." He spoke softly, not sure what to expect. Was she about to pass sentence? He stood up, chains clanking. She turned away.

"Mr. Morrissey, I'd have ye unlock the door."

"Aye, aye, Cap'n." The burly sailor edged past her. He turned the key and stepped aside when the door swung open.

"Bring a light for me."

The man shot her an uncertain look, but he retreated, returning with a lit lantern. Captain Flynt hung it on a hook overhead and faced Farrel. The neutrality of her expression revealed nothing.

"Seat yourself, Mr. McQuaid." She indicated the plank, and Farrel sank onto it. He saw she held his camera neatly concealed in her hand. Mr. Morrissey continued to stand outside the door. "Ye may leave us. I wish to speak to Mr. McQuaid in private."

"Aye, aye, Cap'n." The lieutenant's footsteps faded along the companionway.

"Captain, I'm sorry about what happened up there." Farrel jerked his chin upward. "I had to defend myself. Surely you see that."

"Aye, I suppose I does." Her dark brows lowered. "But ye had no right to touch me then...or after."

"Right. I should have remembered that. I acted out of instinct." He met her eyes again. "I'm truly sorry. This is like some crazy dream I can't wake up from."

She studied him a moment. "Who are ye, Farrel McQuaid? No more lies this time."

"I..." Should he tell her the truth? He could think of no alternative. "When you found me, I thought you were a re-enactment troupe. Where I come from, tall ship regattas are common during the summer."

"And where might that be?"

"York. Or, as I call it, Toronto." Was it possible to lead her into the account gradually and in terms she might accept? "I knew about the capture of the *Chesapeake* because..." He wasn't sure how to continue. "Historically, it was quite a coup for the British."

She lifted the camera, her hand visibly shaking. "Whate'er wizardry ye performed, I want it reversed. Ye must release my...image from this...infernal thing."

He sighed running a hand over his hair. The chains sounded unnaturally loud in the small cell. He rose and held out his hand. She relinquished the camera, pulling back hastily.

"I can erase the image, but it's not a release. You were never trapped." He turned the camera on, watching askance as she recoiled from the musical chimes and sliding lens. He touched the REVIEW button to bring her photo up, then showed her the screen. "Watch. Maybe this will ease your mind."

He pressed the DELETE button. The picture disappeared.

"There. Done." Fighting regret, he set the camera down.

She nodded, though her expression remained wary. He hoped his next words wouldn't earn him a death sentence. "You probably won't believe me, but here's the truth." He drew a slow breath. "My devices—the camera and phone, and the timepiece—you've never seen before because...they're not from this era. Neither am I."

She took a quick backward step. "What are ye saying?"

"Have you ever had a storm push you off course?"

"Aye, 'tis the way of the sea."

"I was caught in a storm, but instead of driving me to a different place, it dumped me in a different time."

"We found you after a short-lived bluster." Her eyes narrowed. "Does ye mean ye lost track of days?"

"Try two hundred years. I come from far into your future." Farrel held his breath as a myriad of emotions crossed her features. Incredulity, shock, fear, then, finally, denial.

"Ye must be mad." She turned to the door.

"No, wait." He surged forward, brought up short by the heavy chains. "Captain, please hear me out." She stopped, her hand on the latch. "I don't blame you for not believing me. I hardly believe it myself." He gestured toward the camera. "But how else would you explain devices that won't be invented for decades yet?" He leaned down to pick it up. "If you come and look, I can show you pictures of the place you found me, and more."

She didn't move, her gaze lowering to the camera. She blinked rapidly, as if remembering how the flash had momentarily blinded her.

"It won't hurt to look at them." He turned the camera back on and pressed the REVIEW button. "Come closer. It's all right."

She edged nearer, as though approaching a wild beast. Farrel turned the display screen so she could see it.

"There's the lightning. Then there's the shoreline." He flipped back through the shots he had taken, coming to photos of the hotel, and a few he'd had Maureen O'Halloran take at the bookstore. "That's me signing a book I wrote. It's why I was in Nova Scotia. These tall buildings are highrises." He looked up, encouraged to see Ravyn hadn't retreated. Rather, she leaned in, frowning as he scrolled through the images.

She stopped him with a fleeting touch of her finger at a photo he'd taken of a park. A few cars stood on the sideline of the image. "What are they?"

"We call them automobiles. Horseless carriages. They travel very quickly. Trips that take days now can be made in a few hours where I call home."

"Ye're teasing. Such a thing cannot be."

"But it is." Farrel turned the camera off. "Those pictures come from two thousand and thirteen. Exactly two hundred years from yesterday. It's too bad neither my watch nor camera show the year. But it does explain why the day of the week was wrong."

They stood in silence for a moment, eyes locked. Farrel needed her to believe him, but he couldn't tell by her shuttered expression.

"Ye've given me much to ponder," she said at length. "'Tis truly a fantastic tale."

"No argument there." His lips twisted in wry humor. "I'm not going to do anything to endanger you or the crew. Truth be known, I'm the one most at risk here." He lifted his shackled wrists in emphasis. "I leave myself at your mercy. I can be useful. Haven't I shown that already?" He waited, but she only gazed at him with questions in her eyes. "I'd like to keep on with the lessons and the logbooks, if you still want me to."

After a moment's consideration, she gave a slow nod.

"I'm still not certain what to think of your wild tale, but I will offer ye the chance to prove yourself." Then she tilted her head to gaze up at him. "When ye...kissed me. Can ye explain what caused that...odd feeling that came o'er us?"

Farrel shook his head. "I don't know what that was." He held her gaze with quiet intensity. "It's only happened since I...arrived here." He lifted a hand in denial. "It really has nothing to do with me." He frowned. "At least, I don't I think it does."

A visible shudder passed through her. "Aye, well, I would like to see Liam's education continued." Her gaze turned severe. "If ye keep the common protocols in mind, I may be disposed to set ye free."

"I apologize for my behavior. I don't know what came over me. Or maybe I do." She gave him a sharp look out of the corner of her eye. "It won't happen again."

"See that it doesn't." Her chin lifted and she met his eyes with direct authority. "If ye conduct yourself with propriety in future, we may forget it e'er happened."

"Of course." He glanced down at his manacled hands.

But he would never forget. He wanted her with an ache so deep, it took his breath away.

Ravyn summoned Mr. Morrissey to release Mr. McQuaid. The lieutenant did so without question, though his expression betrayed bewilderment. She let Mr. McQuaid retain the image device, concealing it on his person as they ascended to the upper deck. There, he faced her.

"May I return to the great cabin? I'd like to make some notes in my journal, if you have no objection."

"Aye, ye may." She glanced to where Mr. Fisher stood on the forecastle, glaring at them, arms folded across his barrel chest. "Conduct yourself prudently, sir."

"I will. Thank you." He gave a small bow and strode away.

She waited until the door of the great cabin closed before returning her attention to Mr. Fisher. He stomped down the stairs to join her.

"Ye released 'im. What're ye thinkin', lass?"

She drew herself up. "Mind your place, sir. 'Tis my choice whether to set him free or nay."

"After what 'e done?" Bushy brows met over his steely eyes.

"He offered apology." She kept her tone even. "He understands the way of things now."

"Does 'e?" Mr. Fisher looked unconvinced. "I'm not trustin' 'im one jot."

Ravyn stared him down, wondering at her own actions. The story Mr. McQuaid told went beyond fantastic. She might even be a fool to believe him. But something in his despair demonstrated he fed her no falsehood, unless he truly was mad. Yet, somehow, she doubted it.

"I knows ye're not a child anymore." Mr. Fisher's murmur diverted her attention back to him. "Truly, a woman worthy of 'er own will. But I'll not be shirkin' the promise I made yer Da. Not like the last time."

"We'll not discuss that." She spoke crisply, averting her face. "'Tis in the past and best forgotten."

"But ye's nay forgotten." She felt his searching look as he studied her profile. "Nor 'as I. 'Twas my shortfallin' that day. I'll not let it 'appen again."

She bent her head, shaking it as a low laugh fell from her lips.

"How often must I tell ye, 'twas not your fault. Ye were in battle, not able to be at my side every minute." She looked up. "Ye must forgive yourself, Eli. I've forgiven ye long since. Not that there was reason for blame at the start."

"Aye, well, I'm not likin' the way that cur dealt with ye. Nor the oddities 'e 'ad on his person, nor the strangeness of 'is clothing. 'E's not to be trusted, I say. If ye won't keep 'im in the brig, ye ought to be orderin' 'im flogged."

He was right. If any other of her crew had assaulted her as Farrel McQuaid had, even in self-defense, they would be dealt forty lashes. But she couldn't bring herself to issue the order, convinced Mr. Fisher would derive too much enjoyment from administering the punishment. Nor would it be a fair call to make on a man not born in their time and schooled in their ways. If that were the truth.

"Ye knows naught of his circumstances, Eli. I've given him fair warning. Be patient. I'm thinking he may prove himself more worthy than ye credit."

She turned and walked away, fully aware of his intent stare following her.

Chapter 11

*R*avyn sat on her bunk, shoulders slumped in weariness that went beyond the physical.

The vivid recollection of Farrel holding her down had awakened the terror that he might ravish her, make her re-experience the terrible way a man used a woman. Then, afterwards, his kiss and his body's reaction to their closeness...

She hid her face in her hands, shuddering with the effort to repress a sob.

She wouldn't cry. Nay. She would ne'er again shed tears over that horrific day. Nor would she be subjected to such degrading treatment. She was Ravyn Flynt, privateer and independent woman, captain of her ship, her own destiny. No man's plaything. Ever.

She removed boots, stockings and waistcoat and sank back with a sigh. Something jumped up on the bed, and a furry head rubbed against her face.

"Sammy." She rolled onto her side and pulled the cat against her. She had forgotten to put him out after Liam fell asleep and lacked the energy to do so now. Settling her hand over him, she closed her eyes. The low rumble of his purr soothed her drifting thoughts, and she let herself flow into the sanctuary of sleep...

Farrel stayed in the great cabin well into the night, writing and trying to sort through his muddled thoughts

It was 1813, not 2013. How could it have happened? He glanced at his camera, touchstone to a reality he could no longer grasp. His whole world was changed beyond recovery. Even returning to shore would only be a new source of confusion. He'd had his life laid out in organized accomplishments, past, present and future.

Now his future...had become the past.

How could he ask Ravyn to believe something he could barely fathom himself? He tipped his head back, closing his eyes.

Before yesterday, she would have been dead for centuries. He gave a bitter, barking laugh. Dear God, he must have frightened her half to death taking that photo. But not as much as she had frightened him.

He picked his camera up. Better preserve the battery as best he could. It wouldn't last forever—he laughed at the incongruous notion—but he'd keep it for the "special" moments in whatever life he had left. Maybe if he kept it charged up by a sunny window, some future descendant might be able to retrieve and reproduce the unbelievable history of his life.

He put the camera, solar charger and cell phone in the drawer, pushing them behind a partition. Later, he would take them to his cabin. If anyone but Ravyn found them, he suspected what life he had left would be short. Might still be, if the overprotective Mr. Fisher had his way.

He wrote nonstop, committing to paper his fall through time and the incredible adventure he had stumbled into. That done, he sank back on the chair, exhausted. The earlier adrenaline rush had leaked away, leaving him achy and ready for rest.

He hoped Fisher had retired. Not much scared him, but that monolith of antipathy put the fear of God into him. Men could disappear without a trace in this time, often at the hands of some unknown enemy. In this case, Farrel knew where the danger lay.

Rising, he extinguished the lamp and opened the great cabin door. Lanterns augmented moonlight illuminating the decks. Farrel peered around but didn't see his nemesis. Only a few men were left on watch, and they paid him no more than passing attention.

Inside his cabin, he leaned against the door, heaving a puffing breath of relief. So far, so good. That in mind, he pushed the bolt into place. No point in tempting fate. He was too tired to deal with more fallout tonight.

He sat down on the bunk and lifted a foot to remove his boot. A sudden feminine cry brought him to his feet and out the door in two strides.

It came from Ravyn's cabin.

Ravyn woke to the sound of sobbing and realized it was herself.

"Cap'n?" Liam's sleepy voice beside the bed coincided with a knock at the door. The boy darted to open it. "Mr. McQuaid." Liam spoke on a half-yawn.

"Ravyn. Are you all right?"

She sat up as footsteps advanced into the room. The cat had fled, probably when the dream had started her thrashing. Her cover was gone, likely tossed onto the floor.

"Aye." She whispered, fighting to control her tears. "'Twas naught but a dream."

"It was about tonight, wasn't it?"

She kept her head bent, unwilling to look at him and acknowledge the truth.

"Is the Cap'n aright?" Liam's voice trembled.

"She's probably had a nightmare. Nothing to worry about, kiddo."

"Go back to sleep, Liam. I'm fine." She stood. "Ye oughtn't to be here, Mr. McQuaid. 'Tisn't proper."

"I heard you call out. I'm really sorry—"

"Mr. McQuaid." The tears still clogging her throat rasped in her voice. "I thank ye for your concern, but 'tis done. Ye may return to your quarters."

"Very well." His head inclined in a nod and he strode to the door. There he paused, looking back, a shadow against the paler darkness. She felt the intensity of his stare and met it, chin lifting, refusing to speak. The door closed behind him.

"Cap'n? Are ye certain ye're aright?" Liam returned to his pallet, still sounding frightened.

"I'm fine, Liam. Go to sleep."

"Where's Sammy? I needs me kitty." His tone quivered on the verge of tears.

"He likely slipped out when Mr. McQuaid entered. Just go to sleep."

The child said no more, and Ravyn settled back on the bunk. She lay listening to the soft music of the waves against the ship and the softer susurrus of Liam's breathing. After that dream, sleep wouldn't come again. Nor did she want it, if that was where it took her.

Rising, she pulled on her stockings and boots. 'Twould be far better to walk the decks than lay wondering when her ghastly memories would revisit her.

Farrel lay on his bunk, angry and at a loss. He'd wanted to reassure Ravyn of her safety, but she had reverted to her stern, invulnerable persona.

He'd known women were treated like property in this era, downtrodden and often abused. The possibility that Ravyn Flynt with her independent nature and austere authority could have been raped inspired a rage Farrel had spent years battling. *Bloody, controlling bastard.* If it were true, he could choke the life out of the unknown son-of-a-bitch himself. Just as he'd wanted to do after his sister's assault.

Grief twisted his heart. Julia hadn't been able to live with the violation. No amount of counseling, no efforts on his part to help her had spared her. She'd taken her life, unable to deal with her sense of helplessness and loss.

And now Ravyn had had a nightmare, probably because of the way he'd held her down. If she had been brutalized in the past, it made sense the reminder would prompt a flashback.

Footsteps passed his door, and he knew without doubt Ravyn hadn't gone back to sleep. Did she spend her nights pacing the decks, pretending to carry out duty while avoiding dreams of a painful past? Fresh fury washed over Farrel.

He rose, pulling on his own stockings and boots and snatching the dress coat from its hook by the door. She wasn't the only one sleep would elude. He'd rather pace the decks with her than try inviting rest that wouldn't come.

Ravyn watched the moon sink over the water, the silvery path it cast disappearing into the horizon.

"Beautiful night."

She whirled with a sharp intake of breath, not having heard him come up behind her.

"Mr. McQuaid." She clenched her hand, halfway to her boot, and pressed it to her breastbone. "Ye should ne'er creep up on me like that."

"Sorry." The moon's pale light revealed his rueful smile. "I forgot your hair-trigger reflexes." He shrugged. "Couldn't sleep and heard you leave your cabin. Thought I'd keep you company. No point in wasting the moonset." He nodded where the orb hovered with its last arc resting on the merging ocean and sky.

"Aye." She spoke softly, regretting her earlier brusque treatment. "It gives me peace watching the moon set o'er the water." He stepped closer, and she felt the heated closeness of his body. She could not repress a shiver.

"You're cold." The rustle of cloth accompanied his words, and his dress coat settled over her shoulders. "You should take better care of yourself."

"Ye're my mother now?" She glanced over her shoulder to his serious expression.

"If that's what it takes."

Biting back a retort, she returned her gaze to the ocean. Above, the sails whispered and snapped in the light breeze, and the low murmur of crew members conversing from their stations punctuated the night's serenity. Farrel leaned his arms on the rail.

"You're a strong woman." He glanced at her with a look like tenderness softening his expression. "But even strong women need someone to confide in now and then."

She lifted her chin. "I need no such thing."

"Everyone needs someone to talk to sometimes. I know I do right now." He stared out over the water.

It occurred to her that if his tale were true, he must feel displaced, lost and uncertain in his new situation. She felt bewildered enough by the revelation, and she wasn't the one claiming to be adrift in a strange time.

"I might have reacted in haste," she finally said. "Your odd device unsettled me."

His abrupt laugh brought her attention to his face. He gazed at her, incredulity in the lift of his brows. "Any more 'unsettled' and I'd be at the bottom of the Atlantic. Between you and Mr. Fisher, I thought I was a goner."

Though not understanding the words, his meaning wasn't lost on her. She smiled in response. "Aye, well, despite my words otherwise, I cannot help but feel glad I didn't stab ye." Her teasing tone sobered as she stared at him. "Were I to believe ye, 'twould bring a new aspect to the situation."

Farrel nodded, frowning. "I suppose since I'm stuck here for the foreseeable future, I'd better get used to living on a ship. I have nothing and no one with whom to connect." His gaze shifted to her. "Except you, of course."

"How would ye e'er return to your time?" His supposed dilemma piqued Ravyn's curiosity.

"I don't know." He looked away again. "If I don't know how I got here, how can I possibly know how to return?" He laughed again, a harsh sound in the quiet night. "It's probably a good thing I'm a historian. At least I know something of where and when I am."

Ravyn couldn't repress a surge of sympathy. "Well, ye have a place on the *Retribution* for as long as ye need it so long as ye follow the rules of protocol."

Seized by a contradictory impulse, she touched his arm, the action hidden by the draping of his coat. He started to pull away then paused, studying her expression with questioning eyes. She kept her gaze on his, giving his arm a gentle squeeze.

When his hand slipped over hers, she didn't withdraw or rebuke him. Rather, she let the warmth of his touch seep into her skin. She steeled herself for the odd sensation that linked them, but nothing happened. Relieved, she relaxed.

"Thank you. I don't know what I'd do otherwise." His fingers caressed the back of her hand, and she shivered.

"Were I not to give due consideration to your fantastic tale, ye'd still be in the brig, or mayhap worse, by now." She met his eyes, "If ye be telling me true, ye must be careful. 'Twould be naught I could do if your...oddities raised doubts."

When he nodded and lifted his hand away, Ravyn experienced a distinct sense of loss.

"I will, don't worry. I rather like living." He stepped back. "You should get some sleep."

"Aye, Mother." Her light, teasing tone brought a smile to his lips. She remembered how those lips had felt on hers, tender and stirring as that strange warm breath united them. She shivered again. "I can look to myself well enough."

"No argument there." He gave a slight bow. "Good-night, Captain."

Once he had walked away, she realized he'd forgotten his coat. She drew it tighter about herself, strangely chilled for the lack of his presence.

Chapter 12

On first waking, Farrel wondered if the previous evening had been a fantastic dream. Opening his eyes to the clang of the watch bell and calls of the crew, he realized the truth.

He assessed his surroundings, trying to absorb the impossibility of it all. A quote from one of Sir Arthur Conan Doyle's Sherlock Holmes stories crossed his mind.

'Once you eliminate the impossible, whatever remains, no matter how improbably, must be the truth.'

Then it occurred to him that the famous author wouldn't be born for a few more decades.

He laughed, throwing an arm across his eyes to block out the morning sun. Whatever happened from now on, real or impossible, he'd been tossed into the middle of it. As Captain Flynt said, he had to be careful and do his best to fit in. Until a viable alternative presented itself, if one ever did, he'd modify his daily life to his new environs. He had no other choice.

He was spared the overbearing presence of Mr. Fisher over breakfast. Farrel hoped it wouldn't be the last time. Liam monopolized the conversation, leaving Farrel and the captain unable to discuss the previous night. She regarded Farrel with quiet understanding, her manner unchanged. For that, he was thankful.

Setting up for the morning lesson, he turned at the sound of multiple footfalls and murmurs entering the room, followed by the scrape of chairs. It appeared some of the crew had taken up the captain's offer of the opportunity for learning to read and write. Ten men, some younger hands, others old salts, ranged around the table, eyes on him in expectation.

"We'll have to do this in turns." He scanned the young, smooth-faced lads and the older, bearded and mustached men. "I only have a few slates."

"Aye, well, they'll be attending 'round their duty shifts." The captain spoke from her place at the end of the table. "We can obtain more slates when we make port."

It would take some creative juggling but wasn't impossible. First, he needed to determine their skill levels and divide the sessions accordingly.

Almost a full-time job. He added it to the daily logs and transferring the older records.

With the afternoon lessons ended and the students departed, Farrel replaced the slates and chalk in the cupboard. When the great cabin door clicked shut, he turned, expecting either Captain Flynt or Liam.

Mr. Fisher filled the space. He held a cat-o'-nine-tails, the nine knotted cords wrapped around the short wooden handle. Tapping it against the palm of his other hand, his steely eyes fixed on Farrel.

"Mr. Fisher." Farrel shut the cupboard door before turning back. "You want something?"

"Aye." The cat-o'-nine-tails slapped against his palm. "I wants to be certain ye knows yer place on the *Retribution*."

Farrel didn't trust the gleam in the big man's eyes. Stepping to the end of the table, he kept its length between them. "I was brought here a prisoner. It's just been my good fortune Captain Flynt found a use for me, as ship's clerk."

"Cap'n Flynt. Aye." The whip handle's tip cracked against the tabletop.

Farrel started, his fear ratcheting up a notch. He firmed his jaw.

"After the way I found ye yester night, pawin' 'er like some common strumpet, me 'and 'as itched to deal out punishment." Again the whip handle struck the table. "She shoulda left ye in the brig or ordered ye flogged fer the boldness, but she pardoned ye." He lifted the whip and unwound the cords. "I 'asn't."

"I apologized. Didn't she explain?" Farrel straightened, resisting the impulse to retreat.

"Too much grog, she said." The bo'sun stood with the whip at his side, the cords dragging on the floor. "I's thinkin' mayhap ye needs a lesson about controllin' yer drink and treatin' the cap'n with proper respect."

Farrel lifted his hands in placation. "She and I came to an understanding. There won't be a repeat of last night."

"Aye, bloody right there won't." Fisher advanced on him. "'Tis true I wants to punish ye in front o' the lads, but the cap'n wouldn't be likin' it. Seems she's a soft spot fer ye and yer uppity ways."

Farrel's back stiffened. His glance flicked from the knots of the whip to the brutal expression on Fisher's scarred, weather-beaten face.

"And what if that 'soft spot' should become something more? Would you deny her affection because you think I'm not her equal?" Though surprised at his anger-fueled boldness, Farrel kept his tone even.

"Ye ain't." Fisher swung the lashes down on the tabletop. The knots passed inches from Farrel's face, striking the table in a staccato of resounding bangs. A hint of old leather mixed with something less aromatic wafted into Farrel's nose. He jumped back. "Take this as fair warnin', McQuaid. If I finds ye's treated the cap'n with familiarity, ye'll be usin' yer fancy talk with the cat." Fisher's eyes gleamed in anticipation. "And she don't 'ave no patience fer excuses."

"Is the captain not free to choose her friends?"

"Aye, but I'm thinkin' ye be more foe than friend."

Farrel met Fisher's eyes. "I'm no threat to her."

The bo'sun's frown deepened.

"I knows what manner of liberties ye be wantin' with 'er. She'll not be allowin' it, and ye'll end with yer back bared to me companion here." He drew the cat-o'-nine's lashes through his fingers in a caressing manner. "When that day comes, sir, ye'll be regrettin' yer misconducts mightily."

What could Farrel say to that? He refused to rise to the bait.

A sneer accentuated the long scar and the vicious glitter in Fisher's eyes. He stepped closer, looming over Farrel and huffing foul breath in his face. His muscular build, shaggy graying hair and drooping mustache made him appear a living mountain. Not the sort one wanted to be on the bad side of.

"I sees ye begins to understand." Fisher grinned, baring his yellow, gap-toothed smile. "Tread careful, McQuaid. 'Twould not be the first she's ordered a whippin' fer oversteppin' o' bounds." His evil grin widened as he stepped back. "An' 'twould be me great pleasure to see ye tied to the grid and at me mercy."

With that, Fisher gathered the cat-o'-nine-tail's cords and wrapped them around the handle. Then, giving Farrel a curt nod, he left.

Farrel stared after him. Evidently, his position was more tenuous than he'd thought.

Did something more exist between Ravyn and Fisher than captain to crewman? The bo'sun's overprotective actions spoke of emotions stronger than simple loyalty. Farrel puzzled over the possibility, not willing to accept there could be a romantic relationship. Fisher was older and not of the same caliber as Ravyn. Farrel smiled to think that. Not long ago, he'd considered her little more than a pirate. But now...

Now he wanted to be the man she looked up to. Astonished yet again at the power of that conviction after their brief acquaintance, he shook his head. He needed to conduct himself with caution. Fisher had the authority—and the means—to rid himself of any impediment another man might pose. Best to keep his desires hidden and establish a safe and respectful distance. Especially from Fisher.

It also occurred to him he was ill-prepared to defend himself. These men, and Ravyn, carried cutlasses, knives and flintlock pistols. Not to mention Fisher's weapon of choice.

As a boy in Nova Scotia, playing pirates with his friends had been a natural pastime with the tales of seafaring buccaneers part of the culture. Once, he had asked his father if he could take fencing lessons, but the question was laughed off and summarily dismissed. He grimaced.

Maybe he should find out who could instruct him in swordplay. After all, if he continued as part of the *Retribution*'s crew, he needed appropriate training. Battles at sea were frequent and bloody in this era, and an unskilled man stood next to no chance of surviving.

And the thing Farrel wanted most desperately was to survive.

While Ravyn settled Liam for the night, Farrel wrote in his journal. When she joined him, they turned to the logbooks, making the entry for the day, then returned to the older ledgers.

Engrossed in a particularly long account, Farrel paid no attention to Ravyn pacing restlessly about the cabin. Once, glancing up, he saw her sitting on the back window seat. She rested her elbow on the narrow sill and leaned her chin on her hand to gaze out over the darkening water.

Farrel returned to the entry, finishing it and moving on to the next. Bewildered by the disjointed notes, he looked up to ask a question. When she didn't answer, he realized she had fallen asleep, head still on her hand. Rising, he neared, intending to wake her. He remembered how little sleep she'd had the previous night and decided to let her rest.

He went back to the log but, unable to decipher the account, set the ledger aside. Turning in his chair, he studied Ravyn's profile. At rest, the tension that seemed an innate part of her features smoothed away. Long, thick lashes rested in a dark crescent against a sun-bronzed cheek, and her full, slightly parted lips were softly pink.

Seized by a notion, Farrel rose and walked to the cabinet containing the slates and chalk. He'd found a couple of graphite pencils and retrieved them along with a penknife. Returning to the table, he flipped to the last page of his journal.

One of his university electives had been an art course, which had included pencil sketching. Farrel had achieved what he considered modest success in his efforts.

He studied Ravyn again, then put pencil to paper, outlining first then filling in features—the soft shadowing of cheekbone and eyes, the deeper shade of brows and lashes, the perfect fullness of lips, pert nose and rounded chin. As he looked up again, he decided to depict her hair differently from the severe braid. In a stroke of whimsy he portrayed it loosely tied at her nape, spiraled tendrils feathering along her face and a few locks draping over her shoulder. He evaluated the sketch, satisfied at his interpretation of her expression, vulnerable and guardedly sensual. A niggling sense of familiarity tugged at him, and he frowned at his work. Suddenly it hit him.

Even unfinished, the sketch bore uncanny resemblance to the one Rowena had left with him. A ripple of déjà vu skittered down his spine.

Had that drawing been his? Had Rowena somehow obtained it and brought it to him? But how? And why? Had she known he would meet the model? Which would mean she knew he would make the shift in time. How? Did some connection exist between them? The questions rolled through his mind with no possibility of answers.

But the sketch wasn't finished. He wanted more detail. Setting the journal aside, he rose and neared Ravyn again. Arm's length away, he hunkered down to better look into her face. A crescent moon sparkled in mercurial fragments on the tossing ocean, illuminating Ravyn's features in muted half-light.

God, she was beautiful. How old was she? Not much more than twenty-five, surely. That she had attained the rank of captain he admired, it being an exception, not only for her sex but her age. Any women reaching that station had been true pirates or successfully disguised as men. Ravyn did disguise herself, but not from her crew. How she maintained control over her rough-and-ready men puzzled him, though he suspected Fisher aided in keeping them in line. Did they truly respect her, or fear repercussion from the menacing bo'sun?

How had she come to a life at sea in the first place? He needed to coax her into telling her story.

Her eyelids fluttered then opened, and she turned to look into his eyes. She started back, her expression tightening. Farrel froze, not sure how to explain what he was doing.

"Mr. McQuaid." Her brows lowered. "I must have fallen asleep."

He straightened. "I was going to wake you with some questions about the logs. You looked so peaceful, I hated to disturb you."

She rubbed a finger across her eyelids then turned her gaze to him. "Ye was looking at me strangely. What was ye thinking?"

His lips curved into a wry smile. Was this the right time to ask?

"I was wondering how long you've been at sea. It's unusual in this era that you've achieved the rank of captain."

She looked away, her brow furrowing, and gnawed her lip a moment before answering.

"I've been at sea most of my life." She met his eyes. "My Da was a sailor. Worked his way up to captain. Mam died birthing me, so Da took me to sea with him." She shrugged, looking away again. "A ship's been my home since afore I e'en walked."

Yes, sailors often took their families with them to sea. The superstition about a woman aboard bringing bad luck was just that—a myth.

"No brothers or sisters?"

"Nay. Da ne'er wed again. I was his only chick." She laughed, a soft, sad sound that touched Farrel. "When he passed nigh ten years ago, I stayed with the crew of his ship, *The Moonraker*. They were my family."

"What happened to him?"

Sorrow cast a shadow across her features. "'Twas a fever took Da. Some months after, *The Moonraker* went down in a storm. Most hands lost. I escaped with Da's bo'sun. We were rescued by the *Sherbrook*, and served on her for a time. The *Sherbrook* made port at Halifax, and we left her to sign on with a merchant ship, *Shannon's Fancy*."

"So, how did you come to captain *Retribution*?"

She turned her face away, but not quickly enough to hide the stark anguish that flickered across her eyes and leeched the color from her cheeks.

"Ravyn?" Farrel fisted his hands to resist touching her.

When she spoke, she kept her face averted, her voice hard and neutral. "The *Shannon* was attacked by pirates. We lost many men, and the ship was ransacked. But those of us left managed to escape and make it ashore." She lifted a hand to rub her cheek, blinking rapidly. "I was unable to bear the thought of boarding her again after the repairs." A sigh accompanied her visible shudder. "Another vessel came up for auction, and a group of merchants purchased her as a privateer. I offered to captain her through the auspices of an agent, and they accepted. They gave me free rein to rename and outfit her."

She turned her gaze to him, her emotions under control once more. "And so the *Retribution* was born." Swallowing, she turned away again. "That be all I wish to say on the matter."

Chapter 13

A hundred questions tumbled through Farrel's mind. "Would it not have been easier for your father to leave you with someone ashore and have you schooled as a young lady?"

"Nay. He ne'er treated me like a girl." A wry smile played at the corners of her mouth. "It may be he wanted a boy, but I was all he got."

"Did you never live on shore?"

"Aye, during some of the winters. Da had friends in Nova Scotia and Jamaica, and we sometimes visited. Otherwise, we took temporary lodgings or lived aboard ship in the warmer climes."

"So, did the people you stayed with have daughters with whom you could socialize?"

Her nose wrinkled. "Aye. They treated me like an oddity." She shook her head. "Mayhap I was in their eyes, always in breeches, ne'er dresses. I was more accustomed to splicing rope and climbin' the ratlines than playing with dolls, as they did."

Somehow, that didn't come as a surprise.

"It just seems strange your father wouldn't have brought you up in the conventional standards."

"Why? I felt no lack. I was happy with Da. None of the crews, e'en before he became a captain, treated me as anything other than one of the lads."

"But I'm sure they knew you weren't."

"Aye, well, I was the bo'sun's child, then the lieutenant's, then the captain's. They were wiser than to try and take advantage." Her lips twitched into a crooked smile. "They knew they'd be tastin' the lash of the cat if they did." Her grin widened to a full smile. "Did ye know another name for the cat-o'-nine-tails is the captain's daughter?"

Farrel laughed. "I'd forgotten that bit of trivia." He thought of Fisher issuing threats with the weapon. "Guess that could put a crimp in a fellow's lusty ambitions."

"Ye does have the oddest way of saying things." She rose. "Would ye like me to look at the notes ye was puzzling over?"

Though he would have liked to continue the conversation, Farrel realized the subject was closed.

As they passed the open journal, she paused, staring at the sketch. "So that's what ye were doing." She bent closer, running a fingertip down the edge of the page. "Is that truly me?"

"Yes." Farrel shifted in embarrassment.

Ravyn lifted wide eyes. "That cannot be me. She's..."

"Beautiful. And that is you."

"But... Ye've shown me as...soft. Delicate. My hair..." Her hand went to the braid draped over her shoulder. "How can ye know how it would look?"

"I guessed. Why did you never cut it? It would have made you look more like a boy."

Ravyn's smile hinted at sadness. "Da said it reminded him of my mother."

"Ah, sentimentality, then." He shrugged. "But Ravyn, there's nothing delicate about you. It's the way I see you through an artist's eyes. And my own." He added the last under his breath, not sure how it would be received.

When she looked up, the glisten of tears in her eyes startled Farrel. "I'm sorry if I've offended you—"

"Nay, nay. 'Tis a lovely drawing. I've ne'er seen myself in the way ye've shown me." Again she ran a finger along the edge of the page.

"It's said beauty is in the eye of the beholder." Farrel offered another smile. "Can't help it if that's what I beheld." He turned away. "But back to the logs..."

As they worked, Ravyn's gaze slid to the sketch several times. Farrel couldn't repress a small, satisfied smile, glad she felt complimented by his rendition. He didn't think it did her justice.

They conferred over several more entries then Farrel sat back, closing his eyes.

"'Tis enough for tonight." Ravyn brushed sand from the page and closed the book. "Ye're straining your eyes."

"Would you join me for a walk about the deck? I wouldn't mind some fresh air."

"Aye. I should be checking on the men anywise."

When they exited, Farrel extended his arm. "With your permission,

Captain, allow me to escort you."

She looked at his proffered arm, then shook her head and started away.

Disappointed, Farrel followed.

They ascended to the forecastle, where Ravyn folded her arms on the rail. They looked out over the water as the moon hovered above the eastern horizon.

Farrel gazed down at her, fighting the impulse to slip an arm around her shoulders and inwardly cursing the protocol that forbid it.

"Have you ever been in love?" He spoke in a low voice, not wanting anyone to overhear.

She looked up, brows arched. "Now, why would ye ask such a thing?"

Farrel shrugged. "It just seems you might have wanted to settle down, have a family, a home of your own at some time."

"The ship is my home, the crew my family. I've wanted naught more."

"Ever?"

She didn't answer right away, giving the impression she held something back.

"Ye ask such prying questions, sir." Her expression flowed into stern lines.

"I just...want to know you better." Farrel looked at the moonlit ripples on the water. "I may be here for the rest of my life. You're the closest I have to a friend. If there's anything you want to ask me, don't hesitate."

Their eyes met and held. Uncertainty flickered across her face then she returned her gaze to the ocean. "There was someone, once. But he died afore anything could pass 'tween us." She cleared her throat.

"I'm sorry." Farrel touched her arm but drew quickly back as her head whipped around. He held his hand aloft, taken aback by the blue fire in her eyes. "No disrespect meant." He let his hand fall, frustrated. "So, how could you have a relationship if your...love interest wasn't allowed to touch you?"

"I wasn't the captain then. He was." She turned and leaned against the rail, arms crossed. "Ye're determined to make me speak of things I find most distressin'. Why?"

He spoke cautiously. "I was just wondering...if there is a...relationship between you and Mr. Fisher."

She directed a puzzled gaze on him. "He's my bo'sun."

"Nothing more? Romantically, I mean."

Her look of shock was followed by an abrupt laugh. "With Eli? Nay, 'tis not the way of it at all."

"But he's so protective of you. Like a predator guarding his territory."

She looked out over the water again. "I told ye Da's bo'sun rescued me from *The Moonraker* when it sank. That was Mr. Fisher. Afore Da passed, he made Eli promise to keep me safe, as my guardian. I've known the man for most of my life."

"But he's like a bear with a thorn in its paw about you. We have a saying for that in my time. Over the top. I know he doesn't trust me, but..." He didn't want to tell Ravyn about the afternoon's confrontation. It would make him feel like a tattletale.

Ravyn faced Farrel, and her lips twitched. "He trusts no man where I am concerned. Nor is he a bad man, only over watchful, since—" She broke off, biting her lip.

"Since...?" Farrel prompted gently.

She bent her head, remaining quiet for a long moment. "There be things of which I will not speak." Her tone was so soft he almost didn't hear her. When she looked at him, her eyes shimmered, as though filling with tears. She drew a shaky breath. "Mr. Fisher has taken his role as guardian very much to heart. That be all I need say on the matter."

Farrel nodded, relieved. That Fisher had assumed a fatherly role made more sense than the other. Not that it made getting closer to Ravyn any easier.

"Is Liam your child?"

"Liam?" Her chin went up and her eyes narrowed. "Nay. I found him on the streets of Dublin. But he's very important to me."

Farrel studied her expression, cast in shadow with the moonlight illuminating one side of her face. "He's an orphan, then."

"Aye. A sorry, ragged little urchin when I brought him aboard as cabin boy. But he's dear to my heart."

Cabin boy. Right. Farrel nodded, repressing a smile. "Guess I should say good-night. Morning comes early around here." Between watch bells, shouts of the men, creaking and groaning of the ship and the constant susurrus of waves, silence was an unknown concept. "Captain." He gave a polite little bow and started away but turned back. "Do you mind if we defer the morning instruction? I'd like to pursue some lessons myself."

"In what, pray?"

"If you have no objection, I'd like to learn how to defend myself. Just in case we run into opposition. I've never used any kind of blade before." It occurred to him that he might need her permission.

"Are ye plotting a mutiny, Mr. McQuaid?" She took a few steps toward him, her brows lowering, but the corner of her mouth twitched, as though she fought a grin.

"Would I tell you if I were? I'd have to have a few allies for that. Liam and Sammy wouldn't be much help."

She chuckled. "I've no objection, I suppose." She tilted her head to study him. "See Mr. Poole. He's my munitions and weapons officer. He'd be the best to teach ye."

"Thanks. I'll do that." He bowed again and walked away.

Ravyn watched his departure, her brow furrowed.

He wanted to learn how to defend himself. Now, was that a wise notion? How much could she trust him? Then she shook her head. As he said, he had no allies, save Liam.

She had watched him work with the little boy, their heads bent together over the slate as the child traced his letters. At one point Farrel laughed and ruffled Liam's hair, a gentle smile curving his lips as he straightened and praised the boy's efforts. The delight and admiration lighting Liam's eyes as he looked up at Farrel revealed growing closeness.

Mayhap if she watched him with Mr. Poole, she could better judge the truth of his fantastic tale of being from the future by how he handled a blade.

He was alone in this place and considered her the closest he had to a friend.

That touched her in an unexpected way.

Chapter 14

"Stand thusly, Mr. McQuaid." Mr. Poole demonstrated the leg stance with feet shoulder width apart, the small sword held out at shoulder height and in line with his body. "Yer startin' guard point."

Farrel imitated him, fingers curled around the sword's grip.

Mr. Poole straightened, scowling. "Ye're holdin' it too tight, man. Should I start ye with sticks, like I does the young lads?"

"No. I want to learn with the real thing." Farrel relaxed his hold as the officer showed him how to grasp the grip with his thumb and first two fingers.

"Ye wants control of the blade." He folded Farrel's other fingers loosely around the hilt. "'Tis the proper way if ye expects to do yer opponent any damage."

About three feet long, the double-edged steel sword rested comfortably once Mr. Poole showed the correct way of holding it. The officer executed simple guards and starting positions to strike different parts of the body. Farrel followed each movement, swinging and thrusting in unison with his instructor. At one point, he saw Ravyn watching from the corner of his eye and stopped to bow in her direction. She acknowledged with a smile and nod.

"'Tis enough for today." Mr. Poole lowered his blade as Farrel began to tire. "On the morrow we'll don the vests and practice together." The man smirked. "I'll try not to skewer ye."

"Thanks." Farrel returned his grin. A number of crude padded vests hung by the blades, but since they were practicing stances and weapon positioning, Mr. Poole deemed them unnecessary. Becoming a swordsman wasn't the easiest exercise, but Farrel determined to master it.

"How did the first lesson go?" Ravyn asked over lunch.

"Well, I think. It's hard to tell with Mr. Poole."

Ravyn laughed. "Aye, he can be crusty and sparin' with the praise. But he is the best for teaching."

"We're using the vests tomorrow. He promised not to skewer me." Farrel grinned. "At least he'll try not to." He chuckled.

They had just finished the meal when a shout came from outside.

"Ahoy. Ship to starboard."

They exited, and the hand who had called clambered down from the upper mast. "She be flyin' a flag o' the Crown, Cap'n."

Ravyn took the spyglass and climbed to the quarterdeck with Farrel close behind. She lifted the glass, studying the distant ship. Farrel's glance shifted from her intense surveillance to the approaching vessel.

"'Tis the *Torrence*, a British ship-of-the-line." She lowered the glass. "I've had dealings with her afore. We best prepare to be boarded."

Farrel couldn't tell by her taut expression whether this development meant impending complications. It left him torn between excitement and apprehension.

She headed for her cabin and emerged moments later in her dress coat and tricorne, most of her hair tucked under it. In her hand, she clutched a rolled parchment.

The massive, three-masted and heavily armed vessel drew nearer.

"Ahoy." The shout came from the crow's nest on the navy ship.

"Ahoy." Ravyn called back. "Come aboard at your will."

Closer now, the anchor splashed down. Orders were shouted to lower the longboats and turn the sails to spill the wind.

Ravyn strode to the lower deck, where the rope ladder was let down. Farrel followed, curious about what would transpire. *Retribution*'s crew completed preparations with aligned precision then formed into a semblance of rank. The air practically crackled with tension while they waited.

Farrel stood behind Ravyn as the Navy men disembarked onto the deck. The dress uniforms of the officers, dark blue and gold-trimmed tailcoats over white trousers and vests, impressed Farrel. He identified the taller man as the captain when he gave Ravyn a salute. She returned it, every inch the ranking officer on her ship despite her small stature and more casual attire.

"Captain Rothchild of the H.M.S. *Torrence*."

"Captain Flynt of the *Retribution*. Ye be new to the *Torrence*, sir."

"Yes. Recently appointed. But I have acquainted myself with previous accounts of your vessel. You're a privateer." Sharp gray eyes raked over her. "You seem young to be captaining a vessel."

Ravyn smiled. "I thank ye, sir. However, I'm older than ye might think.

I've spent most of my life at sea."

"Ah." Once more he studied her. "Have you the required authorization?"

"Aye." She extended the parchment. "My Letter of Marque, Captain."

He took it, untying the ribbon and rolling it out to inspect the contents. Satisfied, he rerolled it and passed it back with the loose tie. Farrel reached for it to secure the band.

"Have you sighted any enemy activity in this area?" His cultured accent indicated the man undoubtedly came from an affluent background, likely the younger son of an aristocrat who had bought a commission and worked his way up the ranks. Judging by the silver threading his hair, visible at his temples under the regimental bicorn, that had been some years ago.

"Nay. Not since hearing of the seizing of the *Chesapeake*." Ravyn kept her voice low and husky, maintaining her masculine disguise.

"Very good. And do you carry any cargo of which the Crown should be aware?"

"Nay. We be heading for port in a few days to take on supplies."

"Where, may I ask?"

"Liverpool."

He gave a terse nod. "You realize we must inspect your vessel."

"Aye. Ye be more than welcome, Captain." Her expression remained pleasant, but a spark of vexation lit her eyes.

Was this the normal protocol, or was the Navy captain looking for something suspicious?

The marines accompanying Captain Rothchild scattered when he waved his hand, disappearing down the hatches.

"And what is your rank, sir?"

Farrel realized he was the target of the question. He flicked a glance at Ravyn, not sure how he should answer.

"This be my ship's clerk, Mr. McQuaid. He keeps the records of the logs for me." Ravyn smiled at Farrel. Following her lead, he gave the Royal Navy captain a smart salute. Rothchild nodded an acknowledgement before returning his attention to Ravyn.

"What has your course heading been?"

"'Tween the state of Georgia and Cape Breton."

Farrel followed at a discreet distance as they walked along the deck, but not so far away that he couldn't hear the conversation.

"You keep your range rather limited." The British captain stopped and faced Ravyn.

"Aye, for the time being. We spent the last winter in the Caribbean rather than go to dry dock."

"Interesting." Captain Rothchild's study of Ravyn intensified. "I should inspect your logs. You say—Mr. McQuaid, is it—has been keeping them?"

"Only recently. 'Tis not one of my finer skills. Mr. McQuaid has been going over them and expanding on the entries."

"I see." The other captain's brows lowered in the suggestion of a frown. The slate-gray gaze flicked to Farrel. "I trust you've been maintaining accuracy, Mr. McQuaid."

"Of course." Farrel nodded. "Captain Flynt has been dictating, along with assisting in the transcriptions."

"Ah. Let us get to it, then."

They retired to the great cabin, where Ravyn laid out the logs, old and new. Captain Rothchild spent some time examining them with keen intensity.

"Very good." He lifted his gaze to Farrel. "You've a fine hand, sir."

Farrel acknowledged the compliment with a smile and a nod. "Thank you, Captain."

"Judging by your speech and penmanship, I take you to be an educated man." Captain Rothchild scrutinized Farrel with new interest. "Your accent is not British or any other Empire dialect with which I am familiar." He canted his head, frowning. "American, perhaps?"

A frisson of alarm rippled through Farrel.

"No, Captain." He spoke carefully. "My home is...York. I've only recently arrived at the coast." He flicked a glance at Ravyn. Tight lines bracketed her mouth.

"How do you come to be on a privateer, then? It seems an odd choice of occupation for one such as yourself."

"I commissioned his services." Ravyn stepped forward. "He's become a true boon."

"Ah." The other captain's gaze shifted from Ravyn back to Farrel. "The Navy could use a man of your caliber, Mr. McQuaid. Perhaps I might... persuade you to consider a change of station."

Farrel's alarm took a swift upward swing. By 'persuade' he had the distinct feeling Captain Rothchild meant to recruit him from *Retribution* for his own vessel, something the officer had the authority to do. He glanced askance at Ravyn. Her features were trained to calm neutrality, but the stiff set of her shoulders betrayed rising tension.

"Mr. McQuaid has become an indispensable part of my crew." She spoke quietly, hands clasped behind her back. "His record-keeping skills are necessary to our operations."

"Assuredly," Captain Rothchild agreed in a pleasant tone, "but a Navy position could offer so much more by way of advancement."

"I would prefer to remain with *Retribution*." Farrel knew he took risk in stating his preference, but the last thing he wanted was to be forcibly removed from Ravyn's vessel—and Ravyn herself. "If," he added in more cautious tones, "it would meet with your approval, sir."

"I think not." Captain Rothchild lifted his chin, looking down his nose in haughty disdain. "Your skills would better benefit the interests of the King—"

"Nay! Nay! Don't let 'im take our Mr. McQuaid."

No one had paid any heed to Liam sitting at the window. He rushed forward, eyes wide, small face pale. He skidded to a stop in front of Ravyn, a pleading gaze lifted to her face. Captain Rothchild stared down at him, frowning. Ravyn made soft shushing sounds, but the child ignored her.

"Please, Cap'n, ye can't let 'im take Mr. McQuaid." Liam's golden curls danced as he shook his head. He turned beseeching eyes to Captain Rothchild, hands fisted at his sides. "'E's teachin' me to read an' write, sir, an' I wants to learn. Please don't take 'im away."

Liam whirled and flung his arms around Farrel, making him stagger. The boy clung as tears welled in his eyes. Farrel rested his hand on Liam's head and directed an apologetic look at Captain Rothchild.

"He's become very attached." Farrel lowered his gaze to the trembling boy, not knowing what else to say. "I have been teaching him his letters and numbers, as well as some of the other crewmen."

"Ye see, Mr. McQuaid is an important addition to my crew." Ravyn touched Liam's shoulder, her eyes on Captain Rothchild. "This is Liam, my cabin boy. Please, accept my apologies for his outburst."

For a long moment Captain Rothchild, his features set in stern lines, gazed down at the sobbing child. Then one corner of his mouth twitched into a rueful smile.

"I have a son not much older than you, and he values his tutor as it seems you do yours." He met Farrel's eyes. "Perhaps we can defer the situation for now. You may reconsider my offer in the future." He reached to ruffle Liam's hair. "Learn your lessons well, young sir. I think you've acquired a fine teacher."

Executing a small, formal bow and salute, he headed for the door. There, he turned back, his expression grave. "I would not wish to separate a man from his woman and child." His mouth quirked at one corner. With that, he exited, leaving Farrel and Ravyn to stare after him.

Her mouth tightened into a grim line and she turned to Farrel.

"Looks like your secret is out." He shook his head.

Ravyn frowned. She followed Captain Rothchild's exit, casting Farrel a look he couldn't analyze.

Farrel crouched and laid his hands on Liam's shoulders.

"Thank you, Liam. I was sure he would take me with them. But you mustn't put yourself in danger of being punished for defiance. Especially before a Royal Navy officer." He tried to look severe, but couldn't maintain it on seeing tears in Liam's eyes.

"I–I couldn't let 'im take ye." The little boy's arms wound about Farrel's neck. He returned the hug, his own shaky relief tempered with tender compassion for the child's fears. He closed his eyes, rubbing Liam's back until the little boy's trembling subsided.

He put Liam from him. "I'd better go join the captain."

When he reached the outer deck, the navy sailors had returned from their inspection.

"All seems in proper order, sir," a young lieutenant affirmed.

"Then you may go on your way." Captain Rothchild spoke in a soft undertone to Ravyn. "You may trust me to safeguard your façade."

Farrel and Ravyn listened to the slap of oars on the water.

"Fascinating," Farrel murmured.

The naval soldiers resumed their ship, and orders were shouted to redirect the sails. Only as distance expanded between the vessels did Ravyn glance askance at Farrel.

"'Twould not have been so fascinating had they found aught to question. Or if Captain Rothchild had insisted on taking ye." She looked back to the ship diminishing in the distance. "There would have been little I could do, whether he thought us family or nay." She looked sidelong at Farrel. "Mayhap that was the deciding point for him. Not all would be so generous."

"I don't know what I would've done." Farrel shook his head, grimacing. "It makes me realize how quickly fortunes can change in this era—and how little say one might have in them." He glanced at Ravyn. Her gaze rested on him, quietly speculative. "Thank you." He reached a hand toward hers on the rail then hesitated, seeking permission with his eyes. She met his gaze then lowered it as his hand covered hers. She let it rest there for a moment before gently drawing away.

"Aye. The Navy can take anyone, or anything, at their whim." She watched the disappearing ship-of-the-line. A small flock of terns reeled over the water, their screeches loud on the afternoon air. "We may also call it fortunate they didn't seize our supplies. Their lot is oftentimes hard with fewer comforts than one would assume the King's officers merit. Life at sea is far from easy for any of us. The lads deserve a true prize now and then, so 'tis not uncommon for some cargoes seized never to reach the Crown authorities."

"So, is that where the stories I've heard of buried treasure come from? I know there were pirates roaming the North Atlantic until the Navy became more vigilant."

"Aye." Ravyn's expression shifted into censure. "There be fewer now, but they still venture into our waters. 'Tis why many believe there be buried treasure along the shores of Nova Scotia."

The inspection having taken up most of the afternoon, lessons for the day were cancelled. Just as well, since the boarding was the main topic of lively conversation.

"You mentioned we'd be heading to Liverpool." Farrel took a sip of grog over the evening meal. "Liverpool, England?"

"Nay. The Nova Scotia port. It would take weeks to reach the English shores, e'en months depending on weather and winds."

He'd visited Liverpool in his time, intrigued by the glimpse into history. He anticipated seeing the town popularly known as the "Port of Privateers" in its historic heyday.

Chapter 15

Ravyn had a difficult time getting Liam to settle for the night. The inspection and near loss of Mr. McQuaid had left him excited and fidgety. After spending the better part of an hour hunting Sammy down, she hoped the cat would calm the little boy enough to go to sleep.

Eager to see if Farrel had finished her portrait, she left Liam once he lay with the purring tabby tucked under his arm.

When she entered the great cabin, Farrel sat at the table, the journal propped open against his knees. His feet rested on the rungs of another chair to support and angle the heavy book.

Approaching, she saw he had started another drawing. The young woman he sketched had light hair and a heart-shaped face, high cheekbones and dark eyes. He wielded the pencil with practiced ease, bringing the subject to life in shades of gray and black.

He glanced over his shoulder at Ravyn.

"You're back." Setting the book on the table he straightened. "Guess we should do today's entry."

Overcome by curiosity, Ravyn leaned in to examine the new image. "She's very pretty. Might I ask who she is?"

"Was." His features tightened. "My sister, Julia."

Ravyn studied his hardened expression. "I thought ye said ye had no family."

"I don't. Notwithstanding that I'm not in my own time anymore, of course." His reluctance to continue piqued Ravyn's curiosity even more.

"But if ye was in your time?" She would allow the possibility for now to hear his response.

A shadow passed over his features. "She's dead." The statement was curt and it appeared he had no intention of embellishing it.

She took the chair he'd been resting his feet on. 'Tis sorry I am for the loss, Farrel." She glanced at the sketch. "Why are ye doing her likeness, then?"

He leaned his elbow on the table, resting his chin on his knuckles. "I got to thinking about everything I've left behind." He let his hand drop and met her eyes. "My house, my artifact collections, the pictures of my family, unfinished manuscripts. I couldn't help wondering what would become of them if I...can't go back." Sorrow deepened his gray eyes to the hue of a lowering storm cloud. "I did a sketch of Julia before—" He gave his head a shake. "In happier times. Drawing you last night reminded me. I wanted to recreate it." He turned the page to Ravyn's image. "Let's finish this."

Ravyn sat in silence as he worked over the drawing, glancing at her several times before adding more shading and finishing the flowing lines of her hair. She sensed his distinct withdrawal as he worked without speaking.

"Done." He tore out the page and offered it to her.

She took it, but her gaze returned to the sketch of his sister, exposed by the page's removal. The young woman looked happy, her lips curved in a carefree smile, a lightness of spirit about her eyes that Farrel had captured. Yet Ravyn sensed something dark from him, seething beneath the surface.

"Farrel..." She pressed her lips together, returning her gaze to her own image. "I thank ye for this." She lifted her eyes again to find him watching her with grave intensity. 'Tis really quite lovely."

His gloomy mood dissipated abruptly. He closed the book, smiling. "You're very welcome. Now, for that log entry."

They completed the account of the day's inspection then tackled the older accounts once more.

When Ravyn retired to her cabin, she set the sketch on her desk. She sat down and studied it by the dim illumination of her hanging lantern, fascinated and touched by the manner in which Farrel had depicted her. He said she was beautiful.

She gave a shaky sigh. It had been so long since anyone had viewed her with such evident admiration. Mr. Fisher said she was a fine woman, but there was a difference between 'fineness' and beauty.

She ran her fingertips along the edge of the image. It seemed strange that Farrel would choose to draw an image rather than use his picture device. Sketching took time and patience, his device required but the press of a button.

Brow furrowed, she settled back in the chair. The pictures in the image device. She wanted to see them again, alone, without him there to influence her impressions. But it was too late tonight. She needed a few hours sleep.

A grimace twisted her mouth. She hoped her rest would be bereft of the dreams that haunted her like malevolent, brutal ghosts.

The opportunity to look at the images presented itself the following morning, while Farrel practiced with Mr. Poole.

For a time she watched as they met in combat, the bulky vests making both men appear larger than their actuality. Mr. Poole called orders as they exchanged strokes, the clang of clashing metal loud on the morning air.

Farrel's features set in dogged determination as he followed Mr. Poole's commands to block his swipes and thrusts. The point of the older man's sword sank into Farrel's heavy protective wear several times. The officer exhibited no restraint in the training. An accomplished swordsman, he would settle for nothing less than total commitment from his student.

The sweat trickling down Farrel's face and the awkward angles he used to fend off Mr. Poole proved he had no experience with blades. At one point he stood with the sword gripped in both hands, legs wide apart, stance tense and brow furrowed as he waited for his instructor's next move. The thrust came at him suddenly, catching the vest at his chest before Farrel could block it. Despite his ineptitude, Ravyn could not help admiring his resolve. A shouted reprimand from Mr. Poole only made Farrel more determined than ever, his features setting into hard lines. The next time the sword came at him in a wide arc, he met it, pivoting so that Mr. Poole had to drop his weapon before his wrist snapped back. Ravyn nodded to herself. He would do.

She left Mr. Hennessey in charge and retired to the great cabin. Taking the image device from its hidden recess in the drawer, she sat down at the table and peered at the buttons. She quickly figured out which one Farrel had used to activate the odd device. When it finished its musical notes, the screen lit with an image of the tabletop. It took a few hit-and-miss efforts accompanied by frustrated, muttered curses before she finally located a sequence of controls that revealed the other pictures.

Passing by the lightning images, the photos of the shoreline and others of gardens and buildings, she came upon a city skyline at night. Inconceivably tall buildings were lit from top to bottom, the other structures joining with a rainbow array of brightness that no lanterns could match. The bright hues reflected in long, rippled lines across the calm bay. He had told her it was Halifax. Certainly not the locality she knew. Though some buildings on the waterfront appeared older than those further back, nothing familiar presented itself.

The next showed the harbor in daylight with a full-rigged ship on the water, the tall buildings spearing into the sky behind it. Something familiar, something not.

The next revealed a partial view of the Citadel, shown once more with the higher buildings in the background.

She went back further, stopping at the picture of a plaque commemorating the taking of the *Chesapeake* by the *Shannon*. That, along with other pictures of statues, public gardens, and the ones of him at the bookstore told his story more clearly than words.

He hadn't deceived her. The rush of acceptance stole her breath.

She turned the machine off and returned it to the drawer, then stood at the window, staring out at the restless ocean.

He had come from a future time. The notion should frighten her, but it did not. Rather, the idea that the things he told her that she had listened to with skepticism were true fascinated her. It explained so much about him; his strange flat accent, his manner of dress, the unusual devices he'd carried with him.

Now, he was her responsibility. A member of her crew. And something more she didn't care to explore too deeply.

Should she return him to that rocky shore? After the first day he had expressed little desire to be taken back, but that could have been due to the threat of punishment if he continued balking her authority. He said he had no family to return to—the sister whose sketch he had worked on was dead—but he surely had a life he would want to resume. A man of higher learning and a writer of books, he would have much to pick up if he made it back to—what was it?—2013. But upon the heels of that thought came a distinct reluctance to see him gone.

She shivered at the notion of the chasm of time that had separated them short days ago.

Had there been a significant woman in his life? Nay, he said he had no ties. A man alone without wife or kin. And why should that matter to her?

A knock sounded at the door and she swiveled with a brusque, "Enter."

The subject of her disjointed ruminations stepped into the room. Farrel had changed from the clothing he'd worn for his lesson. His face was flushed from the recent exertion, or mayhap the burn of the sun on his untempered skin.

"So, how do you think I'm doing?" Excitement edged the question. "I think I'm making progress." He grinned ruefully. "That vest may need some repair, though. Mr. Poole doesn't hold back, does he?"

Ravyn couldn't refrain from returning his smile. "He coddles no one when it comes to the training." She moved to stand part-way along the table. "Ye seemed to handle yourself well, even if he did try to skewer ye."

Farrel chuckled. "Yeah, I think he got some perverse pleasure out of ripping into the vest." He sank onto a chair at the end of the table. "I'm wiped. But lunch should rejuvenate me. We'll start the afternoon schooling after that."

Ravyn regarded him thoughtfully. "Ye said ye taught at a university afore landing here. Does ye find teaching us less challenging?"

One corner of Farrel's mouth quirked. "Truthfully, getting back to the basics is a refreshing change." Then his brow furrowed. "You sound like you believe me. About being from the future, I mean."

Ravyn gave a slow nod. "I looked at the pictures on your image device. They seem real. I believe ye."

He studied her intently. "You're sure?"

"Aye." She paused. "If ye wish, we could take ye back to the beach where we found ye."

Farrel didn't answer for a long, long moment. Then he shook his head, lifting a hand. "I'm not even sure I could get back. What would be the point of waiting on that beach for lightning to strike twice?" His lips thinned as he appeared to consider the matter. "At least with you, I have some connection, a place, a role. There's too much risk in being abandoned in an unfamiliar time and location." He met her eyes with resolve. "I'll stay on the *Retribution*, if you're willing."

"Very well." She couldn't deny the relief that washed over her. Though disturbing in some vague way, it also lightened her heart. "'Tis glad I am ye'll be staying." She stepped to the table and set her hand on it, next to his, not quite touching, but close enough to feel its heat. Farrel looked at it for a few heartbeats then slowly slipped his over it. Ravyn did not pull away. Something passed between them that no words could express.

He glanced up and gave her one of his brilliant smiles that brought warmth to her entire being and that strange flutter in her chest.

"Me too."

Chapter 16

During the afternoon, the temperature soared, the negligible breeze failing to cool the intense heat. By the supper hour, the barrels of fresh water kept on deck for the crew's consumption were drastically depleted. The lack of wind left the ship becalmed, the sails sagging. Even Liam began to wilt. He ate little, and Ravyn consigned him to bed shortly afterwards.

Farrel had shed his waistcoat earlier in the day, and his damp linen shirt clung. When Ravyn joined him, she too had removed her vest, shoes and stockings. Farrel glanced out of the corner of his eye while he wrote the day's log entry, watching her flex unexpectedly dainty feet. She pushed the sleeves of her shirt above her elbows, baring bronzed forearms. Her shirt, though loose enough not to cling, did little to hide the curves of her breasts.

He redirected his thoughts abruptly from the futile—and inappropriate—direction.

The entry completed, he sprinkled sand over the page and sank back in the chair, wiping his sweaty brow with his sleeve.

Ravyn rose and walked to the open casement window, turning her face into the slight breeze. Though minimal, it might dry the perspiration he had noticed trickling down the shirt's partly laced front and between her breasts.

She lifted her profile, closing her eyes and taking a deep breath of the fish and salt-scented air. Resting one knee on the bench, she leaned further into the window's opening.

Farrel pushed his chair back and rose. He had shed his stockings and shoes earlier, making his footsteps silent as he crossed the wooden planking. She didn't move when he stopped behind her. "It's not going to be easy getting to sleep tonight."

Ravyn started, pivoting. As she brought her knee off the bench, she stumbled, falling against Farrel. He caught her forearms to steady her.

Gazing down into the blue pools of her eyes, he knew he should release her immediately.

But the instant his hands closed around her arms, the heated air swept over him in a heady rush, as though it achieved a life of its own. Prickles of pure pleasure danced over Farrel's skin as he stared into Ravyn's eyes. Goose bumps stippled her arms under his hands. Did she feel it too? The arousal accompanying the static-laden sensation held irresistible urgency. He lowered his head, brushing her lips then slanting his mouth over hers.

Somewhere in the back of his mind, he knew this was wrong, but he could not deny how right it felt. He abandoned that sliver of doubt as desire surged hot through his veins.

Deepening the kiss, he savored the soft lushness of her mouth, the tang of salt mingled with a hint of rum. His hands moved with a will of their own, releasing her arms and shifting to her waist, pulling her closer. She yielded, pressing against him from chest to knee. He knew what she felt— his erection against her belly—but rather than curtail him, the insistent contact spurred him on.

Her lips opened to him. Suppressing a groan, he plundered her welcoming mouth.

Through the fog of his passion the realization dawned that the strange sensation they shared had faded. The fervor she returned was given freely, with no more prompting than their mutual, rising hunger. He let the escalating desire overcome reason.

When her arms drifted up to twine about his neck, he spread his fingers to cradle her breasts, his thumbs stroking her nipples. They puckered into tight kernels through the linen shirt. His tongue swept over hers, matching the inciting rhythm of his fingers.

She lowered her hands to his shoulders then between them to flatten against his chest. With a soft cry, she wrenched away, her breathing shallow and quick. Farrel reached for her, but she backed away.

"Mr. McQuaid." Her husky voice shook. "Ye are ne'er to touch me in that manner again." She pushed past him and headed for the door.

"But Ravyn—"

She stopped and looked over her shoulder.

"Ne'er. Else I'll be ordering a flogging."

"But you felt it. I know you did." He took a few steps after her. The rigid set of her back and shoulders stayed him. "Not the weird...thing we share, though I know you felt that too. But it was more. Much more."

Her shoulders hitched, and she choked on a gasp that sounded like a sob she tried to swallow. "Don't make me call for Mr. Fisher."

"Ravyn, wait—"

Ignoring him, she left without closing the door.

Farrel stared after her, bewildered. She had responded. He knew she had. What had caused her abrupt rejection?

He had taken control, at first prompted by that...that...

He had no idea what to call it. Tingle? Current? And what was it, anyway? Why did it keep making him do things with Ravyn he had no business doing at all? Confusion assailed him. Had he succeeded in alienating the one person who knew the truth? The only one with whom he had any true connection?

He laughed, a low, bitter sound. What had gotten into him? Why, after all this time of disregarding his needs, had he suddenly developed the sex drive from Hell? That damned current. It was the only explanation. Yet...she had responded, even after the strangeness faded.

He couldn't blame his actions entirely on that connection. In truth, he desired Ravyn like he needed to breathe. But after such a short acquaintance, what prompted that? Lust? Love? Though he craved her with an intensity both startling and disturbing, he didn't know her. Nor did she know him. They were strangers linked by a peculiar kinetic energy for which he had no explanation. Every time it happened, he felt more drawn to her, keener to develop a deeper relationship with this strong, beautiful woman.

Give it time. If anything were meant to develop between them, perhaps the crucial ingredient was time. Something over which he had no control.

He gazed out at the dark waters, listening to the rush of the ocean.

A lasting relationship had never been high on his priority list. Why not, though? He'd enjoyed the companionship of the women he'd been involved with, both socially and sexually, but never enough to take the relationships any further. Work had been his priority—teaching, writing and collecting artifacts—not marriage and a family.

Was that what he wanted now? Was Ravyn Flynt the woman who had finally penetrated his apathy?

Ravyn strode from one deck to the other, her emotions raw and whirling.

How dared he? She wanted to strike something, imagine Farrel McQuaid's face on whatever surface received her wrath. In truth, she should order him flogged.

Glancing up, she saw Mr. Fisher watching her. Abruptly, she changed direction. Best not let him see the degree of her upset. Not unless she wanted Farrel consigned to the ocean depths.

Nay, she did not want that. Against all reason, even in the face of his effrontery, she did not want that.

Damnation. She thought they'd come to an understanding, that he accepted the limits enforced by protocol—and the limits she placed upon herself.

She drew a deep breath, battling the infuriating urge to cry. She could not do that. Tears betrayed weakness, the last thing she would allow herself to show. Her eyes burned with the effort of holding back the moisture blurring her vision. There was nowhere she could be alone to vent her emotions. Not her cabin, where Liam slept. Nor the great cabin, where Farrel lingered after their embrace.

She closed her eyes, shivering despite the untenable heat of the still night. She should be thankful the moon had not yet risen, that whatever turmoil her face revealed remained hidden in the near darkness.

Farrel had it aright when he said she had felt something beyond that mysterious sensation of warm cocooning. That in itself frightened her, but the fear became lost in the physical lure of Farrel's nearness. Her body had responded to his touch, melted into his hands and lips like some love-starved maid. In that moment she belonged to him, needed him, wanted to relinquish to him all the emotions she held in tight control. Even after that mysterious warmth faded, she would have willingly given her body in that brief interlude of tender yielding.

But it could not be. She knew where such capitulation led. Treachery hid in those feelings of needing, as though a woman's body ached for the torment a man dealt, deceiving with the longing to let him touch her, take him inside her. Ravyn shuddered again.

Her cabin was her only refuge. Liam tended to be a sound sleeper, so her agitated pacing shouldn't disturb him.

The first thing she saw after lighting the lantern was the sketch on her desk. She snatched it up, prepared to crumple it in her shaking hand. But she stopped, staring down at Farrel's depiction of her. He had shown her as soft, vulnerable, but so lovely, as though he saw something beneath the tough, stern exterior she presented. Something of the woman she could have been, had her life been different. But would she have wanted that?

There had always been other women about—the wives of warrant officers sailing with their husbands, the prostitutes invited on board when the ships were in port—but her father had shielded her from such influences. For too brief a time she had found affection that could have become lasting love...

The memory rose to her mind as she stared down at the sketch.

A twilight evening. Standing on the forecastle with Captain Jonathan Moore. He stared out over the water, hands clasped behind his back. His profile, handsome, strong, chestnut hair tied back, his midnight blue eyes fixed on the ocean as he spoke the words she would never forget.

"Lieutenant, you have proven yourself well to me over this past year. I admire your wit, your fortitude, your strength of will even in your feminine state." He turned his head to gaze at her, and a small smile curved his lips before he sobered again. "But I must confess to...a deeper feeling." He looked back at the ocean. "I have always considered myself a solitary man, not one to be bound to wife or babes. You, however, have made me rethink my position." He turned to her, hands still clasped behind him. "I cannot imagine my life without you, Ravyn. Not as crew member, but something far more precious." His hesitation over the next words had her holding her breath. "I have come to care for you, as a woman, a companion, a partner in life." He took her trembling hand and raised it to his lips. "I love you, Ravyn Flynt. That is the simple truth of it." He retained her hand, gazing into her eyes. "Dare I hope you might feel the same in return?"

She had nodded, unable to speak for emotions clogging her throat.

So it had been sealed between them. Jonathan Moore remained the proper captain, the perfect gentleman on that wondrous night, offering no more by way of touch than that token holding of her hand. Their bond, composed, civilized...acceptable. They had never shared kisses or intimate touches as she had with Farrel. Nor had she been swamped by that inciting physical hunger.

But Captain Jonathan Moore had died within a day of telling her he loved her, his life taken in her defense by the same hand that had dealt her unforgivable violence. And if what Will Flemington had done was the physical "love" a man offered, she would have none of it. Her traitorous body would never be debased again.

She opened the top drawer of the desk and slid the sketch inside.

Extinguishing the lantern and lying down on her bunk, she yielded to the exhaustion that weighted her limbs. But though she ached for rest, her thoughts remained turbulent.

Farrel had awakened something deep and vital within her, and her mixed feelings for him warred. Compassion for his situation. Reluctant growing warmth for him as a man. Resentment and anger that he would make such advances when he knew they were not welcome. The longing to allow him to stir her tender emotions. The knowledge that she could not let any of that happen. Not and stay true to her vow.

The tears were unstoppable. She turned her face to the wall and in silence let the scalding drops trickle from her burning eyes.

Chapter 17

*U*nder a cloudy morning sky, ships of all classes lined the piers and rested at anchor on the outer waters of Liverpool's harbor. The wharf buildings teemed with activity, docked vessels and waiting longboats unloading or receiving cargoes. Navy ships floated among the others, their crew's uniforms conspicuous. Beyond the waterfront stood taverns and quayside shops, the Customs House, homes and churches with spires reaching into the gray sky.

The *Retribution* floated a distance from the crowded pier, anchor cast and her sails furled. Farrel stood at the rail, absorbed in the panoramic view.

"Mr. McQuaid." He turned at Ravyn's voice by his side. "Ye be taking an interest in the activities ashore."

"Yes." He returned his gaze to the harbor. "Are we all going in?"

"Some will stay to tend the ship, but aye. I've business to attend to later in the day. If ye wish, ye may accompany me." She stepped away. "We'll take dinner in a tavern where I'm known."

"As a woman?" He looked at her in surprise.

"As a captain." She walked away.

Farrel returned his attention to the shore. Anticipation lent new excitement to the scene.

Late in the afternoon, Ravyn, Farrel and Mr. Fisher set out in one of the remaining skiffs. The bo'sun voiced objections to Farrel accompanying them, but Ravyn stood firm. He cast malicious looks Farrel's way as they rowed to the pier. Though tempted to reprimand him, Ravyn kept her peace. Farrel seemed too engrossed in the surroundings to heed the vicious glares.

Mooring at a small side dock, Ravyn paid the wharf master the fee. They proceeded up a winding street to a tavern called "The Bell and Anchor."

Lanterns hanging from the low-beamed ceiling lit the taproom they entered, and sawdust covered the plank floor. The aromas varied—ale, smoke, lantern oil, unwashed bodies and cooking food being but a few. At round tables, men ate, drank, conversed and gambled. Some wore the garb of sailors, others the attire of town citizens. Uniformed soldiers dined in private corners, oblivious to the hubbub around them. A few women in low-cut dresses with faces painted in a parody of comeliness moved from table to table. They leaned down to speak to patrons and offer their services for a few guineas. "The Bell and Anchor" was more genteel than taverns closer to the wharf, but some natures of commerce could not be discouraged.

Ravyn headed for a dim corner table, trailed by Mr. Fisher and Farrel. No one spared them undue attention.

When a tavern maid approached, her garb less suggestive than the other women's but no less revealing, a smile curved Farrel's lips. Was he amused? Interested? Or savoring the atmosphere?

"Ales." Ravyn gestured to all of them. "Also, bring whatever ye be serving the patrons for dinner." The girl left, hips swaying under her red skirt.

"Captain Flynt." Meg O'Shaugnessy, the tavern's proprietress, drew near. A small, lean woman, her graying hair was hidden under a white mob cap. "How be ye?"

"Right fine, Meg." Ravyn nodded at an empty chair. "Will ye join us for a bit?"

The older woman seated herself. "Has ye just docked?"

"Aye. This morn." Of all the seafarers and landlubbers of her acquaintance, Meg was one of a few outside of her crew—and one reprehensible pirate— who knew her identity as a woman. Ravyn drew off her tricorne and passed a hand over the bandanna concealing the bulk of her braid. She sat with her back to the crowded room in their shadowed corner. "Your children are well?"

"Aye, the girls are all married and settled, my boys either building ships or sailin' on them." Her gaze shifted to Farrel. "Ye've acquired a new hand."

"Farrel McQuaid." He reached past Ravyn to shake Meg's hand. "Pleased to meet you, Meg."

Not being the customary greeting, the woman gave him a quizzing look. "A good Irish lad. Or at least the name. Ye has a strange accent."

"He's not from hereabouts." Ravyn leaned forward. "Meg, I'm hoping ye may be able to provide information I'm seeking."

"And that may be?"

Ravyn looked at Farrel. He needn't be privy to her inquiries. "Could ye allow us a moment, Mr. McQuaid?"

His expression turned mutinous, but then he nodded. "Aye, aye, Captain." He rose and retreated to the far side of the room, leaning against a wall and folding his arms on his chest. One of the ladies sashayed over, striking up immediate conversation. Farrel smiled and responded, even allowing the wench to lay a proprietary hand on his arm.

A flare rushed over Ravyn that made her cheeks unaccountably warm. Anger rose with the sensation. She wanted to get up, go over to them and shove the strumpet away from Farrel.

"Captain Flynt?" Meg's query dragged Ravyn's attention back to her. The woman regarded her with interest. "Ye wished information?"

"Aye." Ravyn forced her eyes away from Farrel and the doxy. "I thought that with ye seeing so many ships come and go, ye might have had reason to serve an...acquaintance of mine."

"And who might that be?"

"He sails aboard *The Ocean's Rage*."

Meg shook her head, a scowl darkening her pleasant face. "That ship went down last autumn, off the reefs of Sable Island during a storm. And good riddance to it."

"He went down with the ship?" Disappointment that the treacherous reefs had cheated her of her revenge twisted in Ravyn's belly.

"Nay. The crew abandoned ship afore she broke up. Last I heard, her captain had secured another vessel, but no one knows its name or heading."

"Damnation." The reefs might have been simpler after all. "Who might know?"

Meg shook her head. "I'll keep my ear peeled, but truth be known, I'd rather not be seeing any from that quarter." She canted her head, studying Ravyn. "What be the name of the man ye seek?"

"Will Flemington."

"Dear Lord!" Meg jumped up, shaking her head. "Ye be seekin' Madman himself? To what end?"

"'Tis my affair. If ye hears—"

"I'll be hearin' naught of that cutthroat pirate. And if ye know what's best, ye'd not be seeking him, either." Her gaze intensified, and she lowered her voice as heads turned their way. "I know your secret, Captain. And I know what that devil spawn would do to ye." She leaned close enough for only Ravyn and Mr. Fisher to hear. "If he learnt what ye are 'neath those man's rigs, ye'd not escape his lust. Neither man nor God nor Lucifer himself would stand in his way." She straightened. "I'll be seeing to my customers. Heed my warning. Best not even say the name of that blackguard aloud, or ye may conjure him like a demon spirit." She flicked a glance to where Farrel continued his interchange with the wench. He laughed over some remark the doxy made, and that searing angry emotion seized Ravyn again. "If ye value the life of your young man there, ye'd not be wishing to cross paths with... him."

"He's not—" But Meg had already turned away.

"That gained ye naught." Mr. Fisher leaned forward as the tavern girl returned and set three tankards and platters of ham, carrots and roasted potatoes on the table. From the corner of her eye Ravyn watched Farrel lift the woman's hand to his lips before rejoining them.

"Did you find out what you wanted?" He sat down and raised his tankard, eyes on Ravyn.

"Nay." Irritation roughened her voice. "'Tis none of your concern, regardless."

"Testy, aren't we?" He took a long drink of the ale and grimaced. "Not exactly the best stock."

"Ye seemed to be enjoying the stock well enough." She directed a pointed look at the whore, who had moved on to her next mark.

"Ah, yes, the lovely Miranda." With a crooked grin, his gaze followed Ravyn's. "She's an interesting one."

"Aye, well, ye know what she be interested in." Annoyance edging her voice, she gave a chunk of carrot a vicious stab with her fork.

Farrel chuckled. "Aye, Cap'n, but I tends to bein' more choosy about the company I keeps."

"Men," Ravyn muttered under her breath, and took a long drink of her ale. "Ruttin' beasts."

"Was that ruttin' or rotten?"

"Both."

Once finished her meal, Ravyn reached into the pouch at her waist and tossed a few coins onto the table.

"We best be returning." She rose and donned her tricorne. "Unless, Mr. McQuaid, ye'd prefer to stay and further the company of the interesting Miranda."

"Not a chance." He rose. "You're not shaking me that easily."

Ravyn canted her head, brow furrowing.

"Leaving me behind."

"I wasn't trying to," she snapped, exasperated.

The cloud cover darkened the evening, the portent of rain strong in the air. Mr. Fisher carried a lit lantern as they traversed the dim, tree-lined streets. Interior lighting from the buildings cast illumination under the gloomy sky. No one spoke while they walked toward the wharf, Ravyn wrapped in perturbed thought.

As they passed an alley between two of the rougher taverns, a feminine cry erupted from the dark passage.

"Nay! Let me be."

Mr. Fisher raised his lantern. A man held a woman backed against a wall. One hand hiked up her skirts. The other tore at her bodice. He was tough, squat of build but burly. A tangle of dirty brown hair stuck out from under a woolen cap. His clothing appeared scruffy and worn.

The woman screamed again as her dress tore. With a coarse laugh, the man pushed the ripped bodice aside and thrust his hand in.

Farrel sprinted into the alley. "Let her go." Grabbing the attacker's shoulder, he pulled him around. He shoved the ruffian, sending him staggering into the street. Growling, the man pivoted. It was easy to see by his swaying that he was none the better for drink.

"Bugger off," he hollered in an ale-laced slur. "The strumpet's mine."

Farrel's eyes lit with an enraged glitter in the lantern's glow. He dove at the man, fist connecting to the stubbled jaw with a loud crack. The man's head snapped back. He stumbled then toppled. Farrel fell on him with a snarl, driving his fist over and over into his target's face. Blood ran from the victim's nose and mouth. A bloodied yellow tooth lay on the ground near his head.

"Farrel, belay." Ravyn darted forward, grabbing Farrel's arm as he drew his fist back yet again. "Ye'll kill him."

"He deserves it." His raspy growl was barely recognizable. "Fucking prick." He tried to yank his arm free.

Mr. Fisher set the lantern down and joined Ravyn's effort. "Get up." He dragged Farrel from the victim.

Farrel blinked, breathing hard. He wrenched his arm free and stared down at the unmoving body at his feet.

He looked at his clenched hand. Blood smeared his knuckles and spotted the sleeve of his shirt. Impossible to tell if it was his or the other man's. Likely the latter, Ravyn decided with a grimace, glancing at the ruffian's battered face.

The freed woman sidled around the corner, hand clutching together the rent edges of her bodice. She looked young and frightened, the torn dress shabby. Mayhap a lightskirt, or a servant. The instant Farrel looked her way, she fled.

"Come. We best go afore anyone takes notice." Ravyn tugged at Farrel's arm. He half-staggered forward, staring over his shoulder at his fallen opponent. "We'll leave him. 'Tis sure some of his comrades will find him ere long."

Her recent dinner sat heavy in her stomach. Farrel had never come across as violent, but there had been murder in his actions and his eyes for the barest instant when she and Mr. Fisher pulled him from the other man. She suspected that left unchecked, there would have been no stopping him until the woman's assailant lay dead.

Back aboard *Retribution*, Ravyn guided Farrel to the great cabin, matching her steps to his mechanical, unfocused movements. He sank onto the chair she led him to, cradling his bloodied fist. She fetched water and a cloth along with the oil of aloe and lavender. Sitting across from him, she took his hand and cleaned away the blood. Bruises showed their beginning in spreading purple and blue patches on his fingers and the back of his hand. Ravyn rubbed the oil in, gentle as she massaged his skin. Only then did she lift her eyes to his face.

"What happened? I've ne'er seen ye in such a lather."

"I saw Julia." His voice was little more than a whisper. "I saw my sister."

She stopped her ministrations to stare at him, uncomprehending. "Your sister?"

He started then shook his head. "I...I mean, when I saw that creep, molesting the woman..." He drew a deep breath, a shudder passing through him. His hand trembled in hers. "I don't know what came over me. I had to stop him, but..." He looked away. "Once started, I couldn't stop myself. So much rage... That wasn't me."

"Aye, ye was like a man possessed." Ravyn lowered his hand to the table and sat back in her chair.

"Possessed. Yeah." He dragged his uninjured hand down his face, his expression as shattered as any Ravyn had ever seen. "If you hadn't stopped me..."

"Ye need not say it." She rose and carried the oil back to the cupboard, her own hands quivering.

"I hope it doesn't cause trouble for you. The woman... She saw us."

Ravyn turned back and leaned against the counter. "I think ye frightened her. The look on your face..." She shivered.

Farrel gave a barking, humorless laugh.

"She probably thought I'd come after her next." He shook his head again as though to clear his muddled thoughts. "No, that's not me."

Ravyn's brow furrowed. "Ye rescued her."

"There were three of us, all men to her eyes. Why shouldn't she think I'd go after her myself? There must be plenty of fist fights over women when the sailors come ashore."

"True enough. But ye need not have subdued him with such violence."

"I'm sorry you had to see that."

"But why did you say ye saw your sister?" Ravyn straightened, watching Farrel's expression.

His gaze slid to her for only a few heartbeats before he looked away again. Then he rose and walked to the cupboard beside her, pulling out the journal he had been sketching in.

Curious, Ravyn followed him to the table. He set the book down and flipped open the back cover. He had finished the sketch of his sister during the intervening days. Her face smiled up at them, carefree, a sparkle to her eyes he had captured. Farrel ran a finger down the edge of the page then sat facing Ravyn again.

"Ye said ye did this drawing in happier times." Ravyn met his eyes. They shimmered with torment.

"Yes." He swallowed and drew a shaking breath. "Before she...was... Before she...died."

"What happened to her?"

The words came out in a flood, as though he had no choice but to set them free.

"It was my second year of university. Julia waited tables at the tavern the students frequented." He stared off into space, his features tightening. "If she was working late, I studied at the library and would stop in at the tavern so I could take her home. But that night I had an exam I was preparing for, and Julia knew how important it was. As a rule, she'd phone me to pick her up, but she didn't bother that time. I think she planned on meeting me." His gaze turned to Ravyn, their light gray altering to a darker hue. "She never made it."

"Why?" Foreboding clenched in Ravyn's chest.

"She was attacked on the shortcut through the university grounds." He swallowed, and Ravyn waited for him to finish. The next words came in a hoarse whisper. "Raped, and left for dead."

Chapter 18

*R*avyn drew a sharp breath. "Farrel—"

He lifted a hand. "The man was never caught." His voice roughened. "Julia recovered physically, but... It was like he killed her spirit—beautiful and cheerful, with the wildest sense of humor. And annoying, but little sisters are wired that way." His lips curved in a faint smile that quickly vanished. "She became depressed, withdrawn, quit her job, refused to even leave the house on her own. We—my mother and I—took her for counseling. It didn't help. She stopped eating and sleeping—had terrifying nightmares when she did. The doctor prescribed a sedative—medicine—to calm and help her sleep." Farrel tipped his head back and squeezed his eyes shut. "Mom came home from work one night and found her, the empty medicine bottle on the night stand by her bed. She'd taken a lethal dose." A tear escaped the pinched-shut corner of his eye and trickled down his cheek.

"Dear Lord." Shock washed over Ravyn in a dizzying wave.

When he opened his eyes, they glistened with more tears. "We tried so hard to help her. I even took a course in psychology to see if she would talk it out with me. We were always close growing up, but I couldn't break through. Mom died of a massive stroke less than a year later. I'm convinced Julia's death contributed."

"What of your da?" It surprised Ravyn to find herself trembling.

Farrel made a disparaging sound in his throat. "He was long gone by then. Left when I was twelve. We never heard from him again."

Ravyn laid her hand on his arm. He stared down at it then lifted his to cover it.

"I thought after this long I'd finally gotten past the rage. There was no closure, no justice for Julia. I wanted so badly to get my hands around that bastard's throat..." He looked into Ravyn's eyes. "That kind of anger eats at your soul."

Ravyn nodded, all the wrenching constriction in her chest allowed her to manage.

"The night I held you down, I saw the same look that Julia had for the rest of her life in your eyes." His voice grew husky with grief. "That is, when she showed any emotion. Most of the time her eyes were...vacant, dead."

Ravyn didn't know what to say. Julia's story mirrored her own so closely it sent prickles skittering up her spine.

"In spite of what happened to you, your survival instincts are stronger than hers."

Ravyn could not contradict him. Somehow, without saying the words outright, he had guessed the truth she thought locked safely away. She bit her lower lip to stop its quivering.

"You don't have to talk about it," he said gently. "I understand. That's all I wanted you to know. But if you ever do feel like talking—"

"Nay." Her answer came out sharper than she intended. She softened her next words. "'Tis grateful I am that ye shared this with me, but I'll not be speaking of it." She rose. "Now, I think ye should rest."

He too got to his feet. He stared at her, his expression serious and, she thought, apologetic. "I'm sorry if I've done things to make you feel I'm taking control from you."

"As when ye kissed me? Touched me?" She hated saying it, but his inference was clear.

"Yes." Holding her gaze, he ran his uninjured hand over his hair. "Please, don't misunderstand my intentions. I can't say I don't enjoy our interludes, but I would never force you to do anything you didn't want. Or didn't seem to want. That look in your eyes... It nearly broke my heart to have you think I could cause that kind of pain. I care about you."

She broke eye contact as slow heat crept into her cheeks. "Aye, well, that...strangeness, when it comes over us..." Even recalling it sent a shiver through her. She gave her head a clearing shake.

"Ravyn..." He extended his good hand, palm up. She laid hers in it, and he lifted it to his lips in the customary gallant gesture. "You're a beautiful, strong woman. I admire and respect you. Please accept that as sincere."

She could not respond past the sudden lump in her throat.

Farrel couldn't sleep. All he saw when he closed his eyes was the coarse face of the man he had attacked, bloodied by his blows, mouth gaping in unconsciousness.

He remembered shoving the man away from the woman, and the swine's possessive claim to the girl. After that, Farrel recalled nothing but a white-hot blaze of madness exploding in his mind. Only when Ravyn and Fisher pulled him away had he come to his senses.

He threw back the light cover and lowered his feet to the cool planking. Funny, the tricks the mind could play under duress. At that instant, the unsatisfied rage that had lain banked like a slow-burning fire flamed high and bright, as though gasoline had been tossed onto the embers.

He couldn't decide how he felt about his actions. Glad he had rescued the woman? Disturbed that he had caused so much damage to her assailant? Or satisfied that he had, for the moment, spent his fury?

Rising, he lit his lantern. Pulling his journal, a quill, ink and sand from the desk, he sat down and began to write, committing his confusion to paper. Then feelings he had never expressed in words flowed onto the page, as though the confrontation had opened a door he'd refused to step through for far too long.

He had never shed tears during Julia's funeral or his mother's emotional collapse. One of them had to be strong. He was the man, the supporting pillar, and whatever he felt, he had suppressed with rigid determination. But tonight he had lost that control.

He sprinkled sand to set the ink, waiting for it to dry before swiping the grains from the pages and returning the journal to his desk. He felt purged of emotion, ready to close his eyes in weary surrender. Then another thought occurred to him.

How had Ravyn felt, witnessing the assault, both of the woman and her attacker by himself? She had been the first to grasp his arm, more alarmed that he might kill the other man than by the scene they'd interrupted. Fisher had looked just as astonished.

"Guess he didn't think I had it in me," Farrel muttered. Then he laughed. "Didn't think I had it in me."

He extinguished the lantern, lay down on his bunk and stared up at the ceiling, watching the shadowy play of waves reflecting against the dark wood.

In little time his eyelids slipped shut and his disjointed thoughts drifted into oblivion.

"Where is our captain today?" Farrel addressed Mr. Lancaster over lunch. Ravyn, Mr. Fisher and some of the crew had departed before breakfast.

"She and the lads are collectin' supplies. We'll be leavin' port later today."

"Oh." Farrel hadn't realized their stay would be so short. "Where are we heading next?"

Lancaster glanced up, his hazel eyes serious. "The Cap'n keeps to a regular course. We'll make south toward the lower American states. We'll likely encounter a merchantman or two carryin' cargoes back from the Continent. Better pickings for prizes if they don't carry the proper port papers or license."

"She never stays long in one place, does she?"

"Nay. There be reason for that but I doesn't know for certain. Mind you, 'tis said she be hunting a pirate vessel, but only Mr. Fisher knows why." Lancaster shook his head. "The Cap'n's protective of her ship and her men, so 'twould seem more sensible to steer clear of pirates. There be danger enough capturing enemy vessels without facin' those as would more likely kill us than surrender."

Why would Ravyn be looking for a pirate? Farrel had a few clues, but not enough to put together a complete scenario. Ravyn obviously intended to reveal nothing. She held whatever drove her too close. Maybe he could be a confidante, a friend, someone who understood.

Eventually, the demons haunting her would demand recompense. He hoped Ravyn wasn't willing to seal that bargain with her life.

Chapter 19

"Ye discovered naught?" Ravyn scowled at Mr. Fisher. They stood on the wharf, awaiting the return of the crew.

"'E's canny about 'is ship's name," the bo'sun responded in a low growl. "I knows a lot o' sailors, but none of 'em could tell me aught."

Ravyn compressed her lips, fighting the impulse to shout. Mr. Fisher's gaze dropped to her hand, clenched into a fist so tight her knuckles stood white against her dark breeches.

"Does he sail a nameless vessel, then? Come and go with the ease of a ghost?"

"'Tis said he takes a new ship and sinks the old, so no one can be sure of the name till 'tis too late." Mr. Fisher's bushy brows met in a deepening glower. "Only the dead knows where to lay blame."

Ravyn turned and stared to where *Retribution* floated on the outer waters. "So every ship is suspect till we knows their intent." She swiveled back to Mr. Fisher. "We proceed as planned, south. Mayhap we'll cross paths in the warmer seas." In gnawing frustration, she clamped her jaw so hard that pain throbbed in her temples.

At dinner, she brooded over her plate, her appetite scant as she pushed the food around. What she did eat seemed flavorless.

She caught Farrel watching her and spared him little conversation. Finishing, she left to take reports. Then she spent close to an hour hunting Sammy when Liam refused to settle.

Aggravated, she returned to the great cabin for the log entry, eager to complete it and find a moment's peace on deck. Watching the sunset always helped her sort her muddled thoughts and resolve whatever vexations colored her day.

"What does this mean?" Farrel ran a finger along a line of an account in one of the older logs.

Ravyn bent to read her muddled scribbling. Her head gave a throb, and the words danced in splitting sparkles before her eyes. Blinking, she straightened.

"Can we have done with this? 'Tis been a long day, and I've little patience for making sense of my notes."

He turned in the chair, perplexity creasing his brow. "You've been cranky ever since you came back from Liverpool. Did something happen? Was there some news of the fight?"

"Nay." She pivoted and strode to the window. "How is my business your affair?"

"Okay. Guess it isn't."

She glanced over her shoulder and saw him shake his head. Putting a hand to her temple, she rubbed at the ache. "I'm sorry. Ye doesn't deserve my temper."

"Are you feeling all right?"

"Only weary. I've much on my mind." She hadn't meant to say the last and cursed inwardly. The last thing she needed was Farrel McQuaid asking questions.

"Why don't you come and sit with me?"

She turned and studied him with narrowed eyes. "What plot are ye hatching, sir?"

"I only want to talk."

She detected no deception in his bland expression and looked away again, sighing. "I've no wish to be talking. My head is aching."

"Do you have willow bark on hand?" His chair scraped on the planking and his voice drew nearer. "The natives use it for pain. It works well for headaches. Made into a tea, you could drink it."

Ravyn folded her arms. "Nay. I might take a little opium, but I don't like doing it."

"Why not let me try a massage?"

She pivoted, not certain she should encourage him. His face betrayed naught but gentle concern. A sharp twinge speared her temple, and she grimaced. The prospect of relief overrode prudence. She strode to sit on a chair.

Farrel fetched the bottle of aloe and lavender oil. Pouring some onto his palm, he smeared it over his hands.

Standing behind her and exerting gentle pressure, he rotated his thumbs on her temples in slowly increasing circles. The pain retreated under his fingers. She sighed, and the tense hunch of her shoulders eased. When he slid his fingers around to her forehead, stroking lightly back and around her ears, she repressed a shiver and tried to shift away.

Farrel bent close enough to skim her ear with his lips. "Relax. Let my fingers do the work."

Goose bumps bristled where his breath brushed her skin. Farrel blew over the tiny prickles, and they spread, rippling down her arms.

She turned her head to meet his gaze. Battling momentary resistance, she faced forward again. He resumed the circles on her temples.

Shifting to her neck, he rubbed upwards with his thumbs. When he pressed in, pain spiked up her neck and into the back of her head. She drew a hissing breath.

Farrel paused. "You okay?" Solicitude threaded his voice.

"Aye." Her response came in a sigh as the pain receded.

He resumed the slow rub along her neck, hands kneading the tenderness she hadn't previously acknowledged. Her muscles quivered into a submissive release, leaving her almost dizzy.

Reaching for the bottle, he replenished the oil. Ravyn watched askance, doubt resurfacing.

What could she be thinking, allowing Farrel to touch her in this intimate fashion? She could not deny that his ministration eased the painful tension. And awakened sensations she would prefer remain buried. She suppressed her misgivings with effort in the face of his marked skill.

He set his thumbs below her neck, exerting pressure and moving across her shoulders. It felt wonderful, heady even, the lavender fragrance flowing and ebbing with the movement of his hands.

He pushed the collar of her shirt aside and kneaded where her neck joined her shoulders. A moan rose from her throat that she tried but failed to stifle. She bent her head forward, the tightness in her shoulders lessening. It found a lower place to settle, throbbing in that responsive cleft between her thighs. She tried to ignore it, along with the warmth that flowed through her body.

Farrel's fingers dipped into the front of the shirt. Jerking her head around, she met his eyes. This went beyond acceptable limits. She raised her hand and closed it around his to remove it.

Then she paused, and her skin prickled. The tenderness of his expression made her chest clench and her breasts tingle.

What was he trying to do to her?

He pulled free and returned to her shoulders. Leaning closer, he slid his hands to the top button of her waistcoat.

"May I loosen this?" His lips brushed her ear this time. "Maybe the shirt too? Just so I can do a proper job of the massage."

She shivered at the light wisp of his breath. Tremors crept down her arms and into her chest, sinking to pool warm in her belly, and lower, to join the throbbing in her core. "Farrel—"

"If I don't ease the tension, you'll have knots on your knots." He lifted his hands back to her shoulders and pushed into the muscles. She gasped at the pain. "You see?" He returned his hands to the button and pulled it open.

Fear and reluctant anticipation warred through her body, but she did not stop him.

The heated current of their mysterious connection flowed over her like tepid bath water, setting her whole body quivering. Her breath hitched as she gazed into Farrel's eyes. Desire overwhelmed fear, enticing liquid heat to her femininity. Her nipples, already sensitive, tightened into hard, aching buds.

He skimmed his hands up her collarbone, along her shoulders and the column of her neck. His fingertips traced her jaw from chin to earlobe. Gently, he cupped her face in his hands and bent until his mouth hovered a hairsbreadth over hers. The sultry heat of their mingling breaths drew him closer. His lips grazed hers, feather-light.

Surely, it was that strangeness compelling him, as it did her, fed by the intoxicating lavender scent swirling around them.

Her eyelids drifted shut, and a shudder vibrated through her. She wanted his kiss, wanted to let him conquer the last vestiges of trepidation and lull it into submission...

Nay, she must stop this. Now. Remind him of his place. Resist the temptation that threatened to undo her. Fight this connection that urged her to surrender. It was like struggling up through heavy water to break the surface of her control.

She pulled free, twisting and rising to face him. "I told ye afore...ye mustn't..." Her words trailed into silence, and she trembled at the hunger that glowed in his eyes, mirroring her own.

A painful twinge along her shoulders traveled up her neck, and she flinched. She rubbed it gingerly and winced at the resurging ache.

"You're still hurting. Let me finish." His voice held a huskiness that had not been there before. "Just undo the waistcoat and loosen your shirt a little." He continued to hold her eyes.

Ravyn stared at the gentle smile curling his lips. Dare she trust that look of innocent concern? That burning desire in his eyes? Her own traitorous body?

Swallowing, she steeled her resolve as that peculiar, arousing bond faded. The air settled into stillness once more.

She could retain authority over herself. However, she would not deny herself the relief his ministrations offered. But only that. Naught else.

Ravyn's expression verged on denial. Then she astonished Farrel by sitting back down, unfastening her waistcoat and pulling the shirt apart a couple of loops lower.

She must really be in pain. He reached to reapply the oil. *Okay, you can do this. Give her what she needs, not what you want.*

What he wanted—no, needed—at that moment was a long, cold shower. Bad enough that he already desired her. He hadn't needed the reminder with that kinetic connection. Or the additional stimulation that had him hard and aching in the suddenly constricting breeches.

He concentrated on kneading her shoulders, trying to distract himself from the thought of pressing kisses to that velvety skin or gliding his hands down the open front of her shirt to the soft, rounded orbs of her breasts, visible between the parted plackets...

He dragged his gaze from the tempting sight. "The next time we're in port, we should find an apothecary and get some of the willow bark, or leaves." He gave her shoulders one last squeeze before breaking contact. "That should be enough. A good night's sleep will help." He stepped back, his body's provocation calming with the desultory conversation.

"Aye, well, sometimes a good night's sleep is far from possible." She turned in the chair to face him.

"You're still having nightmares?" He drew out the chair next to hers and sat.

"Aye." She lowered her eyes but looked quickly back up. "And I've no wish to be talking of them."

Drawing a cautious breath, he decided to broach his deepest worry. "I know you're looking for information on a pirate." He raised a silencing hand when she opened her mouth. "It was difficult not to overhear Meg's reaction to your questions. I didn't catch his name, but she seemed upset you asked about him."

Ravyn jumped up and strode to the windows. "Ye've no right to question my business." She kept her back to him.

"Maybe not." Farrel rose to approach her. "But I do have the right to express my concern. Why take on a pirate?"

She whirled, eyes sparking, features set in hard lines. "Ye'd best not be interfering. 'Tis my affair, not yours."

The revelation hit him with the force of a punch in the gut. "He was the one..." He didn't finish as Ravyn stared at him for a heartbeat then turned away, anguish ravaging her face. "Ravyn, I understand. Hell, I even felt that same need to find and punish the monster who basically killed my sister. It tore me apart, not knowing who it was, not being able to face the son-of-a-bitch and see justice done. What you want to do..." She shot a glare over her shoulder. "I've read enough to know how dangerous this could get. For God's sake, I wrote about the bloody bastards in my book. Who is he?"

She shook her head. "I'll not be telling ye, sir. 'Tis my right to find and face him. Ye'll be having no say—"

He caught her shoulder and pulled her around. She jerked from his grasp, eyes blazing.

"You can order me flogged, but you can't keep me from caring. What will confronting him change? If you manage to kill this piece of filth, it won't restore what he took from you. Is the satisfaction worth the lives of your crew? Or yours?"

"It has to be." Her eyes had gone wide, pupils dilated, her expression so furious that Farrel felt certain he'd have his back to Mr. Fisher and the lash before long.

He yearned to fold her in his arms and offer comfort. But her rigid stance and tightly hunched shoulders forbid any such action. Not to mention the blue fire in her eyes.

"You can talk to me—"

"I'll not speak of it," she rasped. "Ye knows far more than I e'er wanted ye to."

"Julia didn't want to talk about it either. She held it inside, let it fester and grow until it destroyed her. I don't want that to happen to you."

"The only life I'll be taking is his." Her tone was icy.

"And in the meantime, he controls your every action." Farrel knew he crossed a line, but he had to reach her. "You pretend you're out here to capture prizes, but I think the only prize you really want is that damned pirate."

She turned her back on him. "Leave me. Now."

"Think about what I've said. I speak my mind because I care."

"Ye may wish to temper your words in future."

"I'll always be honest with you, no matter how much you may not want to hear. Even if it means I bear punishment for it."

He left, worry submerging the relief of escaping a flogging.

Ravyn clenched her jaw so tight a fresh spear of pain arced into her temple.

Why must he insert himself into her affairs? Though she knew, she did not want to acknowledge it. At times, she felt so close to him, but never more than as a crewman.

He was afraid for her. She recognized that. However, her sole reason for living was to find Will Flemington and make him pay. For killing Jonathan Moore, robbing her of her virginity—for making her suffer yet another loss that had nearly shattered her.

Drawing a shuddering breath, she pushed the heartbreaking memory away. All she must think about was finding that fiend and ending his existence.

She would permit no interference.

Chapter 20

The morning air rang with the clash of connecting steel blades. Farrel danced away from Mr. Poole's broad swing, blocking it. The officer pulled back, executing another wide arc toward Farrel's leg. Though Farrel jerked away, the tip of the cutlass caught his breeches, tearing and scraping across his thigh.

Drawing a hissing breath, Farrel let his cutlass fall. He bent, putting his hands over the wound. Glancing across to the forecastle, he saw Ravyn watching, arms crossed and brows lowered.

"Dammit." It frustrated him that she bore witness to his incompetence.

Mr. Poole set his blade aside. "Sit." He nodded at a rope coil.

Farrel obeyed, still seething with self-directed aggravation. Over the past days, Ravyn had addressed him with no more than cool indifference. His own fault, but it rankled.

"Ye'll get the right of it, lad." The gruff munitions officer fetched a flask as Farrel unfastened the knee strap of his breeches and rolled up the leg. The injury, a short, deep scratch, bled freely. "Learnin' to fight in close quarters takes time and practice."

Farrel winced when the man dripped whiskey as an antiseptic on the cut. "I hope I don't have to prove myself before I'm ready."

Mr. Poole chuckled. "Aye, well, when ye're standin' with a blade at yer throat, ye won't be worryin' as to whether ye're ready or not. Sometimes men learn more in battle than by the practicin' of it."

"Right. And some men die." Farrel shuddered. "I'll keep practicing. I like being alive."

Mr. Poole chuckled again. Farrel answered it with a rueful grin.

The weather remained fair and warm, favorable winds carrying *Retribution* rapidly southward. Ravyn kept distance between the ship and the shoreline, so Farrel had no clear idea where they were. By the increasing heat, he guessed near the lower States.

With afternoon lessons barely commenced, a cry came from outside.

"Ahoy. Ship off portside."

Slates and chalk scattered across the table as everyone scrambled to leave. Farrel followed Ravyn up to the forecastle deck. She took the spyglass from Mr. Morrissey.

"She be flyin' American colors." He pointed at the ship's flag.

"A schooner." Ravyn lowered the glass. "Six men on the decks, but there could be more below." She turned to Mr. Morrissey. "Hoist their colors. Get Mr. Poole to putting the men to arms and gather the grapplin' hooks. We're taking her."

Mr. Morrissey nodded and strode off, shouting orders.

"May I look?" Farrel held his hand out.

Ravyn gave him a cursory glance and passed the spyglass. He made out the American flag on the mizzen mast with its fifteen white stars on a blue background and fifteen stripes in red and white.

He lowered the spyglass. "You're going to capture her?"

"Aye." Ravyn's eyes met his with icy steel. "We've been too long without a prize."

"But—" Before Farrel finished, she strode after the lieutenant.

"Man the long guns. We'll cripple her if need be." She whirled to Farrel. "Take Liam and go to the gunner's store. Ye may help pass up the shot."

Farrel stared after her as she darted down to the gun deck. At the mizzen mast, one of the hands had already lowered the privateer flag and replaced it with the American one. The gunners piled ammunition at the ready. Others gathered cutlasses and strapped on baldrics with braces of pistols.

This is really happening. Alarm flared along with excitement.

Ravyn's gaze flicked to him. "Go. We've no time for ye to be dawdling."

Farrel's eyes ranged over the decks to find Liam. The boy stood by the main hatch, white-faced and visibly trembling. Farrel hurried to him. "Come on, kiddo. You'll be safer below."

They clambered down the ladder and joined Cook in the gunner's room. The ammunition rested in sacks, containing besides cannonballs, any metal shrapnel that served the purpose. Liam sank into a corner, drawing up his knees and hugging them. Cook's limp hampered him, so Farrel handed the heavy sacks up to the men. All the while, he fought anger and humiliation.

Here he was, a full-grown, fit man consigned to work with the youngest and disabled. Granted, the assistance was needed, but he wanted to be part of the action.

"Fire across her bow." Ravyn's strident call cemented his decision.

"I'm going above." He had to shout over the boom of the cannons.

"Nay," Liam shrieked. "Cap'n said as ye're to stay below."

Cook's heavy hand fell to Farrel's arm. "Be careful, Mr. McQuaid."

Meeting the man's eyes, Farrel saw understanding.

He climbed up to the main deck and looked for Ravyn. The gunners reloaded the cannons, using ram-rods to push down ammunition and powder.

The *Retribution* had gained on the schooner. A cannonball had hit the schooner's hull, punching a hole near the water line.

Farrel examined the vessel. It bore no visible armaments. Though not unusual, it seemed foolhardy to leave themselves open to seizure. Men scrambled across the decks and hauled on rigging to turn the sails. It looked like they planned to try outrunning the *Retribution* despite the risk of taking on water.

"Load ball and chain. Aim for the masts and sails." Ravyn shouted from the quarterdeck, directly above Farrel. He took a quick step back, keeping within the shadow of the wall.

The crew scurried to obey, Mr. Poole calling the commands. With flame set to the touch holes of the cannons, the men jumped back. The booming reports left Farrel's ears ringing. The recoil on their carriages rattled like rapid-fire gunshots. Farrel fought not to cough on the pall of smoke drifting from the guns.

Cannonballs joined with chain flew, whining. They connected with the schooner's sails and wrapped around the masts, shredding the canvas. One of the masts, struck by the ball, splintered. It tilted part-way up but did not break.

"Strike your colors," Ravyn shouted. "Surrender, and stand down."

The frantic activity aboard the other vessel increased in a desperate effort to outrun *Retribution*.

"Board her, lads." Ravyn's footfalls descended at a run. Farrel pressed deeper into shadow.

The men lifted grappling hooks on ropes and sent them flying across the narrowing distance. They connected with metallic thunks around the rails and dug into the deck boards. This brought the schooner to a halt. It rocked and listed as Ravyn's men swarmed across on ropes and planks shoved out to join the ships.

They outnumbered the schooner's small crew. The Americans engaged in swordplay in a valiant, last-ditch effort to defend their ship.

"Lay down your weapons, men. We are defeated." The shout from a blond sailor brought Farrel's gaze to the forecastle of the schooner. Though wearing no dress coat or distinguishing head gear, Farrel sensed the man was the captain.

Ravyn leapt onto one of the planks and crossed, cutlass in hand. She had donned her bandanna to hide her braid. Meeting the other captain at midship, she raised her cutlass to his throat, her features set in hard, brutal lines that transformed her beauty into something darker.

The young captain's face paled. "I call for quarter. Spare my crew."

Farrel ventured to the rail as more of *Retribution*'s men jumped onto the schooner and made for the hatches. A few headed to the cabin deck.

A moment later, two men exited, holding a struggling woman. She tried to pull back, shaking her head, chestnut curls dancing. Her eyes were wide, features contorted in fear.

"Andrew." Her cry brought both Ravyn's and the young captain's attention to her.

"Marianne." His gaze flicked to Ravyn. "Please, don't hurt her or the children."

Ravyn lowered the cutlass. A loud wailing issued from the cabin. Another of *Retribution*'s men exited with a crying boy in his arms. Farrel guessed the child's age to be about three. He had the young captain's gold-blond hair. Another man emerged behind them, holding the arm of a tall, black woman with a smaller child in her arms. The little girl, thumb in her mouth, rested her chestnut-capped head on the woman's shoulder.

"Easy with them, lads." Ravyn stepped back.

The men hauled Marianne, struggling and weeping, before Ravyn. They released her, and she ran to the captain, who took her in his arms. He lowered his head to speak in a low, soothing tone.

"Bring them aboard." Ravyn nodded to one of the planks.

Because the schooner sat lower than the frigate, the board rested at a sharp angle not helped by the listing of the schooner. Farrel saw the name of the ship—*Lady Annabelle*.

Ravyn kept her cutlass lowered as one of her men led the captain and his lady onto *Retribution*. She waited until the two with the dark woman and the children crossed before following. She dispatched her carpenters to mend the hull damage on the *Annabelle*.

The men brought up the schooner's cargo—casks, barrels and crates they carried over to *Retribution*. Ravyn ordered two of her lieutenants to remain, along with several hands to man the vessel, while the *Lady Annabelle*'s crew was transported over to *Retribution*.

The young captain took the little boy from Ravyn's man, holding him with one arm, while slipping the other around his wife's shoulders. The black woman stood behind them, her face under a bright turban stoic as she cradled the little girl. They watched the *Lady Annabelle*'s cargo carried over and taken below.

"What are you going to do with us?" Andrew looked from Ravyn to Farrel.

"No harm will come to ye. I'll be taking your papers and logs to make an accounting of your cargo."

"Thieves!" Marianne's green eyes flashed from her place of safety within her husband's arm. "Pirates!" Andrew shushed her, squeezing her shoulder.

"I'm no pirate, mistress." Ravyn's tone was cold. "Only a privateer carryin' out the King's commission."

Moving away, she instructed her men to take two of the *Lady Annabelle*'s injured crew below to the sickbay.

Farrel approached the family, wanting to reassure them. "Captain Flynt has given her word you won't be harmed. She wouldn't tell you false."

Marianne lifted her head from her husband's shoulder, eyes wide and tears streaking her pale cheeks. "That captain...is...a woman?" Disbelief edged her hoarse whisper.

Farrel flinched. He'd spoken without thinking. Guiltily, he glanced to Ravyn in consultation with the men escorting the wounded. Farrel swallowed, hoping she hadn't heard. "She'll make sure the men are tended to."

Ravyn strode back to them. "Captain, I must confine ye to the prison hold with your men. Bringing the cargo aboard should let your vessel float easier while the repairs are done. Your family may return once she's patched up."

"No." Marianne tightened her arms around her husband. "Andrew—"

"Hush, darlin'. It'll be all right." He gave her another quick squeeze then passed the little boy to her. One of Ravyn's crew stepped forward to conduct him below. At the hatch, he turned and blew Marianne a kiss.

She whirled on Ravyn. "Monster! What kind of woman are you, stealing from innocent travelers?" This time, her voice rose in strident condemnation. A hush fell over the deck, all eyes trained on the confrontation.

Ravyn looked taken aback then her expression hardened. She shot a glare at Farrel. He shrugged and offered an apologetic smile.

Ravyn returned a harsh stare to Marianne. "If I am not mistaken, mistress, your vessel carries embargoed goods. We be within rights to seize the cargo and the ship." She returned her attention to Farrel, her look daggers of blue ice. "Mr. McQuaid, if ye'd be so kind as to conduct our guests to the great cabin." She pivoted and strode off.

Farrel reached to take Marianne's arm, but she shrank away.

"Come. We can make you comfortable while things get settled." He nodded toward the cabin.

"I'll not be made comfortable on this pirate's ship." Her shrill denial earned a scowl from Ravyn. Maintaining an air of defiance, Marianne allowed herself and her servant to be conducted to the great cabin.

"Please, be seated." Farrel indicated the chairs. Marianne sank into the nearest one and the little boy wriggled out of her arms. "Allow me to introduce myself. Farrel McQuaid at your service." He gave a polite bow, to find the boy peering up at him with curious green eyes. "And what is your name?" He picked the child up, ignoring a sound of protest from Marianne.

"Stuart," the little boy lisped. "I'm three."

"What is your baby sister's name?"

"Rachel. She's not even one."

Farrel glanced to where the black woman held the child. "She's a pretty wee thing. Looks very much like her mother." He switched his gaze to Marianne. "Could I offer you something to drink? We have fresh water. Or I could send for goat's milk for the children."

"Water will do," Marianne responded stiffly. "I must attend to Rachel's feeding soon."

"Then I'll see you have privacy." Setting Stuart down, Farrel carried the pitcher and tankards to the table and poured drinks. Stuart climbed onto a chair beside his mother and took the tankard in both hands.

"What will happen to us?" Marianne's voice quavered.

Farrel wasn't sure of the answer himself. "All I can say for now is that your husband will be taken before the Vice-Admiralty Court." He spread his arms to indicate uncertainty. "His fate will depend on the outcome of the questioning."

"I appreciate your honesty, Mr. McQuaid." Tears slipped down Marianne's cheeks. "Andrew tried to discourage me from accompanying him, but I couldn't bear to be parted—" Her sentence ended in a sob. "And now it seems we may be parted anywise."

Ravyn entered, her features tight, mouth pursed in a thin line. "Mr. McQuaid, I'll be needing ye to bring the log for the accounting. I'll be settin' a guard here."

"Is that really necessary? I think our guests can be trusted not to attempt an escape."

"Be that as it may, I'll be posting a guard." Ravyn's sharp gaze traveled over the women and children. "Your husband is secured, mistress, and his men being tended to. I'd advise ye not to do anything ye may regret." She turned and exited.

"How can she be so cold?" Resentment edged Marianne's soft voice.

"She hasn't had an easy life. I know your present situation is difficult, but please, try not to judge her too severely."

"She's holding us prisoner," Marianne responded harshly. "What is there not to judge in that?"

Farrel had no response to her accusation.

Chapter 21

Farrel joined Ravyn and they descended to the medical hold.

The injured men lay in hammocks, one with a slashed shoulder, the other suffering a leg injury. Dr. Adam Page, an older man with grizzled hair and a deeply creased face, prepared to stitch the younger sailor's shoulder. Farrel grimaced at the thought of having the procedure done without anesthetic.

"Did you boil the needle and thread?" he asked the sour-faced doctor.

"'Twas enough to pass the needle over the flame." He nodded at the lantern hanging from the low beam.

"You should boil it all first, and use fresh on each patient." Farrel cast a sympathetic smile at the young sailor. He couldn't be more than seventeen. "Make sure the bandages have been boiled as well."

The doctor's bushy brows lowered. "Are ye a physician, sir?"

"He's a professor," Ravyn said. "A man of higher learning."

Detecting a hint of pride in her voice, Farrel glanced her way, startled at the unexpected commendation.

"Phah. Ye be makin' more work than 'tis warranted." The doctor's voice roughened in disgust.

"Diligent cleansing and proper boiling of medical instruments and materials can prevent infection and death." Farrel used his most authoritative tone, recalling too many historical tales of men dying from minor wounds that, through inept treatment, turned lethal. "It wouldn't hurt to open the portlights as well. The air can be foul down here and not conducive to effective healing."

"Ain't ye the fancy talkin' feller." The doctor fisted beefy hands on his hips. "Mebbe ye should be tendin' the wounded."

Farrel shook his head. "I'll leave the stitching to you, sir." He glanced at the boy's blanched face. "Whiskey or rum to clean the wounds, and a little opium so he can sleep through the procedure." Farrel opened the portholes on the outer hull as he continued. "Clean the wounds and change the bandages twice daily, or if you see pus accumulating." He moved to the other hammock. "I need your names and ranks for the records."

"Jeremy Smith, sir. Ship's hand."

"Zachary Metcalfe." The younger man spoke, his voice strained. "Rigger."

Farrel set the log and writing supplies on a counter by the doctor's medical instruments. He suppressed a shudder at sight of the rusty-bladed saw.

Ravyn turned to Dr. Page. "Ye'll do as Mr. McQuaid advises. What he says makes good sense to me."

"Aye, aye, Cap'n." Dr. Page slapped the needle and thread down, glaring at Farrel.

The prison had no portholes. Some of the *Annabelle*'s crew sat on the plank bench, the others on the floor, none of them shackled. The captain remained standing. Two of Ravyn's men stood outside the heavy barred door, cutlasses in hand.

When Farrel and Ravyn entered, the captain lifted his chin. "Are my men being looked after?"

Ravyn gave a tight smile. "Their wounds are tended, and with the advice of Mr. McQuaid here, they should be comfortable."

"Thank you. What of my family?"

"They are safe." Ravyn's voice held quiet reassurance.

One of Ravyn's men rolled a barrel into the room. Farrel set the logbook on top.

"We'll need your names and ranks." Farrel dipped the quill in the inkwell.

"Captain Andrew Marks of the *Lady Annabelle*, out of Norfolk, Virginia." Marks' blue eyes traveled over Ravyn, seeming to take her measure. He introduced the remaining men—chief mate, helmsman, carpenter, boatswain, doctor, cook and mates. "I would like my doctor to assist in caring for the wounded, if you would permit."

Ravyn thought for a moment then nodded. "Aye. But I'll be having one of my own men guard the sickroom."

"Are we to be detained here until you deliver us to the British?"

"'Tis necessary, I'm afraid." Ravyn offered an apologetic smile. "I may have ye brought to the great cabin for dinner. There is much we can discuss. And ye'll be able to see your family is safe."

After instructing one of the guards to conduct the *Lady Annabelle*'s doctor to the sickbay, she and Farrel entered the cargo hold.

"Tea, spices, brandy, wine, cloth, even barrels of grain." Ravyn stood in the middle of the hold, hands on her hips as she surveyed the containers. "'Tis a fine haul."

Farrel sat on a barrel with the log on a crate in front of him, quill in hand. Mr. Hennessey stood by Ravyn, acting as prize master. A few of the mates had shifted the cargo to let them inspect it. One pried the top off another crate.

"Silks and muslins to go with the lace and cashmere wraps in these last two." Ravyn glanced at Farrel as the sailor opened another crate. "More cloth, brocades and watered silks, tulles..."

With the cataloguing completed, they returned above. The carpenter and his men remained aboard the *Annabelle*, performing makeshift repairs to the mast and pumping water from the hold once they patched the cannonball damage. Tow lines were attached to the *Lady Annabelle* until the torn sails could be replaced.

Ravyn and Farrel proceeded to the great cabin. Marianne sat with Stuart asleep on her lap while the servant held Rachel.

Farrel put away the log and writing materials then turned to Ravyn. "Is there somewhere we could let them lay the children down?"

"There are no spare cabins." Her glance flicked from Marianne's militant expression back to Farrel.

"They can use mine. Would that be permissible?" He kept a steady gaze on Ravyn's.

"Aye. Ye may take charge of that. I have yet to retrieve the logs and papers." She departed without giving further instructions.

Farrel led the women to his cabin, and they settled the children on his bunk.

"Is there anything else you need?" Farrel moved his desk chair by the bed to allow the black woman, introduced as Jacynta, to watch over the little ones.

Marianne drew her lower lip between her teeth, uncertainty creasing her smooth brow. "There are some personal items I require from the schooner. But your captain..."

"I'm sure she won't object." He hoped.

They crossed to the schooner.

"Do you keep many slaves?" he asked.

"Jacynta isn't a slave. She's a freewoman. Her parents belong to my husband's family, but she came to us with the proper manumission papers as a nanny."

The spacious cabin they entered held a large four-poster bed, chests of drawers and a cradle bed bolted to the wall. A desk and chair stood to one side of the door, and two large trunks under the windows.

Farrel gazed around. "Our accommodations are poor seconds compared to this."

Marianne wiped a tear from her cheek with shaking fingers. "Poor seconds near my Andrew would be preferable to luxury far away."

"Then if Captain Flynt agrees, you may continue to occupy my cabin."

"That is most kind of you, sir, but I couldn't put you out."

Farrel saw the longing in her eyes. "Not at all. I can sleep elsewhere. Now," he went on briskly, "what do you need taken across?"

It ended up being the two trunks plus another from Jacynta's small cabin. Farrel called on a couple of *Retribution*'s men to help transport the chests then they removed the cradle bed. Once bolted to an unobstructed wall in his cabin and the trunks placed about, little space remained. But Marianne seemed satisfied with the arrangement. Farrel provided fresh bedding and left her to set up.

By the time Ravyn returned, it neared the supper hour.

"Where are ye planning to sleep?" Ravyn inspected the cramped arrangement in his cabin. "The berth deck again?"

Farrel grimaced. "I'll sleep on the upper deck, if I have to. Or maybe a pallet in the great cabin?"

"Aye, that would be permissible." Ravyn slanted him a smile. "Ye be most accommodating."

"Showing compassion never hurts. Mrs. Marks is frightened."

Ravyn stopped and faced him, sighing. "'Twas the last I expected when we seized the vessel. Most men would be wiser than to take a wife and children to sea in the present circumstances."

"They're in love." Farrel's voice softened with sympathy. Ravyn looked away, her features tightening. "What? Don't you remember what that feels like?"

Ravyn refused to meet his eyes. "Men keep their women like property. I am no man's chattel." She strode off.

Farrel stared after her. What had brought that on?

Ravyn ordered Mr. Morrissey to conduct Captain Marks to the great cabin at the supper hour. She took her place at the table, along with Liam, Farrel, and Mistress Marks, whose gaze rested on Liam.

"Liam is my cabin boy."

The other woman gave a terse nod. Ravyn indicated a chair beside his wife for Captain Marks.

Ravyn lifted her fork. "Are ye sailing for the military or a merchant?"

"A merchant. I've only recently been appointed as captain. I didn't expect to face capture so close to home." He took his wife's hand and squeezed it as she lowered her eyes to her plate. "Will I be held for long?"

"Ye'll be expected to testify to the Vice-Admiralty Court. So ye may spend some time in prison. Rest assured, ye'll be treated well while ye're on my ship." Ravyn hoped her smile reassured the captain and his lady. "Did ye visit the injured afore Mr. Morrissey brought ye above?"

Captain Marks nodded. "Thank you for seeing to their care and allowing Dr. Lorriman to assist." His attention turned to Farrel. "You seem an educated sort, sir. I'd be interested to know how you come to be on a privateer's vessel."

Farrel chuckled. "It's a complicated story. As well as serving as ship's clerk, I tutor the crew."

"I see." Captain Marks released his wife's hand to pick up his fork.

"Have ye knowledge of what military maneuvers are planned for these waters?" Ravyn asked.

"None whatsoever. I merely sailed to France, loaded the waiting cargoes, and was on return to Virginia."

"But ye didn't clear the cargo at a British port. I found naught in your papers to state this. Nor a license to carry embargoed goods."

Captain Marks met her gaze. "I had orders to make a straight course from France to Virginia. I knew the risk of avoiding the Crown ports." His mouth twisted in a grimace. "I fear we are all equal victims of government policies."

Ravyn didn't argue. The conversation turned desultory, Mistress Marks speaking little while Captain Marks talked about their home at Norfolk.

During a lull in the discourse, Ravyn ventured onto a different topic. "Has ye heard aught of pirating over the past year?"

Captain Marks gave her a sharp glance. His wife flicked a denouncing look her way. Ravyn chose to ignore it.

"There have been a few attacks. A particularly violent band, so I've heard. The most recent was a Coast Guard cutter near Salem. A nasty business. The crew all killed and the vessel sunk. I must admit such news left me nervous on this voyage."

"Any notion as to who it was?" Ravyn lowered her fork to keep her hand from trembling.

"The name I heard was Will Flemington."

Ravyn pressed her palm flat on the table, training her features to hide her agitation.

"And does ye know the name of his ship?" She kept her tone casual.

"No. If I did, I cannot remember it now."

Ravyn's fingers twitched and she curled them into a fist. How did that fiend manage to keep his whereabouts and sailing identity so close to the vest?

Captain Marks looked from her clenched hand to her face. "I wish I could tell you more."

Ravyn relaxed her hand and waved it in a gesture of dismissal.

"We're well enough armed to defend against that cutthroat. I hoped he might have been captured and executed by now." The evasive answer seemed the best response under the circumstances. But she wanted—nay, needed—to be the one meting out reprisal to that monster.

Over the remainder of the meal, she caught Farrel watching her and tried with pointed looks to discourage the questions in his eyes. Knowing his persistence, he would likely bring the topic up later.

She must make certain the opportunity for his probing would not arise.

Chapter 22

*F*arrel completed the day's log entry once Captain Marks returned below and Marianne retired to the cabin. Ravyn had left earlier to settle Liam. When she rejoined Farrel, her mouth was set in a tense line.

"Come and sit." He indicated the chair beside him. "So...Will Flemington." He gave a rueful grin. "I wrote about him in my book. I think calling him a cutthroat was way too mild."

Ravyn laughed, a low, bitter sound. "Aye. If he had a mother, he likely ate her heart and threw her corpse into the sea."

"If even half of what I learned is true, it'll be a dire risk facing him." He held her gaze.

She averted her eyes. "Did your research say how or when he died?"

The question caught him off-guard. "I found little information following the war. He just disappeared. Maybe you won't find him. Maybe my presence will alter events. The butterfly effect." He smiled at Ravyn's frown. "The simplest explanation of the concept is that a minor change in circumstances causes a large change in outcome. In this case, a time travel paradox. Was history changed before the time travel because it had already happened, or afterwards, because it hadn't?" Judging by her deepening frown, his explanation confused her. "That's just me theorizing."

"Ye've much in your head I cannot understand."

Farrel chuckled. "Sometimes I'm not sure I understand it all myself. But, Ravyn, I don't want you taking unnecessary risks."

"Aye, Mother." Though she answered lightly, Farrel sensed it came as a diversion. "So, if ye wrote about him, does ye know where he might be now?"

Her casual tone didn't fool him. "He kept himself somewhat of an enigma. Anything I learned came from historical records, archived logs and newspaper reports. Some pretty ugly stories. The last accounts I found were nothing more than rumors about an island hideout somewhere in the Caribbean, but with no substantiating facts or dates. After that, he just... vanished. No bodies, no ship, nothing." He leaned toward her, brows lowering. "I understand why you want to find him, but taking him on would be tantamount to a suicide mission. Your life is too precious to throw away on that monster."

"Aye, but it is my life." She looked away.

"Ravyn, I mean it." He fought the impulse to grasp her chin and make her face him.

She rose. "I should look in on the prisoners and see that the wounded are resting easy."

Reluctantly, Farrel decided not to press any further.

If she insisted on hunting Will Flemington, she needed all the support she could get. Her crew would stand with her, but for Farrel, it wasn't enough.

Ravyn heard the baby crying and struggled to find her way through the darkness. Yet, no matter how she strained, she got no closer to the heartrending sound.

The blackness parted suddenly, revealing a new horror.

Will Flemington held the infant in the huge paws of his hands, grinning through the blackness of his long beard. As she watched, frozen, he turned and hurled the child over the side of the ship. The crying ceased abruptly, though she hadn't heard the splash of the tiny body hitting the water.

"Nay!" Ravyn bolted upright in her bunk, tears running down her cheeks. She lifted her hands to her face, becoming aware of soft singing from the cabin abutting hers.

Little Rachel must have woken, and her crying had prompted the dream. Now her mother crooned a lullaby.

Ravyn couldn't bear to listen. Rising, she exited in bare feet. She strode to the great cabin, ignoring the curious stares of her crewmen.

Entering, she took down the lantern to light it. It creaked as she returned it to the hook.

"Ravyn?"

She whirled, exhaling sharply at Farrel's groggy voice. She'd forgotten he was sleeping in the cabin. He sat on his pallet, hair loose, shirt unlaced and open to his waist, legs and feet bare beneath his breeches.

"I disturbed ye. I'm sorry."

"It's okay." He pushed to his feet and swept his hair off his face. "Did something happen?" He reached for the leather strip to tie back his hair.

"Nay. The baby woke me with her crying."

"Oh." Nearing her, he brushed light fingertips along her cheek, tracing the path of her tears. She flinched from his touch. "What's wrong?"

"Naught." She swerved past him, heading for the cupboard where she kept a store of undiluted rum. "I felt in need of a drink. To help me sleep." She pulled out a flask and tankard.

"Okay." Doubt edged his voice. "Care to share?"

She retrieved a second tankard. Setting them on the table, she seated herself. Farrel followed suit, his gaze never leaving her face. She poured two healthy portions and pushed the tankard toward him.

"It may be best to return the captives to their ship now 'tis repaired." She stared into the cup. "Then we may all rest easy."

Farrel remained silent, and she slanted a glance at him. He watched her, brows lowered. "I think taking women and children with the prize disturbs you more than anything else."

"'Twas the risk Captain Marks took in having them with him. I only want to see them safely deposited in Halifax and have the prize assessed. I can leave the handling of it to my agent once the court ruling is made."

Farrel lifted his tankard and took a slow sip. Ravyn wondered what thoughts went through that head of his.

"It seems wrong." He set the tankard down. "Not taking the cargo," he added as she scowled, "but keeping the family separated. What'll become of them in Halifax?"

"The captain and crew will be detained for questioning. Mistress Marks can lodge at an inn or be billeted with a willing family."

"How long will Captain Marks be held at Melville?" Farrel's frown deepened. "I'd hate to see them separated too long, or have him succumb to contagion in the facility."

Ravyn gave a slight shrug. "There's no telling. It could be a matter of weeks or months, depending on the mood of the court."

"Alexander Croke, you mean. I read people respected him for his legal knowledge, but otherwise generally despised him. I hope he's at least a fair judge."

"As a captain, Andrew Marks could be allowed parole. 'Twould mean he'd be obliged to remain in Halifax, but he wouldn't be imprisoned." She drained her tankard and reached for the flask to pour another portion. "I cannot offer any more than that."

"You could let them go." Farrel settled back in his chair, toying with the handle of his tankard. "Release them, but keep the cargo."

"Are ye suggesting I cheat the Crown of its due?" She set her cup down. "I'll not be chancin' that."

Farrel's brow furrowed. "There must be a way." He took another drink before he continued. "You could say the schooner was too damaged to be worth anything at auction." He leaned forward, seeming struck by inspiration. "Or we could make it look as if he took his ship back and escaped. As long as you have the cargo and papers, you could still submit them. His escape should prove his guilt."

"There would be hard questions to answer. His complement of men is scanty, so how would I explain him overthrowing whatever crew I leave to guard them?" Again, Farrel fell silent, thinking, she knew, of a way to circumvent her opposition. "Mr. McQuaid." She made her voice stern. "I know ye feel sympathy for the captain and his family, but there be no other course."

"There has to be. I'll give it more thought."

She rolled her eyes and took a deep swallow of rum. "Ye have to be the most stubborn man I've e'er encountered."

His grin surprised her. "Matched only by the most stubborn wench I've ever encountered," he shot back.

For a few moments, they sat in silence, Ravyn brooding over her rum and taking yet another generous portion.

"You trying to knock yourself out, Captain?" Laughter edged Farrel's voice. "Much more, and I'll be carrying you back to your cabin."

"I defy ye to pass Mr. Fisher on the way." She heard the slur in her retort.

"Right. Your guard dog." He reached for the flask and poured himself another round, emptying the container. "Guess I might as well join you, then." He lifted the tankard. "Cheers."

With a crooked grin, she touched her cup to his, and they drained their tankards. Ravyn relaxed, decidedly lightheaded as she regarded Farrel with a thoughtful, narrowed gaze.

He really was a handsome man, more so in his state of disarray. Her gaze lowered to the sprinkling of golden hair crossing his chest between the parted plackets of his shirt. He seemed equally intent on studying her, gray eyes bright in the lantern's glow. She glanced down, realizing her shirt was more open than her usual wont. She looked up again, running her tongue along her lower lip to taste the last hint of rum.

His eyes captured hers, their warmth charged with tender yearning. Her body responded with an achy restlessness for which she had no name.

Farrel leaned forward and touched her face, cradling her cheek in his palm. She leaned into the caress, her eyes closing. It felt right, this contact. Yet, it did nothing to ease the restlessness. Rather, it stirred an irresistible urge to return his touch. She slipped her hand over his, sighing in pleasure.

The air seemed to take on a life of its own, a rush of warm current making a swift passage from his hand to hers, spreading into a soft, enveloping cocoon.

Her nipples tightened under the damp linen shirt, and a sweet, subtle flutter rippled through her belly, bringing an ache to the core of her femininity.

When Farrel bent toward her, she knew his intent but did not resist as his lips brushed hers. Her mouth quivered under his, and she reciprocated without conscious volition to the sweet communion.

Farrel deepened the kiss, slanting his mouth over hers. He tasted of rum and salt, his tongue teasing her lips until she opened to him. His free hand slipped behind her head to hold her closer as he plundered her mouth. Ravyn's senses reeled in the most delightful fashion.

Breaking the kiss, Farrel rose and lifted her into his arms, eyes riveting hers in a heated, dusky gaze. He carried her to the pallet and sank onto his knees to lay her on it.

He lowered beside her, once more claiming her lips. With one hand, he stroked around her waist then slid it into the open front of her shirt to cradle her breast, brushing the sensitive nipple with his thumb. Ravyn gasped into his mouth as tremors of fire and ice rippled from her breast to her limbs, then lower to blossom in a warm, moist coiling at the apex of her thighs. Farrel answered with a soft groan as his hand abandoned her breast and lowered to the dampness seeping into her breeches. He cupped her there, the heel of his hand exerting gentle pressure. He moved it against her in a way that brought her arching into the caress. She whimpered at the heady rush of desire and slid her hand inside his shirt to tangle trembling fingers in the curling hair on his chest.

He stopped, raising his head to stare at her, his brow furrowed. Lifting his hand away, he sat up, shaking his head.

"What the hell am I doing?" He took her hand from his chest, fingers tightening around it before he thrust it away. "God knows I want you, but not like this." He drew his knees up and rested his elbows on them. With a visible shudder, he laid his head in his hands.

Ravyn's perplexity matched his. Not only had she not fought him, she had wanted his touch. Her body still throbbed with wanting.

"Farrel." She spoke in a husky croak, reaching to touch his arm. He flinched away.

"Go back to your cabin. Now, before this reaches the point of no return." He lifted his head to look at her, his expression anguished. "I don't want you hating me for taking advantage." He turned his face away, uttering a low, bitter laugh. "I don't want to end up hating myself for doing it."

"But, Farrel—"

"It was the rum and that damned...whatever it is that comes over us. I know you don't want this. If I thought you did, I'd even risk Mr. Fisher's punishment." He laid his head in his hands again then ran them over his hair, shaking his head. "Please go. I shouldn't have let it get this far."

She scrambled up, lost for a reply. When the eerie connection had dissipated, she had no idea, the past moments a blur of delightful sensations she had never expected. Nor, in truth, did she want them. But in that moment, she forgot her vows, her fears, her goals. Even now, she ached to have his hands on her again, his lips on hers, slaking some deep hunger she hadn't known she could experience.

She paused at the door, looking back. Farrel still sat with hands at the back of his bent head. She left, pulling the door shut. Her shaky legs, the aftermath of rum and frustrated passion, made her steps unsteady.

It was just her misfortune to meet Mr. Fisher

"Cap'n?" He blocked her way. She lifted her eyes.

"Aye?" She concentrated on maintaining her balance.

His shaggy brows lowered. "Ye was with 'im, wasn't ye?"

She stiffened her back. "I needed a wee drink."

He snorted. "By the smell o' ye, I'd say ye 'ad more than a wee drink. Did McQuaid try 'avin' 'is way with ye again?"

"Whether he did or nay is no concern of yours." Despite her slurred words, she managed to sound stern.

"Aye, well, the man's itchin' for a whippin', and I'm itchin' to oblige 'im."

"Ye'll be letting him be unless I give ye leave. Now, if ye have no mind, I'll be retiring."

She veered around him and headed for her cabin. Her dignity wasn't helped by tripping on the single step and nearly going to her knees. Straightening, she glanced over her shoulder. Mr. Fisher stared after her, scowling.

Inside, she leaned against the door, shivering, arms wrapped across her chest. Whether reaction to the near miss of Farrel's seduction, Mr. Fisher's speculations or her undiminished yearning, she did not know.

Chapter 23

*U*p before full daylight, Farrel donned fresh shirt and breeches. Though clean laundry was a luxury, the hot, close weather necessitated frequent changes. The other men didn't care, but he had no wish to smell worse than the lower holds. He missed his daily showers, cologne and aftershave after two weeks at sea.

Had that been all? It felt longer.

He rolled up the pallet and stashed it in an empty lower cupboard, then descended to the galley. On the way, he passed Mr. Fisher. The bo'sun's glare held a fierce glimmer as it raked over him. Farrel returned a pleasant smile. Fisher had an uncanny knack for knowing everything that happened to Ravyn. The previous night would be no exception.

Right. How would she receive him this morning? Cursing himself, he ascended to the great cabin.

When Ravyn entered with Liam, she gave Farrel a long, searching look.

"Good morning, Captain." He rose and waited for her to take her seat. "Did you sleep well?"

Her look sharpened before she answered. "Aye." The circles under her eyes made him wonder. "Did ye, sir?"

He'd been restless, waking frequently—a mental rather than physical discomfort. Retaking his seat, he nodded. "Are you still planning on returning the captives to the *Lady Annabelle*?"

"Aye." Ravyn didn't meet his eyes. "I may keep Captain Marks, as surety against an uprising by his men."

Farrel couldn't imagine the small crew of the *Lady Annabelle* revolting against Ravyn's tougher men. Nor did he think Mrs. Marks would go without her husband.

"'Tis more common to keep the captured crew in their own brig. But I'll be holding the cargo on the *Retribution*."

"Sounds like you're giving thought to what we discussed."

Ravyn's chin jerked up a notch. "I am not."

Their conversation halted as Marianne Marks entered, accompanied by Stuart and Jacynta carrying their breakfasts.

"Good morning, Mrs. Marks." Farrel rose and pulled out a chair for her. "Did you sleep well?"

"As well as can be expected, I suppose." She darted a resentful glare at Ravyn, then turned her attention to Stuart. Jacynta departed, presumably to return to the cabin and the baby.

The meal was quiet, none of the adults inclined to converse. Stuart chattered with Liam, who responded happily.

"I'll be starting lessons after breakfast." Farrel directed the comment to Mrs. Marks. "Perhaps Stuart could join us?"

"Thank you. That would be lovely." She gave him a ready smile then glanced Ravyn's way. "If the captain would allow it, I would like to spend a little time with my husband."

Ravyn considered a moment then nodded. "Aye. We can bring him above. It may be his men would welcome fresh air as well, once he's secured again."

When Farrel set up, he tore a few pages from one of the primers and brought them with a pencil to Stuart. "Perhaps you'd like to do a drawing."

Stuart nodded, green eyes bright as he took the pencil and started scrawling on one of the pages.

"Thank you, Mr. McQuaid." Marianne touched his arm. "You are truly most kind."

"Not at all. I understand how upsetting this must be for you."

She nodded, tears welling in her eyes.

At lunchtime, Captain and Marianne Marks joined them. She appeared happier, leaning on her husband's arm as they entered.

Too many of the *Retribution*'s crewmen were occupied with duties involving the captives and the other vessel for afternoon lessons. Farrel stood with the Marks family on deck as the prisoners, with the exception of the wounded, were loaded into longboats and transported to the *Lady Annabelle*. Captain Marks watched, frowning, while Marianne clung to his arm, darting condemning glares at Ravyn.

"Ye'll be staying with us, sir, along with your wounded." Ravyn informed the captain. "Your family will return to the *Annabelle*."

"Not without Andrew." Marianne threw Ravyn a dark scowl.

"Ye may find more comfort in your own surroundings." A note of asperity sharpened Ravyn's voice.

"Not without my husband." Marianne tightened her grip on his arm.

"Mistress Marks, may I remind ye that ye are a prisoner." Ravyn's eyes glittered. "If I say ye return to your vessel, then 'tis what ye will do."

Marianne's eyes brightened in panic. "I won't go."

"Marianne, please." Captain Marks slipped his arm around her shoulders.

She lifted her gaze to him, a visible shudder passing over her. "I won't leave you. Surely she cannot make me."

"I can, and if ye won't go willingly, I'll have ye escorted."

"Andrew—" Marianne's voice rose to a shrill cry.

He pressed a silencing finger to her lips. "You mustn't cause a scene, love. Captain Flynt has the right of it."

Marianne shot a glare of raw fury at Ravyn. She met it with blue ice. Marianne burst into tears, burying her face against her husband's chest. He stroked her hair, speaking softly.

Ravyn took two backward steps, agitation flashing over her face. Farrel touched her arm. She spun to him, her features taut.

"Why not let her be? Maybe Captain Marks can get her to see things your way." He directed a commiserating glance at Andrew Marks. The other man met it with silent apology then returned his attention to his distraught wife. "Come on. Let's talk."

"I've no need to be talking about this." Ravyn strode away. "She and the children will return to the *Annabelle*."

Farrel turned to Andrew. "I'll try to get her to see reason." Whether Marianne heard or not couldn't be discerned by her undiminished weeping.

"Thank you." The captain continued caressing his wife's hair. "If you are able to intervene on our behalf, I would appreciate it."

Farrel joined Ravyn at the wheel. She gripped the spokes, her knuckles white against the dark wood, jaw set in grim determination.

He spoke with quiet caution. "Captain, I think you should be more accommodating to Mrs. Marks. She's upset and afraid, and I understand why she doesn't want to be separated from her husband."

"Does ye, now?" She pinned him with her frosted gaze. "And ye doesn't mind bein' put out of your quarters to 'accommodate' her?"

"No. But you seem to have a problem with it."

"I'm not accustomed to being wakened by a babe's crying in the middle of the night." Her fingers tightened convulsively around the spokes.

"A minor inconvenience, all considering"

"Ye doesn't hear it where ye are." She slapped her hand against the wheel. "Mr. Yeates." Her shout brought Mr. Lancaster's assistant running. "Take the helm."

Farrel followed as she descended to the lower deck. "Why do you have such difficulty sympathizing with her? Their whole world has been turned upside down."

Ravyn whirled on him, dark brows almost meeting over her frigid eyes. "I knew girls like her in the families we wintered with. Spoiled, cosseted, used to gettin' their way with a batting of their lashes or a few tears."

"You're also used to 'gettin' your way,' Captain Flynt."

She fisted her hands on her hips. "Tread careful, Mr. McQuaid. Ye be courting a meeting with Mr. Fisher if ye doesn't mind your tongue."

She pivoted and stalked away, leaving Farrel staring after her. His mouth curved in a wry grin. Maybe he should have carried through with the lovemaking. She sure displayed all the symptoms of a sexually frustrated woman.

He rejoined the Markses at the rail. Mrs. Marks had calmed, though she still shuddered against her husband's shoulder.

"The Captain hasn't relented, but I haven't given up. I'll try again when she's more receptive." One corner of his mouth twitched into a grin. "I don't think she knew how to respond to your wife's outburst. She hasn't been around many women in her life."

Marianne lifted her head and sniffed in disdain. "That's most evident. She doesn't seem possessed of any gentle womanly qualities."

Farrel didn't answer, keeping his own counsel as to Ravyn's 'womanly qualities.' Mrs. Marks might be right if referring to a woman of this century. Though Ravyn's unyielding nature frustrated him at times, he admired the strength of will behind it.

His lips twitched in wry humor. Ravyn was the epitome of the feminist movement. Unfortunately, way ahead of her time.

Later that afternoon, the wind carrying the vessels northward died, leaving them becalmed. The sultry air didn't stir with the slightest breeze, and the temperature rose steadily higher, rendering everyone uncomfortable and on edge.

Ravyn watched Marianne Marks where she sat on a sack of sand by the rail, fluttering an ivory fan as she tried to cool herself and the fretful baby. Though itching to send her and the children away, Farrel's reasoning had struck a reluctant chord. The woman looked fragile, as though she might swoon at any moment. Yet another ploy of a cosseted woman.

Liam and Stuart hunkered down in the shade of the forward bulwark to play a game of jack-stones under the attentive charge of Jacynta. Neither Captain Marks nor Farrel were anywhere in sight. Ravyn worried that Farrel devised some escape plan with the other man.

She glanced to the *Lady Annabelle*, sails drooping in the still air. The prisoners moved about the decks, performing their normal tasks with her men assisting or keeping vigil.

Crossing to the great cabin, she found Farrel and Captain Marks standing before the wall chart.

"So, how long from here to Norfolk?" Farrel didn't look away from the map or take his finger from a location she could not see from her position.

"Less time than one would think, but only with good prevailing winds." Captain Marks' gaze shifted from the map to Ravyn in the open doorway. "Captain Flynt."

She faced them with folded arms. "What plot are ye hatching?" The question came out sharper than she'd intended.

"Captain Marks was showing me the route he took along the coast before heading to Europe." Farrel traced the markers for the Gulf Stream current veering off to the northeast. "You must have made good headway to return so soon."

"Between the winds and fair weather, we did reach France more quickly than I anticipated." Captain Marks turned from the chart to Ravyn.

"And ye met no other British vessels on the crossing?" That surprised her.

"There were a few, but we generally identified them early enough that we could change heading to avoid them." He met her gaze. "Before you crossed our path yesterday, I thought ourselves close enough to home that we'd meet no more enemy ships."

She stepped closer to the chart. "There be a sizable navy fleet at Norfolk." She set her finger to the location on the map. "Yet ye have no knowledge as to their plans."

"My mission was purely commerce." He retreated to the table, where two tankards were set out. "I've decided that whatever happens at Halifax, this was my first, and last, voyage."

"What else would ye do?" She followed him with Farrel in her wake.

"I schooled in law." His gaze shifted between them. "My original plan was to set up in practice, but my father and uncle persuaded me to take this delivery as a favor. I've spent a good deal of time at sea. My father owns a small fleet of merchant ships, and my uncle is the merchant for whom I sailed."

Ravyn exchanged a surprised glance with Farrel. "So ye might be the best to represent your interests at the Vice-Admiralty Court." That prospect didn't please her one whit.

"Perhaps." His mouth set in a grim line. "Of course, it's more common for the captain of the captured vessel to seek legal representation from the naval court system within the captor's jurisdiction, so I may not be permitted to represent my claim." His lips twisted into humorless chagrin. "Or, rather, my uncle's claim. He's not going to be pleased at losing this cargo or my father his ship."

"Aye, well, they knew the risks when they sent ye out."

"As did I. Fortunately, thus far the only wound I've earned is to my pride." He lifted his tankard and took a long swallow. Then he set it down, a determined expression replacing his grimness. "May I speak freely, Captain Flynt?"

"Aye."

"It's about Marianne and the children." He hesitated, as though collecting his thoughts. "I know you're within rights to return them to the *Lady Annabelle*, but I would appeal to your compassion to allow them to remain. This is the last I'll have with them before we reach Halifax. There is every possibility I will face a lengthy prison term. Marianne is of a...delicate disposition, and I fear the long separation will be intolerable for her. All I ask is that you grant me this opportunity to prepare her as best I can."

Ravyn frowned, deliberating. It was not unreasonable in retrospect, but would rescinding her order not undermine her authority?

"He has a point, Captain." Farrel spoke in a soft tone.

She flicked him an irritated glance, pressing her lips into a tight line. Farrel moved to stand beside Captain Marks, as though aligning himself with the other man might gain her compliance.

"I'll consider it," she finally relented.

Captain Marks gave a nod, his sea-blue eyes serious and hopeful at once. "Thank you." He bowed. "Now, with your permission, I'd like to spend a little time with my family before the dinner hour."

Ravyn consented with a nod, and he left her alone with Farrel.

"Well, that was an unexpected revelation," Farrel commented. "Captain Marks is more suited to a courtroom than a ship."

"Aye, well, he should have kept to that plan." Ravyn turned her gaze to

Farrel. "Ye seem to have formed an alliance with the family."

"Alliance?" Farrel's brows arched. "I wouldn't call it that. I find talking with Captain Marks a refreshing change. And Mrs. Marks is charming."

Ravyn sniffed. "Charming, ye say. Is that the kind of woman ye prefer? Simpering and shallow?"

Farrel met her gaze with a frown. "I really think you're being unfair. I have no interest in her as a woman." He headed for the door. "Not that it would matter to you," he added over his shoulder.

Ravyn stiffened. Whatever did he mean by that?

Chapter 24

*N*o one ate much dinner. Mrs. Marks excused herself after only a few bites. Captain Marks followed her, with Ravyn's consent.

He didn't return until after the meal, mouth set in a tight line.

Farrel paused in making the day's log entry. "Is Mrs. Marks all right?" He set his quill aside.

"She will be. Jacynta will tend to her much more efficiently than I." The captain lifted the pitcher of water and poured a drink. He regarded Farrel thoughtfully. "You hold an unexpected position. Usually when men are pressed into service, it's for more menial labor than teaching and record keeping."

Farrel chuckled. "True enough. When Captain Flynt discovered I had no usable sailing skills, she decided to utilize those I do have."

"I think there's more to it." Captain Marks gave Farrel a probing study.

"What more could there be?" Farrel spread his hands. "They found me on the shore, brought me onto the ship against my will, and put what skills I have to the best use."

"I've seen the way you look at her. Captain Flynt," Marks clarified when Farrel feigned confusion. "I'd like to believe I look at Marianne the same way."

"So, where did you study law?" Farrel hoped the question would divert Captain Marks from the personal topic.

"William and Mary College at Williamsburg." Captain Marks shook his head. "Why I ever let Uncle Richard and my father talk me into making this voyage is beyond me. Family loyalty, I suppose. Do you have family ashore, Mr. McQuaid?"

"None that I'm aware of." Farrel glanced down at the logbook. "Not now, anyway."

"I think you have a story there."

Mr. Morrissey arrived to conduct Captain Marks to the prison hold, ending the conversation.

Farrel sat in thought. As natural as it would have seemed to research his family history, he'd never taken the time. Nor, with his father abandoning them, had he felt any desire.

A wry smile twisted his mouth. What might he have discovered?

Ravyn stayed on deck long into the night, the baby's fretful crying discouraging her from sleep. The air had cooled little with the sunset. She stood at the rail staring into the darkness, the ocean's usual slapping of waves stilled to a muffled susurrus.

Farrel joined her, leaning on the rail. "You can't sleep either?"

"There seems little point in trying, as ye may hear for yourself." She jerked her head in the direction of her cabin. Rachel's crying had diminished to fussy whimpering.

"It's likely the heat bothering her." He turned to look at her. Lanterns dispelled the total blackness on the decks.

"Aye. I doesn't like this weather. The longer it remains, the worse the storms that follow can be."

"Not sure I like the sound of that." A frown creased Farrel's brow. "It must be pure hell for Captain Marks in that airless hold."

"How else would ye suggest I contain him? I can't have him wandering about free with only the watch on deck."

"You let the crew sleep up here." He nodded to several men sprawled, snoring, against the bulkhead. "Maybe he could stay in the great cabin with me? You could assign a guard if you don't trust him."

"And can I trust ye, sir?" She fisted her hands on her hips. "Ye seem set on granting him more freedom than his present situation warrants. Mayhap you only seek better opportunity to plot his escape." She didn't miss the offended flash of his eyes.

"Have I given you reason to distrust me? I know you don't particularly care about his comfort, but, for god's sake, he's a human being. Where could he go, anyway? He wouldn't leave his family."

Ravyn gave it a moment's thought then shook her head. "Ye may have the right of it. I'll fetch him up." As she walked away she muttered, "My men will think I've lost my senses."

Captain Marks stepped above, his arm gripped by the burly Mr. Morrissey. The young captain looked bewildered, his face pale in the muted light, sweat staining his linen shirt and plastering his blond curls to his head.

"Mr. McQuaid took pity on ye," Ravyn stated tersely. "As long as this heat stays with us, ye may pass the nights in the great cabin with him. Mind," she added as he directed a grateful glance at her, "there will be a guard." She nodded to Mr. Morrissey, "I'd advise ye to conduct yourself accordingly." She started away then turned back. "I've also come to a decision about your request. Your family may remain aboard. Ye may also thank Mr. McQuaid for that." She joined Mr. Lancaster at the helm.

Captain Marks turned his gratitude to Farrel. "Thank you for your intervention on both accounts. I was beginning to feel death stalking me." He glanced to where Ravyn and the helmsman stood with their heads together. "You seem to have a great deal of influence with her."

Farrel chuckled. "Not as much as I would wish. I'm just glad she listened in this instance." They headed toward the great cabin with Mr. Morrissey close behind.

One of the mates brought up another pallet and pillow, and Captain Marks settled on the far side of the cabin from Farrel. The open windows admitted little breeze, but at least the air was fresh. Mr. Morrissey took up a position outside the open door.

At dawn, the sun slid over the horizon, a deep, burning gold. Not a breath of wind offered relief from the heat. After breakfast Farrel expressed the desire to continue his sword training despite the morning's warmth.

Ravyn observed with amusement as Mr. Poole concentrated on teaching Farrel offensive tactics. Captain Marks joined her with Mr. Morrissey to watch Farrel on the deck below.

Ravyn liked Andrew Marks. Though Mistress Marks irked with her simpering, whining ways, the young captain impressed her with his quiet capability and open conversation. The *Lady Annabelle* remained near enough to survey, and his gaze shifted to the schooner. Ravyn couldn't help but admire his concern for his vessel and its fate

"Will ye miss sailing if ye return to practicing law?"

"A little, perhaps, but keeping my family safe is what I must consider above all else." He looked toward the cabins. Marianne and the children had not yet emerged, though Jacynta had earlier delivered the morning meal. 'We can always do some pleasure sailing once this conflict is over." His brow furrowed, "Providing I am free to do so."

Ravyn said nothing, understanding his anxiety. Though American prisoners not connected to the navy were often allowed their freedom, one never knew what whim would influence the Court on any given day.

Her attention returned to Mr. Poole and Farrel on the gun deck below. Mr. Poole made a wide slash at Farrel's shoulder. He blocked the blow with the flat of his cutlass. The clang of the connecting steel brought Captain Marks' attention to them.

"He seems to be taking the training very seriously. I like Mr. McQuaid. He's clever and curious and, to all appearances, intent on becoming a passable swordsman." Captain Marks' gaze moved to her. "He's tight-lipped about how he came to be on your vessel."

"'Tis his story to tell," Ravyn conceded carefully,

The other captain's assessing gaze rested on her for a moment. Ravyn squirmed inwardly. How much had Farrel revealed about his capture and his circumstances?

One day flowed into the next with no relief. Ravyn chafed at the delay, willing the wind to rise so they could complete the voyage to Halifax. The crew became edgy, and Marianne Marks wilted more with each passing day.

Ravyn slept sporadically, disturbed by Rachel's crying, the unbearable heat and her own nightmares. Farrel observed her with increasing concern and she tried to discourage his attentiveness by becoming short-tempered with him. It only increased his watchfulness.

It occurred to her that something had changed between herself and Farrel. She couldn't pinpoint when or how it had happened. Had it been the night she'd been less than prudent in her consumption of rum? When Farrel had touched not only her body, but something deep in her soul she had thought—and fought—never to experience again?

The sweet memory of that night haunted her dreams almost as much as the horror of Will Flemington. One sometimes melded into the other, eliciting a gamut of emotions that woke her, shaking, afraid, yet consumed by a longing she couldn't connect to the dreams.

She prayed for the wind's return, to no avail.

Chapter 25

Ravyn paused by Farrel's cabin. From within, the sound of retching issued, followed by sobs and a soft, soothing voice. Could one of the children be ill?

She knocked, the summons momentarily answered by Jacynta. Behind her, Marianne Marks hunched over a bucket near the window. As she gagged, Jacynta retreated and crouched to stroke her mistress's hair away from her pallid face.

Ravyn stepped inside, letting the door click shut behind her. Stuart sat on the bunk, a wary gaze on his mother, while Rachel slept in the cradle bed, thumb in her mouth.

"Mistress Marks, are ye seasick?"

Marianne drew a gulping breath. "No. I'm..." She sank back on her heels as Jacynta held a damp cloth to her forehead. "I'm...with child."

Ravyn's gaze lowered to the woman's belly, indistinguishable in her crouched position.

"Is there naught that might ease it?" The concern she felt surprised her.

"Sometimes ginger tea helps, but I don't expect you have any." Despite her hard tone, the glance she darted Ravyn betrayed hope.

"Nay. 'Tis not something I have at hand."

Marianne shuddered, closing her eyes. "I want to go home. I want my Mama, and my sisters." She drew a hitching breath. "You keep Andrew from me, and if you have your way he will end up imprisoned." A choked sob wracked her, and she lunged to her knees to retch again.

Ravyn stepped back. A memory long buried surfaced to tear at her heart with the sharpness of a sword.

She tasted the bile and felt the roiling of her stomach that had sent her to her knees in those weeks after the rape. At first believing her sickness reaction to the brutality, the missing of her courses and the slight rounding of her belly told a different story.

The thought of bearing Flemington's babe had disgusted her, yet, in time, she came to see it as blameless and ultimately precious. But after only a few months, she lost it in a painful outpouring of blood and tears. What could have been recompense for a cruel act became yet another penance she paid for her woman's weakness.

No one knew of the infant's brief existence. Not even Eli Fisher.

She shook her head and found Mistress Marks studying her, sudden sharpness in her narrowed eyes. Ravyn realized her hand rested on her own belly. When she blinked, her vision blurred, and warm moisture trickled down her cheeks. She lifted her hands to her face, taken aback when her fingers came away wet with tears. Impatiently, she swiped at them with her sleeve. She pivoted to leave then stopped. The men could not see her weeping.

"Captain Flynt?" Marianne's soft, quavering voice accompanied the rustle of cloth. "You look as if you've seen...a ghost."

Ravyn shut her eyes, dismayed as more tears escaped. Aye, Mistress Marks could not have come closer to the mark. Frustration ate at her that a woman she held in contempt should bear witness to the frailty of her sorrow. Tension churned in her gut like soured wine.

"'Tis naught that ye need be concerned over. I will leave ye to rest." She laid her hand on the door latch.

"Wait." Marianne darted forward and touched Ravyn's arm. Her brow furrowed, and determination settled over her features. She turned to the black woman who stood, a disapproving statue, against the bright morning light spilling through the window. "Jacynta, would you please take Stuart and allow us a few private moments?"

The servant reached for the little boy's hand. He slid off the bunk and Ravyn stepped aside as they brushed past. The door closed, leaving Ravyn snared in Marianne's too perceptive study.

"I lost a child once," Marianne said softly. "Our first. It was devastating, for both Andrew and myself." Again her brow furrowed. "Have you any children, Captain?"

Ravyn's voice roughened. "I've borne no living child."

Gently, Marianne guided Ravyn's hand to rest on her belly. "But you've felt this. A life growing within you. Did your lover know?"

Ravyn snatched her hand back. "I had no such thing. Only a brute who will pay for what he did." She cursed inwardly. She had not meant to say that.

Marianne's eyes widened and she covered her lips with her fingertips. When she lowered her hand, a hard note entered her voice. "One of the men here?"

"My men would ne'er dare." Tightness in Ravyn's chest set her teeth on edge as she reached once more for the latch.

Marianne stepped around her to block the door. Ravyn fought the impulse to shove her out of the way. Scalding teardrops still burned her eyes.

Marianne's expression softened to sympathy. "You poor dear. Something so terrible, and you bore it alone?"

Ravyn glared, determined not to allow the impact of Marianne's compassion to make her lose control of the wellspring within. "We all have sorrows. "

"I grieved for months after I lost the child. Had it not been for Andrew's love..." She swallowed and blinked rapidly, as though battling her own tears. "You are far stronger than I could have been without Andrew and my family." Something glimmered in her eyes that resembled tentative admiration. "To have faced that anguish alone..." She shook her head. "I could not have borne it."

"I had little choice." Ravyn curled her hands into fists at her sides as they threatened to tremble. "Captains must show a brave face to their crew."

Marianne glanced down then back up, her expression earnest. "There may come a day when you will find love and bear another child. That will ease the pain of loss. Having Stuart and Rachel did that for me, though part of me will always grieve for the first one."

Ravyn lifted her chin. "I will ne'er let a man take such undue liberty again."

Marianne cocked her head. "Not even a man such as your Mr. McQuaid?"

Caught off-guard by the question, Ravyn took a quick step back, her breath catching. "I need no man to think he can control me, hurt me at his whim."

"What happened to you is terrible, but that was not love." Marianne's voice dropped to little more than a whisper. "I cannot say Andrew and I haven't had our fumbles. But with the right man, one who is tender and compassionate, the act is no chore." A smile tugged at the corners of her mouth. "What husband and wife share can be true pleasure, even joy." A blush rose to her cheeks. "If you let yourself receive such a gift, perhaps you can find peace in your sorrows, as I have."

"I will find my peace through vengeance," Ravyn growled.

Marianne paled, the curve of her lips diminishing to a thin line. "Perhaps if you abandoned such bitterness, you could attain a measure of happiness. Then your ghosts would be laid to rest."

"I will lay my ghosts with my cutlass." Ravyn leaned in toward Marianne. "Now, let me pass, Mistress."

Marianne shook her head, her mouth trembling into a smile. "Such hardness, Captain. But now I see beneath that. Your woman's heart." She touched her own breast with light fingertips. "Your pain."

Ravyn's chin jerked up.

"You needn't look so vexed." Mariaane's smile turned sympathetic. "We might lead different lives, but in here"—she tapped her chest—"we are very much the same. Love can heal heartache if you will but let it."

"I must return to duty." Marianne's words left her confused, uncertain. She needed to think on them. But she would not allow the other woman to see her agitation.

"Of course." Marianne stepped aside to let her leave.

What was she to make of that conversation? How could a woman who seemed so shallow discern what Ravyn hid from the world? And, she supposed, from herself?

Pleasure, in the arms of a man? Joy in the act of coupling? Was that true? Why would Marianne Marks declare it so if it were not?

She paused at the rail, shivering as she recalled those brief interludes with Farrel. How for a few abandoned moments she experienced that sweet longing, possessed by the hungry ache to let him take her. Deception or reality? Even the recollection brought a warm awareness to her body, a light throb to her core...

The other memory washed over her, the onslaught of a vicious storm swamping the exquisite recollections in an ambush of horror.

Will Flemington, looming over her as she lay nearly senseless, leering like some beast about to devour a helpless bird and tearing at her breeches. His pocked face, almost hidden by the bristling black beard and shaggy hair, yellowed teeth bared in anticipation, his fetid breath huffing into her face with the stench of ale and rot. Black eyes alight with rapacious hunger, his breeches, open, and revealing—

Ravyn shuddered, trying to push the memory back, but it would not recede.

Pain, hideous pain. Her clothing, tattered and soaked in red, blood trickling from the rived juncture of her thighs. Him, thrusting, harder and harder, laughing as she lay unable to fight, her senses still stunned after striking her head. The terrible burning as he ploughed through her maidenhead over and over, the throbbing she still felt in the throes of her worst nightmares—

She went to her knees, gripping the rail as she drew deep, ragged breaths to calm the frantic pounding of her heart.

That other day swept over her—crushing pain and the hot rush of blood, the agonizing realization that her child had died. Cradling the tiny, wizened body in her hands, and in anguish seeing the evidence of a daughter she could have loved and raised, if only she'd known how to keep her safe until the fullness of time. A soft kiss pressed to the wrinkled forehead and a fleeting caress to a cold, blue-tinged cheek, all she could give of love that would never come to fruition.

Weeping as she wrapped the little one tenderly in a piece of soft bleached muslin, then an old wool blanket with a heavy stone, tied shut. Dropping the bundle out her cabin window with a whispered prayer for the wasted life. The shattering splash as it hit the comfortless ocean, to sink into a cold, watery grave. Part of her, lost to the weakness of her body's betrayal. Taking the all-consuming grief and guilt within herself, she had buried it with the infant's memory. More alone than she had ever felt in her life.

She couldn't restrain the sobbing cry that exploded from her lips. "Nay! Oh, sweet, precious one! Please God, nay!" She sagged onto the deck, arms clutched around herself, lost to the devastating grief.

Chapter 26

$\mathcal{F}$arrel spun at Ravyn's cry. He stared, stunned, at her lying on the deck, arms wrapped around herself and knees drawn up, as if in pain.

"Ravyn? What the hell?" His cutlass clattered onto the deck and he sprinted across to her. When he swept her up into his arms, she buried her face against his shirt, sobbing.

"Cap'n? Are ye aright?" Mr. Poole's weathered features creased in concern. Other men paused in their tasks and watched with various degrees of interest.

Farrel knew Ravyn wouldn't want to be on public display as she struggled to choke back her weeping. "I'll take her to her cabin."

He carried her to her quarters and kneed the door open. He set her on her bunk, but she clung to him, shuddering. Farrel disengaged her arms from around his neck and stared into her tearing eyes. She blinked, and drops slid down her cheeks. He brushed the tears away with his thumbs.

"Mr. McQuaid?" Marianne Marks hovered in the doorway, green eyes wide, her face pale. "What happened?"

"I'm trying to find that out." His gaze lowered again. "Ravyn?"

"I'm...fine," she managed between stiff lips. But the way her breath caught in hitching gasps and the unfocused shimmer of her eyes told him something was very wrong.

"Fine, my ass." He darted a glance over his shoulder at Mrs. Marks. "Sorry. Maybe you should let me handle this."

She nodded and withdrew.

Seconds later, the hulking form of Eli Fisher filled the opening. "What've ye done to the cap'n?" The bo'sun's query vibrated with warning.

"Nothing. She collapsed." He glared at Fisher. "If you'll give me a few minutes, I'd like to try to sort this out."

"Ye'll be doin' 'er no harm."

Farrel sighed. "Of course not. We just need a few minutes of privacy."

Ravyn's gaze shifted to Fisher, and she put visible effort into composing herself.

"'Tis aright, Eli." She barely got the words out. "See to the men."

"Aye, aye, Cap'n." His scowl relayed his displeasure at the order, but he stepped back.

"And close the damn door." Farrel kept his worried gaze on Ravyn. "She doesn't need an audience." Other curious faces had appeared behind the bo'sun.

"Farrel," she whispered once they were alone.

"Shh. Just rest a moment." He rose and carried back a tankard of water. Slipping an arm behind her back, he lifted her to take a drink. He set the tankard on the floor and eased her onto the pillow. "What happened out there?"

Ravyn shook her head, unable to vocalize the horror that even now threatened to pull her back into a relentless, clawing grip. Her breath shortened to labored panting as resurfacing panic swamped her anew.

"Whoa. Ravyn?" Farrel's hand clasped her shoulder. She struggled to focus, but her mind sank back into that terrible, dark place. "Listen to me. Tell me the names of your crew. Now."

It seemed his words came from a long distance away. She blinked in confusion

"The men. Come on." Though temperate, his voice held an edge of steel that brooked no quarter for questions. Not while the encroaching darkness held her in its clutches.

"F-Fisher. H-Hennessey. M-Morrissey—" She gasped as the resurging cloud of devastation squeezed the breath from her lungs.

"Christian names. What are they?"

She blinked again, lips parting as she stared into his eyes. They had turned the gray of a stormy sea, of rocks battered by frothing swells.

"Eli." She whispered the first, feeling the roiling horror recede like the early tide. "Gabriel. Alec. Tom. Henry." As she searched her mind for and uttered each name, the wave of pain fell back even more. "Jem. Ian. Franklin." She thought she'd forgotten so many of them, but they tumbled from her lips. "Charlie, Samuel..." The vise of panic loosened and she breathed easy again. "Fergus..."

"Good." Farrel's hand drifted up to her cheek. "That's better." He straightened, his gaze soft with caring.

Ravyn drew a shaky breath. "How...how did ye know to have me do that?"

"It's called grounding, a way of diverting your thoughts from the trauma. When that...feeling comes over you, make a list in your head. What, doesn't matter, so long as you focus on it rather than the fear." He gave an encouraging smile, though his eyes remained serious. "Now, tell me what happened."

Despite the gentleness of his tone, the hint of a plea, Ravyn's jaw clenched. She wasn't going back there. Not now that she had pushed the dreadful memories to their rightful hidden place in her mind.

"You're going to make me guess?" His brow furrowed. "My first thought would be heat stroke, but it's too early in the day. Plus, you were sobbing."

Ravyn turned her face away. That must surely cost her. How could the men respect her authority after this?

Farrel's hand cupped her face to turn her. She resisted the light touch, but he held firm.

"You had a memory, didn't you? Maybe even a waking nightmare?"

Aye, that described it precisely. She gave a jerky nod.

"What brought it on?"

She shook her head in resolute denial. That, she would never tell. She prayed Marianne Marks would keep her own counsel as well.

Farrel glanced away, his mouth tightening, and a muscle twitched along his clenched jaw. When he looked back, a frown puckered his brow. "Stubborn woman. Well, I'm no psychiatrist, but if I had to hazard a guess, I'd think you had a PTSD flashback." Ravyn creased her brow in confusion. "Post-traumatic stress disorder. It usually happens soon after the trauma, but I suspect you've managed to hold it at bay ever since the assault. Except in your dreams, maybe."

"I have to be strong." She drew a hitching breath. "My men—"

"Is that what you think? That you have to deny the memories so you can keep control of your merry band of sailors?" His frown deepened. "You can't bury these things for long. Julia tried, and it destroyed her. Letting your feelings out sometimes can be a good thing."

She struggled to sit up, but Farrel restrained her with a firm yet gentle pressure. "How can this weakness be a good thing?"

"You're not weak, Ravyn. Far from it. But you're not superhuman, either. If you would talk to me—"

"Nay. I will not speak of it, e'er."

"Would you write about it, then? The assault, the dreams, all of it?"

"Nay," she whispered. "I could not—"

"Why? If you don't overcome this, you'll never be free." Frustration hardened his voice.

"I'll be free when I kill him. His death will be my release."

"Will it?" Farrel spoke in a calmer tone, his gaze intense. "Will it erase the memories, restore everything you lost?" She flinched at the brutal reminder, turning her face away. He cupped her cheek and pulled her back. "That didn't come out right." Contrition moderated his voice. "I meant that vengeance isn't the solution. It may make you feel vindicated, but it won't change the person you've become. Conquering your demons is the surest way of getting past this."

She wished she understood everything he said. But the tenderness that softened his eyes... Fighting the infuriating urge to cry, she drew a shuddering breath and lifted her hand to cover his where it rested against her cheek. Damn this weakness.

It seemed his hand became warmer against her skin, a whispering heat spreading in a soft breath along her arm, and his, judging by the way his eyes altered to a silvery hue. His fingers moved in a caress over her cheek as he bent closer.

"Let me help you." His words came out low and earnest. "We can work through this together."

She tried to swallow the tears, to train her expression to stern refusal. But the warmth of his touch continued to brush over her face and along her arm, their connection a palpable thing reaching past her defenses. Tears leaked from her eyes. She gritted her teeth, willing them to stop. It was like trying to hinder capsizing waves in the midst of a typhoon. Farrel wiped the escaping drops away with his thumbs.

Regaining control, she drew a deep breath. "I'll try, but not now."

"Okay." He bent and touched his lips to her forehead. She let the tender gesture pass unchallenged. "You should rest for a bit. We'll talk more later."

"The men. I have to explain—" She tried to sit up, but Farrel kept a light, curtailing hand on her shoulder.

"Let me. What would you like me to say? That the heat got to you?" He shrugged as she frowned. "It makes the most sense and happens to the best of us."

"But my cryin'..." She didn't care to speculate on what they'd think about that. "I have to face them. Ye can't be taking my place." Anger shot through her, shocking in its intensity. She started to sit up again, but once more he urged her down with a gentle, restraining hand.

"I'm not trying to." He rose. "Give yourself time to recover before you face them." At the door, he turned and met her eyes. "There's nothing wrong with accepting help now and then. That's all I'm asking you to do."

When the door shut behind him, she turned to the wall, drawing her knees up and folding her emotions as tight as she did her body. She had to be strong.

Farrel wanted to help her. What worried her was that his help would weaken her resolve.

That could never happen. Not until that vile animal known as Will Flemington lay dead at her feet, her cutlass buried in his black heart.

When Farrel stepped out to the deck, Marianne Marks stood nearby. She looked so pale and anxious that Farrel stopped to reassure her.

"She'll be all right. I think it was the heat and too many sleepless nights. She drives herself pretty hard."

Marianne nodded. "We spoke just before it happened. I hope our conversation didn't overwhelm her."

"What did you talk about?"

A slow blush climbed into her cheeks, and she looked away. "Only female topics. Ones men wouldn't understand."

Farrel folded his arms. "Try me."

She gazed at him with uncertainty, and her jaw set. "N-no, I cannot." A fretful wailing came from within the cabin. "I must tend to Rachel. Please, excuse me." She hurried inside before he could say anything more.

He stared at the closed door, confusion warring with annoyance.

Whatever they had discussed must have been delicate. Or highly indelicate, considering Ravyn's collapse.

He shook his head, frustrated.

Women. Go figure.

Chapter 27

When Farrel entered the great cabin, Andrew and Marianne Marks stood by the open window. She leaned into his embrace, crying as he stroked her hair.

"You should return home, even if I am detained in Halifax."

"But I want you with me. I can't have this baby without you."

About to withdraw, Farrel halted mid-stride.

Marianne Marks, expecting a baby? A board squeaked under his lowering foot, and Marianne lifted her head.

"Oh. Mr. McQuaid." She brushed the tears from her cheeks. "We didn't hear you come in."

"I'm sorry." He turned to leave.

"You don't have to go." At Andrew's voice, Farrel swiveled back. The younger man stepped away from his wife. "I take it you overheard our happy news."

"I did. Congratulations." Farrel walked across to shake Andrew's hand and give Marianne a reassuring smile. "I know the circumstances aren't ideal, but we'll see how things go in Halifax. Take it one day at a time." A thought occurred to him. "Does Captain Flynt know about the baby?"

"Yes. She came to see me while I was ill." Marianne's mouth tightened and she looked down. "But you already know we talked."

Though tempted to probe deeper, Farrel let it go.

"Shall we take a stroll about the deck?" Andrew tucked Marianne's hand into the crook of his arm. "Mr. McQuaid may wish to finish some tasks here."

Farrel didn't contradict Andrew. He wanted to think. Questions rolled around in his head like marbles on a tilted game board. Sitting on the window seat once the couple departed, he stared out at the wide expanse of sun-dappled water.

So, the subject of Marianne's pregnancy had come up with Ravyn. Would that have triggered a flashback? Why?

He recalled her words, ringing clear on the morning air.

"Nay! Oh, sweet, precious one! Please God, nay!"

He had thought her cry was for her slain captain. Now, he wondered.

Had Ravyn borne—or lost—a child? But when—and by whom—could she have been impregnated? A virgin when Will Flemington raped her, her resistance to intimacy made Farrel certain she would have taken no lover since then. So, that seemed to mean...

His thoughts stuttered to a shocked halt.

Had that act of violence led to a pregnancy? Had she given the child up for adoption? Deliberately aborted it? Or miscarried? He couldn't forget the agony in her cry, the despair and grief. He recalled a colleague whose wife had miscarried late in her pregnancy. The pain of loss had been as consuming as losing a living child. He supposed it would be, anticipating that new life, only to have it ripped away.

It would explain so much.

Ravyn refused to rest past noon. She wondered what Farrel had told the men, not missing their wary glances as she passed by. She kept her head high, her expression tight-lipped as she returned their glances with icy severity.

Mr. Lancaster manned the helm, his lean face haggard. Sweat ran along his face and neck.

"I'll take the wheel for a time. Ye go below and rest."

"Aye, aye, Cap'n." He threw her an uncertain glance.

Biting back an angry remark, she harnessed her roiling emotions. Nothing would be proved by snapping at him, save that she was not in command of her disposition.

The tilt of the boards under her bare feet, the whisper of the sails above and the soft rush of the ocean against the hull absorbed her senses. This was her solace, her remedy for agitated emotions. She could be one with her vessel in a way she couldn't with people. Each roll of the deck, every flick of sail and rigging spoke a language she had long understood. Peace existed in this oneness, *Retribution* akin to a living being with which she could communicate. She could let her cares float away, sense each motion of rudder and bow with her hands upon the wheel.

She let her thoughts drift, closing her eyes to give her senses free reign, convinced that even blind, she could navigate the ocean's byways.

"Captain?"

Her eyes snapped open. Farrel gazed up from the deck below. He ascended to stand beside her and look out over the lightly rippled water.

"Why are ye not teaching?" The sun had made little progress toward the west.

"I was worried about you." His gaze shifted to her. "Are you all right?"

"I was better afore ye disturbed me." She avoided his eyes, fixing her attention on the almost non-existent forward move of the ship.

"Sorry. I wanted to make sure you were okay." He paused, but she did not return her notice to him. "I know you talked with Mrs. Marks, before you collapsed."

She turned a wary look to his intent study. "What did she tell ye?" Harsh guardedness threaded the question.

"Nothing. She kept your conversation confidential." Farrel continued to study her.

"Good."

"Something she said upset you, didn't it?"

The sharp spear of anger shot through her again. She faced him, scowling. "I know ye mean well, but I'll not speak of it here or now."

Their eyes met and held. Farrel was the first to look away, his mouth tightening. "Of course. You're entitled to your privacy."

"Ye're nay going to press me about..." She floundered for the phrase he had used but could not recall it.

"No." He started down the steps to the deck below. Halfway, he stopped and looked back over his shoulder. "When you are ready to talk, you know I'm willing to listen." He proceeded out of sight into the great cabin.

Ravyn stared after him, bewildered. That wasn't what she had expected. Usually he pursued a topic with the tenacity of a shark scenting blood.

She did not speak to Farrel for the remainder of the afternoon. Following dinner, while he attended to the log, she took the evening report from Mr. Lancaster. About to descend, she saw Captain and Mistress Marks standing by the rail below.

Andrew held his wife's hand and gazed at her upturned face with a tender smile. Marianne stepped forward as he slipped an arm about her waist to draw her close. He bent and kissed her, first brushing her cheek, then bestowing a lingering caress to her lips.

Ravyn looked away, noting that her crew averted their eyes from the romantic exchange. When she looked back at the couple, Andrew had taken Marianne's hand and drew her to where canvas hung over the deck for shading, with another sheet as a curtain to separate it from the rest of the deck. Though they would not be visible from the level below, enough gaps were in evidence from where Ravyn stood to see them.

Andrew enfolded his wife in his arms, continuing to kiss her, one hand running over her back. When he lifted his head, he spoke softly, the words inaudible from Ravyn's vantage point. But she could not mistake the gentleness of his low voice or his loving manner. Marianne nestled her head on his shoulder, and he stroked her hair, pressing another kiss to her brow.

Ravyn had seen enough. She descended and moved to the forward end of the ship, feeling as though she had swallowed some of the ship's ballast and it had lodged in her chest. She stood at the rail, gazing with unseeing eyes at the rippling vista of ocean.

Over the years, she had borne witness to the men with their women, commonly lightskirts either permitted aboard or met ashore. Never had she seen that manner of affection. The bawdy by-play was more often rough and tumble, though the 'ladies' seemed to revel in it. Most times they were as drunk as the men, all restraint banished and mores non-existent. She could only imagine what transpired in private. Only after her father's death had she observed the randy exchanges. She understood men needed that nature of relief, but the women? Her mouth tightened. If what Will Flemington had done to her was the 'gift' of a man's 'relief,' she would have none of it.

Not even from Farrel in his tenderest of moments.

Yet the weighted longing in her chest did not ease.

Farrel set the quill aside and exhaled a long, frustrated breath. He wanted to believe Ravyn would talk to him eventually, but maybe that was a fool's hope.

"Stubborn effing woman. You hang onto your pain like no one else could possibly understand."

But hadn't Julia held onto her trauma the same way and for the same reasons?

He pulled the journal closer and flipped to the last page. The sketch of Julia gazed up at him, the carefree self she had been before that tragic night.

"Dammit." Farrel slapped the journal shut and jumped up. He paced, hands clenched. "I wish to God you'd let me help you."

Furious, he snatched up the nearly empty inkwell and hurled it at the wall. It thumped off the polished wood, too heavy to break, and rolled on the floor. The residue of ink ran down the wall, reminiscent of black trickles of blood.

He continued to pace, scowling. He had waited for Julia to find her voice. In the end, all she had found was lethal release in the contents of a pill bottle. Ravyn felt that exacting revenge would be her release. In all likelihood, it would bring her death.

Farrel halted, shutting his eyes as an instant of staggering pain speared through him. He couldn't let that happen.

Uttering a sound of exasperation, he scrubbed his hands over his face. If Ravyn wasn't ready to trust him, how could he prevent her making a mistake that could tear her away from him? He needed an ally. Someone she would listen to.

A hoarse shout from the deck brought his head up. He'd recognize that roar anywhere.

Eli Fisher. The only person who might influence Ravyn.

The thought of approaching the irascible bo'sun wasn't on Farrel's list of top ten things to do before he died. Which might just happen if Fisher took offense to his enquiries.

He replaced his journal and the writing implements in the cupboard and stood for a moment, psyching himself up. No time like the present to confront the formidable giant.

Chapter 28

$\mathcal{T}$he sun hung low on the western horizon, a red ball promising another hot day ahead. Farrel spotted the burly bo'sun at the foot of the mainmast delivering a blistering reprimand to one of the younger hands. His harsh, gravelly tones laced the air with menace. Farrel's shoulders sagged. Not a good omen. He thrust away the fleeting impulse to defer his questions to a safer time. As much as Eli Fisher detested him, was there even a safe time? Farrel grimaced. Probably not. Best buck up and get it over with.

He waited until the young sailor skulked away. Taking a deep breath, he stepped forward. "Mr. Fisher."

The bo'sun turned, bushy brows lowering. "Aye?" No welcome in that tone.

"I need to speak with you. Privately."

Fisher's scowl deepened, yet curiosity flickered in his steely eyes. He jerked his head toward the rail.

Farrel had hoped they could retire to the great cabin, but it might be better to remain in the open. At least there were witnesses if the bo'sun reacted violently. The deck was relatively deserted, only a few hands tending to the rigging and smaller tasks. Most would have retired below for the evening meal.

"So, what does ye want?" Wariness edged Fisher's raspy voice.

"I'd like to talk to you about Ravyn...ah, Captain Flynt."

"Why should I be tellin' ye aught of the Cap'n?" If possible, his brows furrowed even more over his sharp, assessing eyes.

There was no delicate way of phrasing this. Farrel took a fortifying breath. "I know what Will Flemington did to her. I also know she's hell-bent on revenge."

"Why should she not be?" Fisher's growl accompanied a grimace that pulled his face into ugly hatred. "That whoreson needs killin'."

"I don't disagree. But do you think she's strong enough to go up against him?"

"She be stronger than many a man I knows." Fisher's contempt was clear in his gap-toothed sneer as his fierce eyes pinned Farrel. "And she'll nay be alone."

"She wasn't the first time, either."

The bo'sun bristled. "What're ye drivin' at, ye bloody good-fer-naught?"

"Only that what happened left her..." He couldn't say 'traumatized' and struggled to find a word to convey her vulnerability. "Susceptible to... episodes like today's. She may be strong, but there are some things the mind cannot fight. If she faces him and has one of those spells..." He shrugged, suppressing a shudder. "What do you think will happen?"

Fisher didn't answer right away. His features creased as if he tried to picture Farrel's scenario. Then he shook his head.

"She's ne'er 'ad fits like that afore. The lass 'as always been a hardy sailor." He frowned again and spoke almost to himself. "Save for those weeks after we met up with Madman."

"What happened then?"

Fisher's attention snapped back to him. "Ye're a meddlesome bugger, McQuaid." He leaned closer in overt threat. "What business be it of yers if she was ill fer a time? The seasickness is common, though 'twas strange the lass suffered it."

"Seasickness." Or morning sickness? "How long did it last?"

Fisher scowled. "I'll be speakin' nay more o' the Cap'n's affairs. If ye knows what 'appened with Flemington, ye already knows too much." He curled one beefy hand into a fist. "Now, be off with ye, afore I tosses ye o'erboard with the rest o' the vermin."

Farrel took a quick step back. Seemed he'd gotten all he was going to by way of information. He hoped he had planted enough of a seed in Fisher's dim-witted brain that he'd consider the possible consequences of Ravyn confronting Flemington. And maybe stop her before it was too late.

He lifted his hands. "Fine. No harm meant."

"Cagey bastard." Fisher followed him, lifting his fist. "Ye're changin' 'er. She's not bin the same since ye come aboard."

Coldness crept into Farrel's voice. "And that's a bad thing?"

"Aye, 'tis." Fisher shook his fist in Farrel's face. "She's a cap'n. She 'as to be strong."

"But she's also a woman. She may have been raised and treated like a boy, made to take on the responsibilities of a man, but there is a beautiful, sensitive woman inside her."

Fisher sneered. "What did bein' a woman get 'er but 'urt? She's nay one o' them weak, willowy creatures. 'Er Da an' me seen to that."

An unexpected insight Farrel tucked away for further consideration.

When he remained silent, Fisher continued in a low growl. "Ye're tryin' to make 'er soft. Make 'er less than she 'as to be."

"Or maybe I'd like to see her become more." Farrel stepped away from the rail.

When he entered the great cabin, Andrew Marks turned from the window. Mr. Morrissey nodded to Farrel and stepped outside.

"It seems you've had an eventful day," Andrew commented with a crooked smile. "Mr. Fisher doesn't care for your interest in Captain Flynt."

"Heard that, did you?" Farrel returned his grin. "He's a bit of a bear when it comes to her."

Andrew chuckled. "Yes, he does bear some resemblance to a grizzly. But you stood up to him. Good man."

Farrel answered with a wry chuckle. "Can't say how much longer it'll be before he decides to use his nine-tailed companion on me." They sat down at the table, turning their chairs to face one another.

"Your captain might have something to say about that." The younger man regarded Farrel thoughtfully. "I still can't help wondering how you ended up on this vessel. Surely once she realized you weren't a sailor, she would have let you go."

Farrel scratched his ear, trying to form a feasible response. "When she found out I could read and write, she decided I'd make a good ship's clerk and tutor. I keep busy enough."

"Indeed." Andrew nodded, his expression becoming serious. "I think you've only told part of your story, though." His searching gaze intensified. "Where is your home?"

Farrel studied Andrew, trying to decide how much of the truth he dared reveal. "I came from...York. Upper Canada. I was a teacher." That seemed safe enough.

"Ah." Andrew leaned forward, clasping his hands on the table. "What brought you to Nova Scotia? It seems an odd place to have been, so far from home."

"I'm...a bit of an explorer." That too could be construed as truth. A rueful smile curved his mouth. "I ended up in the wrong place at the wrong time."

"You do an excellent job of providing just enough information to answer my questions." Andrew returned his smile. "But my lawyer's instinct says there's really much more to your story."

He rose and moved to the cabinets, pulling open a drawer, the one holding Farrel's modern devices. Farrel half-rose in alarm, but Andrew already had the camera in his hand. He closed the drawer and resumed his seat.

"This is a digital camera." He touched the power button.

Farrel stared at him, frozen by shock as the device powered up.

"You weren't born in this era." The captain's eyes met his. "Neither was I."

Once more Farrel watched, dumbstruck, as Andrew scrolled through some of the pictures before shutting the camera off again and setting it down.

"Does Captain Flynt know?"

"Yes. It wasn't an easy reveal." Farrel grimaced at the memory.

"Did she believe you?" Andrew met Farrel's eyes, his own twinkling in amusement. "She must have, or you likely wouldn't be alive to tell the tale."

"Yes, but it took a while. So, how—when did you...?"

"I was—or will be—born in 2008. My home is Norfolk, but I...left in 2016. I was just a child." Captain Marks picked up the camera. "I found this the other day when you left me alone for a few minutes after dinner. My parents...my real parents...had one like it." He rose and replaced the camera to the drawer, then faced Farrel. "You have a cell phone too, not that it's doing any good here." He cocked his head. "What happened to you?"

"A storm. I ended up close to a lightning strike. I think it must have had something to do with the electromagnetic charge in the air. Or it created a rift in the time continuum."

Captain Marks resumed his seat. "Your story doesn't differ much from mine. My parents and I were in a serious car accident. There was a storm, as with you, and the vehicle slid off the road into a hydro pole. The live electrical lines fell on the car. I remembered my father saying I should never get out if such a thing happened.

"We'd spent the day visiting antique shops. I saw a little wooden horse in one, and they bought it for me. I was holding onto it when the accident happened. Whether from the electricity arcing around the car or the storm, I lost consciousness. When I came to, I was lying on the road, a graveled one. Our car was gone. A horse-drawn carriage stopped and a couple disembarked and took me back to Norfolk. Althea and Hector Marks, my parents here.

"The Markses had recently lost a son and were convinced finding me was Heaven's way of assuaging their grief. They raised me, sent me to school, loved and treated me as their own. It didn't take long to accept this as my home and them as my folks." He scratched the back of his neck with a wry smile. "Funny thing, I remember holding that wooden horse when I blacked out, but it was gone when I woke up. A few months later, one came into the mercantile my new parents frequented, and when I said I'd lost one like it, they purchased it for me. I believe it was the same one."

Rowena's ring. Had he really lost it on the trail to the beach, or was it somewhere in this time, waiting to be found?

"Anyway, this is where I belong. I might have been born in the twenty-first century, but the nineteenth is my home."

Farrel nodded. "I may have to accept that too."

"It isn't so terrible, especially if you have a reason to stay." Captain Marks gave Farrel a crooked grin. "I'm glad I found out about you. Perhaps it might have been easier for me because of my youth, but I believe you have the skills, the determination—and the reason—to adapt." He extended his hand, and they shook on their mutual secret. "I wish you the best of luck. With your journey—and your captain."

He could have no idea how much his commiseration meant to Farrel.

After they settled on their pallets, Farrel lay staring up at the beamed ceiling.

Though he had given superficial thought to the prospect that he might never be able to return, for the first time he entertained it as concrete certainty. He should feel a sense of loss for everything left behind, but it didn't manifest. Instead, he could only focus on the challenges surrounding him. After all, what did he have to return to? An empty house filled with remnants of the same past he now occupied? Reminders of loss, pain and grief that could never be resolved? A position filled with detached, transitory relationships?

What he had here seemed far more substantial. Though danger was a constant companion, he had formed connections he wanted to make stronger, deeper, more personal than those in his own time. Most of all, he wanted to save Ravyn—from Flemington, from her fears—from herself.

The realization left him stunned and oddly grounded at once. He closed his eyes, drawing a slow, steadying breath.

How much more peculiar could things get?

Chapter 29

After a restless night, Ravyn stomped into the great cabin. Farrel and Captain Marks sat with their heads together in low conversation. They broke off at her entrance.

"Good morning, Captain Flynt." Andrew Marks rose and waited for her to sit before resuming his chair. He flicked a glance at Farrel, and a slight twitch quirked Farrel's mouth. He hid it quickly by clearing his throat.

"Good morning." Her voice sounded raw and surly even to her own ears. Farrel's brows lowered. She returned his frown. After a moment, he looked away. Her scowl deepened. What ailed the man now?

Mistress Marks led Stuart in by the hand. The little boy broke away and ran to his father. The young captain rose and lifted him into the air with a laugh.

Farrel got up and pulled out the chair next to Captain Marks'. Marianne seated herself, looking at Farrel with curiosity.

"I trust you slept well." He retook a chair on her other side.

"Adequately." She looked at Ravyn. "Captain Flynt?"

"Aye, I rested." She recognized the terseness of her answer but left it at that.

One of the younger hands carried in a tray of victuals and set it on the table. Farrel offered Mistress Marks the platter of eggs before taking his portion and passing it across to Ravyn. As the meal continued, Farrel assured that Mistress Marks had her serving first. Ravyn bristled, thinking it odd and a trifle discourteous that he ignored her, his focus on the other woman. Captain Marks seemed not to mind, his smiling attention on Stuart and Liam's chatter.

Was Farrel deliberately trying to annoy her? To what end? He maintained a lively discourse with Mistress and Captain Marks, saving his most winning smiles for Marianne.

Finishing her meal, Ravyn stalked from the cabin to take the helm. Why should it disturb her that he paid particular consideration to Mistress Marks?

Though he always treated her with courtesy, he had never displayed that degree of...gallantry. Was he becoming enamored of the captain's pretty wife? Ravyn clenched her hands around the wheel's spokes. She loathed the feeling of hot-faced displeasure that washed through her.

Over luncheon, Farrel demonstrated the same courtly observances to Mistress Marks. Ravyn watched Captain Marks for an indication of jealousy, but he seemed to take Farrel's behavior in stride.

At the meal's conclusion, Farrel rose and pulled back Marianne's chair for her to rise. She smiled with a soft-spoken, "Thank you," and left on her husband's arm.

Farrel turned his attention to Ravyn.

"Ye seem overly attentive to Mistress Marks today." She was unable to keep an annoyed edge from her voice. "Tis a wonder Captain Marks doesn't take ye to task."

Farrel's brows rose. "I'm only treating her the way a gently raised woman of this era would expect."

"And ye don't consider me 'gently raised'?" She mocked his words, hands going to her hips. "I suppose 'tis true."

"That's not it at all. You're a captain. My superior. You once said your men didn't consider you a lady. I'm only respecting your position."

Inexplicably, his words hurt. She took a backward step, letting her arms fall. "So ye doesn't regard me as a woman."

Farrel leaned his hands on the table, bending toward her and holding her eyes.

"I see you as that, and more. But it's not what I see that's important." His gaze intensified. "What do you see? When you look in the mirror, who looks back at you?"

"Whom would I see but myself?"

"True enough." He straightened. "But how I see myself changes. Maybe today I'm the studious professor. Maybe yesterday I was the eager student learning to wield a weapon. Last week I could have been happy or buried in sorrow." He gave an expressive shrug.

"Why must ye always muddy the simple things? I doesn't need to look in a mirror. I'm Ravyn Flynt, captain of the *Retribution*."

Farrel walked around the table. Ravyn took a wary backward step once he stood close. A smile curved his lips, but it hinted more at sadness than humor. "You put on such a hard, impenetrable face for the world. But I see beneath that. I see who Ravyn Flynt really is."

Marianne Marks had said the same thing. Ravyn scowled. Was she losing her ability to hide her secrets? How much did Farrel think he knew?

"And who is she, then?" She lifted her chin in challenge.

His smile turned cryptic. "That's for me to know, and you to discover." Unexpectedly, he took her hand, raising it to brush his lips lightly across her knuckles. When he glanced up, Ravyn swore his eyes twinkled. The barest tingle danced over her fingers before he released her hand.

"Ye've a bit of the devil in ye, Farrel McQuaid." The chiding came out husky.

He chuckled and bowed. "Thank you."

"Is that all there is to being treated as a lady? A kiss on the hand, pulling out a chair, being so attentive?" She sniffed in scorn. "I've ne'er expected nor received such blandishments."

"Not even from your captain?"

Ravyn's lips parted then clamped shut. Jonathan Moore had treated her as one of his officers, save on that single night when he had said he loved her...wanted to spend the rest of his life with her...

She thrust the memory away with a huff. "I was his lieutenant. A woman, aye, but he spared me no special treatment." She realized how defensive her answer sounded.

"Too bad. I think you should've been properly courted." Farrel touched her hand with gentle fingertips. "Or maybe he didn't have enough time."

She looked away, blinking rapidly. "I've no wish to speak of him."

"Of course." Farrel backed off. "But the next time you look in the mirror, try to see past your mask. You might be surprised who you find looking back."

As the afternoon waned toward evening, Ravyn took the helm, her thoughts absorbed with Farrel's odd postulations. What did he want her to believe about herself? That she could behave like a woman and remain a strong captain? Her mouth tightened at the ludicrous image such a notion evoked. Herself, clad like Marianne Marks, striding across the deck and issuing commands? Her lips quirked into a wry grimace. Nay, that would never come to pass.

She glanced to Farrel conversing with Mr. Poole on the forecastle.

Neither Captain nor Mistress Marks were visible, but Rachel's fretful wailing from the cabin revealed where the other woman had retreated. Captain Marks had gone below to visit his injured crewmen. The servant, Jacynta, had accompanied Mistress Marks.

A shrill cry from the deck below brought her attention swiveling to where Liam and Stuart had been playing. Liam teetered, on the rail, one hand gripping a shroud line, the other extended. One glimpse of his white, horror-stricken face and the sound of a splash told a terrible story. Her heart leapt into her throat. What—or who—had gone into the water?

All activity stopped, the men looking with narrowed, squinting eyes at Liam's frozen form. Ravyn gestured to one of the gaping younger hands to take her place. She ran down the steps, meeting Farrel by the place where Liam stared down at the water.

"What happened?" She caught Liam around the waist and pulled him from the rail.

"S-Stuart f-fell. I couldn't 'old onto him. We was...w-walking the rail. I does it all the time." The child's explanation ended in a wail.

Ravyn's gaze shot to the water. There was no sign of Stuart. She shuddered, knowing how easily the grasping current would suck him under. No matter the stillness of the day or the almost non-existent movement of the ship, a child's slight weight would be no challenge for the hungry ocean.

Farrel climbed up on the rail, balancing for an instant on bare feet with his arms raised over his head. Then he dove into the water.

"Farrel!" Ravyn lunged to lean over the rail but saw only the widening white-tipped ripples where he had gone in. "Dear God!"

Around her, the low murmur of voices stilled. Few of her crew knew how to swim. She could only pray that in Farrel's time, such a skill would be easily acquired.

"Man overboard!" As the crew galvanized into action, she returned her gaze to the place where Farrel had disappeared. In her mind, she heard that devastating splash again, except this time it came from a tiny bundle impacting the water. Grief sliced through her, nearly stealing her breath. The ocean was a cruel mistress, swallowing victims whole with no compassion for those left above.

Behind her, a shrill cry pierced the air over men's shouts and the thuds of running feet. Mistress Marks. Ravyn could only imagine how panic-stricken she must be. A prayer slipped through Ravyn's mind for the safe recovery of the little boy. And for Farrel.

Nothing could be seen through the murky green-blue of the water. She counted the endless seconds, heart pounding, as the ripples died, leaving the surface ominously still.

Chapter 30

*F*arrel nearly sucked in a watery lungful when he hit the Atlantic, always cold no matter the season. The salt water stung his eyes as he sliced through the shadowy depths. He strained for any sign of Stuart through the minimal light penetrating the surface. Fish brushed past, iridescent scales shimmering in the diffused illumination. The boy had been wearing a white blouse, something that should be readily visible. Even in only a shirt and breeches himself, the current grabbed at Farrel's clothing, tugging him into its vortex.

He changed direction, spiraling against the water's downward draw, searching, groping. Finally, he glimpsed a flash of white below him. His lungs burned. Sparkles danced at the edges of his vision. Pushing harder, he grasped Stuart's sleeve, pulling the little boy against his chest. Turning, an instant of terror seized Farrel as he became unsure of his bearings. Then, seeing brightness above, he kicked with all his strength, paddling one-handed away from the dark, suffocating depths.

His head broke the surface. He dragged in a deep draught of air, shaking water from his eyes. Keeping Stuart's head above water, he stroked toward the ship. Pleas and prayers whispered through his mind.

The men hadn't had time to set a boat into the water. On seeing him, they abandoned the skiff they were untying and lowered the rope ladder instead. Farrel focused on it, quickly reaching the becalmed ship. He caught the ladder with his free hand and secured his feet onto the bottom crossbar. The men hauled it up. One took Stuart, laying him on his side on the deck. Farrel heaved himself aboard and knelt beside the small, still body. Water dribbled from the little boy's parted lips. When it stopped, he rolled Stuart onto his back, pressing two fingers to the child's neck. Nothing. He bent and put his cheek near Stuart's mouth and nose. No breath. He lowered his ear to the little boy's chest. Stillness.

How long had they been under? Was it too late?

"Dammit." He reared up, sweeping his wet hair from his face. Then he pushed up his sleeves.

"Farrel? Is he...?" Ravyn stood over him, all color drained from her face. A cry from Marianne Marks and her running footsteps brushed Farrel's peripheral awareness as he stared down at Stuart.

"He's gone," Farrel croaked. He shook his head, sending water flying. "No, damn it. No bloody way."

"No! Oh no! Stuart!" Mistress Marks reached for her son. Ravyn grasped her arm to stop her, fascinated in watching Farrel.

He tipped Stuart's head back, gripping the child's nose and chin and pulling his mouth open. He thrust a finger inside, swirling it around, then withdrew it. Bending, he put his lips to the boy's. Stuart's chest slowly rose then fell when Farrel lifted his mouth away. Uttering another soft curse, he put a hand to the boy's chest, pushing in quick thrusts with the heel of his hand and counting softly to himself.

"One...two...three..." Reaching thirty, he returned to breathe into Stuart's mouth twice then pushed into his chest again, repeating the dual process several times, face drawn in concentration.

Mistress Marks pressed a hand over her mouth, her eyes wide and tearing. Muffled sobs worked their way around her shaking fingers. Ravyn didn't know what to say. She understood that pain, an icy weight in her own chest.

Suddenly, the little boy gave a gurgling cough, and water spewed from his mouth. Farrel rolled him onto his side. "That's it. Cough it out. Good boy."

Ravyn didn't realize she'd been holding her breath until it whooshed out. Mistress Marks gave a cry, wrenching free of Ravyn's grip to drop onto her knees.

The child continued to hack and spit for a moment, sending salt-water laced bile over the deck. Then he began to wail, his rasping cries blending with Mistress Marks' sobbing as she folded him into her arms.

"My baby. You've saved him. Thank you, oh, thank you!" Tears streamed down her cheeks as she lifted her face to Farrel. He helped her to her feet.

Ravyn flicked a glance toward the hatch leading down to the sickroom.

Captain Marks stood beside it, eyes riveted on his wife and son. He strode to take Stuart from Mistress Marks' arms.

"Thank you." His gaze rested on Farrel with gratitude. The couple started toward Mistress Marks' cabin.

"Keep him warm and check frequently for fever," Farrel called after them, taking a few steps across the deck. "If he keeps coughing or it worsens, let us know. He might contract an infection from inhaling the salt water."

The couple paused in the doorway, turning as Farrel continued issuing instructions. Marianne's lips moved, as though she struggled to say something. Abruptly, she ran back to Farrel. Tears streaming, she took his face in her hands and drew him down to kiss him full on the mouth. Farrel lifted his hands to grip her upper arms, seemingly caught unawares. When Mistress Marks drew back, her eyes widened, and her mouth formed an "O." Color flooded into her ashen cheeks. Ravyn wondered what Farrel must be thinking as they stood frozen.

Ravyn couldn't stop a fleeting anger ripping through her. No matter that it was nothing more than an impulsive gesture of gratitude, how dare Mistress Marks kiss Farrel in that intimate manner? It was unconscionable. Inappropriate.

At the cabin door, Captain Marks watched, brows arched. He flicked a glance her way before carrying Stuart inside.

She suppressed her raw emotion. She was being foolish, irrational.

Mistress Marks' hands fell, her lips moving but no words forthcoming. Whirling, she darted into the cabin. Farrel stood unmoving, fingers resting on his lips, confusion creasing his features. He shook, whether with chill or reaction, Ravyn could not tell.

"You had best go and change." She stared into his eyes. "I'm glad ye saved him with your...unusual skills."

His mouth twitched. "Never thought they'd come in handy." He started toward the great cabin. As he walked, he peeled his dripping shirt over his head. Upon reaching the door, he turned to look back at her.

Ravyn's heart skipped and a stronger pulse beat a rapid rhythm through her body. God's teeth, the man nearly stole her breath. The golden hair crossing his muscular chest caught the sunlight, and a film of moisture glistened on his skin. Though not as brawny as her crew, he still cut a fine figure, his shoulders wide, waist and hips narrow, arms well muscled. Her fingertips tingled as she recalled his warm skin beneath them on the night she had gone to the great cabin for a "wee drink."

He lifted his other hand and pulled the strip that bound his hair free of the escaping tangles. When he shook his head, droplets ran down his chest, glittering in the golden mat crossing it. He turned and entered the cabin.

Ravyn lifted her hand to her throat, the pulse beating there like a trapped bird. Her emotions felt raw, exposed, volatile. Death had come calling, and Farrel had repelled it. She could not help but be impressed by his skill and calm actions. Truly a man of amazing talents.

Had she mistaken some spark between him and Mistress Marks in that kiss? She wanted to shake the other woman, make her claim upon Farrel plain.

Her claim? Her only right of possession was as captain to crewman. Nothing more.

Although, upon consideration, any woman would be hard pressed to ignore Farrel's charms, a quiet vigor most would find attractive.

But that was other women. Not Captain Ravyn Flynt.

She willed her pulse to slow to a cooler rhythm, but it did not still the strange fluttering that persisted in her chest.

When Andrew entered the cabin, Farrel paused in drying his hair. The young captain's drawn expression and furrowed brows over dark eyes sent a frisson of worry through him.

"How is Stuart?" He lowered the towel to dry his chest and back.

"Marianne got him to sleep." Andrew stood with arms folded. "I pray he will recover. Your swift actions spared his life. I don't know what I would have done..." His features twisted in momentary grief. "My family means everything to me. If we had lost Stuart..." He swallowed, and his voice turned husky. "I owe you a debt I can never repay."

"I'm just glad I knew what to do." Farrel studied Andrew's face. He should clear up one issue before it became a misunderstanding. "It didn't mean anything, you know. That kiss."

"Marianne can be impulsive." Andrew let his arms fall, and his features relaxed. He even gave a tight smile. "She has apologized to me over and over again. She's too mortified to face you."

"Please tell her I understand." Farrel tossed the towel aside and combed his fingers through his hair before tying it back.

Andrew astonished him by laughing softly. "Had I been nearer at the moment Stuart drew breath, I might have kissed you myself." His eyes sparked with wry humor. "Though I don't remember a great deal about the time I was born in, I do recall seeing that kind of resuscitation demonstrated." He gave another rueful laugh, "Of course, I couldn't explain that to Marianne. She thinks you must be an angel."

Farrel chuckled. "I'm not ready to collect my halo quite yet." He pulled a fresh shirt out of his trunk. "So, you're not piss...ah, mad about it."

"The kiss? No." Then he added with what Farrel assumed was a feigned scowl, "Although, I had best not find the two of you so engaged again, or I might have to call you out." Then he grinned. "I did note the expression on your captain's face. If anyone was pissed off, I think it might be her."

Farrel laughed. "So you remember some of our more colorful expressions. Good to know. It's been a challenge to keep the modernisms out of my speech around the crew." He pulled the shirt over his head, already having changed into dry breeches. "I didn't see Ravyn's expression." He paused in lacing the placket. "She's a tough one to figure out."

Andrew sat down at the table. "She looked as if she would have liked to push Marianne overboard."

"I'm sure she was just concerned about Stuart." Farrel carried the pitcher of water with two tankards over and poured drinks.

"Again, I think you misread her." Andrew took a slow drink before continuing. "I've watched her, eyeing you these past days. There might be something of the captain's assessment in her study, but I also see a woman's admiration."

Farrel laughed. "She's way more skilled with weapons than I am. I think she's just considering my capability. Even if there is anything more, she won't act on it."

"You want her to see you as more than a crewman." Andrew grinned. "You were teasing her with your attentions to Marianne earlier, and it is certainly hitting the mark." He held up a hand when Farrel started to sputter a protest. "I deduced your ploy immediately." Andrew leaned forward, clasping his hands on the table. "If you have need of co-conspirators to win her, Marianne and I will assist where we can. It's the least we can do after your actions today."

Farrel sighed. "I may give your offer some thought, thank you." He tapped his fingers against his tankard, frowning. "She has so much at stake right now. And more to come, the safety of her life not being the least of it."

Chapter 31

Ravyn stood outside Mistress Marks' cabin with Farrel, a trembling Liam between them. She dismissed Mr. Morrissey and knocked.

Captain Marks opened the door. Beyond him, Mistress Marks sat on the bunk, where Stuart lay tucked up to his chin in blankets. Jacynta stood by the cradle bed, Rachel in her arms.

"Liam has something he wishes to say." Ravyn gave his shoulder an encouraging squeeze.

Captain Marks stepped aside. He looked down at the boy. "What is it, Liam?"

"I-I...wanted to tell ye how sorry I am for...what 'appened." His low voice squeaked. "I'd never wish Stuart any 'arm." His shoulders hitched and he swallowed. "I's come to think of 'im as...as like a little brother. I-I didn't stop to think—" His words ended in a sob.

Captain Marks hunkered down to meet Liam's eyes, his expression solemn. "You realize how much danger you put him in."

Liam nodded, and a tear rolled down his cheek. "Aye. I-I was showin' 'im how I could walk the rail, and 'e wanted to try." Another tear followed the first. "I-I'm dreadful sorry, sir, Ma'am." His gaze shifted to Mistress Marks, who had risen. She frowned at Liam then glanced down at her sleeping son.

Captain Marks set a hand on Liam's shoulder. "I think all can be forgiven if you promise to be more careful in future."

"I should have left Jacynta to watch." Mistress Marks stepped closer, her expression softening. "Stuart is just a little boy, and far less accustomed to life aboard ship than are you." She sighed. "Had I not felt so tired and unwell..." A wispy smile curved her lips. "We must pray he recovers with no ill effects."

"Aye, I will." Liam lifted his eyes to her. "'E's me friend. I'll not let 'im be 'urt again."

"Very good." Captain Marks straightened, shifting his gaze to Farrel. "Once more, thank you."

"Yes, thank you." Mistress Marks did not meet Farrel's eyes, and her cheeks brightened with rosy color. "I-I must apologize—"

Farrel lifted a hand. "None needed."

Mistress Marks nodded, lowering her gaze.

"May I go, Cap'n?" Liam looked with hopeful pleading at Ravyn. She nodded. The boy ran from the cabin.

She returned her attention to the Markses. "Will ye join us for dinner?"

"I'll stay with Stuart." Marianne sat down on the bunk, laying a hand on the little boy's forehead. He moaned in his restless sleep.

"I'll send one of the lads with a tray." Ravyn looked at Captain Marks. "Will ye stay as well?"

"No, I'll join you." He moved to stand by his wife. "The ladies will provide adequate care. But I will return after the meal."

Back on deck, Ravyn looked around, but found Liam nowhere in sight.

"Let him be for awhile," Farrel suggested. "I think he needs time to reflect."

Ravyn uttered a heavy sigh. "I'd ne'er given much thought to how much he might like the company of another boy."

"Maybe he needs a little brother or sister."

Ravyn darted a glance up. Farrel was looking out over the water.

"Are ye saying I should take in another child?"

Farrel's gaze shifted to her, and one corner of his mouth twitched. "I can think of another way."

"Ye keep thinking, then. That 'other way' is not one I am about to consider." With that, she strode away, her emotions once more in turmoil.

The man could have no inkling how much his words stirred her memories. Or how close they brought her to tears.

Ravyn woke from the dream, gasping. Images flashed lightning-fast through her mind. Jonathan Moore lying on the deck, awash in his own blood. Will Flemington leering at her with hungry eyes across his felled opponent. Her efforts to fight him, useless when she knocked her head against the mast and fell, unconscious. Flemington looming over her in his cabin, huffing and laughing at her inability to fend him off as he ravaged her...

Her child, still and cold in her hands...

Panic settled in her chest, stealing her breath, rolling in suffocating waves over her senses. She wanted to scream, but the sound strangled in her throat. The sole cover over her clung like a shroud, tangling as her arms flailed for some—any—purchase.

Then, from nowhere, Farrel's command rang through her mind.

"Tell me the names of your crew. Now."

She tried reciting them in her head, but the darkness intensified, overpowering thought. Another idea formed.

She visualized her terror as a black mist advancing over the water. Then a ship appearing with furled sails, caught in the fringe of the miasma. A sudden recollection surfaced of herself as a girl of six, Eli Fisher at her side, pointing up at the masts.

"Tell me the names of the sails, lass. 'Ighest first."

She whispered them aloud. "Fore topgallant royal, main topgallant royal, mizzen topgallant royal, fore topgallant, main topgallant..." As she said each one, it unfurled in her mind. "Mizzen topgallant, fore tops'l..." As they continued to unfurl, the ship moved away from the panic-fog. Her breaths became slower, easier, less constricted. "Main tops'l, mizzen tops'l..." She went through them all, focusing on each one catching the anomalous wind, carrying the ship further away from the black mist. At last, leaving it behind to dissipate in her mind's nightscape.

Exhaling a shaky breath, she sat up and lowered her feet to the floor. The cool planking grounded her even more.

She stood, eager to escape the cabin's stifling confines.

On deck, a minimal crew stood watch. The moon rode high, into its first quarter so that dim silver light glowed over the water. Two lanterns, one at port, the other at starboard, cast enough illumination to move about with ease. Ravyn stood at the rail, watching the *Lady Annabelle* floating parallel to *Retribution*. One of the lads on her deck waved and saluted, and Ravyn waved back.

She turned at the creak of a board behind her. Marianne Marks approached, little Rachel against her shoulder. The baby's eyes were open and a thumb stuck in her rosebud mouth. Marianne stopped beside Ravyn. She had donned a light dress, and her chestnut hair hung loose around her shoulders.

"Such a lovely night," she murmured. "Rachel was restless, and I didn't want her to wake Stuart. I thought the fresh air might help."

Ravyn stared at the pretty image of mother and child. Unbidden, the memory of Farrel's actions with Marianne earlier in the day, and that kiss, marred the image. Ravyn's mouth tightened as she tried to shake off the notion of Mistress Marks as a rival.

"Ye shouldn't be leaving the cabin alone at night." The reproof came out in a hard snap. "Otherwise, I cannot attest to the conduct of my men."

"I wouldn't, as a rule." Marianne passed a hand over Rachel's curls. "I heard you leave your cabin and felt it would be safe to join you."

"Aye, well, the heat is easier to bear without the sun glaring down on us." Ravyn turned to the rail. "How is Stuart?"

"He ate a little of the broth your cook sent up. He has no fever, but he is restless."

Ravyn looked back as Rachel gave a discontented whimper, squirming against her mother. Marianne shushed her, pressing a kiss to her brow. Ravyn looked away, a sudden clenching in her chest.

"Oh dear, I think she's caught her toes in a buttonhole. Would you hold her for a moment?"

Ravyn swiveled with a decisive shake of her head. "Nay. I've ne'er held a child. I couldn't—" The clench became a twist of pain.

Once. She had held a child once. The image of her stillborn infant, forced into the world too soon to live, flashed through her mind.

"Come, now. It's easy." Ignoring her protest, Marianne transferred Rachel to Ravyn's hesitant arms.

She copied Marianne's way of holding the child, one hand pressing her head against her shoulder, the other supporting her padded backside. Rachel snuggled against her with a little sigh, her breath wispy-warm against Ravyn's neck. She watched Marianne refasten the buttons Rachel's tiny toes had pulled open, aware of the baby's heat penetrating through her clothing. A yearning ache wove through her chest.

"There, you see?" Marianne smiled, making no attempt to take Rachel back. "She doesn't often settle with strangers. She must like you."

"Aye, well." Ravyn moved her hand, and Rachel's downy curls wound around her fingers. "She's very sweet."

Marianne gave a low laugh. "You needn't sound so grudging, Captain. She can be a little curmudgeon when the mood strikes her." She canted her head to study Ravyn. "Have you never wanted a family?"

"My crew is my family." Yet longing continued to stir in her chest as Rachel's breath wisped against her neck. The babe smelled of talc powder and milk.

Marianne glanced around, but no one stood near. She leaned closer, speaking in a conspiratorial tone. "What of the child you lost? Did you want it?"

Ravyn's mouth opened, but no sound came out. Her vision blurred with unexpected tears. She turned her face into the baby's downy hair to hide the grief that contorted her features. The pain of realizing how much she wished her child had lived, how much holding Rachel made her ache for that, unnerved her.

"You did." Surprise threaded Marianne's voice. "I'm so sorry."

Ravyn looked up, training her face to calm neutrality. "Ye needn't be. 'Twas most likely a blessing she didn't live."

"She? But..." Marianne's words trailed off.

Neither spoke for a long moment. Ravyn made no effort to return Rachel to her mother's arms.

At last Marianne spoke. "You could have another child, with the right man—"

"Nay." Ravyn passed the little girl back. "I am not the sort of woman a man could love."

Marianne settled her daughter against her shoulder. "I know you are... unconventional, but someone does care for you." Her lips curled in a coy little smile. "Mr. McQuaid gazes at you with such ardent longing when he thinks no one is watching. He seems a kind man, a free thinker, one who could teach you the...fulfillment of a loving union."

Ravyn regarded her in astonishment. Had she misinterpreted what passed between Marianne and Farrel? "Ye must be mistaken—"

Marianne interrupted, her soft voice persuasive. "Remember what I told you, Captain. If there is love and tenderness, there will be joy." She glanced down at Rachel, to see that the child had fallen asleep. "At last," she murmured on a relieved sigh. "I will bid you good-night." She touched Ravyn's arm. "Sometimes it's difficult to see ourselves as others do. You might be a captain, but I think you've gentler longings, just like the rest of us."

With those astounding words, Marianne turned and walked back to her cabin. Ravyn stared after her.

Blast the woman. She was worse than Farrel. Did they conspire to unsettle her? Was all his excessive courtesy a demonstration for her benefit?

She turned back to gaze out over the water. Everything—and everyone—seemed bent on confounding her. She had no inkling what she wanted. A family? A home of her own? A man to show her the love she had been denied?

"Nay," she whispered into the still night. "Those are dreams." And dreams could so easily become nightmares. She had learned that lesson in the harshest possible manner. Her reality rested in seeking the nightmare's resolution. She would not ache for something that could never be.

But that did not ease the emptiness in her arms, or the tightness lodged in her breast.

Chapter 32

"Cap'n?"

Ravyn turned from watching the men swing the yards, attempting to adjust the sails to catch the minimal breeze. Liam stood behind her, his face creased in a frown.

"Aye? What is it, lad?"

"I heared the men talkin'. They says Cap'n Marks will be put in prison when we gets to Halifax."

"Aye, 'tis likely."

"But what will 'appen to Stuart and his Mum and wee Rachel? Will they be put in prison too?" His lower lip quivered.

"Nay. They will remain free."

"But what of Cap'n Marks? Will 'e be hunged?"

"Hanged?" Her brows arched. "I think not. Where did ye hear such talk?"

"The other fellas." He looked about furtively. "They says Mistress Marks and the wee'uns will be left des...desti...destitute." He brow knit over the word.

She would have to warn the men about saying too much in Liam's hearing. There was no need in frightening him. Crouching, she laid a hand on his shoulder.

"You know from our other captures that the captains are imprisoned for not paying the Crown taxes. This is no different."

"But none o' them 'ad their fam'lies with them." Tears welled in his eyes. "'E be a good man, Cap'n. I knows 'ow much I misses me Da and Mum. I don't want Stuart 'avin' to miss 'is."

Ravyn bowed her head. Liam had not mentioned his parents in a long while. She had begun to think he might have forgotten them.

"Cap'n?"

She looked up again. "Ye mustn't concern yourself over these matters, Liam."

"But..." He caught his lower lip between his teeth, looking past her. Ravyn glanced over her shoulder.

Captain and Mistress Marks exited the cabin. He carried Stuart, still pale and listless. Jacynta followed, holding Rachel. The captain set Stuart on his feet, and he stood gazing in Liam's direction with wide, wistful eyes. A slow smile curved his mouth, and he glanced up at his father. Captain Marks nodded, returning the smile, and Stuart headed in their direction, his steps slow and tentative.

"The fellas says the man who sent 'im out told 'im not to pay." Liam watched his friend, seeming uncertain of his welcome. "Why should 'e be punished when 'e was only doin' as 'e was bid?"

Ravyn straightened with an exasperated sigh. "Liam, ye ask too many questions. Go on with ye."

He hesitated for an instant then ran off. Ravyn stared after him, mouth thinning.

"Wisdom from the mouths of babes."

She started, pivoting at Farrel's voice behind her.

"Ye best be minding your own affairs too, Mr. McQuaid."

"You know how I feel about separating the family. Look at them."

Captain Marks had fetched the ball and stones for jackstones and hunkered down with the boys, encouraging them as they played. Mistress Marks stood over them, smiling. Jacynta set Rachel onto her feet and held her hands as the tot wobbled on unsteady legs. The picture of familial bonding had Ravyn blinking back sudden moisture. She turned on Farrel with an impatient huff.

"I've already stated my case. I've not changed my mind." She started away.

"Did you look in the mirror this morning?"

His question caught her off-guard. She halted but did not turn.

"I'll have none of your nonsense today, sir. Go about your business."

Farrel stared after Ravyn as she stalked away, shouting orders to the men in the rigging.

"Someone's in a mood," he muttered with a wry grin. He joined the Marks family.

Captain Marks glanced up and straightened.

"Stuart seems improved." Farrel nodded at the little boy. Color brightened his cheeks and he played with more energy, tossing the ball into the air and scooping up a stone.

"He had a good sleep and isn't coughing overmuch."

Another strident shout from Ravyn had both men glancing her way.

"Have you given any thought to my offer?" Andrew's mouth curved. "Your captain seems of a churlish temper this morning."

"Everyone's tense. Wish there was something we could do where everyone could participate."

Andrew considered this, brow furrowed. "If there were any aboard of a musical bent, a concert could ease humors."

Struck by the idea, Farrel nodded. "I'll ask Mr. Poole." He intended to take up practice before the day became too heated.

"Do that. I feel in a mood for celebration, despite what lies ahead." Andrew directed a significant look at his son. "Live for today, I say, and let tomorrow see to itself."

Farrel headed off to locate the weapons officer.

"Mr. Fisher."

The bo'sun looked up from unrolling a length of rigging line. "Aye?" His bushy brows lowered.

"Mr. Poole tells me you play the wooden flute." Hard to believe, with those blunt, callused fingers curled around the rope.

"Aye." Curiosity lit his eyes. "Why would ye be askin' that?"

"I thought it might help...ease tensions if we had a bit of music tonight. Mr. Poole also said Artie McNeil has a gift with the fiddle. And Garrett Reeves with the bodhran. All we need is a piper. You interested?"

"Ye be plannin' a ceilidh, McQuaid?"

"A kay-leed? What's that?"

The bo'sun snorted. "Does ye know naught? 'Tis a gatherin', with music and dancin' and mebbe a story or two to tell." Despite his gruff tone, the man's expression revealed anticipation. "Is that what ye be wantin'?"

"Yeah, that's right." Farrel nodded, encouraged.

"Does ye 'ave the Cap'n's say-so?"

"Let's keep it for a surprise." Again, he nodded with a conspiratorial wink. "Does she enjoy music?"

"Aye, we all does." Fisher set the rope down and straightened. "'Er Da used to have the lads play regular. Kept tempers cool." Then his brow puckered. "Ye's bein' cagey again. What be yer purpose?"

"Just what I said. After yesterday, I think we all need to...unwind."

"Ye uses peculiar words," the bo'sun grumbled, "but I thinks I catches yer meanin'." He gave a terse nod. "I'll collect the lads and we'll make a plan."

"Good." Farrel started away then turned back. "Does Captain Flynt know how to dance?"

Fisher chuckled with a shake of his shaggy head. "What need would the lass be 'avin' of learnin' to dance? She wasn't raised fer gracin' gentry ballrooms."

"True." Farrel sighed in regret. "Guess we'll be winging it." He walked away.

"Barmy sod."

"I heard that." He kept walking, repressing an urge to laugh. It seemed the prospect of music had struck a chord with the surly bo'sun.

When he told Andrew and Marianne, they greeted the plan with enthusiasm.

"Just what we need," Andrew concurred. "That should lift our spirits."

"I must choose something festive to wear." Marianne brushed a hand along her light muslin gown. "It's been so long since we attended a soiree or dance."

"Not sure how much dancing there'll be. We only have two ladies to partner, and one of them has apparently had no training."

"Captain Flynt." Marianne looked up with a perceptive smile. "I could provide some lessons this afternoon."

"No, I want to surprise her." Farrel chuckled. "I actually have Mr. Fisher's collusion in this."

"Really?" Andrew's brows arched. "Well, you must recall what Mr. Shakespeare said. 'Music hath charms to soothe the savage breast.'"

Farrel shook his head, grinning. "In Mr. Fisher's case, I prefer the misquote of 'beast'."

Leaving her cabin in the late afternoon, the sound of Marianne's tinkling laughter halted Ravyn. Now, what could be so amusing? Especially after nearly losing her son?

Curious, Ravyn tapped at the door. Marianne opened it, her smile altering to startled wariness.

"Oh! Captain Flynt." She flicked a glance over her shoulder.

Ravyn followed her gaze. An assortment of gowns and undergarments lay across the bunk. Jacynta stood with another dress over her arms.

Ravyn nodded toward the bunk. "I'd no inkling you had so many frocks."

Marianne stepped back. "Please, come in. I was just...laying them out to...air." Her hesitations fed Ravyn's curiosity. "Keeping them packed for so long would leave them irreparably wrinkled."

Ravyn approached the bunk. Her gaze flitted from soft sprigged muslins to plain linens and silks, and a pretty satin creation trimmed with lace and flounces, all with the higher waistline fashionable since the start of the war. She ran a fingertip along a glistening gold-colored satin.

"Have you any gowns, Captain?" Marianne moved to stand beside her.

Ravyn lifted her hand from the dress, shaking her head. "Nay. Da insisted breeches made more sense on a ship."

Marianne's gaze fell to the garments. "I think you would look lovely in a gown with your hair properly done."

"Aye, well, my crew would think it an oddity." She took a step back. "Nor would I wish them to see me as anything less than their captain."

"Oh, my dear." Marianne turned to her, smiling. "I think you would have them agog." Then a sly look narrowed her eyes. "And Mr. McQuaid. He would be dazzled."

Ravyn gave a self-conscious laugh as warmth crept into her cheeks.

"I know what would look perfect on you." Marianne hurried to one of the open trunks, pulling out a muslin and lace gown of a blue so light it was close to white. "This one. It matches your eyes." She carried it back to Ravyn and held it up. It featured a scooped neckline edged with lace and more around the high waistline, short, puffed sleeves, and an overlay of pleated white lace on the skirt. "Andrew purchased it for me in France, but it's simply not the right color for me. Trust a man." She tilted her head. "It will flatter you so much more."

"Nay." Ravyn took a wary step back. "Wherever would I wear it?"

"For Mr. McQuaid." Marianne batted her lashes with a knowing smile. "Let's see how it looks."

"Nay." Ravyn retreated another step. "I've ne'er worn a gown. Nor does

I intend to do so now."

"Please? It's just us ladies here." She laid the garment over her arm and touched Ravyn's hand. "Indulge me, Captain. You might be pleasantly surprised."

Ravyn sighed. It could do no harm, she supposed, as long as no one else saw her. She glanced at the bunk. "I've no idea what needs to be worn with it."

Marianne set the dress down and picked up a long sleeveless cream-colored shift. "This, to start."

Ravyn reluctantly removed her shirt and breeches and let Marianne slip the linen over her head. It felt strange wearing something so soft falling past her knees. Marianne went to the trunk and returned with a stiff, satin-trimmed garment crossed by laces that resembled a starched, body-contoured vest. Ravyn arched her brows in silent query.

"It's a corset." Marianne helped Ravyn slide her arms through the strap sleeves.

When Marianne pulled the front satin ties tight, Ravyn squeaked, the air forced from her lungs. She tried inhaling, unable to pull in more than a tiny puff. "How ever does ye breathe in this contraption?"

Marianne gave a rueful laugh. "It's easier as you become accustomed." She fastened the last of the lacing into a bow and adjusted it so Ravyn's bosom pushed out of the neckline of the chemise. "I will be unable to wear this one until after my confinement."

Ravyn sensed no regret in her words.

After several layers of petticoats, Marianne slipped the dress over Ravyn's head and fastened the tiny pearl buttons up the back.

"Dear Lord," Ravyn muttered. "I feel like a Christmas goose trussed for the oven."

Marianne gave a pealing laugh as she turned Ravyn. The hemline fell shy of the floor, and Marianne moved around her, twitching a pleat into place here, smoothing another there. Though not heavy, it seemed weighty with the layers of petticoats.

"Oh my, it does suit you perfectly." Marianne clapped her hands in delight. "Now, for your hair—"

"My hair stays as it is." Ravyn gripped the thick black plait in her hand.

"It must be properly pinned, at least." Marianne coaxed her to sit in the desk chair while she undid the braid and brushed Ravyn's long, silky tresses.

Marianne fetched a wooden box of hairpins and combs of tortoiseshell and mother-of-pearl from her trunk. With Jacynta's assistance, she rolled and pinned and fussed, leaving a few locks falling over Ravyn's shoulder. Finished, Marianne pulled Ravyn to her feet and walked around her. Ravyn felt ridiculous.

"You should wear this to dinner," Marianne suggested with another conspiratorial smile. "It should make quite the impression on a certain ship's clerk."

"Aye, well, that one requires no encouragement." Ravyn's cheeks warmed.

Marianne laughed again, but stopped at a knock on the door.

Ravyn swiveled, seeking concealment. There was nowhere to hide in the crowded cabin. Marianna answered the door before Ravyn could forbid it.

Captain Marks and Farrel stood framed in the opening. Ravyn wished fervently to sink through the floor.

"Marianne? What on earth?" Captain Marks stared at Ravyn.

Ravyn's eyes shifted to Farrel. His mouth hung open as he looked her over from her neatly coiffed head to her toes peeking from under the dress's hem. Recovering, he strode to her, his eyes sparkling.

"Who are you, and what have you done with Captain Flynt?" He walked around her, and she followed his circuitous examination with uneasy eyes. Returning before her, he dropped to one knee, lifted her hand and kissed it. That familiar tingle danced over her skin. She repressed a shiver. When he looked up, his eyes shone in open admiration. Ravyn squirmed under that approving gaze, not knowing how to respond.

An audible chuckle returned her attention to Captain Marks. He regarded his wife. "Playing dress-up, are we?" he inquired, still chuckling. "I think Mr. McQuaid is about to propose."

Ravyn snatched her hand away, her eyes narrowing. "Ye may rise, Mr. McQuaid. And ye may close the door, sir," she snapped at Captain Marks. He obeyed, eyes twinkling. Farrel rose but had yet to look away from her. What she saw in the soft glow of his eyes, made her heart beat faster as slow heat spread through her.

"You are beautiful. A vision." His hand drifted up to touch her cheek. Her face grew hotter. She flinched from the brush of his fingertips.

"I wish I had my cheval glass," Marianne said. "If you could only see yourself..."

"Nay. I've no wish to see how...unlike myself I look." Ravyn tore her eyes from Farrel to direct a glare at Marianne.

"I'll sketch you," Farrel murmured, bringing her frown back to him. "I think this image is burned into my brain."

"There be no need." Ravyn tried to keep her tone cool, but her voice cracked on the words.

"Oh, there's every need, dear lady." He leaned closer. Her heart gave a traitorous skip. Surely, he wouldn't dare kiss her with the Markses and Jacynta watching. But he whispered at her ear so only she heard. "I knew there was a beautiful woman hiding under all that crust and bluster."

Ravyn put her hand to her cheek where his breath grazed. Though she itched to get back into her breeches, beneath her embarrassment lingered reluctance to lose the glow his words left in their wake.

Chapter 33

*R*avyn settled Liam for the night then ascended to the forecastle. Farrel stood in what little breeze the evening offered and nodded in greeting, a smile curling his mouth. Murmurs from the lower deck brought her attention to the men gathered with their musical instruments. Ravyn flicked a glance at Farrel.

"What be the meaning of this?" She jerked her head toward the crew as more men joined those below.

"I thought it might be fun to have a little music." Farrel's smile widened. "Mr. Fisher's in charge."

Ravyn's brows arched in astonishment, and she returned her gaze to the growing group of men. Mr. Fisher stood in their midst, wooden pipe in hand.

Mistress Marks emerged from the cabin. Her husband joined her at midships. Marianne looked lovely in a pale green gown of pink-sprigged muslin, her hair gathered in soft curls around her face. Captain Marks wore dove-gray trousers and vest, white shirt and pale blue cravat. Ravyn had to admit he looked quite dashing. But no more than Farrel. Though still in bare feet, he had donned clean breeches, a fresh shirt and a blue waistcoat. Ravyn felt underdressed in her own bare feet and rolled-up shirt sleeves.

Captain Marks waved, a cheerful grin lighting his face.

"Let's join them. I'd like to see what Mr. Fisher has planned." Farrel's eyes twinkled in the waning daylight.

It turned out that Mr. Fisher's "plan" involved two wooden pipes, a couple of fiddles and a bodhran hand drum. The musicians spent a few moments with heads together, muttering amongst themselves. Coming to an agreement, they launched into a jig.

Two of the younger hands got up and started to dance, feet flying at a furious pace in tempo with the lively music. Ravyn glanced at Farrel. The look of enjoyment lighting his face as he clapped time left her breathless. So often he appeared tense and worried, but his features were relaxed, rendering him more appealing than ever. It startled her to feel so drawn to him, and she took a reflexive step closer.

Across the water, a cheer rose from the *Lady Annabelle*. The schooner's crew, along with Ravyn's, stood watching and clapping, faces aglow in lantern-light along the deck.

Uttering a sigh torn between exasperation and resignation, Ravyn returned her attention to the dancers. She could order everyone back to their stations, but it seemed a shame to spoil their fun. Instead, she leaned back against the bulwark to watch and listen. In little time, she became caught up in the air of festivity. Someone—she thought it might have been Mr. Fisher—ordered kegs of grog brought out, and drinks were passed around.

Mistress Marks leaned in to her. "Now, don't you wish you had worn the gown to dinner?"

"Nay, I does not." She flicked an irritated glance at the other woman. "You knew of this?"

"Oh, yes." Marianne's gaze slid to Farrel. "Mr. McQuaid wanted to keep it a surprise."

Ravyn turned to him, annoyed at his audacity. He met her frown with arched brows, a shrug, and a grin.

"Did I overstep? Not sorry if I did." He returned his gaze to the musicians and dancers. They took a brief break to fetch drinks, then resumed at a slower tempo.

"Perfect for a waltz." Farrel bowed then held his hand out to Ravyn, palm up. "Shall we?"

"Oh, nay. I doesn't know how—"

"It's easy. Come on." He took her hand, neglecting to ask permission.

She let him lead her out to the center of the deck. Facing her, he set her hand on his shoulder then gripped her other in his. His free hand rested below her shoulder blade, keeping an arm's length distance between them. He began to move in slow, shifting steps, first side-to-side, then back and forth. Though awkward and uncertain, she soon had the flow of the steps.

"Let me lead."

She didn't realize how forceful her movements had become. Glancing at her feet, she nearly lost the rhythm.

"Is this how ye dance in your time?" She divided her focus between the question and the slow steps.

Farrel laughed softly. "If you saw how most of the young people in my time dance, you'd think they were possessed. No, this is a specialized form." Though he continued to smile, a faraway look shadowed his eyes. "Julia took ballroom lessons. They never had enough partners, so she dragged me along. I came to enjoy the lessons. And the history."

"History?"

He gave her a quick whirl that made her catch her breath in surprise.

"The waltz is popular in Vienna, the German courts and in France. It won't be introduced in England for a couple more years. Even then, it's going to be viewed as scandalous." He drew Ravyn into another whirl as she tried to stop her feet at his confession. "If we were in my time, I'd be holding you closer." He leaned in, his breath brushing her ear. "Much closer." His hand trailed along her back to squeeze her waist then returned to its original position.

A wave of warmth rushed through Ravyn at his touch. As they continued to move, she copied the rigid stance of his upper body, but it was impossible to avoid the accidental, casual brush of their legs as she followed his lead. First thighs, then bare calves and ankles as she faltered in the steps. Each contact held an intimacy that sent ripples of heat coursing through Ravyn and her pulse skittering.

The dance ended, and they stood staring into each other's eyes. Ravyn felt under the illusion that they were sequestered in a bubble of quiet solitude. No sound intruded, nor any sense of the others around them. Her heart fluttered as she studied Farrel's tender expression.

Then a shout of, "Bravo," from Captain Marks and Marianne's laughter brought heat flooding into Ravyn's face. She stepped back as the crew clapped and cheered along with the Markses.

The musicians broke into a reel. Captain Marks drew Marianne onto the improvised dance area. Farrel grabbed Ravyn's hand, following the other couple into the swinging figures of the dance. They were soon all breathless and laughing as the women passed between the men.

"I have no clue what I'm doing," Farrel panted when Ravyn came back to his hand, "but, God, it's fun." His broad grin and flushed face revealed joyful abandon that Ravyn couldn't help sharing.

She hadn't felt so lighthearted—or lightheaded—in a long time. The reel ended, and she collapsed into Farrel's arms. She made no attempt to pull away, blaming the grog for her giddiness. Farrel's arm slid around her waist to steady her, and her heart stuttered. She felt as if she were falling, even though Farrel supported her. She wanted to surrender to those sensations and the delight in his eyes.

"Isn't this great?" He beamed at her, face shining with perspiration. "I read sailors loved music. Pirates and privateers alike." He murmured the last near her ear so only she heard.

"What are ye doin' to us?" she asked softly.

"Trying to make you see there's more to life than wars and pain and fear. More to living than work and protocol and worry." His lips brushed her ear. "You need to dance and laugh, be something other than the stern captain now and then." He straightened and looked over his shoulder. "More reels, boys."

Proper form had no place, neither in the dance steps nor general conduct. Some of the younger lads joined in the group dances, abandoning protocol as they changed partners. Ravyn let the misbehavior pass, too caught up in the simple pleasure of flying feet and laughter.

After a few more whirls around their improvised dance floor, Ravyn sank onto a sack of sand to rest. Farrel stood beside her, watching one of the boys perform a hornpipe dance.

"Is no one seeing to duty?" She glanced around. It looked as if all the crew were crowded onto this deck and the one above.

"Don't worry, they're spelling each other off," Farrel assured her.

"I hope they're not too tipsy to be properly tending to the ship—and the prisoners." She directed a severe look at Farrel.

"There's little needs doing while we're becalmed, and as for the prisoners..." He nodded toward the schooner, where all appeared to be enjoying the music, guards and captured crew alike. "I think it's safe to say this shindig might be solving problems rather than creating any."

Though Ravyn refused to admit it, he was most likely right. Even Mr. Fisher appeared less crotchety, mouth twisted into a grin. It truly looked unnatural and a trifle fierce on his scarred face.

Ravyn did not keep track of the time but knew the hour was late when everyone dispersed to take up their stations or retire. She stood with Farrel and the Markses as the men extinguished extra lanterns and returned the kegs to the hold.

"Did you have a good time?"

She looked at Farrel, to see his features creased in anxiety.

"Aye. It was a...heartening change from routine." She remembered how much she enjoyed these festivities when Da had been captain. She had almost forgotten how music enriched the soul and gladdened the heart. "Thank ye, Mr. McQuaid...Farrel."

On impulse, she slipped her hand behind Farrel's head and drew him down to press a kiss to his lips. He tasted of grog, and his musky scent enfolded her. His hands closed around her upper arms, and she deepened the kiss for a few kicking heartbeats. Then she drew back, realizing what she had done as though waking from a dream. Farrel's astonished expression brought fresh heat into her face. She backed away. He released her, his mouth curling into a rakish grin.

She glanced around to see if anyone had noticed. If they had, they gave no indication. Except for Captain and Mistress Marks. They appeared as dumbfounded as Farrel, though after a moment Marianne threw her a knowing smile.

She started when Farrel spoke at her ear.

"We should party more often. I like the effect it has on you."

Ravyn refused to look at him. Her face burned hotter from more than grog and the dancing.

Chapter 34

"The wind is picking up."

Farrel made the observation from the forecastle where he and Andrew Marks stood with Ravyn.

"Aye, so it is." Ravyn squinted into the distance. A light breeze blew from the southwest, but in the northeast, dark clouds loomed on the horizon, scudding steadily southward. It wouldn't be long before they blocked the morning sunlight. "We'd best alter course until this passes. Outrun it, then resume our heading once 'tis over."

Captain Marks nodded. "Do what you must. Safety above all else."

Ravyn strode away, shouting. "Hard alee, Mr. Lancaster. Hands to the halyards. Haul away all. Away aloft. Loosen all sails and wet them. We need more speed."

Some of the men scurried to the lines securing the yards, preparing to turn the beams and redirect the sails. Others scrambled up the ratlines to adjust the sails and rigging and douse the canvas with sea water kept in barrels on deck for that purpose. Still others loosed more sails to catch the wind and push them back south. The sails crackled, billowing into full-rigged glory as they caught the wind. The water stopped it flowing through, and the ship surged forward, beginning its slow arc about.

Ravyn returned to Farrel and Andrew. "It may be best to gather the women and children and take shelter in the great cabin."

Andrew's brow furrowed. "Is there any way I might assist out here?"

"Nay. Ye should see to your family, and Mr. McQuaid to Liam."

Liam already waited by the great cabin door. The boy kept a brave, if pale, face.

Farrel wrestled with frustration at once more being consigned to look after a child rather than serve more useful purpose on deck. But then, she had relegated Andrew to the same.

"How will *Lady Annabelle* fare?" Andrew's gaze rested on his vessel. "That damaged mast may not be strong enough to withstand the wind."

"The men will see what's being done and do the same," Ravyn assured him before moving away again. As they watched, the crew on the schooner copied the activity aboard *Retribution*.

Andrew continued to watch his ship, a frown marring his pleasant face.

Farrel touched his arm. "We'll follow the captain's order for now."

Though they stayed far enough ahead of the storm to avoid the worst of it, the ship pitched on the tossing waves. They fastened the chairs onto wall hooks and secured loose objects. The lantern squeaked as it swung, unlit, on its ceiling hook.

Without light, the cabin soon fell into darkness almost black as night. Marianne, overcome by nausea, retreated to a corner with a bucket and Jacynta to aid her. Captain Marks sat on the floor below the window, an arm wrapped around Stuart and the other cuddling a wailing Rachel on his lap.

Rain lashed the windowpanes. Lightning split the sky, casting the cabin in streaking flickers of brightness. Rumbling thunder reminiscent of echoing cannon fire followed.

On deck, Ravyn shouted orders. The crew returned calls as they fought to keep the ship steady in the roiling swells.

Farrel staggered to the door. He opened it enough to peer out. Men tottered along the tilting, wave and rain-soaked decks.

Venturing out into the stinging rain, he spotted Ravyn at the helm with Mr. Lancaster. In a brilliant flash of lightning he saw they had tied their arms to the wheel.

Ravyn glanced down. Her expression hardened.

"Get ye back inside." She yelled above the roar of wind and waves.

"I want to help." The ship lurched and he stumbled, falling to hands and knees.

On the lower deck, a wave crested over the planking. One shipmate manning a yard line had his legs swept from under him. He slid toward the open edge, still gripping the rope. Hollering a curse, he wrapped the line around one arm and grabbed the rope in his other hand, stopping the deadly slip toward the roiling swells. Farrel heard a sickening snap over the roar of the storm.

The man shrieked, but held on with one hand. The other dangled, useless, in the rope coiled around his arm.

Farrel scrambled to his feet, swaying on the rolling deck.

"Ye can do naught," Ravyn shouted. "Look to those in the cabin. I needs ye to keep them safe."

Farrel stopped in his tracks, hands clenching. Did she think him so useless?

"Mr. McQuaid, heed me. Ye're the only one I trust in this."

He sensed the men around them slowing in their drenched labors to listen. Farrel scraped rain from his brow and drew a steadying breath. Trust... how could he stand against her when she offered that word? Grimacing, he snapped a stiff salute and retreated to the cabin.

He closed the door, repressing a shudder. Could they be swamped by the waves washing across the decks?

"Did you see any sign of the *Annabelle?*" Andrew stroked Rachel's hair as he asked the question.

"No. I wasn't out long enough, and it was raining too hard." Farrel didn't mention the injured sailor. No point in frightening the children any more than they already were.

"I pray she's safe." Andrew pressed a kiss to Rachel's curls.

"I's been in these storms afore, an' worse," Liam piped up as Farrel sank down beside him on the floor. "They's a scary thing, but the Cap'n and the men always sees us safe through." Despite his confident words, an edge of worry tightened his voice.

As much to distract himself as the boys, Farrel told stories of sea adventures he had read while growing up and some he'd written himself. He needed to keep from worrying about Ravyn. She knew what she was doing. It didn't stop his anxiety, though.

"He's a good man, Cap'n."

Ravyn glanced at Mr. Lancaster. His grim expression belied his calm tone, but she knew his focus remained on the danger of the storm.

"Aye, well, oftentimes he can be stubborn as a wharfside mule."

Mr. Lancaster's chuckle brought her glance flicking back to him. He looked out over the ship, the ghost of a smile tugging at his mouth.

"What does ye find so amusing?" Irritation edged her voice.

He shook his head, but the smile continued to play about his lips. Her own mouth thinning, Ravyn returned her attention to steering the ship.

Her arms ached from the pull of the wheel. Soaked to the skin, she shivered as a gust of wind sent stinging beads of rain lashing into her face.

"Ye should step inside." Mr. Lancaster turned a quick look her way, blinking water from his eyes. "Dry off and warm yourself."

"Ye needs me here." Her body shuddered under the unrelenting assault of icy rain.

"We're through the worst of it. One of the lads can spell ye. Mr. Yeates." His shout brought the young sailor bounding up to the helm, swiping water from his face and shaking dripping hair from his eyes. "Untie the Cap'n and take her place."

"Aye, aye, sir."

Ravyn allowed him to loosen the ropes binding her to the wheel. She studied his pale, intent face as she drew her arms free. Anxiety creased his features while she secured him. Stepping away, she rubbed her arms where the hemp had dug in, leaving coiled red wheals in its wake. She looked around at the crewmen tending the lines and sails. They strained under the drag of the wind on the canvas. Lines creaked and the sails crackled, but at least they headed out of the bluster. Glancing up, she noted the gradual brightening of the sky through the disbursing clouds and lessening rain. Her perusal fell on Mr. Fisher, partway up the main mast, catching a swinging line. He met her eyes and gave a terse nod.

She looked back at Mr. Walling. Two crewmen conducted him down to the sickroom to have his arm splinted. He made no sound, but his trembling was visible.

These men were the closest she had to family. They obeyed her commands, working as a valiant unit to bring them safe through the storm. Her heart swelled with pride at their unswerving courage. She could ask no better of them.

Descending, she opened the great cabin door.

"I could not endure if anything happened to you."

Marianne spoke in a rasping quiver from behind the door. Ravyn halted, hand on the latch, her gaze ranging over the cabin.

Farrel sat cross-legged in a corner with the boys, his back to her, while he sang a sea chanty in a low voice. Jacynta stood looking out the window, Rachel asleep in her arms. The air felt heavy, humid, tainted by a slight stench of vomit.

"Nothing will happen, love. It will be all right. The storm is passing, and we're safe." Captain Marks spoke in a soothing undertone.

"But...but that means we'll soon be at Halifax and you will be taken from me. What...what if the court decides to-to..." Marianne hiccupped on a sob. "It was hard enough losing Edward to this dreadful war. Wh-what if they execute you? I-I couldn't go on—"

"Hush, love. There have been few executions. Prison is the worst to expect, I think."

"I don't want to have the baby without you, to raise our children alone." The last ended in a stream of weeping.

"You can return to Virginia. Have the baby there, with your family nearby. I'll be home as soon as I'm able."

His words offered no comfort as Marianne's sobs continued.

Ravyn stepped into the room, closing the door. Andrew stood before the chart wall, Marianne enfolded in his arms. He spared Ravyn a glance and an apologetic half-smile before returning his attention to his wife. Marianne clung to him, what Ravyn could see of her face ashen and streaked with tears.

"Ravyn." Farrel unfolded himself and got to his feet. The boys kept on singing. Stuart giggled at a misused word. "Are you all right?"

"We're still afloat." She caught the drying cloth Farrel tossed her and wiped her face. "We should soon be free of the storm."

Farrel approached, brow furrowed. "You should get into dry clothes."

"Aye." She handed him the cloth. "I'll order supper as well. A cold one, I fear, since Cook will have put out the fire."

She withdrew, nodding to the Markses, and crossed to her cabin.

Over the meal, she watched Marianne with concern. A fragile air enfolded the woman, tense lines bracketing her mouth. She turned a gaze on Ravyn, teary with an unspoken plea as she gripped her husband's hand. If she lifted a bite of food to her mouth, Ravyn did not see it. But then, no one seemed inclined to eat much of the cold meat, cheese and biscuits.

"Should the wind remain promising, we will reach Halifax in a few days."

Ravyn's comment brought Marianne's wide eyes swinging from Captain Marks' face. Mouth opening as if she would respond, she shook her head and pushed her chair back. Jumping up, a sob burst from her. Weeping without restraint, she fled the cabin.

Ravyn stared after her then switched her gaze to Andrew. He half-rose but sat down again, distress clear on his features. Jacynta, who had stayed to care for the children over the meal, rose, scooping up Rachel and striding to follow her mistress.

"I must apologize, Captain Flynt." Andrew gestured toward the open door. "Marianne is distraught at the impending separation. I fear that in her delicate condition, she has little restraint over her emotions." A fleeting grief shadowed his eyes. "She lost a brother in the conflict this past summer.

It has left her terrified of losing anyone else."

Ravyn set her fork down and pushed her plate away, contrition knotting her stomach. "I spoke without considering her reaction."

"It's quite all right." But the worried way he looked at the door belied his assurance.

Ravyn pushed her chair back and rose. "I'll be seeing to the men," she said, her tone crisp.

She stepped out to the deck. The storm clouds hovered over the distant horizon, their threat weakened. It was a great relief to see the *Lady Annabelle*, separated from them during the storm, making a steady advance. The vessel appeared undamaged, and Mr. Hennessey waved an "all's-well" to her.

Around her, men swabbed the decks, sweeping away the excess sea and rainwater and checking the planking for leaks. Mr. Fisher bellowed directions to the riggers. Mr. Lancaster maintained their course, turning into a northern heading again as the sails were reset.

Ravyn's thoughts turned to the Marks' situation. A grimace twisted her mouth. Here she was, watching her "family" work together, while the American family was about to be torn asunder at her jurisdiction.

Their enjoyment of the dance, how they had looked earlier that day, a bond blood family shared. She thought about the terror of Stuart's near drowning, and Mistress Marks' anguish at thinking her child lost.

Tears pricked her eyes. She understood that agony. It was part of her, a black hole of misery she filled with duty and her resolve for revenge.

She had faced so much alone—the loss of the man who loved her, her virtue, her child.

How would Mistress Marks feel, having to give birth without her husband? Though the Court could be lenient, Ravyn suspected that knowingly carrying embargoed goods would earn Captain Marks time at Melville. Liam's fears for Marianne and the children were not without foundation.

Nay, she could not put them through that. She drew a sharp breath at the startling realization. She had to help them. But letting the schooner, the crew and the cargo go was not an option.

Farrel's suggestion echoed in her mind. It might work, with careful planning.

Before she could change her mind, she turned and strode back to the great cabin.

Chapter 35

"I've come to a decision about your family."

Farrel turned from the open window, where he and Andrew watched the *Lady Annabelle*'s rapid approach.

She gestured to the table. "Please, come and sit."

Andrew's brow creased as he and Farrel took seats. Ravyn remained standing at the head of the table.

"I have settled on releasing you." She lifted a hand when Andrew opened his mouth. "Your wife needs her family and ye to be with her. Making her birth a babe in unfamiliar surroundings without kin is asking too much. And that, sir, is the only concession I'm willing to make."

The young captain's brows shot up. "So, just my family, then? Not my ship or crew?"

"Nay. Your ship was a fair capture, and I need witnesses for the Court."

"But…" Andrew ran a hand over his hair. Then he shook his head, jaw tightening. "No. I cannot desert my men, leave them to the Court's mercy while I run off home. There would be no honor in that." His mouth twisted. "But Marianne… She's so frightened."

"Then you should take her and the children home." Farrel spoke persuasively.

"And leave my crew to serve prison time in my place? No, I cannot behave like such a coward." A muscle twitched along Andrew's cheek.

Ravyn leaned forward, hands flat on the table. "I know ye has responsibilities as a captain, but are your obligations to your family not more pressing?"

Indecision and longing warred on Andrew's face. "I would see Marianne and the children safe. They could return home, while I—" He swallowed.

"I don't think she'll leave you behind. Not without a fight." Farrel glanced at Ravyn, who nodded, mouth thinning. "There has to be something else you can do."

"What, pray?" She spread her hands. "I have no influence with the Court. Nay, the only solution is for Captain Marks to 'escape.' And even that is a risky gambit. Remember, my credibility is at stake."

"I appreciate that." Andrew rose and paced the length of the cabin. "But if I do this... What will my crew think? That I, their captain, am a coward and deserter?"

"Maybe it could be explained." Farrel directed his suggestion to Ravyn. "They might understand if they know the circumstances."

Ravyn's thoughtful expression encouraged Farrel. "Would that be agreeable to ye?"

Andrew stopped, his taut expression softening. "May I address them myself? Explain in my own words?"

"Aye, that could be arranged."

"Thank you." Andrew smiled, but uncustomary creases at the corners of his mouth showed his worry. "I am grateful for your offer, but I cannot accept without first weighing the consequences to my men and their thoughts on the matter. That, I know you understand."

Ravyn agreed with a curt nod.

"So, theoretically, how would you orchestrate the release?" Farrel asked.

"I've pursued a little smuggling in my time, and there are coves in the north of Massachusetts where exchanges can be made."

She strode to the cupboards and opened one to a haphazard stack of rolled parchments. Rifling through them, she pulled one out and returned to the table. She rolled it out, setting tankards at each corner to hold it flat.

"'Twill be morn afore we can speak with your crew, but if we make good headway, as the winds seem to promise, we could reach the appropriate shoreline by dark."

The chart showed detailed coastal topography in the northern part of Massachusetts, where it would in future become the state of Maine.

"'Twould be best we stay away from Boston." Ravyn leaned over the map. She pointed to two locations. "These are near villages where we could put ashore. Ye could take the stage or hire a coach to Salem or Boston and make your way from there."

"These contacts of yours. Can they be trusted?" Andrew asked.

Ravyn straightened and folded her arms. "They be good people, your countrymen as well. We could garner their assurance ye'll be safe with a few kegs of that fine French brandy ye carried." At Andrew's raised eyebrows she laughed. "Who is to say but it might vanish with the captain in his escape?"

Farrel chuckled. "You are a devious little minx,"

Ravyn gifted him with a smile, and soft color tinted her cheeks. "Aye, well, one must be prepared to make plans on the fly in these circumstances. More in the way of a raven than a landbound minx."

He laughed at her switch in his comparison and noted with satisfaction that the rosy hue of her cheeks deepened.

"But we will know naught till we speak with the *Annabelle*'s crew," she added.

"Until then, I would prefer to make no mention of it to Marianne." Andrew's mouth tightened. "There would be no point in raising her hopes, only to perhaps have to dash them again."

"Agreed." Ravyn rolled up the map and returned it to the cupboard. "We will keep our own counsel till the morrow."

Ravyn, Farrel, Mr. Morrissey and Captain Marks rowed to the *Lady Annabelle*. The crew gathered in the small great cabin with Ravyn's men.

Andrew presented Ravyn's offer and his reservations in accepting.

"I would feel an utter craven for absconding, but with my wife's delicate condition and my son still displaying aftereffects from his near drowning, I would like to see them safe home."

The men murmured amongst themselves, most frowning, whether with disapproval or indecision was difficult to tell.

Dr. Lorriman spoke. "We knew the risks when we signed on." His kind brown eyes rested on Andrew. "I, for one, understand your concerns."

"But, what of our fate?" A young sailor rose, features creased in belligerence and hands fisted at his sides. "We has as much right as the Capt'n to be freed."

Ravyn stared him down, arms folded and brows lowered. "I will conduct the rest of ye to Halifax to face the Vice-Admiralty Court. 'Twill be the judge's decision to free ye or nay."

"We has families too," another man objected. A guffaw from one of his mates brought their attention to the grinning man.

"I'm thinking those five wenches you service in port would not count as family, Mr. Thorpe," the other sailor retorted. Ripples of laughter floated around the table while Mr. Thorpe glared. Scowling, he sank back into his chair.

Yet another man got to his feet. He was older than the others, his face weathered, with a silver-threaded beard. "The Capt'n can't abandon his duty. Not to us, nor his ship. Not even for the welfare of his kin."

"The ship is already lost." This came from Chief Mate, Quincy Donaldson. "Unless Captain Flynt releases all of us, we must pay the requisite consequences. Mistress Marks has treated us with kindness. If Captain Marks needs to return his family home, I say he should, with our good wishes."

The men continued to argue. Andrew maintained an impassive stance, but oppositional viewpoints flickered in his eyes.

Farrel drew Ravyn aside. "Are you sure there's nothing more you can do? We talked about letting the ship and crew go, even if you keep the cargo."

"Nay." Her stern tone offered no concession. Then a new thought occurred to her. "However, I may put forward an alternative." She stepped back to the table, and the *Annabelle*'s crew quieted when she raised a hand. "I could petition to have ye pressed into service on the *Retribution* rather than a Royal Navy vessel or being confined to Melville. I lost crew members in a conflict some months ago, and that is what I'll base the petition on. The Court may allow it in such circumstances."

Silence greeted her proposal.

"If my petition is successful, ye may return to Virginia too." Her additional compromise met with murmurs of astonishment. "But mind, I make no guarantees. I can but try."

"Then that must be enough." Andrew faced his men. "I will leave it with you for discussion. Whatever your decision, I will abide by it."

Ravyn nodded at Mr. Hennessey and Mr. Donaldson. "If you will oversee the discourse, we will await the outcome on deck."

Ravyn, Captain Marks and Farrel stepped out into the sunshine. Above them, the schooner's sails rippled in the light wind. Ravyn's men tended to the lines and navigation.

Andrew separated from them, taking a position by the rail, back ramrod straight, face tipped up to the sky. Ravyn let him be, deciding the young captain might desire private contemplation.

They waited without conversing. Ravyn strode along the deck, inspecting the repairs and consulting with her men. Andrew stared out over the water, hands clasped behind him as he studied the frothing swells. Little could be heard from the great cabin, save an occasional raised voice signifying dispute.

Ravyn stopped her restless pacing beside Farrel. "They are taking overlong about this."

"You can force the matter. Or let the family go in secret."

"That is not his way." Ravyn studied Andrew's rigid stance. "He respects his men."

"And you admire that."

"Any captain worthy of their station should."

"Not all do." Farrel turned a wry smile on her.

"Then they are fools." Ravyn brushed a stray tendril of hair from her face. "I trust my life to the skills and good esteem of my crew, and they trust me to make the best decisions for the benefit of all. I will have it no other way, nor, I suspect, will Captain Marks." She nodded toward Andrew then strode to join him at the rail.

His profile revealed his tension in the hard line of his jaw and the creases bracketing his mouth. Without comment, she laid a reassuring hand on his shoulder. Though he acknowledged her consolation with a grim smile, he did not speak. He returned his attention to the vista of ocean surrounding them.

Ravyn glanced over her shoulder at the closed great cabin door. The voices had subsided, but the passage of time seemed interminable.

At length, the door opened. The *Lady Annabelle*'s crew filed out, some casting frowning looks their way, others more sympathetic.

Quincy Donaldson appeared last, stopping in the doorway. "We are prepared to render a decision."

His neutral expression gave nothing away. She, Captain Marks and Farrel returned inside, where Dr. Lorriman and Mr. Hennessey waited.

"What is the consensus?" Captain Marks' hands hung fisted at his sides.

"The men remain somewhat divided. However, the majority agree to you seeing your family home." His warm gray-green eyes shifted to Ravyn. "If Captain Flynt will attempt to recruit us, we can endure whatever time we are incarcerated."

"Don't fret about us, Captain," Dr. Lorriman added. "You get your little lady settled in her home and your boy restored to full health."

Captain Marks nodded, his shoulders relaxing in palpable relief.

Ravyn considered the Chief Mate with his strapping build and light blond hair. "Ye'll be treated as any other man in my employ."

Mr. Hennessey nodded, smiling. "They're a good lot and reliable to the maintainin' of the ship."

Ravyn, Farrel and Captain Marks descended to the longboat.

"It may be wise to send the wounded with ye." Ravyn set the oars in the brackets as they neared *Retribution*. "I would not wish to see their injuries worsen from poor care."

"Two more should prove no problem." Anticipation sparkled in Andrew's eyes, and an irrepressible smile curved his lips. "Marianne will be beside herself when we tell her." His expression sobered as he looked back at the schooner. "I cannot help but feel my uncle's and father's welcome will be less than enthusiastic. Especially if they believe I deserted my duty to their venture."

Strange, Ravyn had never pondered her role in that light afore. Profit for her meant loss for the opposing side. Mayhap the lines 'tween right and wrong were not so clearly drawn as she believed.

Chapter 36

"*R*eleasing us?" Marianne's hands flew to her mouth and tears welled in her eyes. "Truly?" At Ravyn's nod, the tears trickled down her cheeks. "Oh, thank you!"

Ravyn found herself wrapped in a tight embrace. She glanced at Farrel, not knowing how to respond. Mouth twisting in evident amusement, he showed she should embrace the grateful woman in return. It proved an awkward gesture, but she followed his lead. When Mistress Marks stepped back, despite the drops glistening on her cheeks, she glowed with happiness.

"When? How?"

"Mayhap as soon as dark tonight." Ravyn smiled at the woman's exuberance. She explained what she had discussed with the men.

"Then I must ensure we have everything ready." Marianne started away.

"Ye may wish to take little," Ravyn called. "There will be overland trekking to reach the nearest town, and the trunks will impede your progress."

Mistress Marks paused, brow crinkled in thought. Then she shook her head. "I need only enough to keep Rachel in dry nappies. You may keep the rest." She ran to the cabin before Ravyn could respond.

Ravyn set one of the younger sail hands to sewing a canvas sling for carrying Rachel. When he delivered it to her near the supper hour, she took it to Farrel's cabin. Upon knocking, Mistress Marks bid her enter.

She walked into a scene of chaos. The cabin looked as if fragments of a shattered rainbow were strewn onto every available surface. Clothing lay scattered on the bunk and over the back of the desk chair. Jacynta stood by one of the trunks, lifting out folded nappies and setting them aside. In the middle of the disorder, Marianne stood with hands on her hips, frowning at the disarray.

"If we have to travel overland through wilderness, I must pick clothing that will allow easy movement."

Ravyn touched a delicate skirt of watered silk. "Ye might find it more practical to wear breeches."

Marianne looked doubtful. "I've never worn breeches. It's not what a lady does." Then she shook her head. "Forgive me. I meant no insult."

Ravyn chuckled. "None taken. But fair warning, a gown will hamper ye."

Marianne studied Ravyn's broadcloth breeks, drawing her lower lip between her teeth. "Very well. I could wear them under my frock and tuck it into the waistband when needs be. Perhaps we should consider the same for Jacynta."

"Done." Ravyn set the sling on the bunk. "We'll see ye properly garbed for the journey."

"Thank you." Marianne frowned again. "I pray we come to no harm. Savages and wild animals roam the forests."

"I'll not send the men unarmed. If ye secure transport, there will be little need to fear the dangers of the wilderness."

"I've never had to do this. My life has been...sheltered." Fear passed over Marianne's features. "What if robbers, or—"

"Ye will find the courage to confront whatever comes your way." Ravyn set a hand on Marianne's shoulder. "If I can withstand battles and storms, ye can withstand this journey. Ye have that boldness within ye."

Marianne lifted her chin, training her features to determination. "Yes, I can. I will. Thank you, Captain Flynt. You are...a remarkable woman."

Ravyn chuckled again. "No more so than ye, Mistress Marks. We see the world in different ways, but as ye told me, we are still the same in our hearts." She dropped her hand and turned away. "I will bring what ye require after the evening meal."

Darkness fell like a black blanket. The *Retribution* floated, eerily silent, only the susurrus of waves and the creaking of the ship betraying their presence. The men moved about the decks with a stealth corresponding to the covert operation, even the deck lanterns snuffed so no light would give them away. Palpable tension vibrated amongst the crew. Though Farrel had heard no word of dissent over the captain's decision, they must wonder at her uncharacteristic choice.

At last, she lifted a shaded lantern and ascended to the quarterdeck. Opening the metal flap, she held the light high. When a dot of light appeared on the shoreline, she waved the lantern back and forth three times. From the shore came the return of three sways, then the light disappeared.

"'Tis safe. Cast the anchor. Shorten sails and spill the wind." Ravyn strode down to the boat deck, where a longboat from *Lady Annabelle* bobbed in the water. The men lowered one of *Retribution*'s vessels.

Along with the 'escapees', Ravyn, Farrel and some of her crew divided between the two boats. The luggage and kegs of brandy were loaded and they set off. With sails hoisted and tillers manned, they made the trip ashore.

Farrel stepped onto the beach and looked around. Lantern light revealed little beyond rock face and a cave's narrow opening. Five men stepped from it. Their single light revealed rough-looking characters in dark clothing, their faces scruffy and beard-stubbled. Ravyn met their leader half-way.

"What has ye brought?" His low, growling voice sounded more cautious than unfriendly.

"An American captain and his family who need to get to Virginia. I know ye can help them make the proper connections." She gestured to the kegs being unloaded. "There be a store of fine French brandy to repay ye for your trouble." She held the leader's gaze with stern warning. "Also, to assure their safety."

His eyes, bright with avarice, rested on the kegs. "There be an inn close by where they can bide till the morrow." He looked to Jacynta with Rachel against her chest in the sling, and Stuart clinging to her hand. "Best be on our way."

Captain Marks set down their ditty bags and stepped to Ravyn and Farrel. "If you ever make it down Norfolk way, please look us up."

Marianne hugged Ravyn. "Thank you. Come and see us when you can. And enjoy those pretty clothes." She slanted a telling glance toward Farrel. He struggled not to grin at Ravyn's bemused look.

Marianne rose on tiptoe to kiss his cheek. "Be good to her," she whispered at his ear. "She needs you."

Farrel smiled and lifted her hand to his lips.

The smugglers gathered the brandy kegs while the "escapees" handled the luggage. They disappeared into the cave.

"It comes out in a copse above," Ravyn explained when Farrel threw her a puzzled glance. "The inn is not far distant."

They concealed the craft from *Lady Annabelle* further ashore, behind a high bank of rocks, before returning to their longboat.

Back on the ship, Farrel entered his cabin. The cradle bed and trunks containing Jacynta's and the children's belongings had been returned to the *Annabelle* that afternoon, along with the cargo. Only Andrew's and Marianne's trunks remained.

"Ye intend to keep them here?" Ravyn spoke from the doorway.

Farrel grinned. "I have the feeling if I send Mrs. Marks' trunk to you, you'll toss her things out the window at the first opportunity."

"Know me that well, does ye?" She leaned on the doorframe, arms folded. She didn't look offended. Rather, her eyes glinted with humor. "Well, I'll have ye also know, I won't be wearing that frippery."

He copied her stance, with arms folded and a wicked smile twisting his lips. "I think I might snatch that cheval mirror. Then you could see how beautiful you are in the 'frippery'."

"Hmph." Straightening, she walked away.

Farrel chuckled. Never let it be said he wasn't up for a challenge.

The next day, a brisk wind drove the vessels steadily northward under a clouded sky. A line of land came into view.

"Another fine day like this, and we'll be at Halifax." Ravyn joined Farrel at the rail. The *Lady Annabelle* had gained on them, and Ravyn's crew adjusted the sails to slow the schooner. They sailed abreast, and Ravyn waved to Mr. Hennessy. He returned an all's-well. "We'll go over the papers and ensure the log entries reflect the changes in situation and prize listing."

"How will you conduct the business of registering the prize with the Court?"

"I needn't be present. Mr. Hennessey, as prize master, can make the proper petitions, e'en to requesting the reassignment of the *Annabelle*'s crew. Most of my affairs are conducted through an agent. He will hire legal services for both sides. Once the Court decision is rendered, I can leave the details of the auction with him and return to sea."

"Could I attend? I wouldn't mind getting a glimpse of Dr. Croke."

Ravyn fixed him with a stern frown. "Only if ye promise not to escape."

"Oh, I promise." He lifted his hand in solemn oath and met her gaze. "No way am I letting you get away from me, Captain."

Heat crept into her cheeks as she turned her gaze to the ocean. "Aye, well. Ye might consider yourself well shed of us." Despite her words, she felt gladdened he preferred to stay. She dipped her head to hide an irrepressible smile.

With unexpected boldness, Farrel slipped cool fingers under her chin to tip her face up. When he spoke, his voice grew soft and husky. "I'd be lost anywhere but in your company."

She drew back, her cheeks growing warmer still. The man had a disconcerting knack for worming past her resistance. Yet, as she looked at him through her lashes, she couldn't stop a surge of smug satisfaction.

She turned and strode off.

Chapter 37

Farrel took out his sketchbook and studied Ravyn's profile where she sat at the great cabin window. With her attention on the ocean, the hard beauty of her features relaxed. Glancing at the sketch he had started, he changed his mind about how to depict her. Turning to a fresh page, he outlined her face as she had appeared in the storm, then her arms tied to the wheel. Instead of her masculine garments, he drew the dress in sweeping lines, setting the folds of the skirt rippling about her legs in an imaginary wind. He paused, evaluating the effect. Beautiful and fierce, dangerous and captivating, more formidable than the storm buffeting her. A force to be reckoned with.

"What has ye so amused?"

He looked up, to find her watching him. He hadn't realized he was grinning, pencil poised over the page. "Oh, nothing." He closed the book. "Your captain... Would you have married him?"

Her brows lowered at the abrupt question. "It never came to that juncture." Though her answer was low and even, the slightest tremor threaded the words. She turned her back to him.

"Was that when you took command?"

She darted a wary glance his way. "Aye. The other lieutenants had been killed. 'Twas a miracle I escaped with my life." A moment of silence passed, a palpable weight, while Farrel waited for her to continue. "The men needed a captain. It was my duty to take charge as next in command."

"You didn't have time to grieve?"

When she spoke, her voice quivered. "I was better kept busy. It was too hard thinking on all that was lost." She made a choked sound, like a sob she tried to swallow. "The nights were the worst. Oftentimes I could barely breathe past the pain."

Her forthright words surprised him. Rising, he moved closer. "Did you worry that being a woman made you weak?"

"There be no room for weakness in a captain, whether man or woman. Da taught me that from my earliest days. Seeing to the men and laying our dead to rest was best. I was ne'er treated like a woman afore Captain Moore."

Farrel stood close behind her without touching her. "But that was your only experience of intimacy? I mean, before..."

A muscle jumped in her clenched jaw. "I saw the lightskirts that came aboard in port, and the women who sailed with their husbands thought nothing of speaking plain in my presence." She refused to meet his eyes. "I knows enough. And after the way Will Flemington used me, I was gladdened I ne'er indulged in such congress."

"What happened to you isn't how it's supposed to be. That was control ripped from you in the most violent possible way." He returned to the table and pulled out a chair. "Come and sit."

Refusal darkened her eyes and her mouth tightened.

"Please." He held her eyes with entreaty. After a moment of clashing wills, she sat. Farrel turned another chair to face her. "Did you see Marianne Marks as weak?"

"She keeps herself submissive to her husband." Ravyn shrugged. "'Tis as she ought to be, I suppose."

Farrel wasn't letting her away with that. "She didn't hesitate to stand up to you. Even after she learned you were the captain."

"Aye, well. She still made me think of those girls Da and I wintered with."

"You said they saw you as an oddity, and you're likely right. They probably talked about fashions and parties and their young men, while all you knew was life aboard ship. They were behaving as they were raised. So were you." He chuckled. "I'll bet you could've beaten the snot out of their gentleman callers."

The corner of her mouth twitched. "Aye. Da had seen I learned to fight with fists and weapons. It kept me safe from unwanted attention." Her expression sobered. "But not when it mattered most."

"It didn't keep anyone safe that day," he reminded her gently. "You weren't the only one who lost a battle. A number lost their lives. Not that that diminishes your trauma. The deceased are free of their pain. You live with yours every day."

She nodded, averting her gaze, her eyes glistening.

"And you lost something else, didn't you? A baby."

She lifted wide eyes, the color draining from her face.

"Mrs. Marks kept your confidence, so don't blame her. And this isn't me prying. I want to be honest with you and let you know I understand." He curled his fingers into his palms to keep from reaching for her hand.

Her lower lip trembled then she clenched her jaw, anger flashing in her eyes. "How can ye know things I haven't e'en said?" Her voice rasped with bitterness.

He shrugged. "Guess I have a deductive mind." He hoped his next disclosure wouldn't shatter this new-found closeness. "I spoke to Mr. Fisher. He said you'd been ill for a time after... After the battle."

She drew a sharp breath. "Ye didn't tell him—"

"Of course not. He didn't know, did he?"

"Nay." She looked away before she spoke again. "It made no sense to burden him...or any of them...o'er something that was...gone. Nor was it their affair, regardless." She closed her eyes, but anguish flickered across them first.

"You went through that loss alone." This time he took her hand. At first, she tugged against his hold, glittering eyes riveted on his. Then she let her hand relax, and Farrel caressed her knuckles with his thumb. "You mourned the baby. Despite the...manner of its conception."

A myriad of emotions flitted over her features too fast for him to identify.

"She was innocent, blameless." The words came in a barely audible whisper. Ravyn closed her eyes again. "She was mine. Not his. Had she lived, he would ne'er have known..." She shivered with a deep sigh. Farrel folded her hand in both of his. "But I was too weak to hold her within me."

"You weren't weak. Sometimes it just happens."

A glistening drop fell to her hand on her lap, followed by another, and another. She made no sound, weeping in silence.

He leaned forward and cupped her damp cheek in his hand. Though she didn't pull away, her eyes darkened warily. "Dear, sweet Ravyn." He risked caressing her velvety skin. She allowed it, her eyes fluttering shut. "You have more strength than a lot of men." He nodded at her doubting expression. "Yesterday, during the storm, I saw Captain Ravyn Flynt standing firm against the elements. You fought and maintained control, resolute in the midst of nature's fury. A fierce warrior wrapped in beauty."

Her mouth trembled into a smile. "I had no inkling ye was a poet."

He turned and opened the journal to the sketch. Ravyn stared at it with a look of wonder.

"How does ye see me as...as..." It seemed she couldn't find the right word.

"Beautiful? Because you are." Farrel gazed into her wide eyes. "Even prevailing against the forces of nature, your beauty shone through. It's something you can't hide, hard as you try. At least, not from me."

Uncertainty creased her features. "Yet...ye put me in a dress. Why?"

Farrel shrugged. "A whim. Me being a man, I guess." He chuckled. "An inescapable character flaw, I'm told. But whether it's a dress or breeches, it doesn't change who—and what—you are. Powerful, compelling, captivating. Stronger than any gale-force wind or lashing rain. A true force of nature." He closed the book again. "And there's no weakness in love. It's one of nature's strongest forces. It should never be something to fear."

"I don't fear love." Her expression softened for a heartbeat. Then it became hard and shuttered again. "'Tis what comes of love I cannot bear."

"What happened to you wasn't love. Not even on the same planet." He leaned toward her. "Maybe someday you'll discover the thing you fear most is what you need to embrace."

Something in the words resonated, but how, he couldn't fathom.

Ravyn stared at him. "Mistress Marks, she seemed happy. Even in her duty to her husband..." Her features creased in consideration. "She said he brought her joy..."

"Mrs. Marks is right. There is joy, and deep satisfaction, in what a couple shares. Strength and vulnerability together. You deserve to be loved."

When her eyes turned sharp and wary again, he feared he might have said too much. After all, it seemed a little soon to be discussing sexuality, even in a roundabout way. Or maybe not. He kept his gaze steady on hers. The sharpness faded, replaced by a flicker of misgiving.

"We should say good-night." He released her hand and stood.

"Aye." She rose as well. "I will think on what ye've said."

"Do that. I know you have a position of power to maintain, but in the right circumstances, letting yourself be vulnerable can have enjoyable consequences." He bowed and lifted her hand to his lips, the kiss a mere brush across her knuckles. A shiver set her hand quivering in his. He released it and straightened. "Good-night, my beautiful warrior."

He hoped she didn't think his compliment too audacious.

Ravyn stared at her hand, where a light tingle played over her knuckles. She reached for Farrel's sketchbook and opened it to the drawing of herself at the helm, standing ramrod straight, expression hard and determined, eyes boring through the rain. The dress as he had drawn it, fluttering around her legs, the bodice sensuously shaped to her bosom, did not detract from the steadfastness of her expression. It created a contrast she found not unbecoming. Womanly. An impression she never thought to connect to herself. It did not displease her. Seen through Farrel's eyes, she felt...gratification? Another unfamiliar sensation.

The things Farrel said... They awakened a wave of desire to discover if more than pain existed in the act of love. But she felt unprepared to confront her fears.

Could Farrel carry her through this? The thought brought heat flooding into her face.

Closing the book, she returned it to the cupboard. Then she retrieved the container of rum. A drink might help her sleep and would do no harm to her troubled state.

She carried it back to her cabin.

Chapter 38

$\mathcal{T}$he click of his cabin door closing woke Farrel. Peering through the feeble moonlight, a shading of white revealed a shirt. Then, amidst the rustle of cloth, a pair of pale legs appeared.

"Ravyn?" His voice came out a sleep-groggy whisper. She walked toward him, her form wavering. He stifled a yawn. "What are you doing here?"

She didn't respond, continuing toward the bunk in a slow stagger. Farrel frowned. As a rule, she moved as one with the ship, her body attuned to its rolling.

The shirt she wore reached to her knees, the lacings loose and open. It looked too big for her, as if meant for a tall, broad-shouldered man. And her hair. Shocked, he realized she wore it unbound, spilling over her shoulders.

When she put a knee on the bunk and leaned over him, he smelled rum on her breath then tasted it on her lips as they found his in the darkness. In initial astonishment, he responded to their softness, along with the silken brush of her hair along his bare chest. Then he drew back, lifting her away by her shoulders.

"How much have you had to drink?"

"Enough." Her rum-laced breath brushed his cheek as she tried to reclaim his lips. He put his hands on her cheeks to hold her still.

"What's gotten into you? Besides a few shots of alcohol."

Her husky laugh sent a heated tremor through him. He steeled himself against his body's automatic reaction as he hardened beneath the sheet.

"I want joy, Farrel. I want it from ye."

She pulled his hands from her face and bent closer. Farrel dodged, tossing the sheet aside and sliding from under it. He'd worn only linen underdrawers to bed, and they weren't doing much to restrict or conceal his arousal. He crossed to light the lantern with shaky hands. Looking over his shoulder, he wished he hadn't.

God, she was irresistible, her hair flowing in dark ripples, the shirt open from neck to navel, hints of the creamy orbs of her breasts visible through the fall of ebony tresses. He ran a distracted hand over his own untied hair.

"Farrel." She spoke his name in a breathless rasp, weaving toward him on unsteady legs. "Make love to me." Walking around to stand before him, she brushed a hand along his shoulder and over his chest, fingers stroking through the hair crossing his pecs. She circled a nipple with a fingertip, tingling heat lingering in its wake.

He clenched his jaw to quell the intoxicating throb of arousal thundering through his blood. Putting his hands to her shoulders, he moved her back. It didn't keep her fingers from their warm exploration. "You don't mean that."

"I does." She gazed at him through half-lidded eyes.

He released one shoulder to catch her roving hand and lifted it to his lips. He had to focus, to think, and she made that bloody hard. Along with other things.

"That's wonderful. But we can't do it like this."

"Surely, we can." She pressed to him despite his restraining hands. Her lush breasts and thighs fired his blood and set his pulse racing. She pushed closer, oblivious to the rigidity of him against her belly, even seeming to relish it.

"God, Ravyn, you're killing me here." He forced himself to step away, turning his back as his erection threatened to erupt from the opening of the drawers. "I don't know what you're thinking. We can't do this without—"

"Joy." She wrapped her arms around him from behind, and her mouth moved against his back, tickling along his spine in small, nipping kisses. Her hands glided over his stomach, making it clench, and came to rest on the waist tie of the drawers.

"Joy. Right." He gritted his teeth. "This isn't the way."

"Then what is the way? I want ye. Now." Her fingers dipped under the light cloth, and Farrel groaned.

He couldn't do this. He had to keep his brain functioning before her caresses and his long denied need switched off rational thought.

"No." He lifted her hands from the danger zone. It took concentration to tamp down his excitement enough to face her again, keeping her hands captive in his. "I wouldn't do it before when you had too much to drink. This isn't any different."

"But I want ye to." She turned the tables, grasping his hands when he tried to let hers go. "Show me there's no pain. Only joy."

He wanted to. God help him, how he wanted to.

She must have read his longing. With a shrewd smile, she drew his hands inside the shirt's placket, settling them over her breasts and holding them there. They burned like globes of pulsing fire, nipples under his palms pearling in invitation. Farrel's breath caught in his throat.

"Ye touched me here afore," she murmured, her husky timbre deepening. "I liked it, whate'er I might have said otherwise."

"Ravyn..." His protest came out a raw croak. He wanted to wrap his fingers around those pliant orbs, knead them, brush his fingers over her kerneled nipples, bend to take one into his mouth... "No." Drawing a ragged breath, he tugged his hands free. They tingled with the lingering impression of her body. "Go back to your cabin. Sleep this off. You'll come to your senses in the morning and be glad I sent you away."

"Nay, I will not." She stiffened her back, swaying. Her chin went up a notch. "As captain, I order ye to make love to me."

Farrel couldn't stop his abrupt laugh. "No." He shook his head, her outraged expression halting his mirth. "That's one order I won't carry out. Not while you're...inebriated." He'd been about to say 'tipsy,' but she was well past that. When her look of indignation altered to hurt, he relented. "If you still feel the same once you're sober, I'll reconsider. But for now—"

Ravyn threw herself against him, and he staggered back. It left no alternative but to embrace her to prevent her taking him to the floor. She twined her arms around his neck, and with one hand drew his head down, capturing his mouth with hers. Sparks danced through him, like flint striking tinder. Startled, he let his lips part, and she thrust her tongue inside, stroking and re-igniting the fire he'd been so close to dousing. He groaned, tightening his clasp around her and returned her strokes, coaxing tiny moans from deep in her throat. His manhood answered, growing harder and pulsing in the flimsy drawers.

Too much. Too much. He tried to pull back, but she had a stranglehold on him.

"Ravyn, stop." He barely got the words out for her hungry lips ravaging his. Breathing in ragged gasps, he pulled her arms from around his neck.

Her features crumpled in confusion as he pushed her away. "Ye doesn't want me?"

Farrel's hands tightened on her shoulders and he hung his head to collect his wits. When he looked back up, he softened his expression.

"God, I've wanted you since you tied me up on that shore. But I won't take advantage while you're not in full possession of your wits." His mouth thinned. "That would make me no better than Flemington." He released her and took two backward steps, wary lest she run at him again. She only gazed at him with wide, bewildered eyes. "Go back to bed. You'll see things more clearly in the morning."

Dumbfounded, he watched her lower lip tremble and a tear trickle down her flushed cheek.

"Don't make me go. I...I doesn't want to be alone."

Farrel stared at her in shock. Where had the aggressive, domineering captain gone? At what point had this vulnerable woman taken her place?

"Ravyn, sweetheart." He stepped to her and drew her into a hug. Her head dropped to his chest, and another hot tear seeped over his skin. He didn't know how to respond, except to hold her and run light fingertips over her hair. She turned her tear-streaked face up to him.

"What did ye call me?"

He had to think before he recalled the involuntary endearment. "Sweetheart. Sorry."

She drew back, but he didn't release her.

"Let me stay," she said, her voice tremulous. "Mayhap ye'll reconsider your refusal later."

Farrel smiled. "I don't think so." He took her arm and led her to the bunk. "You can stay, though."

She sat staring up at him, still the picture of confusion. "Ye're letting me stay under sufferance, then?"

"Oh, there'll be suffering," he conceded with a rueful chuckle, "just not the way you're thinking." Her bewildered expression only deepened. He sat beside her and lifted her hand to kiss her knuckles, then her palm and the soft skin of her inner wrist. "I promise, when you're more yourself, I'll let you have your way with me, Captain. Just not tonight. Okay?"

She nodded, staring where he had kissed her. Did she understand the intimate message the caress conveyed? The commitment he had made that had him semi-hard again?

He took her face in his hands and kissed her, not the deep, penetrating kisses she had given, but a gentle reinforcement of his pledge.

Farrel broke the kiss, rising to extinguish the lantern. The bedding rustled as Ravyn shifted to lie back. He moved over her, pausing on his elbows to study her face in the near darkness. How easy it would be to lower his body, let them be carried on a heady upward tide of desire to completion. But it wasn't the right thing to do.

Repressing a sigh, he settled at the wall side of the bunk. Ravyn curled into him, resting her head on his chest. He caressed her hair. It sifted through his fingers like silk.

"Ye're not like other men." She passed her hand over his chest.

"Oh, I'm not that much different." He pressed a kiss to her brow. "But I'd like to wake up in the morning with a clear conscience." He tapped the end of her nose with his finger. "We'll make love, but not while you're fired up with liquid courage. Okay?"

"Okay."

Farrel chuckled at her slurred repeat of the word so far out of her time frame.

"What're ye laughing at?"

"Mostly me." He settled his arm around her. "Go to sleep. I'll see you back to your cabin later."

She answered with a sigh, and her body relaxed. Soon, her breathing fell into the regular rhythm of sleep.

Farrel closed his eyes, still smiling. Having Ravyn here and wanting him amounted to an improbable leap over a yawning chasm. Even though it appeared the rum had been the impetus, it seemed reasonable it only enhanced existing emotions.

Anticipation set his pulse beating faster.

Ravyn floated in a haze of odd sensations. A gentle thud-thud under her ear, the warmth of another body, an arm holding her close. She opened her eyes and moved her head. A soft mat of hair brushed her cheek. Memory returned like the fragments of a dream.

She lay with Farrel. Had they...? Nay, he had spurned her insistence he yield and give her...joy.

She felt lightheaded, but that must be the lingering effects of the rum.

She stilled, listening to his deep breathing that verged on a snore. Her lips twitched. A memory slipped into her mind; of sitting with Da during an illness. Listening to his raucous snoring had made her wonder how a wife bore with such racket. Mayhap that explained why some occupied separate bedchambers.

She snuggled closer. That would not be her choice. This man had demonstrated restraint and tenderness, expressed respect in a way that sent warmth curling through her. He would never hurt her, never force her to do anything she didn't desire. She had given him every opportunity to slake his lust, but he held it in check. He let her stay, unfettered by obligation. If anyone had been the aggressor, it had been her. She would have no one to blame but herself had he taken advantage in that moment of...

Weakness? Aye, mayhap it had been a mistake to come to him. Thinking about the things Mistress Marks had said, and the way Farrel spoke earlier, had roused her curiosity. And with each successive dram of rum, her curiosity had altered more to the conviction that Farrel possessed the power to replace the bitter memories of Will Flemington.

Truth be known, he had given her an inestimable gift. Mayhap not the nature of joy she sought, but a sense of peace, knowing she could trust this man with her life, her safety, even whatever tattered shreds remained of her virtue.

"Ravyn? You all right?" His sleepy voice tugged her from her musing. When he moved his hand over her hair, she shivered.

"Aye." She sighed. "I wish..."

"I wish you'd come here sober, too." His voice rumbled under her ear. "But this is...lovely just lying here with you." It was his turn to sigh. "I think you'd better get back to your cabin. Before Liam wakes up, and the men start the morning shift. Wouldn't want to damage your reputation."

"Aye, well." She pushed up on one elbow to gaze at him through the darkness but could not discern his expression. "I suppose I should thank ye for being so...gallant."

"Gallant? Right." He swept a hand along her cheek. She sensed more than saw the smile that gave his voice a lift of humor. "I'm a regular Sir Walter Raleigh."

"Nay. Ye're Farrel McQuaid, and I'd have it no other way." She bent and brushed her lips across his.

His hand curled around the back of her head, holding her there as he returned the kiss, deepening it. Ravyn settled over him, breasts against his chest. They ached with the longing to have his hands there again, and mayhap other places he had touched afore.

Farrel ran his free hand down her back, tracing her spine, the indent of her waist, then the curve of her backside. Ravyn's breath hitched as sweet warmth trailed behind his caresses, and settled in a heated throb between her legs. He groaned in return, his arm sliding around to fold her close.

He broke the kiss, gliding a fingertip around her ear.

"Mmm. We'd better stop. Wouldn't want to spoil my gallant image."

"Farrel—" He halted her words with a finger to her lips.

"Stay away from the rum today. If you still want to pursue this, we can get together tonight. Believe me, it will be my pleasure to carry out your order then, Captain."

Heat rose to her face as she recalled issuing the command at the height of her besotted state.

"And," he added, his tone low and husky, "I'll make sure it's your pleasure too."

"I look forward to our tryst." She wondered how she would endure the day with that on her mind.

Farrel chuckled. "Me too,...sweetheart."

He rose and helped her don her breeches when she found herself clumsy and still woozy. He gave her a quick kiss then opened the door. She stepped out.

Glancing around, she saw only one man left on watch, his back toward her. She padded to her door and slipped inside.

Safe.

Chapter 39

When Farrel's door burst open just past dawn, he started up to face two of the hands.

"Ye's to come with us, Mr. McQuaid." The larger man stepped to the bunk. Farrel lowered his feet to the floor, gazing at them in confusion.

"What's going on?"

"We's orders to take ye to Mr. Fisher." Though he kept his tone even, a glimmer of something—sympathy?—flickered in the man's eyes. Farrel looked at his breeches, hung over the back of his desk chair.

"Never ye mind 'bout dressin," the other sailor advised.

"But..." Farrel stared up at their bearded faces, his brow furrowing. "What does Mr. Fisher want?"

"Best not be askin'." Between the two of them they took his arms and pulled him upright.

Jarred fully awake, he attempted without success to pull free. "What the hell?" They half-dragged him from the cabin, sputtering protests all the way.

On the main deck, it appeared the entire crew had assembled. Fisher stood before an upright wooden grate, the cat-o'-nine-tails in his hand. The contained fury darkening his scarred face sent alarm spearing through Farrel.

The men stopped before the bo'sun, keeping a firm grip on Farrel's arms.

A slow, wicked grin twisted Fisher's mouth. "So, ye finally 'ad yer wicked way with the Cap'n." His low growling voice rumbled like an imminent storm. "I seed 'er comin' from yer cabin in the night."

Shit. He hadn't even thought about Fisher when he sent Ravyn back to her quarters. His gaze lowered to the cat-o'-nine-tails lying across the bo'sun's big hands.

"Tie 'im to the grate, lads."

They pushed him against the slats and bound his wrists, arms spread wide, his bare back to the crew—and the lethal whip. He fought, but the burly mates outweighed and outmaneuvered him.

"You've got it all wrong." He glared over his shoulder. "Nothing happened. If you'd let me explain—"

"There be no explainin' what I sawed." Fisher's face was like a thundercloud, gray and vicious. "Ye took advantage of 'er, just as I said ye would." He slammed the whip's nine knotted tails on the planking behind Farrel. "Now I gets to repay ye."

"You don't have her permission, do you?" Farrel injected anger into the question.

"I doesn't need 'er permission. By the time she knows, ye'll be in yer bunk in too much pain to care. If ye're e'en still breathin'. I can make 'er ken this was right."

Some of the crew looked away, while a few met Farrel's eyes with pity. Yet others leered in anticipation.

"Then get it over with, you miserable bastard." Farrel pressed his forehead into the grating, steeling himself for the blows. One of his captors stepped forward and pushed a folded piece of linen into his mouth.

The lashes whizzed through the air before they struck. Agony seared his back. He ground his teeth into the cloth.

The second blow scorched across the throbbing welts already rising. He grunted, closing his eyes in stubborn resistance to the moisture stinging them.

He flinched at the third lash, gulping a deep breath around the linen. Warmth seeped into the waist of the drawers and sweat bit into the open wounds.

Where was Ravyn? Could she not hear this?

He swore the fourth lash cut to the bone, turning his back into a pulsing slab of excruciation. Though nauseous and dizzy, he wouldn't give Fisher the satisfaction of crying out or letting tears fall, though they rose, unbidden, to his clenched-shut eyes.

"Eli! Belay!"

Farrel swiveled his head at Ravyn's cry. He gasped into the cloth.

"'E deserves this." Fisher drew his arm back for the next stroke. Farrel squeezed his eyes shut and sucked in a rasping breath.

"Do it, and ye'll be next." Ravyn's footsteps pounded along the deck to stop at Farrel's side. "And I'll be wielding the lash myself."

Through misted vision, Farrel watched angry confusion twist the bo'sun's features.

"Ye're defendin' 'im? After what 'e done?"

"He did naught." She lifted her chin and glared at Fisher. "Ye has no right to do this without my say." Her cool hand fell onto Farrel's trembling shoulder. "Release him, lads. Take him to his cabin."

His hands freed, Farrel sank to his knees. Agony raked his back like a demon's claws with each heartbeat. The linen was pulled from his mouth, and his arms once more taken by two of the mates. He stumbled, and they steadied him. He kept his jaw clenched tight.

They laid him on his stomach. Ravyn entered with Dr. Page at her heels. She went to her knees on the floor at Farrel's head.

"Farrel, I'm so sorry." Her hand moved over his hair and came away bloodied. She stared at her reddened fingers, her expression going from chagrin to dark fury. "I'll see Mr. Fisher punished for this."

"Don't bother," he ground between gritted teeth as the doctor passed a wet cloth over his pulsing back. Ravyn rose, and her footsteps crossed the room. When she returned, she held another cloth. Wetting it, she drew the locks of his blood-matted hair through it.

"He's cut pretty bad, Cap'n." Dr. Page's gruff voice barely registered past Farrel's suffering.

"Do what ye can. I want no festering to take him."

Farrel hissed when the doctor rubbed vinegar into his wounds. No mistaking that smell. He supposed whiskey wouldn't have felt any better.

"Ye'll be fine, lad. I'll set a poultice to these and ye'll be right as rain in a day or two."

Hard to believe, considering every nerve felt on fire.

Ravyn's hand returned to stroking his hair. Dr. Page uncapped a jar, releasing a vile odor. Then he slathered the concoction across Farrel's back. This time tears did trickle from Farrel's eyes. He clenched his teeth against a foul expletive.

"Where did you come up with that stuff?" It burned like acid, never mind the demon's claws. "Did you raid Sammy's shit pile? Or the goat's?"

Dr. Page chuckled. "It'll heal the cuts quicker than aught else. I'll set strips to the wounds and bind ye. Ye can take opium to let ye rest."

"Aye, 'twould be best," Ravyn agreed. "I may take a little myself. It seems I have a wicked headache this morn."

Despite his pain, Farrel chuckled. "Brought it on yourself. Was it worth it?"

"Not if it means ye suffer for my folly." She ran a fingertip over his lips.

Farrel caught her hand and pressed a kiss to her fingers. "For a night with you, I'd suffer the fires of Hell. In a heartbeat."

"Here, lad." The doctor proffered a cup containing the opium. Farrel downed it, grimacing at the thick, bitter flavor. "I'll look in on ye this evenin'. Ye'll likely sleep through most of the day."

As the drug took hold, Farrel floated in a drowsy fog. He lifted his hand again and brushed it along Ravyn's cheek.

"In a heartbeat," he whispered.

The last he saw before slipping into darkness was Ravyn's eyes filling with tears.

Ravyn stayed on her knees, brushing Farrel's hair from his face, aware of Dr. Page's interested observation.

"He'll recover. 'Tis fortunate Mr. Fisher got only those few strikes at him."

Ravyn rose to her feet. "There was no need for this." Her tone hardened with bitterness. "No need at all."

"I've no inklin' what passed 'tween the two of ye to get Mr. Fisher in such a temper. I'm thinkin' 'twas more than the keepin' of the logs."

Ravyn faced the physician, arms folded on her chest. "He thinks Mr. McQuaid has designs on me." She glanced over her shoulder at Farrel. "E'en so, he can have no say o'er the way of my heart."

"Take this for yer head, Cap'n." He handed her the cup with a lesser dose of the opium and a knowing smile. "As for yer heart, ye must be the one decidin' which way it should go."

He left her studying Farrel. The white strips stood out stark against his back, the salve and blood staining the cloth as they soaked in. His face looked peaceful for the moment, lashes dark crescents against his pale cheeks. She had gotten most of the blood out of his hair, but it stained the drawers in large patches.

She drank the opium then exited, pulling the door shut.

"Mr. Morrissey." The stocky lieutenant hurried to answer her summons. "I needs ye to keep watch here, lest Mr. Fisher tries to further abuse Mr. McQuaid while I'm resting. Does ye know where he is?"

"Aye, 'e went below."

Ravyn stood, undecided whether she should face him now. As her head gave a painful throb, she concluded later might be best. Recriminations would do the megrim no good, nor would becoming sleepy as the opium took effect. She would confront Eli with a clear head.

"It seems Mr. Fisher 'as a bee in 'is bonnet where Mr. McQuaid is concerned."

Ravyn looked across the deck to the grate and the dark flecks of blood spattered on the planking. Her mouth tightened, and she flicked Mr. Morrissey a stern glance. "Aye, well, he'll be havin' more than a bee in his bonnet if he sidesteps my authority again. I trust ye to see that doesn't happen."

"Aye, aye, Cap'n." The man saluted.

In her cabin, she settled on her bunk, the sedating effect of the opium overtaking her. Fleetingly she thought she should have stayed with Farrel, rested beside him to keep him safe, but they would both be in an enforced sleep. Better not to agitate Eli more lest he take it out on Farrel later.

Yet as she drifted towards oblivion, the memory of lying with him warmed her, inside and out. Even as the drug drew her under, her body ached anew for the security of Farrel's solid heat next to her.

Chapter 40

Farrel woke to Ravyn shouting for the anchor to be cast. It appeared to be early evening.

They must have reached Halifax. Disappointment seized him at missing the arrival. As he tried to push upright, searing pain reminded him why he was abed.

"Damn you, Fisher." He answered a knock at his door with a growling, "Come in."

Mr. Morrissey poked his head in, concern etching his rough features. "Ye're awake. The Cap'n'll want to know." He withdrew, and Farrel heard him calling Ravyn.

She entered a moment later. "How are ye feeling?"

"Like I lost a clawing match with a lion."

"Ye're softer than most of the lads." She leaned over him, studying the linen strips. "Ye'll likely be left with scarring."

"Not quite the souvenir I had in mind. How are you feeling? Headache gone?"

"Aye." A blush crept into her cheeks. "I'll be staying away from the rum for a day or two." She crouched to look into his face.

"Good plan." He lifted a hand to caress one pink cheek. She leaned into his touch, her eyes drifting shut. "We'll have to put tonight's plans on hold. I'm feeling a little...rough."

"Farrel..." She raised her head, her brows lowering. "I doesn't regret coming to ye, but we ought to be prudent. The men'll be thinking me... wanton."

"Yeah, I'd say you were pretty wantin' last night." He chuckled. "It was your idea, not mine." He gritted his teeth and rolled to a sitting position, the throbbing pain generating nausea. "I don't want to move, but I'm going to have to take a walk." He grimaced. "The call of nature."

She looked confused then nodded. "I'll fetch a bucket for ye. Ye'll not be wanting to do much walking or climbing for a day or two."

Farrel didn't object. Every motion brought fresh pain scorching down his back, each lash a slice of raw burning. He wondered how many strokes the furious bo'sun would have meted out without Ravyn's intervention. A shudder passed through him.

Dr. Page arrived and examined the wounds, applying more of the noxious-smelling salve and fresh linen strips. Ravyn fed Farrel supper herself, a thick broth he choked down while lying on his stomach.

"The men will think you have a thing for me with all this personal attention."

She tilted her head, brow furrowed. "A thing?"

"Affection. Or maybe they've already guessed that after this morning."

"Aye, well." She looked down at her arms wrapped around her drawn-up knees, color flooding into her cheeks. "Mr. Hennessey will file the affidavit with the Court Registrar in the morn after he turns over the *Lady Annabelle* to the Marshal. He'll be coming aboard later to affirm the papers are in order. Will ye be equal to helping if we bring them to ye?" She lifted her eyes.

"I can probably sit up if I don't have to lean back on anything."

"Aye, and we can wrap ye so the linens don't fall away." She rose and started for the door. "I'll send Dr. Page to help ye."

The doctor wound a length of bandage cloth around Farrel's torso to hold the strips in place, crossing it over his shoulders. Farrel gritted his teeth against the pain. Dr. Page then helped him into fresh drawers and breeches.

"Ye're lookin' pale, Mr. McQuaid." The doctor rested a meaty hand on his shoulder. "Ye're certain ye're equal to this?"

"I'll manage. I want to speak to Mr. Hennessey anyway."

The doctor assisted him to his desk chair, where he settled to wait for Ravyn and Mr. Hennessey. The young lieutenant showed up first, carrying a chair from the great cabin.

"It can be done," he acceded on hearing Farrel's request, "'Twill have to be under cover of darkness. The Marshal will be takin' her in hand on the morrow." He gave Farrel a curious look. "It seems a strange thing for ye to be wanting, sir."

"It's not for me." Ravyn hadn't yet joined them.

"Ah." A slow grin spread across the lieutenant's face. "I hears ye've taken more than a passin' fancy to the Cap'n. And mayhap she to ye."

Farrel returned the smile as Ravyn entered.

They went over the *Lady Annabelle*'s records, the accounting of the cargo and the notes on the "escape." Then they drew up the petition requesting reassignment of the captured crew to *Retribution*. Farrel hoped he used the correct language to state their case in the appropriate terms to persuade Dr. Croke.

He was ready to return to bed when they finished, grateful for the draught of laudanum Dr. Page brought. Too sore to struggle out of his breeches, he settled on his stomach and fell into a deep, pain-free sleep.

Ravyn watched Mr. Hennessy and one of the mates row from the *Lady Annabelle* late that night. By the light of lanterns along both decks she had observed them maneuver a large, blanket-wrapped article into the longboat.

When they hauled it aboard *Retribution* in the canvas sling, she strode to where they stood it upright on the deck. Their careful handling of the object roused her curiosity.

"What has ye there?" She wondered at the look of consternation that passed between the men. Lifting the covering away, she realized what it was. Her full-length image stared back at her, indistinct by lantern light. Her gaze flicked to Mr. Hennessy. "Now, why did ye bring this here?" She had her suspicions.

"Mr. McQuaid said ye wanted it." Mr. Hennessy's grin held a wicked edge.

"Did he, now?" She drew the blanket over the mirror once more. "Put it in his cabin. I made no such request."

She turned and strode away, glancing over her shoulder with a scowl at the sound of muffled chuckles. When Mr. Hennessey lifted his hand to knock at Farrel's door, she called out.

"He'll be sleeping deep. Dr. Page gave him laudanum." They opened the door and put the mirror inside. "Blasted man." She settled her hands on her hips. "Doesn't know enough to desist and gets my crew to aid in his schemes. We'll see how it profits ye, sir."

She remained on deck late into the night, her thoughts a jumble of memories and impressions. Though gripped by chagrin at her bold behavior, she treasured how secure Farrel had made her feel in the end.

Her gaze slid toward his cabin. He had paid a high price for her recklessness. She had yet to reprimand Mr. Fisher. He had avoided her for the remainder of the day. Even now, she knew he busied himself at some needless task below to stay out of reach of her reproof. But he would evade her no longer.

She found him in the sail room repairing torn canvas, a job better done above during the light of day. He looked up as she entered and set the material on the floor.

"Ye knows I could have ye whipped for overstepping your authority this morn. And shaming me before the men."

He held her gaze with a steady steel-blue stare. "Aye, but I knows ye won't. I'm thinkin' the lads will take McQuaid's punishment as fair warnin'."

She folded her arms. "This was not one of the lads shirkin' their duty, nor one of the older men attending their station the worse for drink. This was my affair, nay yours." Eli gave her an arch-browed look. She realized the word she had used was mayhap not the most fitting. She set her jaw in stubborn resolution. "Aye, my affair, if that's what ye believe. Does ye think because Da made ye my guardian ye've the right to decide the course of my life? And I'm to allow ye that liberty?"

His bushy brows lowered as he returned her glare.

"Ye's bin like me own since yer da passed. I won't see no fancy-talkin' bloke usin' ye fer 'is own pleasure. No more'n yer da woulda."

She met his anger with resentment. "Did ye not see 'twas I coming from his cabin, not him from mine? Did it not occur to ye that I chose to be with him? Has ye ever asked if I felt he was using me?"

His dismissive shrug only increased her ire.

"Ye's a woman. Most wouldn't know if they was bein' used or nay." His scowl deepened. "I thought ye'd want no man touchin' ye after Flemington."

"Aye." She unfolded her arms and stepped closer. "But Mr. McQuaid is kind and honorable. He's shown me more caring than I've had in a long while. Not that I doesn't think ye care, Eli," she hastened to add as his scowl deepened. "Ye've been like a da to me, but it may be a da's caring isn't enough any longer. I know ye want to protect me, and 'tis sure I'm wantin' to protect myself, but Farrel McQuaid is a gentleman. Surely ye sees that."

"Aye, well, I's seen some gentlemen as turned out more monster than Flemington. I's thinkin' McQuaid's just bided 'is time, to catch ye unawares."

"I trust him. I think I have from the start. That be all I need say on the matter."

"It won't be all I'll be sayin'. Ye's fallen to 'is charms, lass, but 'e'll only be breakin' yer heart." The anger left his face, replaced by tender sadness. "I's watched ye grow, from a wee girl to a woman, and I's knowed the pain ye's 'ad. E'en to the takin' o' yer virtue. I'll not stand by and see that bugger make ye suffer more. 'E's not good enough fer ye."

"Not good enough?" Her brows arched in astonishment. "He's the most refined man I've e'er had the good fortune to meet. He treats me with gentleness and respect." Warmth bloomed in her chest. She curled her hand into a fist and pressed it over her heart. "Nay, Eli, ye'll let him be. If I needs ye, I'll tell ye. Ye've no right to gainsay whate'er might pass 'tween Mr. McQuaid...Farrel and myself." She turned to leave.

"And what of Flemington?"

She paused, jaw tightening, and shook her head. "I intend to end that vermin's life." She looked at the bo'sun over her shoulder. "Ye'd be well advised to turn your enmity toward that end, rather than punishing a man who has done no harm."

Mr. Fisher snorted. "'E'll rob ye of more than yer honor if ye doesn't uphold yer defenses."

"I say again, that be my affair, nay yours." Not waiting for his response, she strode from the cabin.

But she did not miss his repeated snort and his muttered, "Devil take the scummy bastard. I shoulda ended 'im while I 'ad the chance."

Clenching her jaw, she steeled herself not to whirl back and challenge him. She had made her position clear. To draw it out with Eli would be naught but useless argument.

Once done her business in Halifax, she resolved to intensify her search for Flemington. Mayhap with the monster slain, she could regain her life and explore the promises Farrel offered. Despite Eli's fierce opinion on the matter.

Incredible as it seemed, she longed for that with an ache that refused to leave her.

Chapter 41

*F*arrel woke early. He lay still, gauging his soreness before attempting to move. The instant he sat up, agony scorched along his back. He settled back, cursing. Then he saw the blanket-covered mirror in the corner. His lips curled into a smile.

A tentative knock at his door brought him upright again. "Come in."

Liam slipped in, a tray bearing a bowl and cup in his hands. "I brought ye breakfast, Mr. McQuaid. Cook said as a good stout parritch would help ye feel better."

Seeing the lumpy gray gruel, Farrel wasn't so sure.

Another knock announced Dr. Page and Ravyn. The doctor removed the binding while Ravyn updated him on the day's plans.

"I'll be accompanying Mr. Hennessey into the harbor. He'll convey the papers to the registrar and see the men escorted to Melville. I'll be meeting with my prize agent to arrange for handling affairs after the trial."

Farrel glanced up, brow furrowed. "Is Mr. Fisher going with you?"

"Aye." Her features tightened. "I'll not leave ye unattended with him."

"Thanks." Farrel hissed, flinching as Dr. Page pulled away the linen strips. After washing the stinging wounds, he gave each a thorough, probing examination. Farrel gritted his teeth.

"No festerin'." The doctor nodded in satisfaction. "They broke the skin but weren't as deep as they could ha' been with more strokes applied."

"How many might that have been?" Morbid curiosity prompted the question.

"Sometimes twenty, more often forty. E'en fifty or more, depending upon the offense," Ravyn replied.

Farrel shuddered. Four had been bad enough, multiplied by the nine cords. He couldn't imagine the torment twenty would cause, let alone fifty.

That might kill even a seasoned sailor.

"Guess I got off lucky. Thanks, swee—" He broke off with a rueful grin. "Ah, Captain." He didn't miss the warning glimmer in her eyes, or the speculating glance from Dr. Page. Ravyn left to accompany the men ashore.

Dr. Page reapplied the salve and fresh linen strips to Farrel's back then rebound him. "Were yer hide better toughened, I'd leave off the wrap and let the air at them, but I think ye need the poultice to soak in for a time."

"I'd like to venture ashore soon."

The doctor chuckled and shook his head. "Nay today or on the morrow, lad. Give those wounds time to heal afore ye start exertin' yerself."

Farrel couldn't argue as he sat up and let Liam brush and fasten his hair. The little boy chattered, distracting Farrel from the ache of his wounds. Inevitably, his thoughts turned to Ravyn.

He'd sensed remoteness in her he couldn't justify. After all her care yesterday, it seemed strange she held herself aloof today. He suspected she'd spoken to Fisher about the whipping, and wouldn't be surprised if the bo'sun's response had somehow influenced her attitude. Silently, he cursed Fisher, wishing him at the bottom of the harbor.

Ravyn returned near the dinner hour. After supper, she and Mr. Hennessey joined Farrel in his cabin.

"Mr. Parker thought the petition about the *Lady Annabelle*'s men was curious," Mr. Hennessey said, "but he left it with the papers for Dr. Croke to review. The Marshal put notice to the *Annabelle*'s mast for judgment on Thursday the fifteenth. Not as long as I feared, considering the number of cases still pending."

"I met with Mr. Burroughs to settle for our last capture," Ravyn contributed. "He'll have the funds ready on the morrow."

"Does Mr. Burroughs know you're a woman?"

"Aye, he's one of the few ashore who does. He represents my interests to the merchants who sponsor my voyages."

"Once I'm able to be up and about, we should have dinner somewhere nice."

Ravyn's lips twitched. "The Spread Eagle Tavern wouldn't appeal to ye, then?"

"It sounds...charming." He returned a wry grin. "But I think we'll find someplace a little more upscale."

Ravyn shook her head, still smiling.

"If I might offer a suggestion," Mr. Hennessy interjected, "I hears the Golden Bell be a posh establishment."

"Thanks. I'll check it out when I'm up to an excursion."

"Aye, well, that won't be for the better part of the week." Ravyn's smile dwindled.

"Plenty of time. I don't intend to be kept down any longer than necessary. Can't give the old bugger that much satisfaction."

"Ye'll be staying abed till the doctor says otherwise." Ravyn's tone brooked no argument.

"No more midnight visits?" Farrel hoped she would smile at his bold question with the young lieutenant present. Instead, she rose and stalked out. Farrel stared after her.

"Ye're a fortunate man, Mr. McQuaid. The Cap'n be a fine woman, but she's not shown inclination for any of the men afore ye."

Farrel's brow furrowed at Mr. Hennessey's observation. "You're right, she is a fine woman. But we still have some issues to iron out."

Mr. Hennessey chuckled, shaking his head. "Aye, well, she be a woman, and they has their own dispositions. But she's a good Cap'n, fair when warranted, strict when need be, wise in her ways most times."

Though Farrel agreed, he knew she had far more complexity than Mr. Hennessey's simplistic summation.

"Maybe I should get you to visit the Golden Bell for me. See if they require a reservation for dinner on Saturday." Farrel leaned closer, lowering his voice to a conspiratorial tone as a notion struck him. "Also, find out if they have rooms available. A night away might be good for both the captain and me."

"Mr. McQuaid." The young man's hazel eyes twinkled. "I'm not so certain the Cap'n'll be allowin' that." His expression sobered. "Or Mr. Fisher."

"Just see to the meal and accommodation, please. Let me worry about him. Say nothing to Captain Flynt, though. I'd like to save that for a surprise."

"So, a meal and lodgings." Mr. Hennessey rose to leave, a crooked grin tilting his lips.

Farrel hoped Ravyn would be receptive to his plan.

When she returned, Farrel's curiosity got the better of him.

"About the other night..."

A slow rise of color brightened her cheeks. "Blame the rum. I was thinking hard, and one drink led to another..." She gave a dismissive shrug. "'Twas but a moment of weakness—"

"That's not what I saw." Farrel couldn't help grinning as her dark brows arched. "The woman who visited me knew what she wanted and wasn't about to be sent away without it." A wider grin tugged at his mouth. "I think you would've had me stripped naked in three seconds flat if I hadn't stood firm."

"Farrel McQuaid. What a thing to say." She looked offended and embarrassed in a comical combination of furrowed brow, sparking eyes and rising color.

"Not that I would've minded," he added, still smiling, "but I didn't want our first time to result from a rum binge."

"Our...first time?" Ravyn blinked in bewilderment. "Oh, aye." Her blush deepened.

Farrel took her hand. Her fingers stiffened then relaxed. "Do you still want to do this? Was that more than drink talking?"

Her lips parted, but she clamped them shut on whatever she had been about to say.

"I'm not pushing." Farrel squeezed her hand before releasing it. "That little interlude was...delightful. If you've changed your mind, I'll have to live with that. But I think we've crossed a line we can't erase."

"I should think ye'd be wanting to rest. Surely your back must be hurting."

Her avoidance of the issue didn't surprise him.

"It is, but I know you're hurting too. Here." He laid his hand over his heart. "And here." He tapped his temple with a fingertip. "I think I saw more of the real you the other night than you've ever shown before." He smiled at her stern expression. "Yeah, you had a few jiggers of rum under your belt, but I think that lifted the reserve you hold over yourself like a punishment."

Ravyn sat straighter, her back stiffening and chin lifting. "I act as my position demands. Anything less and I would lose the respect of the men."

"It's what's up here,"—again he touched his temple— "that makes you what you are. Efficient and authoritative, everything a leader needs to be. I don't think the crew would begrudge you some human needs." He reclaimed her hand, running a thumb across her knuckles. "I'm not asking you to change your public image." He lifted her hand to his lips, brushing her fingers with a butterfly-light kiss. "But when we're alone, I'd like to pamper you, court you, within whatever boundaries you set. Treat you as the captivating woman you are." He lowered her hand. "You looked...enchanting in that gown. My beautiful warrior."

Her lips parted, but she made no sound. Her eyes narrowed, and she shook her head. "I've no inkling what to make of ye. Are ye trying to befuddle me?"

"How about a leisurely dinner together in town? No interruptions, no Liam needing to be put to bed. And especially, no Mr. Fisher."

He watched her face, tried to gauge the play of emotions crossing her features. He didn't have time to identify one before another took its place. The only one that held any hope for his cause was a look of longing she replaced with that strange remoteness.

"We'll see how the week progresses." She rose. "Now, I shall bid ye good-night. I'd suggest ye retire."

Farrel returned to the bunk and sat down. Ravyn poured laudanum into the cup on his desk.

"Whose shirt did you wear the other night?"

She hesitated with the cup in her hand. "It belonged to Captain Moore. I kept it...after." She didn't meet his gaze.

He took the cup from her. "You cared for him, then."

"Aye." She didn't hide the flash of pain in her eyes. "It seemed...fitting, considering what he'd told me, afore..."

Farrel glanced down at the reddish-brown fluid in the cup then back up. "How long before you started wearing it?" Her gaze flicked to him, questioning. "I mean, after all you'd been through, you still cared enough to keep and use his shirt like the remnant of a happier past."

"Ye'll be reading something into this like ye does everything else," she muttered. "Drink your medicine and go to sleep."

"We'll talk about it again." He held her gaze.

"Aye, I'm certain we will. Now, drink."

She waited until he downed the sedative and lay back before slipping away. Farrel closed his eyes with a shuddering sigh as the drug carried him into sleep.

With her hand on her cabin's door handle, Ravyn paused. The conversations of the past few days confused her, left her wondering if there was more to her nature than she permitted to show. Mouth thinning, she strode across the deck and entered the great cabin.

After lighting the lantern, she went to the cupboard where Farrel kept his journals. Though he'd taken away his writings, the sketchbook remained. She carried it to the table and opened it to the last one he had done of her at the helm in the dress. She stared at it, bewildered.

Farrel saw her as something more than the commanding captain, softer, yet strong, a 'force of nature,' as he called her. She ran a finger along the edge of the drawing. Could there be truth to his words? Did she wrongly deny her womanhood, viewing it as a liability, when, as seen through Farrel's eyes, it could be a thing of subtle power?

She remembered the enraptured look in his eyes, his astonished then delighted, expression when she wore Marianne's gown. A man under a spell. Her spell.

Her chest clenched with the desire to have him gaze upon her like that again. Recalling the desire in his eyes when she had gone to him, made him touch her, sent a warm flutter curling through her belly and deep into her core.

"Cap'n?"

She started at Mr. Hennessey's voice, whirling and gripping the edge of the table behind her. "God's breath, ye oughtn't to creep up on me like that."

He grinned, one tawny brow arching. "I tapped at the open door, but ye seemed preoccupied." He leaned a little to the side to see past her. "Is that what Mr. McQuaid does? Draws pictures?"

She turned to close the journal, self-conscious warmth rising into her face. It discomfited and displeased her to have her lieutenant see her thus. When Mr. Hennessey reached past her and held the book open, she shot a glare over her shoulder at the boldness.

"He has a talent." Mr. Hennessey straightened. "May I speak freely, Cap'n?"

Ravyn closed the book with a decisive thump. "Aye, but choose your words with care, sir."

The amusement lighting his hazel eyes altered to dark solemnity. "I've been with ye for nigh three years now. Ne'er before has I seen ye pay any man in your command any undue attention." He hesitated, but when she didn't respond, continued. "Mr. McQuaid is a good man. He seems to care for ye a good deal."

"So, ye're counseling me as my da now?" She scowled at him.

He gave a dismissive shrug, his fine moustache twitching as he grinned again. "Aye, well, I'd see myself more as your brother, beggin' your pardon."

Ravyn folded her arms. "So why has my brother sought me out?" She regretted the hard sarcasm edging her voice when Mr. Hennessey took a quick backward step.

"I'm returnin' to the *Lady Annabelle* and will await your orders on the morrow."

She let her arms fall. "I'll row o'er with the lads after first light."

"Aye, aye, Cap'n." He gave a smart salute, the twinkle sparking in his eyes once more. "I mean no disrespect. There be naught amiss with allowin' yourself a little pleasure in life. 'Tis a hard enough lot bein' away from kin for months at a time. I, for one, would ne'er begrudge ye what happiness ye find."

With that astonishing speech, he offered a small bow and another salute before leaving.

Ravyn stared after him, then turned back and opened the journal.

Subtle power. Strength and vulnerability. She saw them all in the sketch. Mayhap there was more to being a woman than she'd realized.

Drawing a shaky breath, she closed the book with reluctance and returned it to the cupboard.

Chapter 42

After a long day in town, Ravyn visited Farrel on her return in the early evening. She found him still abed, half-asleep, a boyish smile curling his mouth. Most likely the lingering effects of the opium.

She drew the desk chair to sit beside him. The scrape across the planks roused him. Blinking, he pushed to a sitting position, wincing as he stretched his back. Though still bleary, his eyes brightened when they met hers. Then he glanced toward the window, where the sun hung low in the sky.

"Did ye rest easy?"

Ravyn's query drew his gaze back to her. "Guess so." He ran a hand over his tousled hair. "You were gone all day?"

"Aye. I had business in town." She opened the pouch at her waist and drew out a small sack. It landed with a clink beside him on the bunk. "I brought ye pay."

He stared at it for a moment then shook his head. "Not quite the reward I imagined for taking a whipping for you. I can think of something better." His eyes when he looked at her crinkled at the corners, as though he fought laughter.

"What might that be?" Her curiosity shifted to wariness.

"Nothing improper. I was just picturing you in one of those dresses—"

That explained the smile. She curled her lip. "To quote something I've heard ye say on occasion, not bloody likely."

"Don't I deserve some compensation? Something better than money." He lifted the pouch. "This can go in my desk."

Snatching the sack, she strode to the desk and shoved it into a drawer. Facing him again, she folded her arms, scowling, "Ye'd be best to take your medicine and go back to sleep." She poured a draught and carried it to him.

He took the cup and drank. His crestfallen expression as he lay back touched her heart, but she refused to let him see it.

"You're such a lovely woman," he murmured in a drowsy fog. "Seems a shame to hide it like you do." He yawned. "Or try to." His eyes slipped shut. "G'night, beautiful."

She stared at Farrel, indecision warring with resolve. He seemed so set on seeing her in one of those damned dresses. Her gaze shifted to the trunk, and her thoughts of the previous night slipped through her mind.

Subtle power. Strength and vulnerability.

Da said a frock emphasized a woman's frailty. To live the life of a man, to be strong, she must dress the part. After the rape, she'd felt no desire to be seen as a woman, fragile and subject to a man's violent, painful will. But considering her talk with Marianne Marks, and her recent experience with Farrel...

She drew her lower lip between her teeth. It would do no harm to look at the foolish things. She lifted the lid, staring down at the folded articles. To one side lay the plain white undergarments, to the other, the blue and white gown. She lifted it, shaking it out, and glanced toward the mirror.

Surprised at her own whimsy, she pulled the blanket from the glass, staring at herself with the gown draped over her arm. Her own clothing, white lawn shirt, dark waistcoat, breeches and boots, hid her curves and lent her no womanly charms. The canvas binding beneath her shirt flattened her figure even more.

She looked up at her face, cheeks still pink after Farrel's teasing, lips full and moist, light blue eyes framed by dark lashes. Her hair, pulled back tight in her habitual braid, made her face all sharp planes and angles.

She recalled Farrel's sketches and wondered that he saw beauty and softness where, to her eyes, none existed.

She held the dress up in front of herself. Astonishment seized her at how the color and gentle draping alleviated the harshness of her features, making her eyes almost luminous, the curve of her cheekbones less stark.

"'Tis nonsense." She fumbled to fold the gown and, frustrated, tossed it over the back of the desk chair. "I'm not that woman."

She glanced at Farrel, certain he slept sound with his face turned to the wall. She stepped to his side, touching his hair and bending over him.

"Ye're a dreamer, Farrel McQuaid. Whate'er ye think ye sees is only in your head." Yet she didn't resist the urge to bend closer and touch her lips to his stubbled cheek. She left, closing the door.

The first thing Farrel spied in the morning was the dress draped over the back of the chair, then the mirror with the blanket on the floor.

He'd thought the vague impression of soft lips pressing to his cheek a dream. Yet seeing the mirror and the gown made him wonder. Maybe Ravyn had kissed him. Warmth expanded in his chest. His gaze slid back to the dress, and he smiled. "Gotcha."

Rather than sit up, he waited for Dr. Page.

The physician glanced at the dress, bushy brows lifting as he returned his gaze to Farrel. His mouth twitched. "Has ye taken to fancyin' ladies garments, Mr. McQuaid?"

Farrel laughed. "Not me." The doctor helped him up to relieve himself. Finished, he adjusted his clothes, washed his hands, and stepped back toward the bunk, brushing his fingers along the lace as he passed. "Guess our captain got a little curious."

Dr. Page chuckled, shaking his head. "I'm thinkin' the Cap'n'd look right comely in a frock, but I wish ye good fortune gettin' her to don it."

Farrel resisted the urge to groan at the doctor's invasive examination. He touched a sensitive spot and Farrel flinched. "No pus formin'. They may require debridin' once closer to healed. Ye'll be sportin' some fancy scars, I'm wagerin'."

"Badges of honor," Farrel responded with a crooked grin. "Not that Mr. Fisher would agree."

"Aye, well, I'd advise ye not to anger the man further." Dr. Page rubbed a lighter application of his malodorous salve over Farrel's back, leaving off the strips and wrapping.

Farrel decided it was time he took a walk about the deck. The sun was a warming balm on his back, despite the greasy salve coating it. He stopped at the rail, gazing over the wharf.

Vessels crowded along the piers with activity both aboard and on the docks. Farrel didn't recognize many of the buildings. He assumed they were destroyed—or would be—in the massive 1917 explosion during World War I. The collision of the Belgian relief vessel *Imo* with the French munitions ship *Mont Blanc* had devastated much of Halifax. The property losses, death toll and injuries had been staggering. Or would be.

Realizing the event he recalled wouldn't happen for over a century came as a shock. His knowledge could change the course of history—if anyone believed him. His mouth tightened. It wasn't his place to alter events. Damned butterfly effect.

He remained absorbed by the activity ashore—cargoes being loaded and unloaded and people, military and civilians alike, hurrying about their business. At the summit of Citadel Hill stood Fort George. From his vantage point Farrel could see the masonry walls and grass-covered earth ramparts. Above them, the dark roofs of the garrison buildings with chimneys spearing into the sky were visible, along with a sentry tower and the flagstaff with the Union Jack fluttering in a lazy breeze. He had visited the modern restoration of the fort. Though he saw no canons, they likely stood in ready evidence closer up.

Further down the eastern side of the hill was the clock tower, a three-tiered, irregular octagon atop a one-storey white clapboard building. Constructed in 1803 and facing what Farrel knew as Brunswick Street, the clock featured a four-sided display of Roman numerals.

In stark contrast to the active harbor, neat avenues of brick and clapboard colonial homes rose to the higher streets, and a few scattered church spires thrust into the sky. Nearer the fringes of the town, smaller, less elaborate dwellings huddled, thatched and pitch roofs dotting the hillsides. Further away still, scattered rough tent encampments sheltered newly arrived immigrants, many of them black Americans fleeing slavery.

"Mr. McQuaid?" He glanced at Liam holding a tray bearing the familiar porridge and a plate of scrambled eggs. "Dr. Page said as I should bring ye breakfast."

Farrel accompanied the boy to the great cabin. Liam left, and to Farrel's astonishment and delight, he returned with a steaming earthenware mug of fresh brewed coffee.

"The Cap'n brought it back yester night," Liam told him. "I can fetch ye some o' Nan's milk, if ye'd like."

"No, I take it black." It tasted wonderful, stronger than his usual choice, but welcome.

He spent some of the morning with the logs then took another turn around the decks. By the time he finished lunch, he felt ready for a nap, his back aching and stinging without protection from the noonday sun. He refused to ruin his few shirts with the salve.

Upon waking near the supper hour, he stepped outside. He saw Ravyn on the main deck with Mr. Hennessey and a short, paunchy man in a dress coat and trousers. A white cravat tucked at his throat failed to contain his double chin. He held a beaver skin hat, and the lowering sun gleamed on his balding head.

Ravyn glanced Farrel's way and gestured for him to join them. Reluctant to do so without being properly dressed, he acknowledged her summons then slipped back into the cabin. Liam appeared in the doorway a moment later.

"The Cap'n said as I should help ye, sir."

"Great. I need to put on a shirt, but that...cursed salve will stain it."

"I can wash it off fer ye." The child moved to the washstand.

Farrel hunkered down to let Liam pass a wet cloth over his back, gritting his teeth at the burn of even that light contact.

"'Tis best I can do, sir."

Farrel inspected the result in the mirror. He winced at his first sight of the crisscrossing scabbed welts. The light washing had deepened their fiery hue.

"Looks good." He didn't want Liam to think he hadn't done a credible job. "I'll get your help with the shirt."

He found one he wore for fencing, mended where Mr. Poole had laid into him on occasion. Liam helped him slip it over his head and onto his arms. It snagged on some of the scabs, and Farrel clenched his teeth as Liam pulled it away and settled it. Farrel left it hanging loose.

"Thanks, kiddo." He gave the boy's hair an affectionate ruffle. "Don't know what I'd do without you."

Liam grinned and darted off.

Farrel joined Ravyn, Mr. Hennessey and their guest.

"Mr. McQuaid, this is Henry Burroughs, my prize agent." She turned to Burroughs. "Mr. McQuaid is my clerk and tutor to the men."

Burroughs shook Farrel's hand. "You must be doing admirably, Captain. 'Tis rare for any but a navy vessel to boast a man of education." Friendly brown eyes twinkled beneath salt-and-pepper brows.

"Aye, he was a fortunate find." Ravyn gifted Farrel with one of her crooked grins. "I'm thinking he might assist in looking over the terms of our agreement for this pending case."

Burroughs turned his attention to Ravyn. Not much taller than the petite captain, his girth compensated for lack of height. "You seem assured of the outcome."

"With the captain escaping and the information we have in his records, I've little doubt Dr. Croke will judge in our favor."

"Very astute," Burroughs agreed with a nod. "Shall we go over the terms, then?"

They retired to the great cabin, and Farrel spent a few intrigued minutes assessing the figures the agent had laid out. He had no idea what the average costs and payouts should be, but knew they often fluctuated.

"We won't have anything final until after the judgment and auction." Mr. Burroughs ran a pudgy finger down the list of figures. "These are but preliminary amounts to compensate myself by way of percentages."

Farrel handed back the papers and looked to Ravyn. "Do they line up with your previous accounts?"

She nodded. "Very close."

The prize agent cleared his throat, looking pleased. "Then we have an agreement, Captain Flynt?"

"Aye. I'll be staying for the court proceedings, but once we know the outcome, I'll be heading out again."

"Of course. Can't waste time ashore with profit to make." He glanced around the cabin. "I'll be meeting with your merchant sponsors on the morrow. They requested I inspect the *Retribution* and report back to them. Is there any damage of which they should be made aware?"

"Naught that can't be tended by the men. We're always replacing sails after storms, but the masts, booms, and yards are sound, and no water damage below."

"They will be pleased to hear that." He turned back to Farrel. "A pleasure, sir. I trust we'll meet again."

They shook hands, and Ravyn left with the men for a tour of the ship. Mr. Hennessey hung back at the door.

"I was able to carry out your request, sir." He grinned and his hazel eyes sparkled. "Dinner and lodging for Saturday." He offered a conspiratorial wink and a bow, then followed after Ravyn and the prize agent.

When Ravyn returned, she seemed surprised to find Farrel still there.

"I thought ye'd resume your quarters." She poured a cup of grog then offered one to Farrel.

"I'm all slept out." He took a sip of the diluted rum. "I need to be up and moving around. Mr. Burroughs seems an interesting sort."

"He's a good man." She sat down next to him. "He has a keen eye for profits and treats us fair. 'Tis more often the court costs that gobble up a goodly sum."

"Typical government." Farrel grinned. "Between taxes and surcharges, I always lost a chunk of my paycheck. If it hadn't been for claiming expenses connected to my writing, I might have been a lot worse off." He sobered. "If I don't make it home, I wonder who will have control of my assets. I didn't make a will. No one to leave anything to." He sighed and shook his head. "Never mind. What's done is done." He took another sip of grog. "I'm sorry I missed you modeling the dress."

She looked taken aback at the abrupt change in topic.

"'Twas foolish curiosity, no more." She rose and moved to the window, keeping her back to him.

Farrel rose to stand behind her. "So, what is there to do on a Saturday night in port?"

She looked up at him, brow furrowed at the switch in topic. "Most of the lads'll be in the taverns, drinking, gamin' or chasin' the lightskirts, and those left aboard will be keeping watch. Why does ye ask?"

"Might be a good opportunity to have that dinner out. Do you know where the Golden Bell is?"

"Aye." She turned and fisted her hands on her hips. "'Tis too grand an establishment for the likes of me, but I knows where it is."

"Good." Farrel gave a decisive nod. "I had Mr. Hennessey reserve a place for us."

"Ye truly want to do this?" Indecision flickered across her features.

"I'm looking forward to it."

"I suppose ye expect me to put on one of those fripperish gowns."

Farrel shrugged. "It doesn't matter to me what you wear. Breeches, dress...nightclothes, whatever your choice. But I intend to dress up."

He couldn't tell from her unreadable expression what her choice might be.

Chapter 43

$\mathcal{R}$avyn spent Saturday afternoon overseeing the loading of supplies then in the chart room with Mr. Lancaster going over their next destination.

As the afternoon wound toward evening, Farrel approached her on the forecastle deck, where she talked to Mr. Hennessey.

"It's almost time to go."

She threw him a glance before turning back to finish her conversation and caught a conspiratorial smirk passing between the two men. On noting her puzzled observation, they moderated their expressions to feign innocence. That raised her suspicions that something was afoot.

Upon entering her cabin, she halted in surprise. The trunk containing Mistress Marks' belongings stood open against the wall. Farrel must have transferred it there during the afternoon. Was he trying to steer her choice?

She strode to the cupboard where her captain's uniform coat and breeches hung. She would dress as she wished, not bow to his desires.

Yet, as she stood with garments donned, her gaze drifted back to the open trunk. A shaft of sunlight fell onto the blue gown, setting it aglow. Drawn irresistibly, she picked the garment up and shook it out. Her mind went back to Farrel's reaction, the gleam in his eyes, the intimacy of his smile. Her stomach fluttered at the memory, and she clutched the dress against herself.

None of the men, not even Jonathan Moore, had objected to her masculine attire, and maintaining that façade was paramount to her. Carrying it off at the Golden Bell might be a challenge, catering as it did to the town's elite. All well and good to play the man in seedy quayside taverns, where drunkenness ruled. With all the doxies vying to catch their eye, why would the patrons look twice at anyone not wearing a skirt?

She drew her lower lip between her teeth, weighing other possibilities. Yet she wanted to see the captivated admiration in Farrel's eyes that made her shivery all over. Would it be so terrible to dress like a woman this once?

She set the gown on her bunk and returned to sort through the garments. Drawers, shift, the damnable corset, petticoats, stockings and garters. She set them out, and digging deeper, discovered a pair of kid slippers. These too she set aside, hoping they fit. She thought back to what other women wore. Gloves, a pair of dainty lace ones. A bonnet? Again, she dug down in the trunk. In a round box she found a wide-brimmed bonnet trimmed with pale blue ribbons and silk roses.

It took time and numerous whispered curses to don all the layers. She tightened the corset's laces the best she could, adjusting it as she recalled Marianne doing.

Satisfied, she pulled on the silk stockings and tied the ribbon garters above her knees. Her pensive gaze shifted to her boots beside her clothing cupboard, and her weapons laid out on the adjoining countertop. After a moment's consideration, she added one more piece to her attire.

Though she would have preferred donning her boots, she suspected they would appear out of place. She slid her feet into the slippers, close enough in size for comfort.

Then she hesitated, a cashmere shawl in her hands. Her hair. She had no idea how to fix it as Marianne had. In the end, she wrapped her braid around her head and fastened it in place with hairpins. The bonnet fit over it, and she tied a bow under her chin before drawing on the shawl.

She waited for Farrel to knock. Let him think what he liked, she would make it clear the decision had been hers.

It pleased Farrel that Andrew Marks' clothes needed no alterations. Though the younger man was broader in the shoulders and chest, the looseness allowed Farrel's still tender back more ease of movement. He donned a white shirt with a ruffled front, light buff trousers, waistcoat, white collar and neck cloth and navy blue tail coat with a pair of lace-up shoes.

As an afterthought, he pulled out a small kit bag and packed a few toiletries—brush and comb, his shaving razor and soap, and a jar of alum tooth powder. He tucked the sack of coins in the satchel as well. Then he picked up a beaver skin hat, carrying it as he exited, the bag slung over his shoulder.

When Ravyn answered his knock, he stared at the vision she presented in the gown, complete with bonnet, gloves and wrap. Her beauty and the flashing look of defiance she cast him from under her lashes made his chest clench, chasing words in the pleasure of sensation.

He took her hand and bent to brush his lips over the glove. "You're breathtaking."

"I didn't do it for ye." She lifted her chin.

"Of course not." Though he kept his tone mild, he couldn't help a surge of satisfaction and an irrepressible smile. "Shall we depart, my dear?"

She flicked a glance at the bag he carried then back up with a question in her eyes he chose not to answer. Then she nodded.

Farrel settled his hat on his head and tucked her hand into the crook of his arm.

The men aboard gravitated toward the cabins, gawking at the unprecedented sight of their captain in gown and bonnet. Judging by the comical slack-jawed stares, the dress had the effect Farrel thought it would.

"Cor, Cap'n, ye looks like a princess." That came from Liam in his innocent, piping voice. Mutters of agreement rippled through the crew. A becoming blush suffused Ravyn's cheeks.

They moved to the gangplank descending onto the pier.

"Don't wait up for us." Farrel dared a wink over his shoulder at the gaping men. Some of them exchanged knowing looks. "I plan on showing the captain a night on the town." The punch Ravyn dealt his arm made him stumble. "What?"

"Ye'll be giving them indecent notions," she hissed. "Hold your wheesht."

As Irish as she was, he grinned at her use of the Scottish admonishment.

"Ye'd best be takin' good care of the Cap'n," Mr. Lancaster called. "When Mr. Fisher finds out, there'll be hell to pay." The bo'sun had departed for town earlier in the day.

"Aye, well, hell after a night of heaven might be worth the price." Farrel kept his teasing tone low enough for Ravyn alone. Nevertheless, she punched him again. "Ow! You trying to bruise me, woman?"

"I'm tryin' to shut ye up afore my reputation's in tatters with the men. They looked at me like they'd never seen me afore."

"Your reputation's safe. I'll make sure of it."

"Aye, well, I'm not so certain as to that." She lifted her face, eyes sparkling. "I think ye've more in mind than dinner."

"Mmm. I was planning on dessert, too." He chuckled as her blush deepened.

They found a carriage for hire as they left the pier. Farrel handed her in and gave the driver their destination.

The Golden Bell Inn stood on a street on the upper side of Halifax, its wooden sign with the namesake bell swinging in the evening breeze.

Farrel helped Ravyn disembark, smiling as she set each slippered foot to the cobbles.

The foyer they entered opened into a spacious public dining room, where guests of the establishment were seated.

"Have ye come to dine with us this evening?" The elderly, stoop-shouldered man who greeted them had a pleasant face and temperate voice.

"I had a messenger make a reservation, under the name of McQuaid."

"Aye, I remember." The man nodded. "Lodgings along with dinner. The room is ready for ye."

"Room? Only one?" Had Mr. Hennessey misunderstood his intentions?

The innkeeper frowned. "The young sir requested but one." He spread gnarled hands, looking worried and apologetic. "There are no more to spare tonight."

Farrel glanced at Ravyn, bracing for heated opposition.

She met his gaze, her expression neutral. The glitter in her eyes and the tight creases at the corners of her mouth spoke more of uncertainty than resistance.

"I do apologize, sir. It has been uncommonly busy, what with the troops and the Vice-Admiralty trials. During the summer season, our rooms tend to fill quickly."

Farrel turned his gaze to Ravyn. "I leave the choice to you, my dear."

She gave an almost imperceptible nod, though her expression did not change. "We will stay."

"Very good." Relief edged the innkeeper's voice. He smiled, offering an ingratiating bow.

"Would it be possible to have a bath brought up?" Farrel didn't miss Ravyn's questioning glance. "If it comes at an additional cost, 'tis within our means."

"Aye, sir." The innkeeper registered mild surprise. "We can have the copper tub taken up. However, it will take some time for the girls to heat and deliver the water. Would ye partake of supper while ye wait?"

"Of course." Farrel tucked Ravyn's hand into the crook of his elbow and turned toward the public dining room.

A bath? Ravyn's brows lowered as she looked up at Farrel. He met her stare with a smile and drew her to a table by the window. The other diners, some couples and a few military officers, paid them little heed. Farrel pulled Ravyn's chair out to seat her then took his own.

She slipped the cashmere wrap from her shoulders to settle it over the back of the chair, and Farrel set his hat aside on the table. She looked around again, on edge lest anyone recognize her. It disconcerted her to find two soldiers studying her with interest. Her shoulders tightened and she returned a sharp look.

She started when Farrel's hand touched hers on the table.

"Relax. Don't blame them for noticing a beautiful woman." His voice warmed her despite her nerves, and her mouth quivered into a responding smile. "That's better." He lifted her hand to his lips, brushing a light kiss over the glove. Despite the covering, her skin tingled at the caress. "You have no idea how lovely you are, do you?"

Her lips parted, but before she could reply, a serving girl approached with a flagon of wine and two goblets. She poured and withdrew.

Ravyn stared at the elegant, etched glass. Once more she looked around, but the men had returned to their meals and conversation.

"You see? Now that they realize you're taken, they'll pay us no mind."

"Taken?" She bristled at the presumptuous remark. "I am not taken, sir."

Farrel chuckled. "You misunderstand. What I meant is that seeing us as a couple makes you unavailable. Whether or not you are."

Ravyn weighed his words, not liking them, but deciding to accept them.

Farrel raised his glass. "A toast, sweetheart." He waited until she raised her goblet then spoke in a husky undertone. "To a night we'll never forget."

Heat crept into Ravyn's face. She touched her glass to his and sipped, meeting his ardent gaze over the rim. She set her glass down, unfolding the linen napkin and spreading it across her lap as the serving girl set platters before them.

They ate in relative silence, enjoying the inn's sumptuous fare of roast duck, potatoes stewed in mushroom sauce, steamed vegetables and a dessert of pastries filled with strawberry preserves.

Ravyn stole glances at Farrel, to find his gaze on her face and occasionally lowering to the expanse of bosom exposed by the dress's scooped neckline. She fidgeted under his scorching study, fresh heat rising into her cheeks, and wished she had made use of one of Marianne's lace fichus to conceal her décolletage.

They finished their dessert, and the girl returned to retrieve the dishes. The host approached and gave Farrel a key. He assured them that everything was ready.

As they exited, Ravyn's hand tucked into Farrel's elbow, the officers once more turned their attention her way. She fought not to stiffen, though her hand tightened on Farrel's arm. Lifting her chin, she sent them a look that both challenged and defied. The younger man glanced away, shrugging, while his older companion held her gaze with a deliberate smirk.

Farrel tried to hide his smile, but his lips quirked up anyway. Ravyn might bear the appearance of a proper lady tonight, but the captain maintained the fire of command. Farrel met the soldier's grin with a nod and smirk of his own. Those fellows had no idea of the petite firecracker he led out on his arm. No simpering miss here. Just more woman than they would know how to handle.

Amusement and pride swelled in his breast.

Chapter 44

The chamber they entered was larger than Farrel expected. He gazed about, noting the size and apparent comfort of the four-poster bed. Candles and lamps, set about the room and in the middle of a table with two chairs by the casement window, cast a subtle golden glow. Another flagon of wine and two goblets waited on the table.

The end of the copper tub extended beyond a folding screen, wisps of steam drifting up from the water. A tray holding jars, bottles and soaps stood on a stool at the foot of the tub, towels and washcloths stacked on the floor beside it.

Farrel bolted the door and turned to Ravyn.

She stood with arms folded across her chest, her expression taut. "I shall have a few words with my canny lieutenant upon our return for conspiring in this."

"Don't be annoyed with him. He only did as I asked, though I think he misunderstood about the lodgings."

One black brow arched. "Did he, now?"

"Maybe you're right. He did have a roguish gleam in his eye when he left my cabin." Farrel shrugged. "But isn't this what you wanted anyway?"

Rather than answer, she undid the bonnet and pulled it off. Her gaze shifted from him, to the bed, then to the tub.

Farrel chuckled at her bemused expression. "I thought you might enjoy this luxury you never have aboard ship. Most ladies enjoy a hot, fragrant bath by candlelight."

Ravyn stared at him with increasing wariness. "Are ye not accustomed to my smell?" She sounded more dubious than offended.

Farrel drew out a chair and gestured for her to sit. When she did, he pulled the other to face her. "I know all this is new to you." He took her hand

and lifted it to his lips. "Do you feel safe with me?"

After a moment, she nodded.

"Good." Farrel rose and stepped to the stool. He lifted the stoppers from some of the bottles. Myriad fragrances wafted to his nostrils—flowery, spicy, and musky. When he opened one of rose-scented oil, he turned to Ravyn.

"Roses. They will always remind me of you." He poured some of the oil into the water and inhaled the perfume. "Perfect." He set the tray on a half-round table and returned to Ravyn. "Now, can you enjoy a little pampering?"

She gazed into his eyes for a long moment then started to kick off her slippers.

Struck by inspiration, Farrel dropped onto one knee in front of her. "May I?"

The tip of her tongue slid over her lower lip before she nodded. He took her foot in his hand, drawing off the slipper, then lifted her other foot to do the same. He ran his hand a little way up her calf and paused. Her pupils had dilated at the light caress. At last, her head moved in a jerking nod.

He slid his hand further up, finding the ribbon garter. Unfastening it, he rolled the silk stocking down. He didn't miss the catch in her breathing as his fingers brushed her skin. He glanced up to see her lips parted and her eyes half-lidded.

"You like?" He slipped the stocking over her toes and set it aside.

"Aye," she whispered on a hitching breath.

He went after the other garter, focused on titillating her. Startled, he paused as his fingers contacted a sheath holding one of her stilettos, tied in place with the garter. He pulled it free and sat back on his heels with the weapon across his palms.

"You came prepared." He wasn't sure if he should smile or remain serious. "For what?"

She shrugged. "One never knows what manner of cutthroats might be encountered on the streets."

He set the knife aside, hiding his smile. He couldn't picture her lifting her skirts to retrieve the blade in the middle of a public thoroughfare. However, he understood her putting self-protection ahead of modesty.

He resumed his tender task, rolling down the second stocking and laying it with its mate.

"There." He straightened and took her hands to bring her to her feet. "May I help with those dress fastenings?"

She turned and let him undo the dress. He pushed the tiny puffed sleeves down her arms, and the gown slithered in a seductive rustle to pool around her feet. She stepped out of it and pivoted to him, eyes wide.

Farrel took her face in his hands. He brushed her lips with his, surprised to feel hers quiver. Drawing back, he studied her face, thumbs stroking her cheekbones as he gave a reassuring smile. Again, he kissed her, making it firm yet gentle.

Ravyn's hands drifted over his, and her lips parted. She tasted of wine and strawberries, her mouth soft and responsive.

Farrel withdrew, lowering his hands to the ribbons fastening her petticoats. He untied them as he continued to savor her lips. She lowered her hands to grip his, stopping him.

Drawing away, she retreated a step, her breathing shallow, eyes misted. "I–I'll finish disrobing behind the screen," she murmured, her tone husky, as she took another backward step.

Ravyn removed her undergarments and hung them over the screen. Stepping into the tub, she lowered into the water's enveloping heat.

"This is heavenly," she said with a sigh. "Thank ye, Farrel."

"You're welcome."

Submerging deeper and leaning back, she closed her eyes. This was luxury, the warmth soothing the tension from her body. She listened to Farrel moving about the room, the clink of glasses and pouring of liquid, then the rustle of cloth. She exhaled a deep, relaxing breath, letting her thoughts drift.

"I thought you might like me to wash your back."

Ravyn gave a tight gasp at Farrel's voice from beside the tub. Her eyes flew open and she stared up at his serious expression. In wary trepidation, she noted he had shed his upper garments, leaving his chest bare. Her heart fluttered at the fascinating sight.

She sank further into the water, snatching the washing cloth to cover her breasts.

Farrel went to his knees, picking up the bar of perfumed soap from its metal holder hooked onto the tub's edge. He reached for the cloth, hand hovering above it. "May I?"

After a slight hesitation, she lifted her hand. He scooped up the cloth, and Ravyn splayed her fingers over her breasts. Her effort at concealment was aided only by the oil and soap skimming the water. Flicking a glance at Farrel, she realized he focused on lathering the cloth rather than her nakedness. Even so, she sat up with slow deliberation, leaning forward to better conceal her bosom.

"Baths in this time period are not the most common event." He looked up, a playful grin tilting his mouth. "Nor is it usual for a couple to share one." He moved the soapy cloth over her back in slow circles. "Quite scandalous, really." He shifted it along her shoulders then down her side, brushing a feather-light caress along the base of one breast. "Do you feel up to a bit of scandal?" He wiped the soap away and bent to touch his lips to her nape.

Ravyn shivered, her heart thumping. She hunched her shoulder but didn't push him away.

"You okay?" He halted, hand against her ribs.

"Aye." She heard the tiny catch in her voice. When he started to draw back, she covered his hand with hers to stop him. She turned her face up with a tremulous smile.

Given that encouragement, Farrel stroked once more along her breast, then with more boldness, under it, continuing to caress her neck and shoulder with his lips.

Ravyn drew a slow, deep breath, easing against the high back of the tub. Yet she gripped the edges so tight, pain lanced through her knuckles. Farrel lifted the nearest hand to bestow a soft kiss first to the back of her fingers then her palm. She shivered, but did not draw away, wanting his gentle seduction. He replaced her hand on the edge of the tub. She let it remain supine against the warm copper.

Farrel stroked light fingertips over her breast. It tingled and ached, feeling heavy and fuller. When he passed over the already pearled nipple, it tightened even more. Tendrils of sweet pleasure snaked into her belly, and she uttered a breathy gasp.

"You are so beautiful," he murmured at her ear. Gooseflesh stippled over her neck with the brush of his breath. He slid his hand along her belly. It quivered, sending a frisson of heat into her core. His fingers slipped into the curls at the juncture of her thighs, and she drew a sharp little breath. This touch, flesh to flesh, set her head spinning.

An unwelcome needle of fear pierced her pleasure.

For an instant, she was back on that cursed ship, helpless, afraid, in the merciless clutches of a brute. But only for an instant. She focused on the sensations, the thrill of anticipation. Opening her eyes, she saw uncertainty crease Farrel's face as he paused, fingers unmoving. He would never hurt her. Determined, she swallowed the fear and put effort into easing her tension. Her body relaxed with a shudder.

Farrel parted her to stroke the crux of her femininity. The tiny nub throbbed and ached, already primed by his tender attention. She uttered a quavering moan, her hips lurching in the water.

"Farrel." She met his eyes, and a renewed flash of fear gripped her.

He tried to pull away, but she stopped him with her hand, inadvertently pressing his fingers tighter against her. Sparks danced through her body.

"That feels so...strange." She closed her eyes on a breathless laugh.

"Pleasant, I hope." Farrel kissed her ear, sending fresh goose bumps over her.

"Oh, aye." She removed her hand, and Farrel drew his finger along her. Gasping, she could not refrain from moving to increase the pressure and accompanying pleasure.

"And that's just the beginning." He repeated the caress, sending molten heat rushing through her. She trembled when his free hand slipped around to bathe her other breast.

So much to feel, her body a thrumming mass of wanting. Impossible to focus on one place, one sensation, every part of her yearning for Farrel's touch. Even that most secret place where she had yet to permit him entry.

He drew his finger along her once more and stopped.

"Time to finish up." His voice had deepened to a husky rumble. He gave her a lingering kiss, running his tongue over her lower lip before sitting back on his heels. "I'd like to wash up too, so don't be long."

He straightened and retreated, leaving her in an agony of bewilderment. Why had he stopped? Her body remained charged with the hunger he had awakened, restless and unfulfilled at his withdrawal.

Sighing, she sat up and reached for the cloth. It disconcerted her that her hand trembled.

Farrel strode back into the room, his trousers, previously comfortable, tight with his arousal. Though he'd ached to coax Ravyn into a spontaneous orgasm, he wanted her to have the control he feared losing himself. She deserved that.

He sipped his wine as she splashed through the remainder of her wash. His erection, undiminished, reminded him in painful throbbing how long it had been since his last sexual encounter. Too long, he reflected, his mouth twisting in rueful humor. His only mistress for the past two years had been history.

He set the glass down, racking his brain for some distracting thought, anything to redirect circulation away from his arousal.

The outline for his next book, the one he might never write now.

When Ravyn emerged from behind the screen in her shift, he set his glass aside. The filmy garment clung to her, outlining her curves in a sensuous display of which she seemed unaware. "All done?"

"Aye." She followed his gaze down the ankle-length shift. Her crisp tone matched the spark in her eyes. "I only dressed for dinner."

"We could still go back—"

She silenced him by putting her fingers to his lips. "Nay."

He caught her hand and kissed it. "Would you mind returning a favor? I don't want to scrub my back."

She nodded, flicking a glance to the screen. "Tell me when ye're ready."

He took that to mean he should disrobe out of her sight. Once settled in the water, he did the main wash then squeezed the cloth over his shoulder.

"I'm ready." He positioned himself with knees bent and another cloth concealing his manhood. He would let her decide when—or if—she was ready for the full reveal.

When she stepped around the screen, her gaze roamed over him. She dropped to her knees, lifting the cloth and lathering it to run it over the sores on his back.

"They seem better." She drizzled water to rinse the soap and let the cloth drop back into the tub. Their eyes met, and Farrel smiled, one brow arching in silent query. She returned the shyest look, her gaze lowering once more to his back. She seemed as bashful as a schoolgirl, uncertain how to act or react.

"What's wrong?" He lifted one hand to cradle her cheek.

"Naught." She leaned into his touch. "I...I know not what ye expect of me."

"I think the important question is, what do you expect of me?" He let his hand drop to the edge of the tub. "I poured you a glass of wine. I'll be out in a minute."

She rose and retreated. Farrel stood up and reached for one of the drying cloths, securing it around his waist, and stepped onto the woven mat by the tub.

He joined her at the table, pulling out the chair and sitting to face her.

"Are you sure you're okay?" He took her hands, feeling them tremble

"I know where ye're wanting to take this night, and I...I'm not certain I'm ready after all." Though she met his eyes, hers glimmered with anxiety.

"Do you trust me?" He kept his tone gentle.

She studied his face before answering. "Aye," she whispered, nodding, "but I'm still..." Her lips moved, but she couldn't seem to say it aloud.

"Afraid?" Farrel raised her hand to his lips. "No need to be. Not of me. I understand your apprehension. Let things happen naturally. You can say 'no' or 'stop' at any point, and I promise we'll stop." Even if it was the last thing he wanted to do. He kept his gaze steady and gave her hand a reassuring squeeze before leaning in to kiss her. "Can we do this?" His lips grazed hers with the question.

Her answer was the quivering return of his kiss.

Farrel broke the kiss and rose, lifting her into his arms. He lowered his head to kiss her again, conveying desire and tenderness in the caress. Her arms slipped around his neck, and her lips parted, allowing him entry to the sweetness of her mouth. He made the exploration slow and intense.

When he raised his head and met her eyes, he read misty reciprocation of his ardor as he carried her to the bed.

No matter the outcome, this night was for her. However far she allowed it to go, he vowed to be content.

Chapter 45

Ravyn felt her heart would pound out of her chest as Farrel carried her to the bed. She stared up at the tender yearning darkening his eyes, the gentle curve of his lips, his features cast in shadow and gold-tinged candlelight.

She wanted him to make love to her. But even as the thought lodged in her mind, the leering face of Will Flemington flickered before her, a demon vision superimposing itself on Farrel's temperate features. She shivered, burying her face against his shoulder.

Could she do this? She trembled harder as Farrel lowered her to the bed.

"Ravyn? What's wrong?"

Lifting her head, she gazed at Farrel's creased features. This was Farrel, not Will Flemington. Yet that hated, black-bearded countenance once more slithered across her vision. She turned her face away, closing her eyes tight against the panic that rose to douse her desire.

"Ravyn?" Farrel's hand came to rest against her cheek but only to caress her.

She forced her mind to dredge up an image of the room, focusing on naming each piece of furniture as she pictured it. Her lips moved in silent recital, her breath ragged, almost panting.

Farrel released her and the mattress sank as he sat down. "We don't have to do this."

Ravyn lurched up, throwing her arms around his neck. "We does. Now." She forced command into her voice, but underlying desperation quavered through it. She met his gaze with fierce resolve. "Please." She ran her fingers along his stubbled jaw, determined to reawaken what she had lost.

"You're certain?" His hands drifted along her sides and settled on her waist.

"Aye. I want..." Her voice cracked. "I want ye to make love to me."

"Remember, we can stop if you need to."

Though she heard the edge of reluctance in his words, she cherished his reassurance. But she would not stop him. She trusted Farrel.

She lay back, wincing as a hairpin stabbed her scalp. Reaching up, she pulled a few of them out.

"Here, let me." Farrel took over, running his hand around the braid and removing the offending pins. He dropped them onto the night table by the bed then unwound her braid. With a smile, he untied the ribbon fastening the end and drew his fingers through, unraveling it to spread her hair along the pillow.

He stretched out, leaning on his elbow, one hand fisted under his cheek as the other moved to the ribbons securing her shift. He untied them to her waist, letting the edges lie undisturbed. Ravyn swore her heart hammered hard enough to set the flimsy material aflutter.

He smiled, his hand sliding under the edge to lie against the mound of her breast, warm and strong. Her breath caught in her throat, and she swallowed. Farrel bent and touched his lips to hers, the kiss tender. He slanted his mouth, increasing the intensity and skimmed the tip of his tongue along the seam of her lips.

She opened to him, willing, wanting, and met his tongue stroke for stroke. His hand slid over her breast, fingers coaxing the nipple into a taut kernel. The familiar tendrils of fire and ice flowed into her belly, then lower. She sighed into his mouth, arching to encourage his caress.

"So beautiful," he whispered, lips brushing hers. He swept the front of the chemise open to bare her breasts. When he bent and took one nipple into his mouth while continuing to tease the other, she gave a small cry. Fire arced from his hand and the slick heat of his mouth to every extremity, bringing a tight, exquisite coiling into her belly.

Farrel lifted his head, eyes dusky with desire. "May we get rid of the shift?"

She let him pull the skirt up and moved to accommodate the garment's removal. Farrel tossed it away, and it whispered onto the floor.

She felt exposed, vulnerable, as his devouring gaze roamed the length of her naked body. Her hands fluttered to the thatch of curls at the juncture of her thighs. That place where heat gathered and pooled under his searing gaze. Farrel drew her hand away.

"My beautiful warrior angel." Once more he bent to run lazy kisses along her throat, her shoulder, down her breastbone, again taking her nipple into his mouth. His hand wandered over her quivering belly, fingers sliding into the curls and parting her to touch that throbbing pulse he had found in the bath. She moved against his hand, closing her eyes and drawing a slow breath. Her whole body felt charged with...wanting.

His fingers slipped inside, stroking and stretching. She gasped as the coiling pressure tightened almost to the point of pain. But not a hurting pain, more a physical longing for...something...more. Deeper.

She knew what that was. The thing Will Flemington had done to her. The mental image she fought to resist washed over her. A low sob burst from her lips.

Farrel's head came up, and he stilled his caresses. Lamplight played over the curves and planes of his features. He withdrew his fingers, and she whimpered at the bereft, empty feeling.

"Are you all right?" The anxiety in his voice brought tears to her eyes.

"I know ye won't hurt me," she whispered, "but I'm..."

He stopped the words with a kiss. "Please let me try to replace those memories." He kissed her again, the amorous heat of his lips and the light touch of his fingers on her skin seeking her consent.

She did not want him to halt. The longing seemed too much to bear, sending the welling tears slipping over her lashes. She could do this, let Farrel banish her nightmares.

"I want ye, Farrel. Ye promised me joy. I want that." She drew another slow, deep breath, and more tears trickled from her eyes. "So, so much."

His smile was like sunshine breaking on the far side of a dense, dark cloud. "Then it's joy you'll have."

He moved down her body with butterfly kisses, kindling new fire with each fleeting touch of lips and tongue. Coming to her legs, he stopped. When he looked at her, mischief lit his eyes and curled his lips. He ran a hand along one outer thigh, then the other, watching her all the while. She shuddered at the light, brushing stroke of his fingers. Then, lifting away, he used his hands to part her thighs. He lowered his gaze to her most delicate flesh. It throbbed as his eyes darkened to a promising heat.

When he kissed and licked his way up her inner thigh, her breath caught. The air seemed too heavy to breathe.

Upon reaching that tiny thrumming place, he flicked it with his tongue, and she closed her eyes, gasping in the headiest pleasure. Each touch, the increase of tempo and intensity, blazed through her entire body. Her legs felt weighted, yet restless. She wanted to move them, not to push away, but to bring him closer. Instead, she arched under Farrel's ministrations, the deep, coiling hunger making her rock with him, against him. The tension built, drowning her in a vortex of sensation until something erupted within her. Fire burst into an explosion that ravaged her from head to toe, making her surge up to his plundering as she fisted the bedclothes in shaking hands. Her low moan reverberated around them.

She felt suspended as he continued his caresses, the ongoing ripples of release carrying her on a tidal wave that at last set her with astonishing gentleness on the shore of completion. A delicate sense of peace washed over her, leaving her feeling boneless.

But Farrel wasn't finished. She opened her eyes, startled to find herself gazing into his. Her glance flicked down to where the drying cloth he'd worn around his waist hung off the edge of the bed, leaving his backside cast in shimmering golden light.

She became aware of him then, a ridge of hot solidity nestled to the softest part of her, where a slow trickle continued to pool. So velvety, yet so firm. She drew a sharp breath, her body tensing.

"Can we do this?" He stroked her cheek with trembling fingertips.

Looking into his eyes, she read his desperate longing, the slight creasing at the corners of his mouth, his tender, yearning expression as he gazed at her.

"Aye. I–I'm willing, but..." Her whisper ended on a tremulous sigh.

"Still afraid?" He answered her jerking nod with a crooked grin. "We'll do this a little at a time, then." When he pushed against her opening, the heated tip of him glided in, smooth and painless. She clenched around him, and he stopped. A frown furrowed his brow. "Does it hurt?" She shook her head and focused on relaxing. He pushed deeper, stretching her. She tightened around him again, and he paused. "Now?" Once more, she shook her head. "Almost there." He moved his hips in the final thrust then held still, filling her. Not only her body, but her senses, her heart, even her soul. He drew a slow breath, lowering his head to give her a quick kiss. "This won't last as long as I'd like," he rasped in a breathless husk. "But later it will. I promise."

Ravyn couldn't stop the tears. But they were of joy, relief, a sense of release from some dark, unspeakable prison into a place of beauty and light.

Farrel moved slowly at first, teasing with a sensual glide that soon had her moving with him, loathe to let him withdraw yet eager to feel that silky virility slide into her. She gazed up at him as he quickened the pace, finding herself carried back into the upward pull of passion. This wasn't surrender. This was something so freeing she could think of no word to describe it.

A growing distension had her thighs falling further open to accommodate him as she neared her sensual apex. On reaching it, spiraling ever higher, she arched up to him, glorying in the sensation of oneness. Her core squeezed around his manhood, tugging as though to draw him deeper into her.

He closed his eyes, groaning as his head fell back and his features clenched. His response lent her a sense of power, as though in some indefinable way, she held Farrel at her mercy. A flux spilled into her, not burning, as she had experienced before, but warm, almost soothing as she floated from the pinnacle of satisfaction. He groaned again, burying his face against her shoulder, lips moving in an ardent caress as he too drifted from the coupling.

A sob burst from Ravyn that she tried to control, but it held its own sway. Farrel lifted his head, pulling her into his arms and rolling them onto their sides.

"Ravyn, I'm sorry. I didn't mean to hurt you. What can I do—"

She put her fingertips to his lips. "Oh, Farrel," she breathed, "ye did not hurt me. My tears,"—and she choked back another sob— "are for...joy. What ye've given me is...wondrous."

A smile lit his face. "That's how it should always feel." He kissed her mouth. "Wondrous." He tucked her against him, their legs tangling as he reached and drew the covers up. "So, you understand now what it means to have a man make love to you?"

"Aye." Her answer came as a breath. "Ye're a fine teacher, Professor."

"And you've passed the course with flying colors." He chuckled. "Not a subject on the regular curriculum. But there will be plenty of post-graduate studies." He kissed her. "And exercises." He kissed her again. "Oh, yes, lots of exercises."

She laughed when he bent to kiss her throat, her lips, the tip of her nose. At that precise moment, the lamp sputtered and the flame died, plunging them into darkness.

"I think that's a hint." Farrel pressed his lips to her cheek before settling his head next to hers on the pillow. "Thank you."

"For what, pray?" she asked, yawning.

"Just for being you." He hugged her tighter, and she let her eyes drift shut. "Sweet dreams, angel."

It was the last she heard before deep, surfeited sleep overcame her.

Chapter 46

*R*avyn woke to Farrel's heat against her back. His arm curled around her, hand cradling her breast. His breath tickled her nape, and she squirmed to readjust her position. Farrel's proximity, the security of his body wrapped around hers, comforted her. She wasn't alone in the dark.

Exhaling a shaky sigh, she covered his hand with hers. They had made love. Remembering that brought an ache of longing to experience that miracle again.

Farrel shifted his hips, pressing the hot length of his shaft against her. He made a low sound deep in his throat. A responsive thrill rushed through Ravyn.

"Farrel? Are ye awake?" He must be, considering how...ready he seemed.

"Mmm. I am now." His murmur at her ear sent goose bumps prickling over her neck. "You okay?"

"Aye. I didn't mean to rouse ye." She started to wriggle away, but he tightened his hold, a soft chuckle sending more gooseflesh skittering over her.

"Well, rouse me you did, sweetheart." He pressed a light kiss to her shoulder, at the same time prodding against her backside again. "You wanted something?"

Oh, the man was a devil!

"Aye...nay. I but thought... Ye're so...hard." Heat crept into her face.

Farrel laughed, squeezing the breast he cupped. "That sometimes happens to a man when he's sleeping, especially if he's holding a dark-haired temptress in his arms."

Ravyn turned onto her back, trying to see his face in the darkness. But not even residual moonlight illuminated the room. "I-I didn't know."

All humor left his voice. "Of course you didn't. I am your first, after all."

Ravyn opened her mouth to correct him then paused. Truth be known, he was her first. The first to make love to her, transport her to a place of bliss.

"Aye, so ye are." She touched his face, feeling the corner of his mouth lift in a smile. "And for that, I thank ye."

"You're welcome." He bent and kissed her. "Now, back to my original question. Did you want something?"

She heard the laughter in his voice. Aye, she did want something. Badly. His touch, his kisses, the awareness of him filling her, her body climbing higher on the wings of passion. Her breath caught.

She turned on her side to face him, curling a leg across his hip. The tip of his manhood brushed her core, awakening an urgent throb. When he stroked his hand along her thigh, she shivered.

Chuckling, Farrel slid his hand up to cup her buttock. "Is that an answer or an invitation?"

"Both." She touched her lips to his shoulder.

She laughed as he dipped his head to kiss her throat then sighed when his mouth shifted to her breast. She stroked his hair, pressing him closer. After a moment, he put his hands on her hips and rolled onto his back, pulling her to straddle him.

"What're ye doing now?"

"Teaching you another way. I think you'll like this one." He hoisted her up with one hand and she let him, giving a little gasp as he used his other hand to position himself at her pulsing cleft. "Slowly." He returned his hands to her hips as he lowered her to take him in by degrees until sheathed within her. She sighed, feeling his fullness as though part of herself. "Now you have control."

"What...what does ye mean?"

"You choose the pace, the intensity, the depth you take me in." A husky breathlessness accented his words.

She began to move, at first tentative, rocking away then back onto him. As her senses spiraled, she accelerated her movements, finding that, not only did it increase her quickening, but seemed to bring him fuller inside her. His hands left her hips to cup her breasts and tease her nipples. Once more it seemed there wasn't enough air in the room, nor sufficient space to contain the euphoria she soared toward.

"Oh, Farrel." Her soft cry sent her tumbling over the edge. She quivered with the release, every nerve from hair to toe awakened to explode, shiver. But this time he didn't follow her over the precipice. When she would have collapsed onto his chest, panting for breath, he held her upright, his hips surging under her in ongoing propulsion to her reeling senses. He gave her no time to collect herself before plunging her into the rapturous chasm yet again. Tears slipped down her cheeks. She tried to still herself, to gather her wits, but Farrel seemed intent on driving her even further on to the pinnacle of bliss. He slipped his hand between them, stroking that sensitive place where their bodies met. It propelled her even higher, her whole being careening toward completion.

Reaching the crest nearly shattered her. Finally, he let her slip to rest against his chest. She remained acutely aware that he maintained his fullness within her. His heart thundered under her ear as he caressed her shoulder and the nape of her neck.

"Enough?" He pressed a kiss to her forehead.

"Aye." It came out in a breathy gasp. "'Tis sure I am ye're tryin' to kill me."

"But 'tis sure I am ye'd go to your grave with a smile on your lips. We're not done yet, sweetheart."

He rolled her onto her back without pulling from her and began his own movement, thrusting so deep she felt him touch her womb. Yet it carried her again to the heights, and she marveled that her body withstood such onslaught. Her wits must surely fly away from her, like escaping birds, leaving her as weightless as clouds on a warm summer day.

The release, a softer float from the pinnacle, coincided with his, their moans blending as one. They lay quiet for a time, cuddling in sated tranquility. Ravyn gave a deep sigh of gratification.

"Ye've given me a precious gift." She pressed a kiss to his chest.

"And what might that be?" His hand moved over her hair.

"Joy." She closed her eyes, relaxed in the drowsy afterglow.

"As promised." His hand slid under her chin to turn her face up for a languid kiss. "All the joy you can handle, angel."

Ravyn didn't respond, content to listen to his heartbeat. She felt utterly buoyant, as light as the feathers in the bed's ticking, warm and safe in Farrel's embrace. She would never again fear this intimacy, not with him.

She was safe. In the storm of her fears, Farrel had become the sheltered harbor to which she steered, where she longed to cast the mooring lines of her heart. He washed her in the soothing swells of his care and concern, awakening her to new horizons of feeling she had resisted experiencing. He had carried her away from the tempest of her fears and lifted her on gentle surf to set her feet upon new white-sanded shores. In his arms, she could cease trembling as the victim of the past.

A smile curled her lips as she slipped into sleep.

When Ravyn opened her eyes, sunshine spilled across the bed. She reached for Farrel, only to find him gone. A soft humming and a scratching sound caught her attention. She looked toward the small dressing table across from the foot of the bed.

Farrel, clad in his trousers, stood before the mirror, drawing a straight razor over his soap-smeared cheek. In the stark light of day, he looked so tall, his broad shoulders hunched as he bent close to the glass. She noticed renewed redness around the welts across the middle of his back. No fresh bleeding, but the discomfort must be great. Though not brawny from the kind of hard labor her crew endured, the muscles of his arms were clearly defined and his chest firmly sculpted. Her heart skipped into a quicker beat, and she drew a slow breath. His reflected gaze met hers.

"Morning, sleepyhead." His reflection grinned at her. "Thought you might be planning on sleeping the day away."

She sat up, holding the covers above her breasts. "What time is it?" She ran a hand over her tousled hair.

"Time for church, judging by the bells that woke me up." Finishing, he rinsed and dried the razor then turned to her as he toweled his face. "I've already ordered breakfast brought up." His eyes sparkled. "Or maybe we should put it off for a bit."

"Nay." She swung her feet to the floor, retaining her stranglehold on the covers. "Where is my shift?"

"Here." He moved to the opposite side of the bed and picked it up. "You want some help?"

She reached across to take the garment from him. "Nay, I think ye're too willing."

"Killjoy." He retreated to the settee for his shirt.

"How is your back feeling?" While he was distracted in his struggle to get the shirt over his head and arms, she let the covers drop and drew the chemise on, fumbling to tie the ribbons.

"I'll live." His head appeared through the loose neck of the shirt. "Ravyn?" She looked up from tying the last ribbon. "Why the frown?" He began to tuck the shirt into his trousers then hesitated. "Are you sure I didn't do something wrong? Or would you like me to take you back to bed? I'm up for it, you know."

She flicked a glance to the distinct bulge at the front of the trousers then looked back at his face. She opened her mouth to retort, but a knock at the door stilled the words.

"Damn." Farrel pulled the shirt out again so the loose hem hid his eager manhood. While he stepped to the door, Ravyn ducked behind the screen to pull on the rest of her undergarments. She heard him speak and a woman's response, then the door clicked shut. Ravyn stepped back out to the room.

Farrel set a tray on the table. "We could stay another day." She didn't miss the hopeful note in his voice. "Maybe go for a walk, explore the town, come back here for a little...afternoon delight?"

Her heart fluttered at the suggestion. She would enjoy showing him about, and even more returning to their haven of bliss. Though tempted, she shook her head.

"'Twill be difficult enough persuading Mr. Fisher ye don't deserve another whipping. Stayin' away longer isn't going to help."

Sighing, he lifted the cloth from the tray. "You had to bring him up, didn't you?" He set out the platters of eggs, back bacon, fresh buttered scones and home fried potatoes along with mugs of steaming coffee. "Well, come and eat. Every condemned man deserves a hearty last meal."

Ravyn sat in her petticoats, reluctant to risk soiling the gown. The aromas of the food awakened her hunger, and she dug into the fare with gusto. Farrel grinned at her over a forkful of potatoes.

"Amazing what a little romp does for the appetite." He cast a twinkling glance toward the rumpled bed.

Ravyn swallowed quickly, warmth rushing into her cheeks. "Aye, well, our...romping should give the maids aplenty for gossip."

Farrel laughed. "And maybe our neighbors." He waggled his eyebrows at her. "We might have provided some midnight inspiration."

Ravyn's blush deepened. Aye, they had been far from quiet in their passion. She could imagine the speculative stares they would receive upon descending. Gazing into Farrel's eyes, her initial mortification was overshadowed by a resurgence of desire. She looked down to scoop up more eggs.

With their meal done, they finished dressing. When Ravyn stepped into the gown and reached back to fasten the buttons, Farrel stopped her.

"Let me." He took his time doing up the tiny pearl fastenings. "How did you manage this yesterday?"

"I fastened most of the buttons then pulled it over my head and did the rest." She glanced over her shoulder. "Ye seem well accustomed to fiddling with the fastenings of a lady's dress."

He chuckled. "Is that a roundabout way of asking if I've gotten many women out of and into their clothes?"

"Aye, well." She looked toward the window, surprised at the twinge of jealousy that heated her face. "Ye does come from a different time."

"True enough. A far more liberated era than this." He bent to press a light kiss to the side of her neck. "So you shouldn't be shocked to realize I might be acquainted in this way with others of the fairer sex." Laughter edged his words.

She turned to gaze up at him. Though he smiled, the light in his eyes reminded her of the moment he had seen her in the gown that first day. The jealousy ebbed into gratification, and she lifted a hand to touch his face.

He covered her hand with his. "But I must say, I think this time has been the most enjoyable."

Few patrons occupied the dining room when they descended, the rest most likely attending church. Out in the inn's courtyard, they found a conveyance to return them to the docks.

Farrel spent the drive gazing at the passing homes and commercial buildings. She, in turn, studied Farrel. He was a handsome man, with his strong, rugged profile and tanned complexion. Remembering their intimacies of the night brought light warmth to her face. He had been tender and patient, yet, in the end, so passionate. She fought not to fidget—or sidle closer to Farrel—as the reflection awakened a tingling awareness in her body, of breasts and belly, and the throbbing place below. That she was even able to experience this enthralled her, and she let herself succumb for a moment to the overwhelming seduction of her own desires.

She could accustom herself to this, to being treated and loved as a woman. But with that realization blossomed another far more startling one.

She loved Farrel McQuaid. She couldn't name the day when it had happened, but there it was, plain and true. In teaching her the pleasure of making love, the joy and peace of lying safe and protected in his arms, he had lodged himself into her heart. She wanted to shout her joy to the world but tucked it tightly away, convinced such public expression would be undignified

A sobering thought intruded on her elation.

What if he found a way back to his own time?

Her heart thumped in dread. She could not bear to lose him. Should he one day vanish, it would leave her with a void as yawning as the vast ocean 'tween here and the Continent.

She clenched her hand in her lap, quelling the impulse to touch Farrel, to hold him fast to this place and time.

Nay. She would not let her newfound ardor be troubled by such dire contemplation. Farrel was with her now. She would think of naught else.

Squaring her shoulders, she determined to live in the moment.

Chapter 47

Farrel tucked Ravyn's hand into the crook of his arm as they walked along the pier to the *Retribution*. They hadn't spoken of the recrimination awaiting them, but he sensed Ravyn's dread about confronting Fisher. He too felt trepidation, but determined not to show it, to stand tall and face his culpability. He hoped it didn't land him in the ocean for an unplanned swim—or in some nineteenth century morgue.

They saw the bo'sun long before reaching the gangplank. He stood at the top, arms folded on his barrel chest, his scowl fierce.

"Uh-oh. Looks like Dad's been waiting," Farrel murmured. Ravyn gave him a sharp glance. "No gun or cutlass in his hand. Is that a good sign?"

"Farrel, ye've naught to fear. He'll be angry, aye, but I think if he understands—"

"If he takes time to understand." Farrel gave a wry shake of his head. "Did you think to hide the cat before we left? And I don't mean Sammy."

She slanted a frowning look at him. "I'll not let him hurt ye."

"Thanks, Captain. I'll remember that when I come to after he decks me."

Ravyn's shoulders shook then she laughed out loud, the low, rich sound carrying on the morning air. Farrel, watching Fisher, swore his scowl deepened to murderous proportions.

They started up the gangplank, Farrel working out some way to slip past the blockade Fisher presented. No such luck. He did step back, but in no way were they getting past him. Ravyn kept her hand tucked in Farrel's elbow.

"So." That simple word carried the impact of a gunshot. "Where has the two o' ye bin?" His eyes held Farrel's with the pointedness of a blade to his throat.

"We spent the night at the Golden Bell." Ravyn held her head high. "Ye needn't be so churlish. As ye've said yourself, I'm not a child any longer."

"Aye, but neither are ye this cur's doxy. Bloody wastrel. I'll flog ye within an inch o' yer worthless life."

"Ye'll not." Ravyn scowled, her eyes blue ice under puckered black brows. "I went willingly with Farrel. Ye can have no say in that."

"And what would yer da be sayin'? Would he be wantin' to know his wee lass slept with...him,"—he snarled the word— "outside the marriage bed?" He spat on the deck at Farrel's feet. "Mebbe we should be remedying that."

"Mr. Fisher...Eli." Ravyn placed her free gloved hand on his arm. It looked incongruously small against the man's bulging muscles. "I am a woman fully grown and able to make my own choices, whether they be right or nay. E'en Da wouldn't be denying that." She glanced at Farrel. "This one felt most right."

Farrel patted her hand, forcing a smile to his stiff lips.

"Aye, well, the poor man'd be turnin' in 'is grave if'n he knowed." Fisher's piercing gaze shifted back to Farrel. "Ye's disgraced 'er, McQuaid."

"Not at all. If anyone's done her harm, it's you."

"Farrel..."

He ignored the warning in Ravyn's voice. "You're nothing but a bully. You'd keep Ravyn locked in emotional misery rather than living her life to fullest advantage." Ravyn's hand squeezed his arm, but he couldn't stop himself. "Why can't you let her be free?"

Fisher's gaze flicked to Ravyn, then back to him. Though still dark with fury, his features creased in bewilderment. "Free? To be tumbled by the likes o' ye at yer lecherous whim? Nay, I'll be seein' ye dead afore that 'appens."

Farrel didn't like the evil grimace that contorted Fisher's scarred face as he planted beefy fists on his hips.

"Eli." Ravyn withdrew her hand from Farrel's arm to match Fisher's stance, brows lowering under the brim of her bonnet. It really looked comical, but Farrel repressed his smile. Better not make Dad's surrogate any madder. "I am still captain here, and I order ye to stand down."

"Cap'n, are ye?" The steely eyes raked over her. "Ye looks more some prissy town miss to me."

Uh-oh. Farrel didn't like the sound of that.

"Eli Fisher, if any other man spoke so to me, ye'd have him tied to the grid and flogged afore he could turn tail and run." She undid the bonnet and snatched it off, throwing it onto the deck with a huff. The vicious look she shot Farrel had him taking a quick backward step. "I told ye I shouldn't be wearin' a dress in front of the men."

"Sweetheart—"

At Fisher's growl, Farrel swallowed the rest of his protest. Ravyn's glare didn't make him feel any more secure.

"Now, I'll be changing out of these foolish rigs and hearing reports." She stalked to her quarters, slamming the cabin door.

"I shoulda ended ye that first night," Fisher rumbled, "but I bowed to her wishes, as Cap'n and her da's daughter." His glower intensified. "Ye's likely ruined her. Turned her soft, more woman than cap'n."

"Why can't she be both? She's the strongest woman I've ever known. In here." Farrel tapped his chest over his heart. "You have to let her go. Let her live without the constant reminders about her father's expectations."

"Ye thinks ye 'as all the answers. Ye and yer 'igh an' mighty learnin'." He lifted a fist to brandish it in Farrel's face. "This be all she needs at sea. This'll keep 'er alive, not yer fancy words nor deeds. Ye're jest teachin' 'er to be weak. Missish. The men'll not be respectin' that. Ye should go back to whate'er milksop life ye came from afore I tosses yer entrails to the fishes."

A wave of pure, blinding rage washed over Farrel. Before he even realized his intent, he balled his hand into a fist, drew it back and sent it flying toward Fisher's maddening face. The cracking connection to the bo'sun's granite jaw jarred all the way up his arm. The man didn't even flinch. Farrel yanked his hand back, cursing aloud at the agony of his throbbing knuckles.

Fisher snorted, unfazed. "Mollycoddled whelp," he taunted as Farrel cradled his fist in his other hand, teeth gritted against the pain. "Ye's softer'n rotting fish guts. Not e'en worth wastin' me weaker fist o'er."

He stomped away. Farrel glanced around. Many of the mates stood about, silent and in some cases, revealing expressions of sympathy.

A strident cry issued from Ravyn's cabin. Farrel snatched up her bonnet from the deck. He entered her quarters, not bothering to knock.

She stood in the middle of the room, buried beneath the rustling folds of the dress as she struggled to pull it over her head. An ominous rip accompanied another sound of frustration.

"Sweetheart, don't." Farrel tossed the bonnet, kit bag and his hat on the bunk. He caught the gown's hem and eased it over her head. "The dress is lovely. Don't ruin it." He backed away with it draped over his arm as she turned to him. Her haunted expression nearly broke his heart.

"Ye must stop callin' me that. 'Tis not becomin' in front of the lads."

"Sorry. It just slipped out." He set the dress aside on the bunk and on impulse took her into his arms. She didn't protest or pull away, though she remained stiff and unresponsive.

"I said they'd think me soft if I dressed like this."

"It's only Mr. Fisher thinks that."

"But I feel soft. Ye gave me so much, but I'm...changed somehow."

Farrel cradled her face in his hands. "There's no reason you can't be leader and woman. I admire both of you. The hard, controlling captain and the sweet, responsive miss. Don't lose her. She's an essential part of you." He bent and kissed her lips, a gentle caress without demand. Straightening, he felt gratified when she returned a feeble smile. "Get into your ship's garb and you'll be back to your crusty self."

"If ye say so." An edge of reserve tightened her voice. She pulled away, and Farrel left her to finish changing

Looks of speculation greeted him on exiting the cabin. He met them head-on with a dismissive shrug.

When Ravyn emerged in her breeches, Farrel couldn't help but smile. Her features had resumed their former hardness, yet something had indeed changed. Despite the severity of her expression, her eyes, when she glanced in his direction, showed new warmth, a reserved vulnerability—exactly what he had depicted in that first sketch.

"So, the two o' ye will be marryin' while we's in port."

Fisher's blunt statement redirected Farrel's attention to him. He stood at midships, arms folded across his massive chest.

"Nay."

"No."

Their coinciding denials brought Farrel's gaze back to Ravyn. Her eyes met his, something flickering across them that vanished too quickly to identify.

"Aye, well, ye's nay worthy of the lass anywise." Fisher stomped away, leaving them to stare at each other.

"No?" Farrel repeated, bewildered.

Instead of answering, Ravyn stalked past him, refusing to meet his eyes.

Now he was really confused, and maybe a little hurt. Why such quick rejection of marriage, especially considering the morals of this era? He wanted to follow her, to ask what had gone through her mind, but felt it best the leave it alone for now. Marriage wasn't exactly on his priority list either. And yet...

He frowned, unsure how he felt about the notion. Ambiguous came the closest.

Unsettled, he entered his cabin and sat down on the bunk. Glancing down at his still throbbing hand, he saw tinges of blue and purple blooming on his knuckles. He shook his head with a rueful grimace. So much for defending

Ravyn's honor. He'd likely have to marry her to do that.

He had to consider the complications—and the possible consequences. If he married Ravyn, he couldn't return to his time. Not without leaving her behind. But he might have no choice. Time itself might catch him up in its tangled net and carry him away. What would happen to Ravyn then? And how would he feel about losing her the way he had lost everyone else in his life?

No, it was one thing to awaken Ravyn's sensuality, another to tie himself to her in what was referred to as 'the parson's trap' in this era. Ridiculous for Fisher to even suggest such a solution. And yet...

He laid his head in his hands, his senses, emotional and physical, stirring at the recollection of their night together. What did he truly feel for her? Admiration, yes. Compassion, certainly. Empathy, as much as possible in relation to his own circumstances. But love?

Running his hands over his face, he stared at the window with its view of other moored ships.

He cared for Ravyn in a way he hadn't about anyone for a long time. Even his other relationships hadn't motivated this intensity of connection. Was it only because of Julia and his determination to not let Ravyn fall victim to her fate?

He shook his head to clear the muddled thoughts. It didn't help. He wanted Ravyn to be as free as the bird her name emulated, to live the full, rich life she deserved.

Was he meant to share that life beyond what they had achieved already? Only time would tell.

Chapter 48

$\mathcal{F}$arrel heard Ravyn's raised voice from the great cabin. A few moments later, Mr. Hennessy exited with hunched shoulders and a hang-dog expression.

He shrugged off Farrel's apology with a rueful grin.

"She's the right of it, I suppose. but sure, if ye asked me, I'd help ye again."

"Thanks. It ended well and meant a lot. To both of us, even if she won't admit it."

Mr. Hennessey studied him. "Ye're a good man, no matter Mr. Fisher's opinion. Mind, I might be sleepin' with one eye open the next few nights, were I in your position. 'Twouldn't be the first some hand Mr. Fisher took a dislike to ended up takin' an endless midnight swim."

"Warning noted." Farrel grimaced. "No need of a sheriff with him aboard."

"Aye, he's judge, jury and executioner. I'll see ye in the morn, sir." He gave Farrel a long, considering look. "I hope."

Dr. Page inspected Farrel's back before he went to bed.

"Ye've a welt showin' some festerin'." He pressed one of the cuts in the middle of Farrel's back. Farrel hissed as pain speared out from the wound. "It requires lancing to release the pus."

"Then get it over with."

The doctor lifted out a small, curve-bladed scalpel from his medical kit.

Farrel eyed the finely honed, ivory-handled implement. "Sterilized?"

"Aye." The doctor's sharp gaze met his. "I've been doin' as ye recommended and boiling everything. I can clean it with whiskey, though, if ye're still doubting."

"It wouldn't hurt."

The doctor left and returned with a flask. He poured some of the alcohol on a cloth and ran it along the blade.

"Now, lie down. Ye might want to bite on somethin'." He passed the alcohol-soaked cloth to Farrel. "No point wastin' good whiskey."

Farrel laughed as he lay down and took the wet cloth in his teeth. Between the strong odor of the alcohol and its biting taste, he nearly missed the quick slice on his back.

But not quite.

He groaned, tears pricking his eyes at the sharp incision. The doctor ran his fingers along the severed edges, sopping up whatever oozed out with another whiskey-soaked cloth. Farrel yelped at the burn, the sound muffled by the cloth between his teeth.

"What's goin' on here?"

Farrel lifted his head at Ravyn's voice from the open door.

"I'm tendin' my patient." Dr. Page straightened, casting a measured look her way. "These sores shoulda been properly treated last evening."

Farrel spit out the cloth. "Put on some of that blasted salve. I'll get over it."

Ravyn studied Farrel. "Ye should have said something." She stepped close to the bunk. "I thought they looked worse this morn."

"I'm fine." Farrel winced as the doctor rubbed the foul-smelling salve into the open sore. "Take it easy there, doc."

"Aye, well, ye'll be takin' it easy if ye dies of brain fever." Dr. Page pressed harder.

Farrel fought the urge to clout him one.

"Ye should be stayin' abed," Ravyn told him.

"Offering to keep me company?" Farrel waggled a brow at her. She turned her back, flinging her hands in the air with a snort. He couldn't tell if it was amusement or irritation.

The doctor chuckled, shaking his grizzled head. "Ye're a corker, Mr. McQuaid. Not a whit of sense about ye at times, sir, but a corker nonetheless." He pulled out a linen strip and set it to Farrel's back.

"Just can't get enough of a good thing," Farrel growled as the pressure of the doctor's hand heightened the wound's sting. "If I'm going to die, I'd like to die happy." He turned his head towards Ravyn's rigid back. "And satisfied. How 'bout it, angel?"

Her glance flicked to the doctor. "Give him some laudanum. That should hush his tongue."

"I'd rather have the whiskey." Farrel sat up, throwing her an injured look. "You're no fun, Captain."

Uttering a beleaguered sigh, Ravyn headed out the door. "Aye, well, we're nay on a pleasure cruise."

"Best be conductin' yerself with caution," Dr. Page advised as he repacked his supplies. "Ye may ha' had the Cap'n 'neath ye yester night, but tonight she's yer better."

Farrel darted a glance at the doctor. "Had her on top, too."

Though he made no sound, the man's broad shoulders began to shake and a wide grin split his cantankerous features as he stared into his kit bag.

"That explains the raw condition of yer back. I'll leave the whiskey. Don't be taking more'n ye can handle."

Farrel drained the flask and settled on his stomach for what he hoped would be a peaceful sleep. The reopened sore throbbed, but he managed to rest until sometime through the night.

He woke with the impression of no longer being alone. Recalling Mr. Hennessey's warning, he started up, expecting to find Fisher looming over him. Instead, Ravyn stood by the bunk.

"Did you change your mind?" He yawned, giving his head a shake to rouse himself fully.

"About what, pray?" She spoke barely above a whisper.

"Staying with me." He turned over and sat up, lowering his feet to the floor.

"Ye're a man of single-minded determination. I but came to see ye weren't coming down with fever." She put her hand to his forehead, fingers cool against his skin.

Farrel caught her hand before she could withdraw. He kissed her palm, then her inner wrist, satisfied when she shivered.

"Stay. That way you can be sure I'm not coming down with a fever." He grinned, "At least, not from the wound."

"I cannot." She pulled her hand away. "What we do ashore is one thing, but here on the ship, in the presence of the men—"

"So, they can go ashore and screw their brains out, but you can't have a little one-on-one time with me on the ship? C'mon, Ravyn. You're the captain. What you do is your own business."

"On the ship, what I do is the business of all," she told him, her tone severe.

"What if we were married?" The question, unexpected even to him, seemed to catch her by surprise.

She drew a sharp little breath. "But we aren't."

"Yeah, and you were pretty quick to reject Fisher's rather strong suggestion. Guess I wasn't much better, though." He tried to discern her expression, but it was too dark to see more than the pale oval of her face. "Is the thought of being married to me repugnant? Or just the idea of being married?"

She sat down beside him. "I meant no insult to ye. 'Tis only that..." She sighed. "A woman becomes subject to a man's authority upon marrying. I fear my crew would not view my leadership as absolute if I put myself in such a position. Or allowed another to order the union."

She was probably right. Wives in this era were subordinate to a husband. But did that mean her crew would see her as any different than the strong, commanding, and independent woman she was?

"The men respect you. Mr. Fisher's the only one who has a beef with our being together."

"Aye, and isn't he problem enough for ye?"

She had a point. "Did he see you come in?"

"Nay. He went below afore I came to ye." She bent her head. Farrel slid his hand under her chin to turn her face up. Though he couldn't see her clearly, he felt the hitch in her breathing.

"I don't think having a husband would diminish you in the eyes of your men. Despite what Mr. Fisher says."

"Mayhap not, but I'll not be letting him dictate when or whom I wed. If I e'er do marry, it will be my own choice."

"'Atta girl." Farrel slipped his arm around her and pulled her closer. She didn't resist, lowering her head to his shoulder.

She took his other hand and lifted it to run light fingertips over his bruised knuckles. "How is your hand?"

"Still sore. But I'd punch him again." He bent and kissed her hair. "He has no right to treat you like that. Especially since you're his captain."

"Aye, well, he was my guardian afore I became captain." She lifted her head to gaze at Farrel. "If 'tis ship duty, I am the commander, but if 'tis about my place in the world as his ward..." She shrugged.

"Why on earth would your father choose a lout like him as your guardian?" This had puzzled Farrel for some time.

"They grew up in the same village on the coast of Clare. Ran in the same smuggling crew."

"Your father was a smuggler?"

"Oh, aye." He heard the smile in her voice. "'Twas how Da came to life at sea. And oftentimes 'twas the only way families survived, by the profits of the trade." Her tone sobered. "But there came a day when the British caught them and, rather than condemn them to the noose, pressed them into service on a Navy vessel."

Intrigued, Farrel waited for her to continue.

"Da used his wits to connive his way to first lieutenant. When the captain died of ship's fever, Da assumed command. He and Eli returned to Ireland, and Da married his childhood sweetheart. My Mam." She gave a shuddering sigh. "He had to return to duty afore I was born, and Mam died shortly after birthing me. He took me with him when I was but a few months old, weaned to goat's milk. Rough as he is in looks and ways, Eli was like an uncle to me, Da knew he loved me as his own. 'Tis why Da made him my guardian."

"Would it not have made more sense to have him serve on another vessel? Fewer complications for you."

"Aye, well, one captain tried it. A cruel man Eli suspected had designs on me." She chuckled. "They ne'er did find his corpse. No one tried to separate us after that."

Farrel shuddered. "So he's been your protector all along."

"As much as he could." Her voice tightened. "He's ne'er forgiven himself for not protecting me from Flemington. We were apart in the heat of battle, at opposite ends of the ship. Eli curses himself constantly for letting that happen."

"Nevertheless, he's going to have to realize you have the right to a life of your own, even if he doesn't approve."

"I've tried to tell him I'm safe with ye, that I trust ye, but he's not in a mood to hear it."

"But you do feel safe with me."

"Aye."

"Good." He bent, touching his lips to hers, brushing them then, when her lips parted slightly, slanting over her mouth to taste the salt and her sweetness. Her hands framed his face as she returned his kiss, a shudder vibrating through her.

"Stay." His whisper grazed her lips. "Just for a little while."

He lay on his side and heard the thud of her shoes hitting the floor as she kicked them off. She settled facing him, hands tucked against her chest. Farrel took one and laid it over his heart. Her fingers curled into the furring there, and Farrel drew a slow breath. He ached to hold her skin to skin, aware of her reluctance. Yet he felt it came from their location rather than the heat sizzling between them.

He released her hand, cupping her thigh and drawing her leg across his hip. It brought her closer, the warmth at the juncture of her legs settling against him. She didn't resist. Rather, she curled closer, her head nestling into the hollow of his shoulder.

"There's nothing wrong with wanting each other," he murmured against the top of her head. "It doesn't—or shouldn't—undermine who you are as captain. It just makes you human." He ran his hand over the curve of her buttock with a low growl. "You feel so good."

"Farrel..." She tipped her head back, and he silenced the imminent protest with a kiss. She lifted her hand to cradle his cheek as she pulled back. "Ye needs to rest. I'm not wanting ye to fall ill."

"So, what do you want?" He moved his hand over her backside, brushing the seam of the breeches between her legs. A tiny patch of dampness seeped into the material. "Mmm. I think I know."

"Nay, not while we're aboard ship." She tried to pull her leg away, but he caught her thigh and held it.

"Who's going to know? Most of the men are ashore—"

"I will know." Though she made no further effort to pull away, her body stiffened. "If ye've any respect for me, as ye claim my men do, ye'll not press the issue."

Frustrated, Farrel released her leg. She drew it away. "What do you really want, then?"

She met his challenge with a moment of silence, her face becoming distinct as the sky lightened with the first coral fringes of dawn. He read the emotions warring in her eyes—reluctance, desire...capitulation.

"I do want ye to make love to me," she whispered. "But not here. Not now."

"Guess we should've kept the room." He rolled onto his back, wincing as the lanced wound chafed against the bedding.

"Nay. Ye needed your back tended." She moved her hand along his arm, letting her fingers twine with his. "'Tis well ye did. Untended festering can bring a man low."

"So can untended needs." He pulled her down to kiss her mouth, making the caress brief and undemanding. "Okay. I'll let you off this time. But I'm considering this unfinished business."

She stared at him without answering, then sat up on the edge of the bunk.

"I must get to my quarters. Liam will wake soon." She picked up her shoes and headed for the door on stocking feet. She paused with it partly opened to peer outside.

"Sweet dreams, angel," Farrel murmured. She glanced over her shoulder, her expression revealing nothing of her thoughts.

When the door clicked shut, Farrel closed his eyes.

Sometimes it felt as if he dealt with two diametrically opposed natures in Ravyn, one so repressive it neared frigidity, the other so warm and tender it could break his heart. Captain and woman, he supposed. Somehow, those two natures must merge to make her whole. Not just for the sake of their mutual gratification, but for the sake of her sanity—and his.

Chapter 49

$\mathcal{F}$arrel woke, restless and edgy after Ravyn's predawn visit.

She was gone ashore when he went to breakfast, so he spent the morning and part of the afternoon with Liam over lessons.

As the time for supper approached, Ravyn had still not returned. He wondered if she was avoiding him. Her mercurial mood shifts confused him, yet he understood. Keeping up appearances with her crew outweighed their passion.

She admitted wanting him, but refused to let herself go in the place she should feel most comfortable. Or maybe that was the point. At the inn, no one had known them. No appearances to keep up, no reason to hold back.

Hearing voices through his open door, Farrel padded barefoot out to the deck. Ravyn and the men had returned. Mr. Hennessey carried parcels to Ravyn's cabin, greeting Farrel with a nod along the way.

On the pier, several men struggled to lift an item from a box cart. Surprised, Farrel realized it was a hip bath. When Ravyn joined him, he glanced at her, brows arching and a grin tugging at his lips.

"You've been shopping. Decided you liked to bathe, did you?"

"Aye, well." A rosy blush tinted her cheeks. "It has its advantages."

Farrel laughed, and her color deepened. Pivoting, she directed the men to take the tub to the hold then caught Liam before he could dash after them.

"Liam is outgrowing his breeches and shirts. I found a haberdashery that caters to young lads." She smiled at the boy. "Come, try on some of these."

Farrel followed them to her cabin. Ravyn lifted out knee breeches and linen shirts. Liam happily shed his worn breeches for the new ones. Ravyn opened another box, removing a child-sized tailcoat and vest.

"For fancy dress," she said. "I'll take ye into town for new shoes and boots on the morrow."

Liam put on the vest and coat, appearing comical in his bare feet with the formal wear.

"How does I look?" He directed the question to Farrel, who chuckled.

"Come and see for yourself." He led them to his cabin, pulling the blanket from the cheval glass and positioning Liam in front of it. "Quite the handsome gentleman." Farrel stood behind Liam and laid his hands on the boy's shoulders.

"I likes it." Liam looked up at Farrel in the glass, then at Ravyn. "Thank ye, Cap'n."

Farrel stared at their reflection, struck by a sense of familiarity. He recalled a photograph, taken with his father when he wasn't much older than Liam. They had stood in almost that same pose, and for the first time Farrel realized how closely his own features resembled his father's. Liam bore many of the same—gray eyes, square jawline, the straight, patriarchal nose. Even the color of his hair reminded Farrel of his own, lighter until his teens, when it had deepened to the darker, gold-tinged ash-blond.

"Go and change. 'Tis nearly time for dinner."

Ravyn's order to Liam interrupted Farrel's contemplation. Liam ran off, and Ravyn turned to follow.

"Ravyn, wait."

She pivoted back. "Aye?"

"I've been giving some thought to our...unfinished business. May I discuss it with you before we go to dinner?" He swept his arm as an indication for her to enter his cabin. When she did, he pushed the door to, leaving it ajar.

"So, what has ye determined?"

"We need somewhere on board we can consider private."

"Ye knows how I feel—"

"I do, but it won't always be possible to go to an inn. We need another solution. Here's what I'm proposing. We make my cabin neutral territory. No ranks. Just you and me, a woman and a man, free to conduct ourselves as we please. Out there,"—he nodded toward the door—"we resume our professional positions. In here, we assume...other positions." One corner of his mouth quirked up.

Ravyn frowned. "But we cannot do as we please, whenever we please. The men will know—"

"Yeah, the men will know—they're inveterate gossips—but we'll be discreet. We'll set some ground rules. We won't do anything you don't consent to. But whatever happens, happens." Farrel shrugged. "Or doesn't."

He waited for a response, but none came. Her neutral expression gave no indication of her feelings.

"I'll think on it," she said at last. Exiting, she left him no choice but to follow.

Ravyn toyed with her food as she considered Farrel's proposition. On one hand, it made great sense and created a tempting compromise, yet on the other, it still contravened her standing on ship conduct.

Mr. Hennessey, Mr. Fisher and Mr. Lancaster had joined them for the meal. She heard little of their conversation. Every time she cast oblique looks in Farrel's direction, his proposed scheme brought warmth flooding into her face. Once, he met her glance, and his lips curled into a slow grin. Her face burned as memories of their night together assailed her.

She left without finishing, her stomach churning in uncertainty, to hunt down Sammy with Liam and settle the boy for the night. All the while, she mulled over what to do.

She wanted Farrel to make love to her. She yearned for his touch, his tender words, the sweet exhilaration of falling apart in his arms. What would it cost her, though? All at once, it wasn't only the respect of her crew, but her rigid self-control.

Then she recalled her conversation with Mr. Hennessey on the night he saw the sketch Farrel had done. Mayhap she put too much weight on what the crew would think were she to indulge herself with Farrel. Her lieutenant felt she had the right to a loving relationship.

Still undecided, she wanted to discuss it with Farrel, ascertain he understood her concerns. She tucked Liam in and bid him good-night.

Farrel's door stood open, and he sat at his desk, writing. Dusk had fallen, and his lamp bathed him in flickering illumination.

"Farrel?"

Looking up, he set the quill in the inkwell. "Come in."

Ravyn pulled the extra chair closer and sat down. "How does your back feel?"

"Still sore." He turned to face her. "Liam seemed happy with the new clothes."

"Aye." She smiled, tenderness for the child light in her chest. "I always want him looking his best."

"Did you get anything for yourself?" He grinned. "Besides the tub.

Maybe something pretty?"

She shrugged, glancing away. "I've naught to be vain about."

"Oh, I beg to differ, sweetheart." Farrel rose and took her hand to draw her over to the mirror. He closed the door and pushed the bolt into place.

Ravyn's eyes narrowed. "What are ye about?"

He gave her a long, serious study before answering. "Look at yourself."

She did, but saw nothing remarkable, only her usual garb. Shrugging, she shook her head.

He retreated to fetch the lantern and hung it on a hook above the mirror. Before, with the light behind them, they had been indistinct silhouettes. In the direct illumination, her sharp features became more apparent.

Farrel stood behind her. He lifted a hand to run his fingertips along her cheek. She shivered at the soft touch that left a trail of warmth in its wake. Then he skimmed over her mouth. Bending, he brushed a kiss to her cheek. "The set of your jaw and that fierce glimmer in your eyes...that's your command but also your beauty."

His hands drifted around to the front of her vest, and he undid the top button. Ravyn's breath hitched. He lowered to the next button.

She pressed her hand over his. "If ye're meanin' to seduce me, 'tis not the time for it."

"I'd like nothing more than to make love to you, but that's not what this is about." He indicated the mirror with a gesture. "This is about you seeing yourself."

Ravyn tried to read the look in his eyes. She could discern nothing from his inscrutable expression.

"Very well." Her chin went up and she squared her shoulders. She could manage this. "I agree to your earlier suggestion. But we'll do only what I permit."

"Of course." His breath brushed her ear.

Ravyn shivered, already anticipating his touch.

Reaching around and undoing the buttons, he drew the vest down her arms. He dropped it to the floor then turned his attention to the laced fastening of her shirt.

"Farrel..." She lifted her hands, intending to stop him. Regardless of the desire luring her into its thrall, and no matter their new agreement, she would not yield so easily.

"See yourself without the trappings of captain." He kissed her ear, and a spear of liquid fire shot through her. She tried without success to steel herself against it.

"I needn't be disrobed to do that." Her hands trembled over his, and she struggled to keep her breathing slow and steady.

"Call it an uninhibited inspection, then." Though Farrel didn't move, his breath against her cheek teased her senses. Gently, he took her hands. She let him lower them to her sides. Slipping the lacing from its loops in the shirt's placket, he drew the edges apart enough to reveal the curving of her breasts and the shadowed hollow between.

"You are so beautiful." He kissed the soft skin connecting neck to shoulder, and she shivered as heat spiraled to her breasts, her belly, and lower to pool, hot and throbbing, between her thighs. Prickles danced over her skin, making it itch. Her clothes suddenly felt confining.

Farrel cupped her breasts over the linen. She had discarded the canvas wrapping before settling Liam. Now, seen like this, her breasts filled Farrel's hands, seeming to belong there. She gasped as his thumbs passed over her nipples, already pearled and craving his touch. He slipped his fingers into the shirt's placket and pulled it aside, baring her to her waist. Her momentary discomfiture dissolved as Farrel again cupped her and stroked the sensitive peaks. She arched forward, pushing into his hands, hungering for his caress as much as for her next gulp of air.

God's breath, the man stole every shred of modesty she possessed!

"A goddess," he whispered against her neck. He withdrew, leaving Ravyn disappointed and curious. What could be his intent now?

He lifted the end of her braid, untied the ribbon, and unraveled her hair, drawing his fingers through the tresses and spreading them over her shoulders and down her front. It felt silky and warm against her skin.

"Farrel..." She started to turn, but he put his hands to her shoulders, holding her in place.

"Do you like what you see so far?"

Ravyn licked her dry lips. Had she looked like this the night she came to him? Features softened by the loose fall of her hair, breasts barely hidden by the ebony tresses? Her nipples, dusky and erect, peeked from among the dark strands, as though seeking more attention. Ravyn released a breath she didn't realize she'd been holding.

Farrel brushed her hair back over her shoulder, leaving one breast bared.

"I...I think ye've made your point."

He laughed softly. "Not quite. There's still more to see."

Tugging the hem of the shirt free, he pulled it over her head. The soft fall of hair as it slid from the opening and resettled created the illusion of stroking fingers. The throb between her thighs ratcheted up to a searing ache.

"Mmm. Perfect." Farrel ran his hands over her back, along her belly and to the waist of the breeches. Ravyn couldn't stop shivering at the heady sensation and sight of his gliding hands

"Farrel... I doesn't want... We oughtn't to..." Speaking became more difficult with every pass of hands, each phrase torn between protest and longing. Her body belied any objections as Farrel once more caressed her belly. It quivered, and she gasped. Her skin felt too sensitive, tingly, and unbearably warm.

"This isn't about sex." He undid the buttons of the fall on her breeches and parted the front placket. A grin twisted his mouth. "You wore drawers today."

She opened her eyes, trembling. "Aye. I does when I go to town." The natural huskiness of her voice deepened.

Farrel crouched and lifted her foot to remove first one shoe, then the other. Put off-balance, she reached back to lean on his shoulder. He unfastened the knee straps of the breeches, sliding his hand under to release the garter and slip the stocking down. Ravyn watched in the mirror, shivering at the feel and the sight of his hands gliding along her calf. He pulled the stocking off and repeated the process with the other, then drew her breeches down. She expected him to go after the drawers too, but he straightened to gaze at her reflection. A hint of mischief brightened his eyes and curled his mouth. She stepped out of the breeks, and Farrel shoved them aside with his foot.

"Almost there." When he lowered his fingers to the tie of the drawers, Ravyn turned to face him. Despite the irresistible craving Farrel's words and touch ignited, she would not relinquish control.

"It hardly seems just that I'm the only one to be disrobed." Summoning a smile, she put her hands to the placket of his shirt, already unfastened. "If we are to consider ourselves equals here, should you not shed your clothing as well?"

Farrel stared at her for a heartbeat then his lips curved. "If you think it will help."

She guided the shirt over his head and arms and dropped it to the floor, eyes riveted to his chest, visible above the binding. Sighing, she laid a hand over his heart then furrowed trembling fingers through the crisp hair crossing the taut muscles. Lifting her gaze, she caught a shimmer in his eyes he hid by lowering his lids.

Struggling against the urge to throw caution and authority to the wind, she ran her hands along his upper arms and shoulders, relishing the firm, sculpted musculature under her palms, and his warm skin. Though the distraction aided in tamping down the rampant desire licking through her, it lurked beneath the surface, a soft beat of need.

Slipping her fingers into his bandage, she freed the end and unwound it by walking around Farrel. He stood still, only turning his head to watch. She dropped the wrapping on the floor and stopped before him. Putting a finger to his chest, she circled one dark nipple. It hardened instantly, and he drew a slow, hissing breath. She followed the line of golden hair down to where it disappeared into his breeches.

Pausing, she looked at his face. His eyes had darkened, and moisture glistened on his upper lip.

"Ravyn..." Her name came out raspy, and his hands clenched at his sides. "I thought you didn't want—"

"I does." She stepped closer, sliding her arms around his waist and pressing to him. The ridge of his arousal rested hard against her belly. These feelings he awakened...they were too strong to fight. Her mind might still seek control, but her body hungered to yield.

Her fingers glided back to the buttons on the fall of his breeches. Instead of undoing them, she ran her finger down the throbbing length of him over the cloth. His responsive gasp and the twitch of his cock sent fresh tendrils of heat flickering through her.

"I want ye," she whispered, letting her hand rest lightly on the steady pulse of his manhood.

His head lowered and his mouth claimed hers. The kiss, long and inflaming, turned the heat engulfing her into a blaze that could not be denied.

She drew back, her fingers hooking into the top button.

Then, like the stab of a knife, the memory of Will Flemington's brutalizing cockstand flashed through her mind, shattering that moment of abandon. Not one of her spells, only a spark of recall, enough to set her hands trembling.

She couldn't do this—could not look upon Farrel's full arousal. She feared it would drive her back into that dark, terrifying place.

But it did not dull the desperate craving for Farrel that must be satisfied. She tried to undo the button, but her fingers quivered too badly.

"Ravyn? Are you all right?" Concern edged Farrel's husky voice.

Heart pounding in frustration and apprehension, she looked up at him.

Chapter 50

$\mathcal{F}$arrel saw a glimmer of...something cross her features that she tried to hide by glancing away. He lifted her hands from his breeches. They trembled in his grasp.

"Ravyn? What's wrong?" He released a hand to cradle her cheek and gently pulled her around to face him.

"Naught." Her wide eyes were dilated, but no longer distressed. They burned the fiery blue of a gas flame with longing. "I want ye to make love to me." She turned her head to kiss his palm, lips soft and inciting against his skin.

"You're sure?" His own desire teetered on a raw edge, thundering through his blood. But he refused to push her into anything.

"Aye." Her gaze flicked to the lantern above them. "May we douse the lamp?"

That caught his attention. "Why?" He studied her face.

Instead of answering, she glanced at the front of his breeches, where his erection made itself blatantly apparent. Her breath hitched.

Farrel's thoughts tumbled over one another as he fought to discern her reasoning.

They had made love two nights before. He had been inside her, so she knew what it felt like. So, what disturbed her now?

The light. That was it. She hadn't seen his erection.

"Is it this?" He indicated it with a sparing gesture. "It's nothing to be afraid of."

"I am not afraid." Her vehemence startled him. It also answered his question.

"Okay." He lifted his hands in placation. "But can you be honest with me? Tell me what the problem is?"

Ravyn gnawed on her lower lip, her gaze darting about as though she sought some means of escape. She sighed, releasing her bite. The indentations of her teeth showed on the soft pink skin. "Douse the light. When we're in the dark, I don't see...him."

"This could be the last sliver that has to be pulled so you can heal." Farrel put his hands to the fall of his breeches, ready to bare himself. She took a quick step back, a flash of panic racing across her face. He let his hands drop. The direct approach was obviously the wrong one.

"Surely we can still do this, in the darkness." Her fear faded to open yearning.

"Not until you can look at me without cringing." Farrel slipped his fingers under her chin and tipped her face up. "I want to make love to you in the light, watch your eyes mist with passion, your skin glow as if lit from within." He bent and touched his lips to hers. Though she accepted the kiss, her mouth quivered. "I want to see your expression when you climax in my arms."

"I want that too," she whispered, "but I cannot look...not yet..."

"Then we have to figure out how to get past this."

She looked so lovely and vulnerable in her state of undress, yet the tight set of her shoulders spoke of the strength she struggled to maintain. "I want the pleasure you gave me at the inn."

Beneath her affirmative tone, Farrel sensed a plea. Much as he wanted to accommodate her, to lift the lantern down and kill the flame, he felt certain that wasn't the answer. After all, she hadn't yet looked at herself completely nude. How could he expect her to look at him?

"How about we focus on you for now."

Ravyn let Farrel turn her to the mirror. Her face gazed back, cheekbones stark with the rigid set of her jaw and eyes shimmering, light as a summer sky. The momentary distraction had blunted the sharp edge of her desire, yet it continued a soft, alluring singing through her blood. Farrel had promised her pleasure. She wanted it with a hunger that disconcerted her. She should not let those feelings control her, but it was like falling into a whirlpool that sucked her deeper into its vortex, helpless to escape...

Not wanting to escape.

Farrel's hands lowered to the ties of the drawers, pulling them loose with agonizing slowness. Sliding his fingers into the waist, he drew them open. They slipped in a whispering pool around her feet. Ravyn stepped out of them, eyes riveted to her reflection, her breathing shallow and uneven at the sight of her nudity.

Besides her face, neck and forearms, only a deep V on her chest and her legs below the knees were bronzed by exposure to the sun. Everywhere else, the lantern light washed her in pale, gold-tinged cream. A slow blush rose to her cheeks, and she made a futile attempt to cover herself, folding one arm across her chest and lowering the other hand to the dark triangle of curls.

"Oh, no you don't." Farrel caught her hands and spread her arms wide. "That's perfection. No need to hide it from me. Or yourself."

She shook her head. "I-I doesn't see what ye find so wondrous." Her tanned, sun-weathered complexion defied the dictates of womanly beauty, as did her robust build. She lacked the voluptuous curves so admired by men. That in itself did not disturb her, but Farrel must recognize her faults as clearly as she.

"I find you magnificent." He glided his hands over her waist and hips. She shivered at the warm sweep of his palms and fingers on her skin. "You've been raised to think being a woman is weakness, but that is so wrong." His hands skimmed over her belly and up to cradle her breasts. "This is power. Enough to influence kings and tempt saints, to seduce the angels sent from Heaven to guard humanity, to incite wars and bloody feuds. A woman has the potential to sustain the future in her body and bring it into the world as a man cannot." He brushed his lips over her ear. "There's more power in what you hide under your captain's rigs that can bring a man to his knees than wielding a blade or firing a pistol."

Stunned by his poetic words, she could not think of a response.

He moved his hands down to the black curls shielding her femininity. She watched in fascination as his fingers dipped into them, finding her throbbing center and gently stroking. Surrendering as fire lanced through her, she leaned her head on his shoulder and closed her eyes, her breathing ragged.

"I'll give you what you ask," Farrel whispered into her ear as he kept up his caresses, "but I want you to do something for me. And maybe for yourself."

"Aye? What?" He met her panting questions with a low chuckle that tickled over her skin.

"This may sound kinky, but I want you to watch in the mirror."

"Kinky?" Ravyn opened her eyes and turned her gaze to him, puzzled.

"I'll explain later. For now, I'd like you to see what I see when we make love."

Moving to stand in front of her, he went to one knee. He put his hands to her hips and drew her forward, then lifted one of her legs to settle it over his shoulder.

"Remember how I pleasured you before I entered you?"

"Aye." That memory sent fresh heat spiraling through her.

His eyes sparkled and he grinned. "Watch yourself while I do it again."

That discomfited her, seeming too personal, somehow...unnatural.

She tried to pull her leg away, but he caught and held it in place. He stroked her outer thigh with his fingertips. "Let me do this." He turned his head and pressed a hot, lingering kiss to her inner thigh. Ravyn couldn't stop the tremor that ran through her.

He moved forward, slipping his free hand to cup her buttock and draw her to his mouth. The instant he touched that sensitive place nestled amongst the curls, she quivered, her head arching back as fire blazed through her.

"Remember to watch." The warmth of Farrel's breath against her most private flesh set her shaking. She turned her head, gasping at the image of herself so sweetly pleasured by Farrel. He moved his hand from her thigh, reaching around and sweeping his fingers across the weeping opening of her core. A sob escaped her trembling lips as he encouraged the responsive throb of her passion. Heated blood pounded a steady rhythm in her ears. She lurched against his mouth as he slid his fingers inside, stroking, caressing, finding the place that ached for him. Watching made her feel strangely outside herself, as though the couple locked in the erotic act in the mirror had no connection to their physical selves. Yet the sensations were real enough, magnified so her whole body felt vibrant.

The tight coiling in her belly spread, becoming close to painful as her body sought the pinnacle toward which Farrel pushed her. The leg she stood on began to tremble, the shocks of impending release arcing like wildfire through her limbs and curling her toes. She clutched with shaking fingers at Farrel's hair. She didn't want to cry out for fear of being heard outside the cabin, but as the tension built to a driving force, it didn't matter anymore. A soft groan escaped as her whole being seemed to expand and contract, falling in on itself then exploding in throbbing shards of fire. Her reflected face gazed back, pupils so dilated her eyes seemed black, glazing over as the spasms took her. Even so, Farrel did not let up, his ongoing stimulus at last bringing his name to her lips as the convulsions became too much to bear.

"Farrel! Oh, please! No more!"

Her quivering leg began to collapse under her. Farrel lifted his head and caught her, letting her slip to her knees. She stared into his eyes, her fingers still tangled in his hair, tugging it from the leather strip so that wisps hung loose around his face.

"You okay?" His brow furrowed to match the concern in his voice.

Unable to speak, she nodded.

He laughed softly, leaning forward and kissing her mouth. She tasted the musky flavor of her own juices on his tongue and returned the kiss with dreamy passion.

"Did you see how gorgeous you look in the mists of rapture?" he murmured as their lips parted.

She tried to speak, but nothing came from her throat. Sighing, she lowered her head onto his shoulder, shivering in ever-diminishing throes.

"Overwhelmed you, did I?" Again, she nodded, and he laughed. "Good to know."

Rising, he gathered her into his arms and carried her to the bunk. He set her down and pulled the light cover over her before lying down and taking her into his arms.

Ravyn felt as though her bones had melted, a fuzzy-edged languor enclosing her. Farrel drew her head onto his shoulder.

"Farrel…" She moved enough to look up at his face. The dim illumination cast his profiled features in planes of light and shadow. "What of…ye? Could we not…finish, as afore?"

"Not tonight." He kissed her forehead.

Ravyn glanced down, noting the undiminished bulge tenting the fly of his breeches. "But ye're still…hard."

Farrel chuckled. "Sure am. But I don't want you worrying about that."

She returned her gaze to his face. "Ye knows I'm willing."

"I think we've done enough for tonight." His tone, soft and infinitely gentle, touched her heart. He tapped her lips when she parted them to respond. "I can wait a little longer. Another day or so isn't going to kill me. Maybe hurt a bit," he added with another rueful chuckle, "but I'll live. I want you to be completely comfortable with me. All of me."

Ravyn settled her head on his chest, listening to the regular, strong thud of his heart. "What does the word kinky mean?"

His laugh rumbled through his chest. "In this context, I think the closest is…unconventional. Some might say perverted in the sexual sense. What we did was different. Interesting. And enlightening, I hope."

"Oh, aye." Warmth flooded into her cheeks. "I looked so…lost and vulnerable. And yet…" She searched for the right words. "Anchored fast, though it seemed my soul sought to flee my body in that moment of... release."

"*La petite mort.*" Farrel stroked a hand along her hair. "The little death. The ultimate gratification." He ran his hand along her arm. "Feeling relaxed?"

"Aye, and tired." She sighed, catching his hand and twining her fingers with his. "I'll soon have to leave." She gave an expressive yawn. "I want to sleep. Mayhap I should go now."

"Stay." Farrel tightened his arm around her. "Have a little nap. You'll feel more refreshed." He lifted their hands and kissed her knuckles.

Ravyn had neither the strength nor inclination to argue. She closed her eyes, letting her body go limp. It felt good to simply be held. To feel warm, safe, secure and loved...

Chapter 51

"Ye've reopened that wound," Dr. Page growled when he examined Farrel's back in the morning.

"Have I?" He supposed it had happened during the night. Or maybe Ravyn's heel had irritated it as he made love to her. He couldn't repress a smile.

The doctor stepped back, hands fisted on his hips. "Ye and the Cap'n was at it again, wasn't ye?"

Farrel chuckled. "You might say that."

The man sighed, shaking his head. "Ye're a lecherous devil, McQuaid. Careful, lest ye get our Cap'n in the family way."

"Shit. I never thought of that." Farrel's grin died. Then he shook his head. "What we did last night wouldn't get her pregnant. Only happy."

"Aye, well, I'm thinkin' Mr. Fisher might have a thing or two to say on that score." Dr. Page spread ointment over Farrel's back, concentrating on the lanced wound. "I'm not wantin' to be doin' this on a regular basis."

Farrel grimaced as the salve stung the tender welt. "You think he'd get used to the idea she's happy, fulfilled."

The doctor snorted. "Fill her too full, sir, and ye may be thinkin' different yerself."

Farrel tried to recall what contraceptive methods were available in this century. A wry smile twisted his lips. "Maybe I should have a serious talk with my lady." He winced as Dr. Page pressed a fresh strip onto the wound. He sat up to have his torso rewrapped.

"Aye, ye might be wise to spend more time talkin' than applyin' yer rod to 'er."

"Sir, I object to your phrasing." Despite his protest, Farrel grinned. The older man chuckled, clapping him on the shoulder.

"Aye, well, ye has the right of it when ye say she's happier. She smiled at me this morn, somethin' she's not done in a while."

"Good. It's working, then."

The doctor shook his head. "Ye're a cheeky bugger, McQuaid. But I think I likes that about ye." He paused at the door to look back. "If ye make her happy, that's all to the good, I say. And I'll tell Mr. Fisher so if he says otherwise."

"Thanks." Farrel rose and pulled on a shirt. Most of the welts were healed enough to allow easy movement, but the one in the middle of his back stung when he stretched. Remembering the enraptured expression on Ravyn's face made the pain bearable.

"Mr. McQuaid."

Farrel spun around. He hadn't heard the door open.

Fisher's menacing growl set his pulse skipping. The bo'sun wore his usual belligerent expression, heavy brows lowered over glittering eyes.

Farrel didn't bother trying to be pleasant. "What do you want?"

"Ye's been swiving the Cap'n again." Fisher stepped further into the cabin.

Farrel stood his ground. "How can you know that? You were in town last night."

"Aye, well, the lads left on watch said she spent a long while closeted with ye." He sneered. "Does I need to bind and gag ye in the brig after the evenin' meal to spare the lass yer lecherin' trickeries? Ye ought to be 'ung from the yard by yer bollocks."

"As if Ravyn would allow that. Why can't you let her be happy?"

"She is 'appy. Or was, afore ye come aboard. She'll rue the day she took ye from that shore."

"Or maybe she'll be thankful. I know I am."

Fisher snorted. "Aye, I'll wager ye are, ye lustin' bastard. Keelhaulin'd be too good fer ye."

"The captain and I have the right to our own business."

Fisher's thick lips parted in a yellow-toothed grin. "More fool ye, McQuaid." He turned away then looked back over his broad shoulder. "I'll be keepin' rope 'n rag at the ready." He stomped out, slamming the door.

Tucking his shirt into his breeches, Farrel paused.

Rope and rag, was it? Bind and gag him? He'd only surrender that privilege to one person, and it wasn't the angry bo'sun.

Striding to the sea chest, he dug inside until he found the items he sought. "Thanks for the inspiration, Fisher, old boy."

"Are you still going into town?" he asked Ravyn over breakfast.

"Aye. I needs to get Liam's foot gear, and it may have to be made."

"Excellent. I'm coming with you."

"Are ye certain? 'Tis but a day more than a sennight since..." Her mouth thinned as she flicked a glance toward Fisher.

"I'm tired of being confined to quarters. I want to explore. We didn't get much chance over the weekend." Farrel aimed a deliberate wink at her.

Fisher gave a low growl, glaring over his mug of coffee.

"If ye thinks ye're equal to it." She appeared unconvinced.

"More than equal, swee—ah, Captain."

Across the table, Mr. Hennessey snorted.

The day was sunny and warm. He and Ravyn walked with Liam between them, the boy exclaiming over everything they saw. Farrel shared his enthusiasm as they made their way from the harbor to the commercial district. They soon found a bootmaker's shop and ordered boots for pick-up after the court judgment. They visited more shops, Farrel engrossed by commonplace items that in his time would be priceless antiques.

At the Citadel, soldiers lined up for inspection by a stern-faced colonel who strolled along the rows of his regiment. Many appeared young, standing ramrod straight with rifles at their sides.

Living history, Farrel thought, giddy with repressed excitement.

They wandered among the vendors on Market Square, buying fresh bread and cheese for lunch, along with fruit from the tropics—oranges, mangoes, and lemons. The air was redolent with meat cooking over open fires, spices and other aromas. They found a grassy knoll and sat in the shade of an oak tree to eat.

"This is wonderful." Farrel leaned back on his hands gazing at the busy harbor below, while Ravyn placed the remains of their meal in a rucksack. "I could get used to living here."

"Could ye?" Ravyn paused, and Farrel caught a pensive expression on her lovely face. Then she smiled, shaking off her seriousness. "Aye, Halifax is grand, but surely not compared to...your home."

"I could be happy here, given the right circumstances." Farrel held her gaze. "I've pretty well resigned myself to it."

"Has ye?" She ran a hand along the bandanna covering her rolled-up braid. "Nay regrets?"

"None I care to dwell on." On impulse, he clasped her hand. "I feel like I belong."

"Aye, well." She gently withdrew and pushed to her feet. "We'd best be movin' on. The foodstuffs won't keep in this heat."

Farrel enjoyed their meandering return to the harbor along residential avenues, admiring the colonial architecture. Nearing the wharf, the structures became rougher, with no colorful gardens or manicured lawns. The populace changed from strolling residents to sailors. Soldiers moved among them in their bright regimental coats. The taverns teemed with customers, loud conversation and raucous laughter floating out of open windows and doors.

Farrel wanted to visit the Great Pontac House. It served as a community center, housing everything from a grand hotel to a ballroom and theater, even providing stabling for horses and carts in its center open court. Farrel had stayed at the twenty-first century hotel and longed to visit the location in its historic heyday. However, by the time they reached the *Retribution*, Ravyn protested it was too late in the day.

"We could stay at the hotel," Farrel suggested with a rakish grin. "Maybe there'll be a play going on."

"Ye can't see everything in one day. Ye've tired me with all the walking, and ye should be resting yourself."

"I'm too keyed-up to rest. We've just got tomorrow then the court, and you'll want to get underway."

She gave an indulgent smile. "Mayhap on the morrow we can visit the Pontac. I'm ready to put my feet up, and we're at the opposite end of the harbor."

"We could hire a carriage."

Ravyn dashed his hope with a shake of her head, still smiling. "Ye're like a child with all this excitement." She leaned forward and patted his hand. "If ye're a good lad and go to bed as ye ought, we'll see about going to the Pontac in the morn."

He grinned. "Okay. I give. But as for that part about going to bed..." He widened his grin to a leer. "You might have to tie me down to keep me there. You up to the challenge?"

"Lord, would that I had half your spunk today." She flung her hands up, laughing. Farrel loved the way her face lit and her twinkling eyes crinkled in the corners. "I thought ye'd be worn out after..." A blush crept into her cheeks.

"Mmm. Not quite, sweetheart. Remember, I didn't get my share of the action."

Ravyn rose from her seat on a coil of rope, rolling her eyes in exaggerated vexation. "Are ye tryin' to kill me?"

"Only with kindness." He caught her hand as she started to walk away. "Admit it. You loved it." She pulled free, her blush deepening. "Are the boys going out tonight?"

She snorted, covering her mouth with her hand to stifle an outright laugh. "Ye doesn't give up, does ye?"

"Giving up is definitely not my strong suit." He took her other hand and tucked it in the crook of his arm as he leaned closer to her ear. "Especially when persistence can turn out to be so damn much fun. Besides, I have a surprise for you."

"Another? Does ye not think I had enough last eve?"

"One can never have enough surprises. At least the pleasant ones. And I guarantee this one will be pleasant."

One corner of her mouth twitched into a grin. "It had best be worth my attention."

"Oh, it will, sweetheart." He patted her hand with a broad smile. "Shall we go in to dinner? You may need the nourishment for this."

Ravyn had no inkling what Farrel intended. However, he had snared her curiosity with his oblique promise.

Every time he looked her way over the meal, his eyes sparkled a light, dancing gray, and his provocative smiles sent prickles up her spine. Most of the men remained ashore, only enough on deck to keep watch.

She settled Liam with Sammy curled in his arms. Opening her cabin door, she almost collided with Mr. Fisher. "I thought ye was going to town."

"Aye, but I wanted to see ye wasn't goin' to let that blighter McQuaid use his lecherin' guile on ye."

Ravyn stepped out and pulled the door shut. "Why would that be your concern?"

"It isn't."

They both looked at Farrel standing outside his open door, arms folded across his chest.

Mr. Fisher returned his gaze to her. "Come to town with me. 'Twould be safer fer ye."

"Sounds like fun." Farrel sidestepped Mr. Fisher to her. "However, the Captain and I have plans." He smiled, but tense lines bracketed his mouth.

She tucked her hand into the arm he offered. "Go on with ye, Eli. I'll be alright."

Steely glare shifting between her and Farrel, Mr. Fisher bared his teeth in a grimace. "Aye, well, I think ye be makin' a grave error, Cap'n, if ye'll pardon me sayin' so."

"'Tis my error to make."

"Don't let us keep you." Farrel nodded at the glowering bo'sun. "Have fun. I know we will." He winked at Ravyn.

Mr. Fisher's chest puffed out as though drawing breath to bellow then deflated just as quickly. "Aye, aye...Cap'n." One corner of his mouth curled into a sneer as he turned away and stomped off. Ravyn stared after him, frowning.

"Don't worry about him." Farrel tugged her toward his cabin. "I won't."

"Ye might be regrettin' that. He's not one to let an offense go unpunished. But ye be well aware of that."

Inside the cabin, he released her hand and shut the door. "I refuse to let him spoil our evening."

"Aye, and as to that..."

"I think I've come up with a way to get you past that last inhibition." His lips twitched into a wry grin. "We can thank Mr. Fisher for the idea." He turned the chair and gestured to it. "Come and sit."

She complied, watching him curiously. "So, what is this...idea?"

"I think what you need is to discover for yourself the...intricacies of the male anatomy. What you see in your nightmares has likely become exaggerated beyond reality." He held up a hand when her lips parted. "Men are essentially made the same, though some are more...generously endowed. Maybe you need control over when and how you see me aroused. Then maybe you can look upon my fearsome member without reservations. Or not so fearsome, depending on your perspective."

"So, what is it ye're proposing?"

He reached past her to the desk. When he straightened, he held a long red silk sash and a gray bandanna cloth in his hands. His smirk hinted at mischief. "You're going to tie me up and blindfold me."

She flicked a glance to the material then back to his grinning face. "What manner of game are ye playing?"

"You want to make it a game?" His brows lifted, then he assumed a musing expression. "I've never done the role-playing thing before, but it could be...interesting. How about...you make me your prisoner? I've been your captive in one way or another since that first day." He held the sash and kerchief out to her.

"But...to what end?" She stared down at the cloth pieces, torn between wariness and curiosity.

"To give you complete control. If I can't touch or see you, then whatever you choose to explore is entirely at your discretion. I can help verbally, if you need it."

"Or mayhap I should gag ye as well." An impish note entered her voice. "Ye does have a habit of talking overmuch at times."

Farrel laughed. "You've been taking lessons at the Fisher School of Seafaring Torture, I take it." He cocked his head. "It's up to you."

"I will allow your lips freedom for now, though I've no inkling what ye expect me to do." She glanced down, warmth rising into her cheeks.

His fingers slipped under her chin to tilt her face up. "You'll figure it out."

Ravyn stared at him, her stomach quivering as though a flock of hummingbirds had taken up residence.

Could she truly do this?

Chapter 52

*R*avyn rose and took the sash and kerchief from Farrel. "How does ye wish to go about this?"

Farrel assumed the seat and laid his arms along the armrests of the chair. "Tie my wrists with the ends of the sash. But first..." He leaned forward and pulled off his shirt, dropping it to the floor, then he started unwrapping the bandage around his torso.

Ravyn put a hand out to stop him. "Your back. Ye ought to leave it covered."

"It'll be fine. Bring a pillow and put it behind me."

She snatched up the one from the bunk, settling it behind him with the linen bandage over it.

"Tie my wrists."

Ravyn gripped her lower lip between her teeth as she fastened first one wrist then the other to the arms of the chair with the ends of the sash, draping the rest behind.

"Now, the blindfold."

She folded the cloth and fastened it around his eyes.

"I am now subject to your will. You may plunder and pillage to your heart's delight. But I draw the line at whips and sharp implements."

Ravyn stared at him, not certain what he expected of her. She knew the destination of this 'exploration' but felt in no hurry to reach it.

"Ravyn? You want to get past this, don't you?"

"Aye, but..."

"Then it's up to you to take the initiative." His tone vibrated with gentle encouragement.

Stepping forward, Ravyn ran light fingertips along his jaw, the rasp of his late-day beard stubble rough under her fingers. Then she caressed his lips, and they curved into a smile. He did not speak or kiss her fingers.

She drew them down his chin and throat, delving into the crinkly hair crossing his chest. Circling one brown nipple in its gold-hued nest, she heard a catch in his breathing, and watched the nub harden as she stroked it again. Her body responded in kind, nipples tightening and tingling beneath her lawn shirt. Emboldened, she bent and passed her tongue around and over it, again aware of a catch in his breathing.

Dropping to her knees, she continued to where the line of hair disappeared into his breeches. She halted, pondering whether to brave the reveal. She flattened her hand over his navel, his skin warm under her palm and the light furring tickling her fingers. Lowering her gaze to the fall of his breeches, she noted the bulge there.

Nay. She was not ready for that yet.

She looked down at his bare feet, for the first time noticing how long and narrow they were, actually, quite elegant. She sat back on her heels and skimmed her fingers over his toes, smiling as they twitched, then ran her finger along his instep and down to follow the high arch.

A stifled snort brought her eyes to his face. He jerked his foot away.

"Ticklish, are ye?" She returned a speculative gaze to his foot.

"It wasn't my foot I thought you'd go after."

"Aye, well, ye said I should explore. One must begin at the farthest boundaries of new territory before plunging into the heart of the forest." She caught his little toe and wiggled it.

Farrel chuckled. "Afraid of encountering a wild animal?"

She went still, the unwelcome vision of her dream flashing across her mind.

"Ravyn?"

Giving her head a clearing shake, she swallowed the lump that clogged her throat. "Nay. Only a wee beastie needing to find its way home." She kept her tone light.

"Wee beastie, huh? You don't spare a man's ego any quarter, do you?"

"Only if he merits it." She folded her hand around his ankle. "Now, bestill yourself. I have more terrain to cover."

"Cover away, then." He moved his other foot to nudge her leg.

Ravyn grabbed that foot then ran her hand up his calf. Reaching the buckle at the knee of his breeches, she undid it and slid her hand under, to his upper thigh. His bare upper thigh. A tight gasp brought her attention to his face again.

"Ye aren't wearin' your drawers."

His mouth twitched into a grin. "Disappointed?"

"Nay, I..." Warmth rose into her face she was thankful he could not see. "Nay." That last came out a soft husk. "But...I thought ye didn't like going..." She tried to remember the word he'd used. "Commander?"

"Commando. Tonight's special. Thought I'd make it easier to get to the good stuff."

"Oh. Aye." She lowered her gaze to the 'good stuff' in question. Despite their mundane conversation, the bulge had increased in both size and activity, straining tight against the button fly. "The wee beastie seems anxious." Her lips quirked up. "Shall I mayhap set it free?"

"By all means." The rasp of his tone belied the casual words.

"All in good time." She pushed to her feet, and drawing a fortifying breath, seated herself across his lap. "I think the northern border bears further investigation."

Wrapping her arms around his neck, she leaned in and pressed her lips to his. He exhaled in a sharp breath redolent of mint that enticed her to open her mouth. Taking the initiative, she coaxed his lips apart and thrust her tongue in to stroke his, amazed at how wonderful he tasted. He returned the caress without demand. Yet the tension rippling through his body revealed escalating desire.

Drawing away, she laid her hand to his cheek. "Ye taste of mint."

"We purchased it for Cook, remember? I snitched a couple of leaves to chew on after supper. You like?" The gravelly note in his voice sent a tingle down her spine.

"Mm, aye." She kissed him again, quick and light, before bending and running her tongue along the heavy pulse in his throat. He groaned, low and soft, and his manhood prodded her thigh. She bent lower, finding the bud of his nipple, and closed her lips around it, drawing it to immediate attention. Farrel trembled, and the insistent nudging at her thigh increased.

She lifted her head to look at him. A tic along his clenched jaw betrayed the control he exerted. Ravyn smiled. So, she could bedevil him as he had her over these past weeks. She reveled in a sense of power. Farrel was truly at her mercy. Not only did she find it exhilarating, but arousing as well.

Slipping from his lap, she dropped back to her knees, pushing his legs apart to position herself between them.

She could do this. It was no longer a question of confronting fear, but yielding to the appeal of holding him in her hands, subject to her will and desires.

She glided her fingers along the ridge of his length over the broadcloth breeks, keenly aware of the throb that greeted her touch. Once more her body answered, a heated beat blossoming at her core. Slowly she hooked her finger under the top button and flicked it free. The second came undone as easily. Lifting her eyes again, she watched a taut smile curve his mouth. Returning to the task at hand, she undid the third and fourth closures.

One more button, but her fingers hesitated. Resting her hand against him once more, she felt a distinct jerk under her palm. She pulled back with a startled gasp.

Farrel chuckled. "You're making it do that. See how much power you have over me?"

She drew a sharp breath. Had he read her thoughts?

She lifted her other hand and with a determined tug, unfastened the last button. She parted the breeches, and his shaft sprang into her hand. She nearly jumped back, but made herself stay, letting it quiver under her fingers. A low laugh escaped her.

"So, this is the wee beastie." She clasped him, marveling that something so solid could feel like velvet.

"Aye, 'tis a terrible, ravening dragon," Farrel whispered, feigning an accent. Merriment underlay the excitement in his voice. "Beware, Captain, lest it devour you."

"Then mayhap I should devour it first." An image flashed through her mind that she couldn't quite deal with. When she glanced up, Farrel's mouth hung open.

"I can't believe you said that."

"Aye, well, there be many kinds of devouring. I think ye'll favor the one I have in mind." She exerted minimal pressure on the 'beastie,' the last of her trepidation dissipating in the sensation of pulsing heat. She trembled with a need so strong she wanted to divest them both of their garments and draw his throbbing member deep into her body.

But first...

She continued to stroke him, exulting in the way his cock grew even more in her grasp. As she caressed it, a drop of white, iridescent fluid oozed out. She stared at it then touched it with a fingertip. Warm and viscous, it came away on her finger. She lifted her head at a groan from Farrel.

His jaw was clenched tight. The muscles of his arms bulged against the bonds at his wrists, a clear indication of how she affected him.

"Am I hurting ye?"

"No," he said between gritted teeth, "but it is excruciating torture."

Intrigued, she returned her attention to his shaft. "What shall I do to ease it?"

He barked a laugh. Another milky drop trickled along the scarlet-hued skin. "Take the wee beastie home to its warm cave. Don't forget to give it a good stroking first."

She laughed. Giving him a last caress, she rose and tugged her shirt over her head then stepped out of her breeches. Setting her hands to the waist of his breeches, she pulled them down when he lifted his backside off the chair. Sliding them off, she set them aside.

"Ravyn? You can untie me now." His voice had lowered to a croak.

A slow smile curved her lips. "Nay. Ye'll stay bound and blinded while I have my wicked way with ye." She slid along his legs between hers, eliciting a gasp from him.

"I think I've unleashed a beastie myself. Ravyn, sweetheart, is this how you want to play it?"

"Aye." She bent to kiss his mouth, pressing her breasts to his chest. His heart pounded against her, stirring her even more, tendrils of liquid heat flowing deep into her. "Ye said I could have control."

"So I did. Okay, then. Go for it."

Pulling herself onto her knees on the wide seat of the chair and putting her hands to his shoulders, she hovered above him, glorying in the feel of him brushing along her sensitized core. Pushed forward as he was by the pillow behind him provided easy access. Using a hand to guide him, she lowered herself slowly, taking him in by gradual degrees. He trembled under her, not thrusting up, but keeping still. She moved into the heady sensation, pulling away then retaking him.

After a moment, he began moving with her. The feel of him driving into her spurred the sparking tendrils into full-blown flame.

She bent to kiss him, parting his lips with her tongue and playing the aggressor. He let her, but the way his body shuddered betrayed the effort of his restraint.

Her tension spiraled until she wanted to cry out in pure joy. Instead, she moaned as the release overtook her. Her whole body tingled with it, and as Farrel spilled into her, the sensation enfolded them both, sizzling against their skin where they met, inspiring yet another immediate climax. She buried her face against Farrel's shoulder to stifle the cry she couldn't repress. He groaned, his head falling back as he continued to pump into her. Spent, his body sagged under hers.

Finally at rest, she turned her head and kissed the side of his neck.

"You are a feisty little thing," he murmured. "Now, do you think it's possible I might have the use of my hands and eyes back?"

She laughed against his neck. "I think I prefer ye this way."

"I have created a monster." His lament ended in a rueful laugh. "A fair trade-off, I suppose. You got to confront your demon; now I have to deal with my diminutive dominatrix."

Lifting her head, she frowned. "What is that, pray?"

Farrel threw his head back and laughed until dark patches blooming on the blindfold evidenced tears in his eyes. "You're such an innocent." He shook his head, still chuckling. "If you don't free me, I'll never tell you."

She rose and unfastened the blindfold, then released his hands. Farrel rubbed his wrists, his gaze roving over her with open admiration. Rather than making her feel shy and exposed, it filled her with pleasure. Aware of a slow, sticky trickle along her inner thighs, Ravyn pivoted and mince-walked to the washstand. She cleaned herself, warmth flooding her face at the realization of what she washed away.

When she turned back to Farrel, he had risen. Ravyn saw bloodstains on the bandage over the pillow. "Ye've opened the wound again."

"It'll heal." He took her hand and lifted it to his lips. "I'd say this was well worth it. Now, my dear Captain, I suggest we rest for a time. The wee beastie is worn out and needs a nap." He scooped up the pillow and drew her with him to the bunk.

Farrel turned her so they lay in a spoon position. He drew the light cover over them and slid his arm around to cup her breast in his hand.

"The men will wonder what I'm about, so long confined to your cabin."

He pressed a kiss to her nape. "It shouldn't take them long to figure it out. Besides, we agreed that in here, we can do as we please. Or as you pleased, tonight."

Ravyn closed her eyes in fleeting chagrin. Then she let the momentary vexation pass. She had agreed to his terms about when and where they could share intimacies. And she had relished their lovemaking as much as Farrel. Mayhap more, considering.

"So," she began on a yawn, "tell me, what is a dominatrix?"

Farrel wasn't sure when they fell asleep, or even if Ravyn did. He woke to find her gone, the bed still warm where she had rested.

He thought about their lovemaking. Ravyn finding the courage to look upon him, touch him, even tease him in their exchange, filled him with elation. Maybe now she could embrace the freedom to release her fears and inhibitions. To fall in love and live the life a woman of her dynamic spirit should enjoy.

But would he be around to bask in her new emancipation?

The thought that he might not made it difficult to draw a deep breath past the tightness in his chest. If he had freed her, she had captured him in a way that left him confused and a little unnerved.

Thunder rumbled in the distance, echoing his disquiet.

Chapter 53

It started to rain during the night and continued into the morning.

Dr. Page arrived in fisherman's hat and oilskin slicker, medical kit tucked under his arm. He took one look at Farrel and snatched off his dripping hat.

"Ye've nary a lick of sense in that educated head." He regarded Farrel with slitted eyes. "That wound will ne'er heal if ye doesn't keep it covered."

Farrel endured the physician's rough examination, gritting his teeth when Dr. Page pressed heavily onto the wound.

"No pus, but that makes ye fortunate rather than shrewd. Judgin' by the Cap'n's cheery mood this morn, I knows the nature of luck ye be enjoyin'."

"I confess. She and I have an irresistible attraction."

"Aye, like the moth to a bonfire." In spite of his growling tone, Dr. Page chuckled. "Beware, lest Mr. Fisher sets ye ablaze and tosses ye o'er the side with the excuse of dousin' the flames."

"Let him try. I think he'll face opposition from more than one quarter."

"Aye." Dr. Page's expression dissolved into serious lines. "Ye've earned a place with the Cap'n and much of the crew. She'd not take kindly to foul play against ye."

Farrel appreciated the doctor's backing.

The rain persisted throughout the day, confining activities to shipboard. Just as well, Farrel supposed, despite disappointment at not visiting Pontac House. His anticipation for the Admiralty Court buoyed him up in spite of the weather.

The morning of the Court dawned cloudy, but the rain had stopped. Dr. Page redressed Farrel's back and reapplied the bandage wrapping.

Farrel donned the finest Andrew Marks had left—another lawn shirt, collar and neck cloth, gray trousers, a white waistcoat and deeper gray coat. The day promised to be warm and humid, but he wanted to look his best.

Ravyn had already left when he took breakfast. Mr. Hennessey joined him.

A short carriage ride took them to the Cochrane Building, located on George Street and facing onto Market Square. It stood three stories high, mullioned windows overlooking the avenues and the busy square. Outside, vendors sold everything from fish, fresh produce, cheeses, breads and grain to kitchen wares and other household necessities. Inside, plank flooring creaked underfoot beneath low beamed ceilings. Henry Burroughs awaited them. They exchanged cordial greetings and entered the courtroom on the ground level. Benches divided by a middle aisle gravitated toward a front dais, where a heavy oak table stood, a massive wooden chair behind it.

They took seats midway down the room. After a short time, three black-robed men in white periwigs filed in and took places at the vacant front bench on one side. Soldiers escorted prisoners to the bench on the opposite side, where the uniformed men stood guard.

Mr. Hennessey leaned close to Farrel. "The *Annabelle*'s Chief Mate, Quincy Donaldson, is here to represent the interests of the owner. Dr. Croke will have already reviewed the paperwork, so Mr. Donaldson's presence is mere formality."

Farrel nodded, intent on the proceedings.

The bailiff entered, ordering all to rise for the High Court of Admiralty commencing session. A man in a red robe with a white collar and wearing a long gray court wig strode in. Taking his seat in the chair behind the table, he scanned the room with sharp eyes. Though his features gave the impression of a temperate nature, rumor had it that he was considered brilliant, cynical, and, ironically, grasping.

The court attendees seated themselves, and the proceedings began.

Farrel listened, engrossed by the judgment passed in Dr. Croke's expansive, often overwordy deliverance. History played out before Farrel's eyes, an experience he wouldn't have missed for the world.

The cited case against a vessel named *The Eunice*, which had taken in cargo on her return from Lisbon, came to a swift conclusion. The ship and its goods, unprotected by a license or other regulated documentation, were condemned.

Following a brief recess, the bailiff pronounced their case. Dr. Croke made quick deliverance of the judgment.

"In the case of the *Lady Annabelle*, captured the twenty-third day of June by the privateer *Retribution*, this vessel, with a cargo of French brandy, wines, silks and other goods, the manufacture and produce of France, and sailing from the Port of Bordeaux with a voyage destination of Norfolk, Virginia, without license or the appropriate British port clearance documentation, is in clear violation of the Order of Council of the twenty-sixth of April of this year, and is hereby condemned under these same orders."

Dr. Croke shuffled through the papers in front of him while the court waited in respectful silence. At length, he picked up the petition for reassignment of the *Lady Annabelle*'s crew. Farrel recognized the document at once. Dr. Croke scanned it, his brows lowering and mouth thinning before he looked up.

"By whose authority has this petition for reassignment of the captured crew been issued?"

Mr. Hennessey rose. "By Captain Flynt and myself, Gabriel Hennessey, as prize master, Your Honor."

"This request is highly irregular. Is the composer of the petition present?"

Farrel rose, hat in hand, his heart beating faster. "'Twas myself, Your Honor." He adapted his speech to the best of his ability.

"And you are?" The judge's stern gaze pinned him.

"Farrel McQuaid, clerk to the *Retribution*, sir." He twisted his hat in his hands. What could Dr. Croke need to know?

"I require a clearer explanation. The normal course of action is to detain the prisoners at Melville or press them into service on the ships of our navy. For what reason should I give consideration to a privateer?"

Farrel swallowed, his mind scrambling for the right words.

"Your Honor, the crew in question was on a commercial voyage. They carried minimal arms and had no military aspirations. Their captain escaped with his family. This April past, the *Retribution* met in conflict with an American vessel and lost a number of crew in the fray. The petition is made in the hope that these numbers can be restored without resorting to press actions within the general populace." Farrel tried to assess the judge's reaction by his expression. However, the man had the ability to appear neutral, whatever his thoughts might be.

"Captain Flynt is in agreement with this?"

"Aye. The Captain, in fact, made the suggestion. It seemed the ideal solution to the problem of replenishing the vessel's complement of men."

Again, the judge studied him. Farrel remained standing, sweat running down his chest and back and soaking into the binding.

"How, might I ask, did Captain..." Dr. Croke glanced at the records, "...Marks manage such an escape? Surely he would have been kept under stringent watch."

"We...encountered a storm along the coast of Massachusetts. Much of the crew of both ships was occupied with keeping the vessels on course. Once it had passed, repairs were necessary. We believe the captain managed to slip away under cover of darkness while those not busy with repairs were resting. A regrettable oversight, to not have assigned more vigilant guard on the prisoners." He spread his hands. "We saw no reason to think he would attempt such a gambit."

"I...see." The judge's eyes narrowed, and Farrel's palms dampened. "You seem an educated man, Mr. McQuaid. How is it you became part of a privateer crew?"

"An unexpected turn of fortune, Your Honor. I am well satisfied to remain part of the *Retribution*'s crew."

Dr. Croke's brow furrowed. "From whence do you hail, sir?"

"Upper Canada, Your Honor. York, to be precise."

"York." Dr. Croke settled back in his chair, one corner of his mouth lifting in a wry smile. "It seems you are a long way from home."

"Aye, Your Honor. A very long way."

"Do all the residents of York speak with your flatness of diction?"

"Some. York is host to a...variety of languages."

The judge leaned forward and rescanned the petition. "Though it is irregular, I will allow the conditions of this petition to be implemented. The prisoners will be released to the custody of the *Retribution* on the morrow."

"Many thanks, Your Honor." Farrel offered a polite bow and sat down, giving an inward sigh of relief.

"Ye handled yourself admirably," Mr. Hennessey praised after the court adjourned. Henry Burroughs had advised that he would see Ravyn the next day to firm up the figures for court costs and whatever other levies might apply. The auction was set for a date more than two weeks away.

"We won't be staying for the auction, will we?" Farrel settled back in the carriage, taking off his hat and pulling a handkerchief from his pocket to wipe his brow.

"Nay. Once the business affairs are settled with Mr. Burroughs, the Cap'n'll be setting sail on the next fortuitous tide. Another capture will bring us back to Halifax, and by then, he should have collected the proceeds from the sale." Mr. Hennessey grinned. "Ye've a gift for words, Mr. McQuaid. I'm not certain I could have persuaded Dr. Croke with the ease ye did. 'Twill serve ye well when we go before the court again."

Farrel remained silent, caught up in contemplation.

Would he still be here for that? Unless he discovered some way to return to his own time, it would seem so. Did it disturb him, the thought of going back?

Only in the probability of leaving Ravyn behind.

Suddenly, that seemed the worst possible outcome.

Chapter 54

*R*avyn sat in a dusky corner of the Spread Eagle Tavern, a tankard of ale before her. She toyed with the handle, attuned to the hum of conversation. Clad in her ship's garb, she blended with the other patrons. Nevertheless, she kept her head down so her tricorne shadowed her face.

Though early afternoon, the seedy tavern abounded with customers. At one table, three drunken men sang a bawdy off-key sea chanty while at another, two tattered sailors argued the merits of sloops over ketches.

This establishment, rarely quiet, provided refuge for privateers and pirates alike. It was also the best place to hear gossip about ships, their crews and nefarious activities at sea or ashore—and mayhap word of Will Flemington.

She had partaken of food and lingered over her ale. No telling when the Court would adjourn.

A pair of men entered and settled at a nearby table. They bore the roughshod appearance of common sailors, their faces scruffy, clothing dirty and unkempt. One wore an eye patch, the other a gold hoop dangling from his ear. After ordering ales and food, they resumed their discussion, close enough for her to overhear.

"'Twas fortunate Cap'n Burke be acquainted with Flemington. Otherwise, we mighta ended at the bottom."

Ravyn tensed, hand tightening on her tankard.

The man with the eye patch nodded, his mouth thinning in a grim line. "'E 'ad ta be in a jolly mood, or deep in his cups. Does ye know why 'e was askin' the Cap'n' if 'e'd crossed paths with a woman workin' a ship in 'is travels?"

"Aye. I 'eard some o' their talk. 'E's lookin' fer the wench. Said she's captainin' a privateerin' ship. A black-haired beauty with eyes lighter blue than a midsummer sky wearin' britches bold as any man. Says 'e 'as a claim to 'er."

"Captain? A woman?" Eye Patch's single grizzled brow arched. "'Ow can that be?"

"I's no inklin', but I's 'eard sailors in other ports talkin' 'bout 'er. Say she thinks she's foolin' 'em, dressin' like a man. They daren't cross 'er, though. Say she 'as a big bo'sun as'd kill any man lookin' sidewise at 'er."

Eye Patch snorted. "Flemington'd make short work o' that one. Then the wench'd be 'is fer the takin'."

"But 'e don't know where ta find 'er. 'E said 'er ship was some big frigate, but 'e don't know the name. Nor that of the woman, save that 'tis some kind o' bird."

Eye Patch grinned. "I'd pity any bird caught in that shark's net. Or any man fool'ardy enough ta be layin' with 'er now if Madman finds 'em."

Gold Earring grimaced. "Aye, 'e'd be rippin' the blighter's bollocks off with 'is bare 'ands an' makin' 'er watch."

Ravyn's dinner of beef stew suddenly weighed like lead in her stomach.

"'E's a rare one fer drawin' out the torture afore lettin' the poor bloke die. 'Tis said they begs fer it in the end. An' it don't need the reason of some woman fer 'im."

"'E said she was a sweet piece o' baggage." Gold Earring gave a salacious chuckle. "Trust Will Flemington to be diddlin' a comely one. No ugly wenches fer 'im."

"Well, I's glad 'e let us go unhurt."

"'E tol' Cap'n Burke 'e was settin' course fer Nassau an' 'opin' ta find 'is quarry along the way."

"I can tell ye, I wouldn't want to be the luckless bugger comin' 'tween 'im an' the strumpet." Eye Patch shook his head.

The barmaid sashayed over with their dinner. Talk ended, and they set to eating.

Ravyn sank deeper into her chair, her heart pounding and chest clenching.

So, Will Flemington looked for her as diligently as she sought him. Nor did her identity appear as safe as she thought. Who would have betrayed her? Or was her guise more transparent than she believed? The mere thought of falling back into that demon's clutches...

She set her jaw, curling her hand into a fist. Nay, she would not fall into the terrible darkness. She would maintain control of her emotions. Yet she could not prevent the memories that boiled to the surface. They flashed across her mind akin to the frozen images on Farrel's picture-taking device.

Flemington's lusting black eyes blazing at her over Jonathan Moore's blood-drenched body.

Waking in the malodorous confines of his cabin, her clothing ripped from her body. Him looming over her like a hawk prepared to devour a helpless mouse.

Ravyn came back to herself, the metallic taste of blood on her tongue. She had bitten her bottom lip hard enough to break the skin. But the memories would not stop.

Locked in the cabin, wrapped in a numbed cocoon of disbelief that this could have happened to her.

She drew a slow, deep breath, trying to force the images away. Her stomach churned, as though she might be ill. Swallowing bile, she had no choice but to let the images play out.

Eli Fisher bending over her, his scarred face drawn in fury. Then bundling her in a sheet to spirit her from the pirate's vessel while the brigands reveled below.

The long row of canvas-wrapped bodies on their own deck, readied for their eternal sleep.

Eli's face set in grim lines as he gripped her shoulders, reminding her of her duty to the remaining men.

Stepping from the cabin that had been Jonathan Moore's, swallowing the last vestiges of grief and shame to take her rightful place as captain.

And now Will Flemington sought her, to reclaim her as his own. She shuddered.

Nay. She would never let herself, nor any of the men in her charge, fall into those brutal hands again. Especially not—

Her determined thoughts stuttered to a halt.

Farrel.

Fear squeezed her chest, ousting the impending panic.

Even if no one bespoke their relationship, Farrel's actions alone would betray them. She had no doubt he would rise to her defense. But he would never withstand the unscrupulous tactics Flemington employed. His death would be unavoidable, whether a quick kill or slow torture.

Ravyn's breath clogged in her throat. Any hint of attraction 'tween her and Farrel would be sufficient to inflame Flemington. Farrel would die.

She could not let that happen.

God willing, she would send Flemington to the Hell he deserved.

Farrel glanced around the tavern's squalid surroundings, nose wrinkling. The place reeked of cooking food, ale, lantern oil and unwashed bodies. The soiled sawdust on the floor looked as if it hadn't been changed for weeks, maybe months.

"'Tis not the most auspicious establishment." Mr. Hennessey spoke at his elbow. "But 'tis where many of our ilk meet on occasion." He nodded toward a dim corner. "There be the Cap'n."

Farrel had intended to return to *Retribution*, but curiosity won out over prudence. He followed Hennessey, glancing at the shabby patrons. Pulling off his hat, he sat across from Ravyn.

"I feel distinctly overdressed." He gave a crooked grin.

Mr. Hennessey chuckled, lifting a hand and gesturing to a barmaid. She carried tankards of ale to the table, hips swaying, her generous bosom nearly falling out of her low-cut bodice.

"So, how did it transpire?" Ravyn leaned forward.

"The judge condemned the *Lady Annabelle* and her cargo," Farrel supplied. "Dr. Croke agreed to release the crew to us tomorrow."

"Mr. McQuaid did a fine job of convincin' him." Mr. Hennessey nodded his approval. "Better than any lawyer, I'm thinkin'."

"Good." Though Ravyn appeared pleased, a pinched look tightened her mouth. A small, fresh scab marred her full lower lip. Had something happened to worry her?

"He set the auction for a fortnight hence. Mr. Burroughs asked that ye meet with him on the morrow." Mr. Hennessey lifted his tankard.

Farrel looked askance at a nearby table, where a pair of burly sailors watched them with cagey interest. "I don't think we should stay long. They're eyeing me like I'm their next paycheck."

"Aye, well, ye said ye felt overdressed." Ravyn offered a tight-lipped grin. "They likely think ye a well-heeled gentleman perched in the wrong quarter."

"Sure feels like it." He redirected his attention to her. "You look anxious. Something happen?"

"Nay." Her attempt at smoothing her features didn't fool Farrel. Wariness that hadn't been evident in the last week or so sharpened her features. "Finish your drinks and we'll take our leave."

Farrel drew a deep, cleansing breath once outdoors, the prevailing odor of fish preferable to the stink of the tavern.

Aboard *Retribution*, he changed into breeches and a fresh shirt.

"By the time we have the men assembled and ready for setting sail, 'twill likely be Saturday," Ravyn said to Mr. Hennessey and Mr. Fisher over dinner. "I'll meet with Mr. Burroughs while ye fetch the *Annabelle*'s crew. We also need to be sure we've taken on enough stores to last for a time."

"You plan on being at sea awhile?" Farrel leaned toward her.

Her expression shifted from business-like to something Farrel couldn't name. It looked like pain. She tried to hide it by glancing down at her plate, where she had done little more than push her food around.

"Aye. 'Tis the best season for capturing prizes. We may head further south than our usual course."

That got the attention of Mr. Hennessey and Fisher. They stared at her with undisguised curiosity.

"How far, pray?" Mr. Hennessey spoke softly.

"Mayhap as far as Nassau." She rose. "I'll be hunting Sammy and putting Liam to bed if ye need me."

When the door closed behind her, Farrel turned a questioning gaze to Mr. Hennessey, noting the younger man's pensive frown. "Nassau? Has she gone that way before?"

"Nay, not in more than two years." He turned to Fisher. The bo'sun's bushy brows sat low, and a scowl drew his scar into crooked relief. "Does ye know what her thinkin' is?"

"Nay." Fisher rose and exited.

"That clears it up." Farrel set his fork down. "What's at Nassau?"

"I've no inklin'." Mr. Hennessey shook his head.

"I know it's a British stronghold now. It's not a haven for pirates anymore, if that's what she's looking for."

"Pirates?" Mr. Hennessey's brows flew up. "Whatever would make ye think she be huntin' pirates?"

"Ask Mr. Lancaster." Farrel wiped his mouth and threw his napkin down. He hadn't meant to say that much, but he'd gotten the impression that all the men suspected Ravyn hunted a pirate's vessel. Only he and Fisher knew the whole story. "If you'll excuse me."

He found Ravyn in the galley. Sammy sat at Cook's feet, tail twitching as he waited for tidbits to drop.

"Here, let me." Farrel scooped up the cat and draped him over one arm. Sammy lolled without complaint, his yellow eyes fixed on the ham Cook chopped. Grinning, the man held out a few pieces in his callused hand. The cat scarfed them down. "Spoiled rotten, you are." Rubbing behind Sammy's ears, Farrel left the galley with Ravyn.

"Ye wanted something, Mr. McQuaid?" She faced him in the narrow companionway at the ladder to the deck.

"Why are you heading for Nassau?"

Her eyes narrowed. "There are prizes to be found that far south. Sometimes the currents carry them into British waters. Moreover," she added in a crisper tone, "it truly be none of your concern where I set course."

She took the cat from him and ascended the ladder one-handed. He let her go on to her quarters with Liam and remained at the rail, staring out over the harbor.

Had she been like that this morning? Not having seen her, he didn't know. But something had happened.

He was sure of it.

Chapter 55

Jonathan Moore stood between her and Flemington, weapons clashing as the young captain leapt to her defense.

She watched, frozen in horror, as Jonathan's form flickered, settling into Farrel.

A thrust at Farrel's throat had him swinging his cutlass up to deflect the blow. Flemington feinted, slashing across Farrel's chest then plunging the blade into his belly.

Ravyn screamed, the clatter of Farrel's cutlass hitting the deck a death knell to her ears. "Nay! Nay!" Falling to her knees, she cradled him, awash in his blood as life left his eyes.

Flemington wrenched Farrel's body from her, kicking him aside. Laughing, he hauled her up. She pummeled his chest.

"Ye're mine now." He bared a yellow-toothed leer. "No man fer ye but meself."

Repulsed by the stench of his breath and his overwhelming body stink, she struggled, screaming epithets.

"Release me, ye bloody—"

"Ravyn, wake up."

Farrel's voice from the dead shocked her. She continued to fight, convinced that Flemington could somehow mimic Farrel.

"Release me." Striking out again, her fist met a warm, bare chest. Not Flemington's filthy shirt.

Farrel grunted, catching her hand before she could strike again. "C'mon, hon, wake up." He pressed her hand against his chest so she felt the thud of his heart.

Her eyes flew open. She drew a gasping breath, staring at Farrel's anxious face, visible by moonlight spilling through her window.

"Farrel?" She pulled away, still caught in tangled fragments of the dream. Then she flung her arms around his neck. "Ye're safe."

"Of course I'm safe. So are you." He rubbed her back, his touch gentle and reassuring.

The last wisps of nightmare faded, leaving her shaking and bathed in cold fear-sweat. She burrowed her head on his shoulder.

"It's okay now." His lips brushed her temple. She drew a hitching breath, finding comfort in that simple caress.

Footfalls pounded from the outer deck. Ravyn lifted her head, pulse jumping. Two of the mates left on watch appeared in the doorway. Mr. Fisher pushed through, cutlass in hand.

"What 'as ye done to 'er?" He hoisted the weapon, glaring at Farrel.

Ravyn pulled away, back stiffening, and drew a slow, calming breath. Though her heart still pounded fit to burst, she controlled her voice.

"Naught. I but dreamed." Her gaze flicked to Farrel then back to Mr. Fisher and the gawking men. Determined to assert her authority, she stood, refusing to yield to her quivering legs. "Ye may resume your stations."

The two mates disappeared. Mr. Fisher stood his ground.

"I's not leavin' till I knows ye're aright." He lowered the weapon, glowering.

"I am quite recovered." She licked her dry lips.

"You're still shaking." Farrel took her arm and drew her gently back down. He rested a light hand on her shoulder. "Liam, would you bring a cup of water for the Captain?"

Liam, round-eyed, scrambled up from his pallet. He poured water from a pitcher and carried the pewter cup to them. She reached to take it, but nearly dropped it.

"Here, let me." Farrel put the cup to her lips. She rested her hands over his to steady her tremors. She could not afford to let Mr. Fisher witness her vulnerability. She sipped, grateful for the cool water trickling down her parched throat.

How long had she been crying out? Shuddering, she pushed the cup away.

Liam retreated, wary eyes on her. Farrel beckoned, and the boy neared cautiously once more.

"Are...are ye aright, Cap'n?"

"Aye, I am...f-fine." She cursed inwardly at her faltering voice.

Farrel put an arm around the boy's shoulders. "Why don't you go to my cabin for the rest of the night? I'll stay with the captain."

"Nay, ye doesn't have to... I doesn't need..." But even as she protested, Liam headed out the door at a run, pushing past Mr. Fisher.

"An' ye be aright lettin' the lecherin' sod stay?" the bo'sun rumbled.

Ravyn opened her mouth to tell Farrel he should go back to his bed. But staring at his face, the terrifying scene of his death replayed across her mind. A shiver rippled through her. She did not want to go back there. Nor did she want to be alone.

"Aye." She turned to Mr. Fisher. His disapproving grimace and the bulk of his form in the half-light reminded her of a fairytale ogre. She kept her gaze steady on his, her chin kicking up a notch. "I want him to stay."

"I wasn't planning on leaving, sweetheart." Farrel touched his fingertips to her hair then ran them over her cheek.

His caress warmed and chilled her at once, the convergence of a flesh-and-bone man and the remnant of a ghost. The impression sent gooseflesh stippling over her.

"You heard the captain, Mr. Fisher. You may go. And shut the door, if you please."

"Sweetheart. Phah." The bo'sun stomped away, leaving the door open.

Farrel sighed. He rose and closed the door.

Ravyn's shoulders slumped now that they were alone.

Farrel sat down and took her hands, letting them rest loose in his. "Do you want to talk about the dream?" The concern softening his eyes nearly overset her.

"Nay." Her hands quivered, and Farrel squeezed them.

"You sure?" His unwavering gaze seemed bent on searching her soul. She looked down, refusing to let him see how deeply the dream's memory unsettled her. Her chest tightened with the familiar panic. She swallowed, focused on forcing the darkness away. She would not let it rule her.

"Aye." She drew her hands free and wrapped her arms around herself. Farrel pulled her into his embrace. She leaned into him, bolstered by his solidity.

"Let's lie down." He started to pull her back.

She resisted. "Nay, I...I doesn't want to—"

"I only want to hold you." His voice vibrated with a note of wry humor. "Is that all right?"

"Aye." Relenting, she allowed him to draw her down. She settled her head into the curve of his shoulder and laid her hand on his chest. The crinkly dusting of hair, the warm, firm muscle beneath, his musky scent and the regular thump of his heart calmed her more than his words of reassurance. He was alive. Safe.

But for how long?

Farrel lay awake after Ravyn drifted into uneasy slumber, her body tense in his arms.

Now he knew something had happened. She hadn't experienced such a violent nightmare in nearly two weeks, waking or sleeping. But why had she expressed so much relief over his safety?

He remembered how Julia's nightmares had wakened him and their mother as she fought her attacker in the unconsciousness of sleep. As with Ravyn, he'd only been able to offer reassurance. However, Julia had shrunk away from any physical contact. At least he could hold Ravyn.

Strange, how he had been carried into an almost identical situation. However, Ravyn knew the identity of her attacker and deliberately hunted him to exact revenge. Whether she admitted it or not, that must prey upon her mind.

Closing his eyes, Farrel drifted into a half-sleeping state, his senses on high alert for the least tremor, the slightest hitch in her breathing that might indicate a return to her place of torment. But she rested in his arms, her breathing at last slow and steady, body warming as she nestled against him.

The violation was something she would never get over. No matter how tender and passionate their relationship, part of Ravyn would remain trapped in that terrible time and place. Moved by that insight, Farrel made a vow.

She need never face the traumatic memories alone again. Even if it meant never returning to his time—a situation he accepted—he would stay at her side, day and night, to rescue her as no one had when it happened.

Whether tossed into her life by predetermination or happenstance, Ravyn would not fall victim to Julia's devastating fate.

Perhaps, in some inexplicable way, this had been his destiny all along.

Dawn's pale glow lit the cabin when Ravyn opened her eyes. She tensed, astonished to find herself wrapped in Farrel's arms.

The dream and its aftermath flooded back. She swallowed a gasp.

She looked up at Farrel's face, his tousled hair, the taut lines creasing his features. She couldn't lose him. Not like that.

But how could she keep him safe? There seemed only two alternatives— forfeit her hunt for Flemington, or leave Farrel in a safer situation.

Neither appealed to her, but she had to choose one.

Forfeit her revenge? She crushed the light coverlet in her fist. Nay, she could not allow that shark to live.

Leave Farrel behind? Her chest ached at the thought. It would be abandoning part of her soul to sail away without him.

She passed her hand lightly across his chest, ruffling the crisp hairs and molding her fingers to the strong muscles beneath. Stopping over his heart, she felt its powerful throb under her palm.

She studied the fine stubble on his jaw, the curve of his lips, his sharply defined cheekbones, the dark golden lashes that would glitter in the sun. A longing to touch his face, to cradle it in her hands, seized her. She resisted, not wanting to wake him. The moment was too perfect to disturb.

Sighing, she nestled her head against his shoulder.

"You okay?"

She started at Farrel's soft question. "Aye." A shiver passed over her. "I remember I...dreamed."

"You sure did. Your cries woke me up."

"The men on watch. They heard as well." She clenched her jaw, self-directed anger heating her face.

"They did. And your guard dog."

She sighed. "Farrel...ye mustn't refer so to Eli."

The breath from his low chuckle tickled her ear. "Okay. But Dad wasn't happy when I said I was staying. Thanks for letting me, though."

"I ought not to have. The men will be thinking me soft, weak, like... like..."

"Like a woman in need of comforting?" He cradled her cheek in his hand. "Are you ashamed of that?"

She gazed into the temperate gray eyes so close to hers. "Not...shamed." She couldn't put a name to the feeling of discomfiture. "The men must see me as a strong leader, not-not..."

"Not human?" Farrel tightened his embrace, resting his chin on the top of her head. "You don't have to go through this alone."

"I should be rising—" She started to pull away, but Farrel stopped her.

"It's early yet. Sleep a while longer." He settled his arms around her. "Besides, I'm enjoying this."

"Farrel..."

"No seduction this morning. I'm tired, you're tired, and it's enjoyable resting here with you in my arms." He kissed her forehead. "I could get used to waking up like this."

She relaxed into his embrace.

Though she would never admit it aloud, it was pleasurable to rest in his arms. No demands, no expectations, no fiery passion, just simple coziness. Her heart ached with the realization that it couldn't last.

She treasured Farrel too deeply to let any harm befall him. And harm him Will Flemington would.

She slid her arms tighter around Farrel and buried her face against his chest, inhaling his masculine scent as she blinked back tears.

He said she need not face this alone. But that was her only means of keeping Farrel safe. Flemington must never know she loved another man.

Finding Flemington and ending him must be her only goal.

Alone.

Her heart broke with the knowledge.

Chapter 56

"While I confer with Mr. Burroughs, I'll have ye retrieve the prisoners." Ravyn directed the order to Mr. Hennessey over breakfast.

Though blue circles shadowed her eyes, she acted as if the past night hadn't happened. Fisher cast dark glares Farrel's way, leaving him certain that if looks could kill, he would have been struck dead the moment he entered the great cabin.

"Aye, aye, Cap'n." Mr. Hennessey swallowed a last gulp of coffee and rose. "I'll gather the lads and be off."

"Is there anything I can do?"

Ravyn met Farrel's questioning gaze. "Ye can keep Liam occupied. There'll be too much commotion for him to be underfoot."

"Babysit. Okay." Farrel shrugged, grinning.

"Nay, teach." Ravyn rose. "'Tis what I pay ye to do."

Farrel flinched at the curt reprimand.

He and Ravyn had fallen back to sleep, waking when Liam crept in to change into fresh breeches and shirt. Ravyn shooed them out so she could dress. Farrel offered to help, but she refused without the return of his teasing humor.

Mid-afternoon, a commotion from the outer decks heralded the arrival of the *Annabelle*'s crew. Farrel stepped out and watched them conducted aboard. Though not restrained, nearly double the number of Ravyn's men guarded them. Farrel met Dr. Lorriman's bright brown eyes, and the man waved. Farrel acknowledged it with a nod and a smile before the 'prisoners' were taken below.

Ravyn returned before supper. Over the meal, she conferred with Mr. Hennessey and Mr. Morrissey about the *Annabelle*'s men. "I expect them to work their share till we reach our destination."

"Aye, Cap'n. There's plenty to do afore the morn, so I'll be gettin' them at it." He, Mr. Morrissey and Fisher departed, leaving Farrel with Ravyn and Liam.

"I need to speak with Mr. McQuaid," Ravyn told the boy. "Ye go and find Sammy."

Liam darted from the cabin.

"What's on your mind?" Farrel poured grog into their tankards.

"I've been giving a deal of thought to...things." She lifted the cup and took a slow sip.

Farrel paused with his drink half-way to his mouth. "What things?"

She set her tankard down, gaze fixed on the contents, her expression tight and guarded. Suddenly, Farrel had the feeling he wasn't going to like this conversation.

"I spoke at length with Mr. Burroughs today. Your handling of the court matters impressed him." She toyed with the tankard's handle. "He'd offer ye a position if ye'd stay in Halifax. I told him ye're a teacher of higher learning, and he said there may be opportunities for tutoring or even startin' a school."

"Leave the *Retribution*? But—"

"Ye've been a boon to us. But it may be your talents are wasted here." She lifted a hand, forestalling any response he might have formulated. "It may afford ye the chance to find your way...home." Something flickered across her eyes, and she looked away.

"I'm not interested in staying in Halifax."

"But ye said ye could get used to living here." A tremor edged her voice. "Said ye felt ye belonged."

"That's not what I meant, and you bloody well know it." He leapt up, almost overturning his chair. "I belong on the *Retribution*. With you."

She rose. "'Tis a grand opportunity. I think ye should—"

"Why are you trying to get rid of me? We've become so close. You want to give up on that? Abandon me? Us?"

"Nay, I–I..." She swallowed. "Ye could achieve so much more—"

He fisted his hands and pounded the table hard enough that their tankards jumped. "This is bullshit. Why are you really doing this? It's Fisher, isn't it? He's a mean-spirited bully, and I'm sick of the way he manipulates you."

"And what is it ye've done?" Her eyes flashed. "Ye've seduced me at every opportunity. Compromised the respect of my crew—"

His own anger raised his voice to a shout. "Your crew still respects you.

Dammit, woman, I love you!"

The impact of his words stopped him cold.

He loved her. More accurately, he was in love with her.

Ravyn retreated a step, her lips parting in a reflection of his shock. She drew a sharp breath, and her eyes softened. Her hands unclenched, trembling at her sides. Then her expression hardened again, and she shook her head. "Ye've swept into my life like a tidal wave. I need time and distance from ye." She strode to the window, turning her back. "When we set sail on the morrow, I want ye gone."

"So, I'm to stay here, while you sail off to God knows where, for God knows how long, and into God knows what danger? No flippin' way!" He stalked up behind her, pulling her around and into his arms. He claimed her mouth in a harsh kiss, anger and his sense of betrayal roughening the caress.

Ravyn stiffened, her fists coming to rest on his chest and pushing as a sound of protest rose from low in her throat.

Farrel drew her tighter, trapping her hands. He lessened the intensity of the kiss, turning outrage into a plea. Though she didn't relax, her mouth softened. A long moment passed before he broke the kiss. He didn't loosen his embrace.

"I can't lose you." He lowered his forehead against her hair. "You're part of me. And, I swear to God, I've never felt or said that for any other woman who wasn't family."

A shudder passed through her. "Ye must give me time to think. I can't with ye so near."

He released her, stepping back. "You're not leaving me behind."

Her expression turned cold. "Then I'll have ye forcibly removed."

Farrel ran a hand over his hair. He stared at her, trying to fathom what lay behind this sudden turn. "I won't go willingly, nor do I think the men will put me off. Ordered or not."

"They'll do as I bid."

When she started forward, Farrel caught her arm. She tried to wrench free, but he tightened his hold. "You're not calling the men. We're going to talk this out."

Her eyes met his in a blaze of fury. "Release me. Now."

Farrel pulled her, resisting, to a chair. "Sit down and tell me what's really going on." He allowed her no choice except to drop onto the seat, scowling at him. He stood before her, arms crossed. "I can be as stubborn as you, and I intend to find out the truth."

Ravyn's hands gripped the edge of the chair seat so tight her knuckles whitened. She looked away from him, lips thinning.

He sighed, pulling out a chair to face her. He uncurled her fingers and held her hands. "Don't shut me out."

She darted a glance at him before tugging her hands free.

Farrel wanted to shake her but reined in his impatience. He thought over the past week, the intimacies they had shared, the sweet camaraderie that had blossomed between them. He could find nothing that might have offended her. Only in the past day had constraint grown between them. After she set her course for Nassau...

It hit him like punch in the gut.

Flemington. The pirate sailed those waters, raiding any vessel unfortunate enough to cross his path, as Farrel had learned in his studies. "You're going after Flemington."

She didn't speak, but a tic along her clenched jaw gave him the answer.

"Dammit, Ravyn, why didn't you just say that? It's no reason to put me off."

Her wide-eyed gaze turned back to him. "Ye haven't the skills to face that beast or his crew. They'd cut ye down as easily as a scythe through wheat."

"You're willing to risk the rest of your men."

"They knows the danger they face. Ye has no inkling—"

"Shouldn't I have the right to decide if I'm ready?"

She shot to her feet, and Farrel rose. The torment in her eyes reminded him of Julia's night terrors and Ravyn's own nightmares. 'Ye're no warrior. I'd spare ye the peril of conflict if ye'd but let me."

"If that's your reason, I'm still not leaving. I'm not a coward." Anger gnawed at him that she'd think him too weak to fight.

"But ye knows we'll be back." Though she spoke with confidence, trepidation darkened her eyes.

"Nothing is sure in life. I've lost enough to know." He took her arms in his hands. "I'm not losing you. I refuse to be left again."

Realization slammed into him.

He had become emotionally attached, so much that the thought of being separated from the object of his love was too much. He would risk everything—even his life—to stay and protect her. Having her sail away without him was not an option.

"I don't want ye harmed. Or killed." Ravyn's voice quivered on the last words.

"No, you just want to cut my heart out and throw it away. I'm not letting you. We face this together."

She dodged around him, heading for the door. "I'll not let ye sacrifice yourself."

He lunged after her, catching her arm in a steely grip. "You're treating me like a helpless child. I'll keep practicing. I'm sure Mr. Poole would be willing to step up the sessions."

Ravyn stilled, staring at him with haunted eyes.

"He'll kill ye," she whispered. "Torture ye an inch at a time and make me watch." She choked back a sound that verged on a sob. She straightened, regaining her composure and lifting her chin. "I overheard talk in the tavern. Flemington searches for me, thinks he has a claim on me." She swallowed. "If that brute learns we are lovers..."

"I get it. I know the kinds of tortures pirates use. Not pretty. But I refuse to cower on shore waiting for you to come back. If you come back." The thought of never seeing her again made him pull her into a tight embrace. Though she did not refuse the enclosing circle of his arms, the tension in her body remained palpable. "If you put me off, I'll follow you. I'll borrow the money to hire a ship, if I have to. I'm not letting you go into this without me."

Ravyn slipped her arms around his waist and rested her head on his chest. Her heartbeat, strong and quick, thumped against him. Farrel stroked her hair. What thoughts were going through her head?

She sighed and eased away from him. He released her, watching her face. The hardness of her expression diminished, though Farrel couldn't help thinking it looked forced. Her lips trembled into a smile.

"Very well. If I cannot convince ye, I suppose I must yield the issue." She stepped back, taking his hand. "I should be seeing to affairs on deck. Will ye accompany me?"

He squeezed her hand, thankful she had conceded. "I'll always stand by you. Whatever the cost."

The words felt right, though the concept of being in love still astonished him. But he would take the risk he had avoided for so long, accept the potentials love offered. No matter how ugly the obstacles they faced.

When they stepped out to the deck, furtive glances flicked to him and Ravyn, though the men moved about their tasks with quick efficiency. Their argument must have been overheard.

Retaining his hand, Ravyn led him to Mr. Morrissey, standing with a few of the crew. Nearby, Mr. Hennessey and Mr. Poole appeared deep in conversation but looked up as Farrel and Ravyn approached.

"Mr. Morrissey, I'd ask ye and two of your hands to escort Mr. McQuaid ashore with me."

"What? No." Farrel yanked from her hold. "I thought we came to an agreement."

She faced him, hands curling at her sides.

Despite obvious bewilderment, Mr. Morrissey directed two of his assistants to take Farrel's arms. When Farrel tried to shrug them off, they tightened their hold, looking to Ravyn for further orders.

"Cap'n?" Mr. Hennessey glanced from Farrel to Ravyn.

Farrel stilled, focusing on Ravyn. "Have you told them the real reason you're heading so far south?"

Ravyn's eyes sparked a warning.

Farrel turned his gaze to Hennessey. "The ship Captain Flynt served on came under attack by Flemington about three years ago. They killed many of the crew members, including the captain Ravyn was pledged to marry."

"Cap'n." Mr. Hennessey spoke softly, his hazel eyes sympathetic. "Ye ne'er told us."

She glared at Farrel.

"She thinks I can't handle myself if it comes to facing off with Flemington. But I should decide whether I stay or go. After all, I am a full-grown man." He shot angry looks at the two crewmen holding him. They lessened their grip but did not release him. Farrel scanned the assembled men to locate the weapons officer. "Mr. Poole, do you think I'm capable?"

Mr. Poole stroked his chin. "Mayhap not at this moment, but with more rigorous practice—"

"That be the cap'n's say." Fisher stepped from behind the mainmast, where he had remained unnoticed in its shadow. He took a belligerent stance in front of Farrel. "Ye's no right to gainsay her orders." His features twisted into an ugly grin. "I'd be more'n 'appy to take 'im in 'and fer ye, Cap'n." Fisher pulled his cutlass from his belt. "I can show the whelp 'e'd stand no chance against a bloody pirate." His eyes gleamed in the lantern light.

Farrel's gaze lowered to the cutlass. Its blade glinted, an evil, curving sneer in the dim illumination. Some of the men moved back, while others leaned in with anticipation, like schoolyard boys waiting for the bully to start a fight. A scene Farrel remembered all too well as the target in his youth. Well, this time he'd be no one's whipping boy.

"Pass me a weapon," he ground out, tugging at his arms.

The men released him. A cutlass passed into his hand. Letting his anger rise, he took a step closer to Fisher.

"Farrel, nay—" Ravyn laid her hand on his sleeve.

He shook it off. "If the old bugger wants a fight, I'll give him one."

"So, ye thinks ye can stand against me." Fisher chuckled, his grin contorting his face into a menacing mask. "Summon Dr. Page, Cap'n. Ye'll be needin' 'is services shortly."

"Bring it on." Farrel gritted his teeth and raised the cutlass.

He blocked the first slash with little effort, the metallic clang of the connecting weapons loud on the quiet evening air. A jab aimed at his gut missed the mark as Farrel dodged to the side and spun, arcing his own blade toward Fisher's shoulder. The big man's arm swung out to block the blow. For all his size, Fisher moved like a snake.

Sweat ran down Farrel's neck at the realization that this had evolved into real battle. Fisher could—and would—kill him with no hesitation.

Farrel avoided Fisher's onslaught for a few moments. But as he began to tire, his movements slowed, reflexes sluggish under the constant, unrelenting attack. A swift thrust aimed at his right shoulder sliced through his shirt and into the flesh. Farrel stumbled back, blood trickling down his arm. A collective sigh whispered through the surrounding men.

Farrel clenched his jaw against the pain and moved in on Fisher again. But the man had done enough damage that lifting his arm sent fresh pain streaking into his hand. His cutlass clattered to the deck in the spasm's wake.

Fisher drew his cutlass up and back in both hands, triumph on his scarred face.

Farrel knew the next blow would take his head.

Chapter 57

Before Eli's lethal swing could connect, Ravyn stepped between them, her own cutlass drawn. The clang of Fisher's blade against hers rang as she easily deflected the blow.

"Enough! Stand down, both of ye." She flicked a glance at Farrel then turned to stare at Fisher. He lowered his weapon, scowling, but stepped back.

One long stride brought her to Farrel. She caught his arm in an unyielding grip. "Come. I'll tend to that wound."

"But—" Farrel tried to hang back. Ravyn refused to surrender her hold as she drew him toward their cabins.

"I said, enough." She looked at Fisher over her shoulder. "Ye've made your point, Eli. Return to your duties."

"Aye, aye, Cap'n. Back at it, ye lazy gomerels." His surly growl sent the men scattering.

Ravyn didn't speak, her profile cast in tight lines. She pushed Farrel into his quarters and followed, lighting the lantern over his desk. Pouring water into the washbasin, she carried it to the bunk, peeled the shirt from his shoulder and wiped away the blood to examine the injury.

"It's nothing," Farrel muttered. "A flesh wound."

"Enough to slow your hand." She lifted her eyes, shimmering with unshed tears. "Does ye not see? Ye're far from ready."

"Bind my shoulder. I'll keep practicing. I'm not leaving."

"Ye're a mulish man, Farrel McQuaid."

"Thanks." He slipped the fingers of his good hand under her chin to raise her face. "One of my better qualities."

"Will 'e live?"

Fisher's sarcastic rumble brought their attention to the open door. Ravyn sighed, straightening.

"No thanks to you," Farrel answered. "I know you hate my guts, but you'd better get used to me hanging around."

"Aye, well, hangin'd be too good fer ye." Fisher leaned his massive frame against the doorjamb, folding his arms on his chest. "I knows more fittin' ways to dispose of a cur like ye."

"Eli, I said, enough." Ravyn shot to her feet. "There'll be no disposing of anyone."

"Ye wants to spoil me fun?" Malice twisted Fisher's features. "Ye said ye wanted 'im gone. I can oblige ye so ye ne'er 'as to see 'is soppish face again."

Farrel repressed a crude response. With Ravyn's back to him, he couldn't assess her expression. The tight hunch of her shoulders told him all he needed to know.

"You don't have the Captain's permission." Not the comeback he wanted, but he hoped it reminded Fisher of his place.

"And who can say but ye chose to leave in the dead o' night? I needs no permission fer that." Hatred flashed across Fisher's eyes. Straightening, he turned and stalked away.

"Well, I feel safe." Farrel glanced at his shoulder where blood seeped from the wound. "Not." He looked up at Ravyn. She faced him, lips drawn in a thin line. "He doesn't scare me."

"Ye'd be safer—."

"No." Farrel rose. "If I go anywhere, it's to bed. Here." He grinned, trying to lighten the mood. "With you, maybe?"

She seemed about to object, then her shoulders slumped. "It might be best." She strode to close the cabin door and threw the bolt into place. "Not better than sending ye ashore. But if ye're determined to put yourself in danger..." Her eyes pleaded for him to reconsider.

He squared his shoulders, ignoring the stab of pain rippling down his arm. Taking the few steps separating them, he stroked her cheek with his thumb. "I love you, Ravyn. No one is coming between us. Not Fisher, nor Flemington."

Bending, he captured her mouth, setting free the wonder of this newfound love in the tender savoring of her lips. Her tension melted as she responded, body relaxing against him. He slipped his good arm around to pull her away from the door. "Let's go to bed."

"Your shoulder." The breath of her words on his mouth sent a tremor through him that brought him hard in his breeches.

"Damn the shoulder." To prove his forbearance, he scooped her into his arms. The wound twinged in protest but he ignored it, carrying Ravyn to the bunk.

"I'm still vexed with ye." The shimmer in her eyes, however, spoke of a different passion.

"Nothing like a little healthy anger to add fire to the make-up sex."

She sighed. "I swear ye does most of your thinking with your wee staff."

"Hey! No insults, woman. I prefer to call it my blade of glory." He lowered himself beside her and drew her into his embrace.

"Impudent oaf."

"Tempting vixen." He reclaimed her mouth, making promises he fully intended to keep.

Ravyn listened to the shouts of the men from the outer deck. With hours yet until dawn, she lay in the darkness, enfolded in Farrel's arms. He slept, breaths slow and even along her temple. Against all reason, they had made love, passion soaring between them with the ease of an eagle's wings lifting it into the sky. She did not regret the interlude, though recalling her resolve to see him safe ashore, her mouth tightened in self-directed recrimination. Her plan had gone so awry, Eli's threat compelling her to cast caution to the wind.

She edged away from Farrel. Sitting up, she looked for her discarded clothing. It lay scattered amongst Farrel's. Quietly, she dressed. Leaving the cabin, she drew the door softly shut. She stood for a moment, checking her surroundings. All seemed in order, some men adjusting the rigging lines while others secured the trappings of the deck.

"Cap'n?" Mr. Hennessey descended from the quarterdeck. "We be nearly set."

"Good. We'll leave afore the dawn."

The first lieutenant regarded her with head slightly canted, lips quirking into a grin.

"What?" she asked.

"Will ye be retirin' again?"

"You bet she will."

Ravyn swiveled.

Farrel stood in the open doorway, clad in his breeches. "The captain needs her rest." Ravyn swore he winked in Mr. Hennessey's direction.

"I needs to oversee preparations." She turned back to the young officer. "Ye should be retiring yourself."

"Nay, I'm hale and hearty and ready for the next adventure." He saluted her. "Mr. McQuaid has the right of it." He returned Farrel's wink with a chuckle. "And ye'd best be seein' the cap'n gets some sleep, sir."

"She will." Farrel took her arm. "Come back to bed. You're my insurance against the threat of bodily harm."

She followed the direction of his gaze, seeing Mr. Fisher suspended in the shrouds, a line dangling from his hand. He scowled, and a low growl rumbled up from his chest.

"See? I told you. Guard dog." Farrel steered her toward his cabin. "Even sounds like one."

"Ye bleedin' sod." The thump of Fisher's feet hitting the deck brought them back around. He stood with fists raised. "I'd pummel ye to a weepin' mess if ye wasn't hidin' behind a woman."

"Mr. Fisher." Ravyn wrenched her arm from Farrel's grip and strode to the bo'sun. Fury churned in her gut. "Remember your place, sir. I am more than a woman on this ship. I am your captain, and I will not bear your insults."

"But ye'll bear 'is bastard if ye keeps crawlin' into 'is bed. Ye'll rue the day ye let 'im 'tween yer legs."

The crack of her hand striking his cheek resounded like a whiplash. All talk around them ceased, and Ravyn became aware of the utter silence. Even the water seemed to still its restless whispering.

"If we wasn't preparing to sail, I'd be sending ye to the brig with orders for a flogging at dawn," she seethed through stiff lips, ignoring her stinging palm, "I may yet, once we're under way." Turning, she strode back to Farrel. "Come, Mr. McQuaid." She took his arm and pulled him back to his cabin.

Farrel leaned against the door once it closed behind them. "That was impressive. Hope his face hurts like hell."

Ravyn rounded on him. "Ye see what ye've done? If Eli doesn't respect me, how can the rest of the men?"

Farrel ran a hand over his tousled hair, wincing at the movement of his wounded shoulder.

"Damn and blast." She took his arm again and pushed him toward the bunk. "We ne'er did bind that wound."

He sat down, peering at the long slash. Blood had crusted over his shoulder and fallen onto the bed sheet in dark blotches. Fresh blood trickled along his arm and chest from the reopened gash.

Muttering, Ravyn fetched the pitcher and poured water into the ewer. She cleaned the wound carefully then snatched up his shirt from the floor and tore it into strips.

"Hey! I have few enough clothes without you using them for bandages. Guess I should've bought more while we were here."

"Ye could acquire them on the morrow."

"Nice try. Not happening." He sat still while she wrapped the strips around his shoulder and tied them in place.

"I should fetch Dr. Page. This needs to be better cleansed." She stepped back, giving her work a critical examination. "Mayhap stitched, as well."

"It's not that deep. I'll have the doc inspect your handiwork in the morning." He drew her to sit beside him. "Don't worry about the men. You haven't lost their respect."

"They'll be seeing me different now that ye've taken me to your bed." Averting her face, she studied the scrollwork around the edge of his desk. "If ye gets me with child..." Tightness in her chest strangled the words. "How can I be the captain I ought?" The words sounded husky and uncertain, even to her.

Farrel curled his hand around her cheek and drew her to face him. "I know the perception of a woman's place is different here than in my era. But there's no reason you can't have a family and be just as strong a leader as you are now. I've known women in high-powered positions who had children. They didn't let that interfere with their jobs. Neither should you." His eyes glowed with tenderness. "But would you mind? Having a baby, I mean?" His voice grew soft, wistful, and his features echoed his pensive tone. "My baby?"

Pain, sharp as a knife, stabbed into her chest. She lifted her hand and pressed it over her heart. Did she want another child? Could she even conceive? Her breath caught in her throat as she stared into Farrel's eyes. She had no inkling at that moment what she wanted. Save to find Will Flemington and end his blighted existence. She let her hand fall. "This is not the time for such thoughts. Are...are there ways of preventing it?"

"In this time? I'm not sure." Farrel released her and turned away, but she saw the flicker of disappointment in his eyes. "In my time, a pill solved that dilemma. Now... I don't know." His profiled expression was neutral. "You want me to ask Doc?"

Ravyn rose and paced to the window, staring out over the harbor. "There is one sure way I know." Turning, she studied him.

"Abstinence." He sighed. "Guess I never considered the consequences." He met her eyes across the room. "It may already be too late."

Ravyn's heart gave a hard thump, and her lungs constricted. She might already be with child. A flutter of dread quivered through her belly. A baby. Farrel's child. She lowered a trembling hand to her abdomen.

"Ravyn." Farrel's hands came to rest on her shoulders. "If you're pregnant, I'll do the right thing. I won't leave you."

"But what—" She had to swallow the lump in her throat before she could continue. "What if ye return to your time?"

"If it hasn't happened by now, it's not likely to." He touched his lips to her earlobe. "Besides, I'm not going anywhere without you. Or my child, if one exists."

"But what if the choice is taken from ye?" She turned to look into his face. Swamped in her own emotions, she could not fathom his.

"Let's take this one day at a time, okay?" Bending, he brushed a light kiss across her lips. "Now, just to be on the safe side..." He moved to the Markses' trunks by his desk. Using his good hand, he dragged the biggest to the door and pushed it against the panel. "That bolt might be sound, but I don't trust Fisher any further than I could throw him. With my luck, he'd land right back on me."

She couldn't repress a grin. "So ye're holding me prisoner now."

Farrel chuckled. "Guess so. It raises interesting possibilities."

"Farrel..."

He held up a hand. "No more romping tonight. I'm wiped. You must be, too."

"Aye. Mr. Hennessey has things well in hand, so I'll leave him to it."

When they lay together, her back to his chest and Farrel's arm curled around her waist, she relaxed, borne down by the weight of exhaustion. So much had happened. Farrel had declared himself and raised the possibility of a child. Though that prospect filled her with an ache torn between fear and longing, she could not dwell on it tonight, nor even on the morrow.

It was a long time before she slept. She felt the lurch of the ship as the sails caught the wind and pulled from the harbor, heard the shouts of the men as they adjusted the rigging lines.

She couldn't help but wish Farrel had stayed in Halifax. Safe. Protected. A contrary part of her rejoiced that he rested warm at her back. She wrapped her hand around his, praying for this voyage to end swiftly. If she had a future with Farrel, she wanted it to be free of the chains from her past. Free of the threat and the terrible memories of Will Flemington, if that were possible. And even if total escape weren't possible, at least she had Farrel to assuage her fears and give her peace.

If they survived.

Chapter 58

Farrel gazed out his cabin window as the sun rose, casting shivering golden reflections along the restless water. The start of a new day. For him, a fresh beginning in having found—and recognized—deep, all-encompassing love. He breathed in the clean ocean air, more relaxed and at peace than he could recall in a long time.

He'd been awake for a while, his throbbing shoulder hindering further sleep. The movement of the ship under sail sent relief through him. Ravyn wouldn't be putting him off now.

His gaze shifted to where she lay with a hand tucked under her cheek and the other on the coverlet. He jumped as a fist pounded against the door.

"McQuaid." Fisher's bellow brought Ravyn bolt upright, the cover clutched to her chest. "When're ye settin' the Cap'n loose?"

"I'm keeping her here for the whole voyage."

"Ye wicked, lustin' blighter," Fisher growled loud enough to be heard through the thick panel. "Ye'd best be openin' this bloody door."

"What if the captain doesn't want me to?"

"Farrel, belay." Ravyn dropped the cover and rose. "I needs to be on deck."

"Maybe we should have breakfast in bed. Lunch, too. And dinner..."

She lifted her chin. "Ye're a terrible man, Farrel McQuaid." She snatched up her breeches from the floor and pulled them on over the shirt she'd slept in. "I has to get to my tasks."

"Spoilsport." A grin accompanied the accusation.

She made a sound of frustration. "The men'll be thinking their captain no better than a harlot, regardless."

"You need me to make an honest woman of you?" Farrel gave the idea serious consideration. "Mrs. McQuaid. Or would you still want it to be

Captain?"

"I've no inkling what I want." She tugged her waistcoat on. "I wanted ye ashore, then I wanted ye inside me." She gave her head a shake. "I'm still vexed with ye, sir."

"Mmm. If that was vexed, I might not survive happy." He stepped forward and turned her face up for a quick kiss. "You're a spitfire. My spitfire."

"Aye, well, Madman Flemington might have a thing or two to say as to that." A shiver passed through her.

"Right. My training. Best get to it after breakfast."

"After the doctor inspects your wound. Ye may have to rest that shoulder."

"Not if we're going into battle. I'll work through the pain."

He could not assess the expression that tightened her jaw and creased her brow. If it was doubt, he vowed to prove her wrong, no matter what it took.

"I need your advice." Farrel sat on a chair in the surgery, shirt tossed over the table top with its ominous dark stains in the worn wood. Dr. Page removed the makeshift bandage and proceeded to probe the wound. Farrel winced.

"Aye, well, I'd be advisin' ye avoid crossin' blades with Mr. Fisher." The doctor moved to the counter and returned with a threaded needle. "'Tis not a deep wound, but I'm thinking a few stitches would prevent ye openin' it again if ye insists on keeping up the swordplay."

"I have to." Farrel turned his gaze to the porthole, wishing for a better anesthetic than the whiskey Dr. Page poured over his shoulder. Drinking it would likely do more good. "That's not the advice I need." He paused, gritting his teeth against the hard prick of the needle and the nausea generated by the thread drawing the edges of the slash together. "This is kind of...delicate." He drew a hissing breath at the second stitch. "I need to know how to keep Ravyn from getting pregnant."

The doctor paused. Farrel glanced over his shoulder. Dr. Page stood with the needle in mid-air, grizzled brows drawn in a frown.

"I...I mean, I have nothing to use myself, so I just wondered..." He let the sentence trail off as Dr. Page's scowl deepened and he returned his attention to the stitching.

"There be one sure way of preventin' it." The doctor stabbed the needle through Farrel's skin. He grunted at the deliberate rough pinch. "That be keepin' yer rod in yer trousers."

"But is there nothing we could use? Some kind of... sheath? Or something for Ravyn?"

Intent on his work, Dr. Page didn't answer. Farrel maintained silence with gritted teeth. This wasn't as bad as the whipping but ranked a close second.

The physician knotted the thread and cut it before he spoke. "We keep no French letters aboard. 'Tis something more likely acquired ashore when the men visit the ladies."

French letters. Right. Farrel should have remembered the archaic term for condoms.

"As fer the Cap'n..." Dr. Page gathered his supplies and returned them to the counter. Opening a cupboard, he took out a wad of yellow sponge. Tearing a small piece off, about half the size of a golf ball, he held it out to Farrel. "Ye could give her this, along with some vinegar to soak it in. If she puts it in her body, the vinegar should kill yer seed afore it can enter her womb."

Farrel accepted the offering, staring at the sponge. "Vinegar, huh? Not exactly aromatic."

"Aye, well, ye could try whiskey or undiluted rum instead. More to yer taste, mayhap?"

Farrel hoped the warmth rising to his face wasn't a blush. The doctor's chuckle didn't reassure him.

"Fer a man who has a way with our cap'n, ye seems to know little about a woman's private issues."

He would have known what to do in his own time, but he couldn't share that with Dr. Page. "Maybe you should take this to her and explain—"

Dr. Page snorted. "I'll not be talkin' to her about such delicacies. I knows tendin' wounds, cuttin' off rotting limbs and curing fevers. Woman troubles I has no dealin's with. Ye're her man, ye do the talking." Dr. Page fetched a fresh bandage and wrapped Farrel's shoulder. "Now, take care with that wound. And our cap'n. We needs her well and strong."

"We have to talk."

Ravyn turned, lifting her finger from the chart of the Caribbean she had been studying. The great cabin was empty but for herself and Farrel.

"Aye?" She leaned against the table, arms folded on her chest. She wondered at Farrel's discomfited expression. He should be elated, having gotten his way about staying aboard. Her gaze shifted to the bulk of the bandage visible beneath his shirt.

"I spoke to Dr. Page about how we might prevent a pregnancy. That is, if it hasn't already happened." His look of discomfort intensified.

She straightened, gaze lowering to the floor, not sure she wanted to have this conversation. "Did he suggest we not engage in that particular activity?"

"He did. And if it's what you want..."

His hesitation had her looking up. His eyes held hers, the longing in them clear. She hoped she didn't look as doe-eyed in return. She resisted a strong impulse to step closer.

"So, what else did he suggest, then?"

"This." He opened his hand. "Apparently, if we soak it in vinegar..." The color in his face deepened to a sunburned red.

"Are ye sayin' I should put that in my..." Heat rose to her face. "I think not."

"But...short of not making love..."

"I heard some of the women talkin' in the past, saying that their men would...pull out afore they spilled."

"The withdrawal method. Not very reliable." Farrel glanced down at his still opened hand then closed his fist around the sponge. "So, that's it? We abstain."

Ravyn wanted to kiss away the disappointment that tightened his mouth. Instead, she looked past him.

"Mayhap that would be best." She turned back to the table and rolled up the chart. "I am grateful for what ye've given me, but I won't risk conceivin' a child. At least, not now." She added the last to herself.

Farrel's heavy footsteps crossed the cabin and the door thumped shut.

Regret surfaced in the sting of tears. Making love with Farrel had become the sweetest joy. Denying herself—and him—that soul-deep comfort would be the greatest pain. But until they found Flemington and dispatched him, there could be no true rest for her. And knowing she must somehow protect Farrel from the peril he faced as her lover—

She shook her head, hands clenching tighter around the parchment roll. Distancing herself was the only solution if he insisted on staying aboard. That, or finding a way to yet get him off the *Retribution* afore they reached the southern seas...

Passing her tongue across her lips, she tasted a salty trace of tears.

Above all else, she must keep Farrel safe. And alive.

The winds turned fickle over the next days. Though they should have reached Massachusetts, no matter how the sails were trimmed or how often, the wind changed direction or died for hours at a time. It pushed them further out to sea rather than south. No sign of pirates, though they crossed paths with other British privateers and a few Royal Navy vessels.

During the afternoon of the seventh day out, a cry came from the crow's nest.

"Ahoy! Ship to starboard. She's aflame!"

Ravyn ran to the rail. The day had clouded over, but the gray billows failed to obscure black plumes roiling off the water. Though still distant, she saw the orange flicker of flames and heard their crackle. A mast split with a sharp snap and plunged over the side.

"God's breath," she whispered. Hands fell onto her shoulders, and she glanced at Farrel. He stared at the tragedy in progress, the color drained from his face. She pulled away, heading for the helm. "About ship."

Mr. Lancaster threw her a worried glance but swung the wheel to turn toward the burning wreck. Other men scrambled up the ratlines to redirect the sails.

"All hands on deck," Ravyn called. "Doctors, make ready the surgery."

As they drew nearer, objects floating in the water came into view. Closer still, much of the debris revealed itself as bodies, some missing limbs, others, heads, a few barely recognizable as human. They bobbed amidst the ship's wreckage, staining the swells red and tipping the waves frothy pink.

The ship's hull sank deeper, hissing steam. The fire was burning out, more smoke than flame now. Visible between the drifting black clouds, Ravyn glimpsed broken masts and shattered rails. Holes gaped in the vessel's side like mouths crying out to the heavens. She coughed in the smoke-laden air and rejoined Farrel at the rail. He couldn't tear his gaze from the devastation despite a greenish hue to his skin.

"Sweet Jesus," he whispered when she stood at his side. "Is that...a child?"

The body, smaller than the rest, floated on its back, arms flung out, head nearly severed, mouth agape in a frozen scream. Most likely the cabin boy, fair-haired, like Liam, mayhap a little older. Despite the waves washing over him, blood stained his clothing in large, dark blotches. "Aye."

"Who could've done this?"

Ravyn would have answered, but a piece of wooden hull bobbing nearby caught her eye. On it, a whole body lay face down. The head moved and one arm twitched, hands clinging to the edge of the makeshift raft.

"Man overboard!" She hurried to the open side of the lower deck. A couple of the hands released one of the smaller skiffs and scrambled into it. Rowing to the debris, they caught the man under his arms, dragging him into the boat.

Blood stained him from chest to groin, making it impossible to tell to what class of crew he belonged. Other hands lowered the canvas sling to hoist the man aboard.

Both doctors arrived, dropping to their knees on each side of the victim. The sailor gasped for breath. Ravyn despaired, recognizing the sound of death rattles. She went to her knees beside Dr. Lorriman.

"Sir. Can ye hear me?"

He struggled to open his eyes, a clouded, unfocused blue. He gave a jerking nod.

"Who attacked your ship?"

"Mad...man. Fl-fleming...ton."

"His ship. What is its name?" The one piece of information she'd been unable to ferret out from any of her sources.

He opened his mouth. A single wracking cough accompanied the gout of blood that spewed from his lips. He tried to draw breath, but managed only a choked gurgle. The last vestige of life faded from his eyes.

Dr. Page pressed fingers to his neck and shook his head. He passed his hand over the dead man's ravaged face to close his eyes.

Ravyn sat back on her heels, consumed by helpless rage. They had missed the devil by scant hours.

"Ravyn?" Farrel assisted her to rise.

"'Twas Flemington." She looked into his blanched face. "Ye sees what he does? We'll find no more living men here." She glanced to the ship. Only the tip of the stern struggled up from the water. Black smoke still churned into the air from the shattered evidence of cannon fire. White steam rolled over it like newly formed fog.

Farrel cursed and took her into his arms. She couldn't decide which of them trembled more.

"We'll give the man a decent burial. As to the rest..." She swung her arm out in a gesture of futility. "The ocean has them now." She pulled away and strode to the helm. "We'll resume our heading south."

"Captain Flynt?" Quincy Donaldson, the *Annabelle*'s Chief Mate, stood at the foot of the steps.

She waited until Mr. Lancaster adjusted their heading before descending. "Aye?"

"Are you certain we can't stay and assist in your search for Flemington? Many of our own countrymen have lost their lives to his brutal tactics."

"I promised Captain Marks to see ye safely delivered. I can't say every extra hand wouldn't be appreciated, but I should like to keep my word."

He nodded but remained tight-lipped. "We're not cowards, Captain. He'd understand."

"I'll think on it." Her gaze shifted to where the ruined ship had disappeared beneath the waves.

"Vengeance is an ugly thing." He accompanied her return to the forecastle. "But I can't say I disagree with your view on the matter." His Virginia drawl became softer and more pronounced as he glanced to Farrel staring over the smoke-limned water. "I've watched Mr. McQuaid these past days. He'll serve you well, if any of you have the chance to survive an encounter with Madman."

"'Tis in my plans. The choice of whether or not ye fight with us may be taken from our hands if we meet up with him on the way."

"We'll stand with you, regardless." He gave a small bow and a quick salute before he walked away.

Chapter 59

"God, that had to be the scariest thing I've ever seen." Farrel took Ravyn into his arms once they were alone in his cabin. He needed to feel the solid living reality of her. "You sure we can't find a nice little place ashore to settle down? Let someone else put an end to him?"

"Ye knows I can't."

He sighed. "I know. But, Jesus, I've never seen such horror. All those mangled bodies. That poor little boy. That dying wretch you pulled from the water."

"And likely more burned to death aboard." She shuddered. "'Tis Flemington's way, leaving one alive long enough to spread word of his brutality. He may have e'en espied us in the distance and let us find the wreck, just to confirm 'twas his handiwork."

"Shit. That close?" Farrel hugged her tighter. "Would he come about to take us down too?"

"The devil alone knows. He may spare us on a whim, but we may not fare so fortunate again. I'll be tellin' Mr. Hennessey to double the watch. If we make it to the Massachusetts cove, I may send Liam with the *Annabelle*'s men to Captain and Mistress Marks for the time bein'."

"Excellent idea. I'd hate to think of anything happening to our little boy."

"What an odd thing to say."

He pressed a kiss to her brow. "Not so odd. I love him as much as I love his surrogate mother."

She gave a soft laugh, her breath warm and wispy against his skin in the open V of his shirt. "Ye're a man of quick affections, Mr. McQuaid. Dare I trust such impulsive emotions to last?"

"Forever. Whether in your time or mine."

The weather proved more in their favor over the next two days, bringing them back to the Massachusetts coastline. Ravyn gathered the *Annabelle*'s men on the afternoon of the planned disembarking, along with Farrel and Mr. Hennessey.

"Mr. Donaldson expressed an interest in staying with us to hunt Flemington." She scanned the faces around the long table. "I'd more like to keep my word to Captain Marks. But for those of ye who do choose to stay, ye'll be given fair compensation."

"Or ye could forfeit your lives with the rest of us," Mr. Hennessey put in judiciously. "Ye've a few hours to think on it."

Ravyn turned to the doctor. "Also, sir, if ye're willing and choose to return to Norfolk, I would ask if ye'd take Liam to Captain and Mistress Marks. I'll send a letter of explanation and hope they will keep him for however long it takes to finish this business."

The doctor nodded. "I'll keep him myself if they are unable. I have no wife to return to—she passed on two years ago—but I have two boys and a little girl awaiting me with my sister and her husband. Save for them, I'd stay."

"And I comprehend your reasons for choosing not to." Ravyn gave a nod. "Then 'tis settled. I'll have Mr. McQuaid draw up the letter."

The men dispersed, but Farrel stayed with Ravyn to compose the correspondence. Together, they packed a ditty bag with Liam's belongings.

The little boy watched with wide, timid eyes. "I'll be missin' Sammy." He hugged the cat so hard Sammy growled and gave a warning hiss. "Can I take 'im with me?"

"Nay, lad, we've nothing for ye to carry him in." Ravyn didn't turn from packing, her heart heavy.

"But-but, what if..." He gave a hitching sob, burying his face against the cat's fur. "I doesn't want Sammy to die."

Ravyn paused, glancing over her shoulder.

"We'll keep him safe." Farrel crouched and passed a hand over the wriggling cat. "I know Sammy's important to you, but you're way more important to us."

"I'm scared. I won't know anyone."

"You know Stuart. And you know Captain and Mrs. Marks." Farrel patted his tear-streaked cheek. "Even if they can't keep you, you've gotten to know

Dr. Lorriman. He has children too. Please, Liam, this is for your own good."

"Ye're going, whether ye wants to or nay. We know what's best."

The boy ceased his mourning, though he refused to let Sammy—or either of them—out of his sight.

When Ravyn chafed at the child being constantly underfoot, Farrel took her aside.

"It's not only Sammy he's afraid of losing. It's us, the people he calls family. He just can't bring himself to say it. That might make it real."

Ravyn nodded, swallowing the lump in her throat as she looked at Liam.

While Farrel helped Liam gather his belongings at the rail, Ravyn called the crew she'd chosen to accompany them for a brief conference. They met what she had to say with exchanged glances of bafflement.

"But, Cap'n..." Mr. Hennessey stared at her with an intensity that made her want to squirm. "Why would ye do this now?"

"I've told ye my reasons. I'll thank ye not to question them." Her chin went up, and she met his bewilderment with calm authority. "Ye'll do as I ask. All of ye."

"I'll not gainsay ye." Mr. Hennessey's jaw clenched. "But I'll not betray a man I consider a friend."

About to reprimand him, Ravyn set her own jaw. She turned a sharp glance to the other men. "Will any more of ye countermand my orders?"

"Nay, Cap'n," they answered in unison.

Though they appeared no less confused, she felt assured of their accord.

As darkness fell, she ascended to the quarterdeck to signal the smugglers. They returned the safe-to-land. A longboat was lowered into the water once the anchor had been cast.

Most of the *Annabelle*'s men opted to stay, though in the end, three who had young families decided to leave with Dr. Lorriman. Farewells were said then the men, along with Ravyn's crew, descended to the vessel. She invited Farrel, making the excuse that he might help if Liam balked at the last minute. She had another reason for taking Farrel. The encounter with the shipwreck had redoubled her fears.

This would not be an easy parting.

The longboat slid onto the stony shore. Two sailors jumped out to pull it from the water.

Farrel stepped out then lifted Liam from the prow. Three men appeared around the base of the cliff, pistols in hand, the leader carrying a lantern. Seeing Ravyn, he gestured his followers to holster the weapons. Farrel released a slow, relieved breath.

"We meet again." The smuggling leader stepped forward, casting a glance over their group. "I'd no inklin' ye was dealin' in human cargo."

Ravyn swept her hand toward the crew of the *Annabelle*. "These men are your compatriots needing to return home."

The leader chuckled and shook his wool-capped head. "The Crown'll be wonderin' why so many are escapin' their prisons if ye keep on."

She returned his laughter. "Aye, well, 'tis but the honoring of a promise I made the captain we brought afore."

He gave a gap-toothed grin. "The innkeeper above will be thinkin' himself well heeled."

"As to that..." Ravyn lifted a sack out of the boat. It clinked with coin. She tossed it to the smuggling captain, and he caught it. "A wee somethin' for your trouble and the men's lodging."

He hefted the sack and nodded. "Crown currency, I'm wagerin'."

"Aye. There should be no difficulty turning it to your Yankee blunt."

"Nay," he agreed with another chuckle. "We're not particular about where the gold comes from, only that it be of good measure."

Ravyn turned toward Liam, who gripped Farrel's hand. "Ye'll be safe, lad. Dr. Lorriman has promised to deliver ye to Captain and Mistress Marks."

Liam's hand tightened.

"It's only for a little while, kiddo." Farrel hunkered down and folded the child's hand in both of his. "You'll have fun with Stuart."

Liam's wide gray eyes shifted to Ravyn. She crouched, and Liam pulled from Farrel to throw himself into her arms, nearly overbalancing her. Righting herself, she hugged him as his arms wound around her neck. "They'll keep ye safe till we come for ye."

"Ye will come back?"

"Of course we will." Farrel laid a hand on the boy's trembling shoulder. "It's gonna be okay." He looked toward the *Annabelle*'s doctor. "Isn't that right?"

"Of course." Dr. Lorriman directed an encouraging smile at Liam. "We'll have a grand adventure along the way."

"You have the letter for Captain Marks?"

"I do." The doctor patted the front of his coat. He proffered a hand. "We owe you and Captain Flynt more than we can ever repay."

Farrel shook his hand. Ravyn straightened to receive the gesture of gratitude. The other men murmured their appreciation.

Dr. Lorriman extended his hand to Liam. The boy stepped reluctantly to slip his hand into the doctor's. They started away, Liam staring back over his shoulder. Suddenly, he pulled free and ran back to throw his arms around Farrel. Touched, Farrel crouched again and hugged him back.

"I'll miss ye," Liam whispered. "Ye're most dear to me heart."

Farrel blinked as moisture stung his eyes. "You're dear to me, too." He held the boy's cheeks. "Now, go on. We have to get back."

As Liam returned to the waiting doctor, Farrel straightened. He watched until the group disappeared around the base of the cliff.

Turning, he faced a row of drawn cutlasses, blades glinting in the light from the lantern Mr. Hennessey held. He brandished no weapon, looking unhappy at the development. The tip of Ravyn's blade hovered a few inches from Farrel.

"Seriously?" He ranged an astonished gaze along the line of men.

"I wants ye to go with Liam." Ravyn's hard tone brought his eyes back to her. "Ye can keep him safe, along with yourself."

"Until when? After you meet up with Flemington?" He spread his arms in frustration. "We settled this when we left Halifax."

"I've changed my mind." Ravyn's eyes glittered in the light. "Once we've dealt with Flemington, we'll fetch the two of ye."

"If you deal with Flemington." Farrel's hands curled into fists. "Dammit, I'm tired of you treating me like I'm as helpless as Liam. What if the pirates kill the lot of you? Or Flemington carts you off to his lair?"

"Aye, and takes ye with me to cut ye up, piece by piece, while he makes me watch?" She shook her head. "Nay. Ye'll go where ye'll be safe."

He stepped closer, until the tip of her cutlass dented his waistcoat. "If you want to leave me, you'll have to wound me. Enough to stop me. And won't that defeat the purpose of ditching me here?"

"Ye'd heal from my wounding," she rasped. "Ye wouldn't from the terrible things he'd do to ye."

"Okay. Go ahead." He lifted his arms in surrender. Their gazes locked, and a flash of anger crossed her eyes. Farrel inched forward, until the cutlass pierced his waistcoat and shirt. The deadly tip rested cold against his stomach. "You might as well. Abandoning me would about kill me anyway."

"Quite the dramatic, aren't ye?" She made no move to dig the blade in deeper. "Why won't ye do as I ask?"

"Because I'm not letting you face him alone." He flicked a glance at the men. "I know you'll be there for her. I want to be there too." He returned a glare to her. "Don't I have the right to decide if I want to put myself in the line of fire?"

The anger in Ravyn's eyes brightened to fury.

The men muttered amongst themselves. After a moment, Mr. Hennessey spoke.

"He has the right of it, Cap'n. We agree he should be free to choose."

Her heated gaze shot to the lieutenant then returned to Farrel as murmurs of agreement rippled through the group. "Are ye plotting a mutiny, Mr. McQuaid?"

A wry grimace twisted his mouth. "Sure am, sweetheart. This time, it looks like I have friends to back me up."

Fisher sneered. "Ye wants ta be cap'n? Ye's naught the mettle nor wits. End 'm now, Cap'n, afore he sets these turncoats agin ye." He cast a contemptuous glower over his shoulder at the crew.

"Nay." Mr. Hennessey shifted, agitation creasing his features. "We're formin' no mutiny, Cap'n, only allowin' the man his place in the world."

"Ye thinks that place should be cap'n?" Fisher returned a fierce look. "Not so long as I has say in the matter."

Palpable tension filled the standoff. Farrel took a cautious risk, hoping to defuse the friction. "Hmm. Captain McQuaid. I kinda like the sound of that." He chuckled, despite a rumbling growl from Fisher, relieved when the other men grinned and echoed his amusement.

Fisher studied him, scowling. He set a hand on Ravyn's arm. She flicked him an affronted glance when he shifted her blade away from Farrel.

"Let the boy 'ave 'is fun." His hard gaze locked on Farrel. "'Tis sure Madman will teach 'im 'is place an' save me the trouble. Green as 'e is, ye'll likely be consignin' 'im to the deep alongside that blackguard."

"Yeah, you'd like that, wouldn't you?" Farrel held the bo'sun's glare. "Maybe I'll put him in his place if you get me ready. If it comes down to it, you don't want her hurt or abducted any more than I do. Like it or not, we're on the same side." Again, he looked at the other crew members then back to Ravyn. "You once told me the crew is your family. Well, they're mine now, too. Even if there is a wicked stepdad in the mix."

Ravyn's gaze flitted from him to Fisher and to the rest of the men as they again muttered agreement.

"I'll keep on trainin' with ye," Mr. Hennessey affirmed, and the others nodded. "We'll get ye ready, Mr. McQuaid." He smiled, hazel eyes twinkling. "No offense meant to ye, Cap'n."

"Let's go home." Farrel started for the longboat. The other men followed, only Ravyn and Fisher hanging back. Farrel turned and beckoned with a lift of his arm. Fisher shrugged his massive shoulders. He took Ravyn's arm and drew her toward the vessel.

Farrel felt giddy with relief. He should be scared stiff, knowing what he did about Flemington. But at least he'd be where he belonged. At Ravyn's side.

They made it a little more than halfway to the ship when he picked up a cutlass from the bottom of the boat and lifted it over his head.

"All for one..." He glanced at his companions. "Anyone here named Dumas?" They all shook their heads. "Good. All for one and one for all."

A roar rose from the crew. Not a great idea when they were carrying out covert activities, but they echoed his enthusiasm in the battle cry.

"What's got into ye, Farrel?" Ravyn regarded him through narrowed eyes. Her hands clenched around the edge of the bench in a white-knuckled grip, her taut posture evident even in the subdued light of the crescent moon creeping over the horizon.

"Nothing but friendly camaraderie, sweetheart."

"Farrel..." Her frown deepened.

"Aw, he's family now, Cap'n." Mr. Hennessey's voice shook with repressed laughter. "Let him call ye what he will." He met the glower she threw him with a grin and a careless shrug.

"Okay." Farrel began a list, curling his fingers in one at a time. "I'll call you beautiful, strong, charming, delightfully funny, sexy as hell—"

"Farrel McQuaid." Her voice rose in outrage.

"Aw, Cap'n, I think 'twas a compliment," Hennessey supplied, still chuckling. "Was it not, sir?"

"Aye. A great compliment indeed." Farrel gave Ravyn a wide smile and a bold wink. "Now, where was I...? Oh, right. Sexy as hell... Wait, I already covered that one." His smile expanded, and he leaned toward Ravyn, speaking in a low tone. "But it's well worth repeating, angel mine."

Chapter 60

*F*arrel watched in uncomfortable silence from a seat on the quarterdeck steps as Ravyn paced the decks. Her boot heels pounded a steady rhythm along the planking and her fist struck the rail in hard punctuation. He flinched at each dull thump. "C'mon, Ravyn. It isn't that bad. Liam will be safe."

She halted, eyes blazing brilliant blue in the pale light of the quarter moon. "But nay ye." She faced him, hands on her hips. "Ye think I've treated ye shabbily, but 'tis only that I fear for ye. Ye saw what Flemington did to that ship. Ye saw the corpses."

"You think I'm not ready?"

Her severe stare spoke volumes.

"Okay, maybe not. I'll keep at it, though." He rose. "But I have something to say to you."

"Lord, ye does more talkin' than women gossiping around the town well," she snapped. "What is it now?"

"Come with me." He ascended the quarterdeck steps. When she joined him, glaring, he lifted his hands to frame his mouth. "Everyone. I want your attention."

The low conversations across the decks ceased until only the creaking of ropes and the snap of the sails in the breeze blended with the ocean's steady wash.

"I have a question for the captain." His voice carried the length of the ship. Some men moved to the lower deck, while others in the rigging clung to the ratlines. "It should be a private matter, but since what happens to the captain affects all aboard, I'm making it public."

He dropped to one knee and took Ravyn's hand, gazing into her bewildered face.

"I love you, Ravyn Flynt, with all my heart, body and soul. You've made my life complete, given me something I thought lost forever—community, companionship, family...love." He lifted her hand and pressed a kiss to first the back then the palm. "I know we're living in uncertain times, so to me it seems the best time to ask this question." He drew a steadying breath. "Will you do me the honor of becoming my wife?"

Ravyn's mouth dropped open, and her hand quivered in his. Had he truly asked her to marry him? She stared at his face, breath barely passing her parted lips. His eyes, oh how they shone. Her heart thudded in her ears. Even the air stilled in breathless anticipation.

Ravyn closed her mouth, love and a pang of sorrow dampening the shock. Though his words answered her wish for his unconditional devotion, she could not ignore the deadly obstacle that blocked their path. She shook her head, blinking back moisture. "Nay, 'tis not the time—"

"It's the perfect time." He pressed her hand in both of his. "We don't know what the future holds. When better than now to validate our love with a firm commitment?" Raising her hand to his lips, he kissed her knuckles. "I love you, Ravyn. I want that to guide us." He stared into her eyes, his own earnest. "I know you love me. If you didn't, you wouldn't care if I live or die. But you do. And I care so much I can't let you go into danger without me. So, I offer you my heart, my soul, and the strength of my body to protect you. Will you accept them?"

Ravyn's chest knotted. His words, spoken with tenderness and conviction, moved her beyond measure. Could she truly turn her back on the depth of his caring? She drew a shaky breath. Nay. 'Twould be foolish to let even the briefest prospect of happiness pass them by.

She fought tears. Futile, as one slipped from her lashes to roll down her cheek.

"Aye. I will accept." She spoke so softly she was sure only he heard. "Should we survive this, I will be your wife."

He surged to his feet, clasping her in his arms, and pressed a fervid kiss to her tremulous lips. The men cheered and clapped, calling ribald comments that brought warmth flooding into her face.

"You've made me the happiest man in any century." He gave her another resounding kiss then turned to the cheering crew. "Break out the grog. Time for a celebration."

"We can't be drinkin' with danger so close." Ravyn shifted in the arm he held around her shoulders. "The men must be sober—"

"They know. Give them this night. We don't know what tomorrow will bring."

From the deck below, Mr. Fisher let out a loud "Harrumph," He stood with hands clasped behind him, his usual scowl uplifted into a grin.

"'Tis well past time ye made an honest woman of 'er, ye bloody reprobate."

Farrel returned his gaze to Ravyn. "I wish we had an official to marry us, here and now. I don't want to wait."

"We'll find a chaplain when we go to port. If we had one on board..." She shrugged, unable to ignore a tug of regret. Though seeming impulsive, her heart echoed Farrel's eagerness to marry. Who knew how much time they would have together afore finding Flemington? No amount of joy could erase that quavering fear. Not for herself so much as for Farrel.

"Forgot that in your recruiting, did you?" Farrel sighed. "Guess the captain can't do the honors, seeing she's the bride." He bent and kissed her forehead. "We'll figure it out."

"Ye could handfast."

Both of them looked at Mr. Fisher.

"Handfast?" Farrel's brow furrowed. "I've heard the term, but I'm not familiar with what it involves."

"'Tis an old ceremony, not so official as marriage by clergy, but more bindin' than a betrothal." Mr. Fisher pinned Farrel with his steely glare. "Since ye's already bedded the lass, 'twould be fittin' to pledge yerself to 'er, and she to ye till we put ashore."

"But... Is there an actual ceremony? Vows?" Farrel looked at Ravyn.

"Aye. 'Tis as Eli says, but I've no inkling what words need be said—"

"I'll show ye on the morrow."

With that cryptic promise, Mr. Fisher stomped away, gesturing to a couple of the lads to follow him into the hold. They returned with kegs of grog.

"I'll do whatever it takes." Farrel hugged her again then accepted two tankards. Giving Ravyn one, he lifted his toward the assembled men. "To a victorious battle and future joy with my beautiful bride-to-be." He touched his cup to Ravyn's. Her heart lurched at the love shining from his eyes. The men echoed his toast, and the celebration commenced.

Ravyn marveled at the lightness of her spirit. She refused to let fear hold reign this night, her heart too filled with love to grant it room.

Their tankards were refilled again and again. Farrel kept her close to his side, whispering sweet promises and heated suggestions in her ear.

"Let's retire for a private celebration." His breath against her ear sent goose bumps rippling over her skin. "Hmm?" The tip of his tongue traced her earlobe, and a shiver rushed through her.

"Farrel..." Though tempted, she wanted to remain alert and watchful. One never knew where Flemington might be hiding or when he would attack. Darkness made an ideal cover.

"C'mon, angel. There's no reason the men can't keep watch while we..." He licked that tender place under her ear, sending a shot of desire to her core.

She squeaked when Farrel scooped her into his arms and started for their cabins.

"You're in charge, Mr. Hennessey," he called over his shoulder, ignoring Ravyn's sputter.

"Aye, aye, sir." Mr. Hennessey made no effort to hide his merriment. "Ye see to your betrothed. We'll heed the watch."

"Good man." Farrel kneed the door of his cabin open to calls and laughter from the men.

"Ye're giddy as a schoolgirl after her first champagne," Ravyn scolded when he set her on her feet.

"So I'm drunk with joy." He shrugged, advancing on her with a smirk. "I've got some of that undiluted rum you're fond of. Meant to use it on the sponge, but maybe we should drink it instead. How 'bout it, angel?"

"Not tonight, sir. We may be facing too much danger on the morrow to be courtin' a headache. Nor does I think I should be encouraging this disposition ye're in."

"Once we're married, I'm teaching you to loosen up." He gave her a broad smile. "Married. Never thought I'd use that word for my situation."

"Aye, well, we've a battle to get past afore that. We should be resting—"

He pulled her into his arms. "Later. First, I'm going to tire you out."

"Blasted man," she muttered, her words muffled as his mouth claimed hers.

"Intoxicating wench," he returned, the response equally stifled.

They didn't speak for a long time after that.

Fisher was already at table when they went for breakfast. A small leather book, worn with age, rested at Farrel's place. Farrel threw Fisher a questioning glance.

"Me Mam and Da handfasted. Ne'er churched, but wedded nonetheless." The man's voice turned gruff. "Mam wrote the words to keep."

Farrel opened the book to pages of flowing script, verses and instructions outlining everything in minute detail. A sentimental keepsake contrary to Fisher's abrasive personality.

Farrel looked up at Fisher. "Who do we get to officiate?"

"If it be yer wish, ye could assign Mr. Hennessey here to do it."

"'Twould be an honor," the first lieutenant murmured with a smile and a nod.

Farrel glanced back at the book. "Okay. Except for...the cord and rings, we're set." He looked at Ravyn with a wider smile. "This is a dress-up occasion."

"But what if we sight Flemington's ship? I can't be fightin' with a dress tangling 'round my legs." Misgiving tightened her mouth.

"If he interrupts my wedding—er, handfasting, he's definitely a dead man." Farrel bared his teeth.

Fisher chuckled. "Aye, well, ye might want to keep a primed pistol tucked in yer trousers, then."

Chapter 61

*R*avyn stepped onto the main deck, her stomach fluttering. She'd chosen a white dress with embroidered sprigs of pink flowers adorning the scooped neckline and skirt. She had marveled at her image in Marianne's mirror. Could the beautiful woman in the glass truly be herself? Captain and woman. Farrel's words filled her with renewed strength and confidence.

Most of the crew crowded on the decks, others suspended in the lower ratlines of the rigging. Mr. Lancaster saluted from the helm. Even the Americans stood at quiet attention.

She ascended to the forecastle, where the lieutenant, Farrel and Mr. Fisher waited. Mr. Hennessey wore his dress uniform of dark blue tail coat and buff breeches, looking handsome and solemn.

The handfasting ceremony book rested atop a barrel. Beside it, she noted with wry amusement, lay the sash Farrel had made her use to tie him up.

As she joined them, Farrel removed his hat and set it behind the book. If he felt as nervous as she, it didn't show. He smiled, his eyes alight.

"You're a vision." He lifted her hand to his lips.

Her skin tingled at the light brush across her knuckles, and her heart constricted with emotion. Though she had met his proposal with uncertainty, this felt right. As though some force beyond their ken had brought them to this juncture.

Mr. Hennessey cleared his throat. "We come together to witness the union of Cap—er, Ravyn and Farrel. Though they have lived oceans—"

"And times," Farrel mouthed, leaning close enough that Ravyn heard the soft words.

"—apart, the universe has brought them before us today. Please face each other and join hands."

As Mr. Hennessey intoned the next lines, he lifted the sash and wound it loosely about their linked hands and arms.

"These are the hands that will love and cherish ye, that will wipe the tears of sorrow and joy from your eyes. These are the hands that will comfort ye in illness, and hold ye when fear or grief wracks your mind. These are the hands that will hold ye tight as ye struggle through difficult times, give ye support and encourage ye to chase your dreams. Together, everything ye wish for can be realized." He tied the ends of the sash in a knot between them.

Ravyn gazed into Farrel's eyes, the tenderness glowing back making it difficult to breathe. She lowered her gaze, remembering how they had used the sash to release her fears.

Mr. Hennessey looked at Farrel. "Farrel, do ye come freely to become the partner of the woman who faces ye?"

"I freely do." His strong affirmation resounded over the decks.

Mr. Hennessey turned to Ravyn. "Ravyn, do ye come freely to become the partner of the man who faces ye?"

"I freely do," Ravyn responded softly. Her chest tightened as she fought unexpected tears.

They repeated the next vows together with frequent glances at the book.

"You cannot possess me for I belong to myself
But while we both wish it,
I give you that which is mine to give.

"You cannot command me for I am a free person
But I shall serve you in those ways you require
And the honeycomb will taste sweeter from my hand.

"I pledge to you that yours will be the name
I say aloud in the night
And whose eyes into which I will smile in the morning."

The thought of waking at Farrel's side as sleep left her every dawn had Ravyn drawing a shaky breath of joy. She could think of no better way to greet each new day.

"I pledge to you the first bite from my meat
And the first drink from my cup.
I pledge to you, my living and my dying, both equally in your care."

That final line sent her heart into a stutter of fear. She had wanted to protect Farrel, to keep him safe, but he, in his passion to defend her, would willingly throw himself into the face of danger. There could be no greater sign of his love than that, even if it did terrify her.

"I will be the shield for your back and you for mine.
I shall not slander you, nor you me.
I shall honor you above all others.

"And when we quarrel, we shall do so in private
And tell no others of our grievances.
These are my vows to you.
This is a marriage of equals."

Mr. Hennessey laid his hands over theirs.

"These promises ye make by the sun and the moon, by fire and water, by day and by night, by land and by sea. With these vows, ye swear to be full partners, each to the other. If one drops the load, the other will pick it up. If one falls ill, the other will become the caretaker. If one is sad, the other will share the tears. And when one is joyous, the other will celebrate their joy." He lowered his hands. "Who holds the ring?"

Farrel shook his head. "We don't have—"

"I does." Mr. Fisher stepped forward, opening his hand. On his broad, callused palm rested a simple band of gold and silver plaited together.

Ravyn lifted her eyes, astonished. "Where did ye find that?"

Mr. Fisher's gentle smile left him looking oddly vulnerable. "'Twas yer Mam's. Yer da gave it me afore he passed and asked that I keep it fer ye."

Tears filled Ravyn's eyes. "My Mam's?" She lowered her gaze to the ring once more. "And ye ne'er said aught to me?"

"Ye was ne'er a lass fer wearin' baubles. But a bride, e'en a handfasted one, needs a ring." He turned to Farrel. "To seal yer pledge."

Farrel gave a nod. "It'll do until I find my own to give." He turned a bright smile on her. "And it's significant, being your mother's."

"Aye." She barely got the word past the lump in her throat.

"Then proceed." Farrel nodded at Mr. Hennessey.

Mr. Hennessey picked the band up. "May this ring be a symbol of the difficult times, the problems that come into a relationship. It will be like the refiner's fire that drives away the impurities, leaving only the precious gold of your love." He turned Farrel's right hand palm up and set the ring into it. "Farrel, repeat after me."

Without dislodging the sash, Farrel took Ravyn's left hand and slid the band onto her finger, gazing into her eyes. "As a sign of my commitment and the desire of my heart, I give you this ring. May it always be a reminder that I have chosen you above all others and from this day forward, you are my life partner and I am yours."

They rejoined hands, and Mr. Hennessey recited the last words in a low, reverent tone.

"May the road rise to meet ye. May the wind be always at your back. May the sun shine warm upon your face. May the light of friendship guide your paths. And when eternity beckons at the end of a life heaped high with love, may the good Lord embrace ye with the arms that have nurtured ye through your joy filled days. Today, may the Spirit of Love find a dwelling place in your hearts." A smile curved his mouth. "'Tis my honor to pronounce ye life partners." His eyes twinkled as he looked at Farrel. "Farrel, ye may kiss your mate."

They loosened their hands, and Mr. Hennessey pulled the sash from their arms to set it atop the book.

As Farrel embraced her for a long, tender kiss, the decks and ratlines erupted into cheers from the crew.

When Ravyn and Farrel parted, still holding hands, Mr. Hennessey looked from one to the other with a solemn nod. "Congratulations, sir, Cap'n."

"Thank ye." Ravyn looked from him, to Farrel, and then to Mr. Fisher. The man grinned from ear-to-ear, looking as proud as though he truly were her Da.

"Ye'll be takin' proper care o' the Cap'n now." He clapped Farrel on the back hard enough that he staggered.

"That's a promise."

In the great cabin, Cook set out a festive meal. Ravyn fidgeted while they ate, desirous of getting back into her breeches. Though the men on watch reported no unusual sightings, she didn't want to be caught with no time to rid herself of the cumbersome clothing.

Once they had eaten their fill, Farrel leaned in to her. "Let's go change. I can see you're itching to get out of your pretty clothes."

Upon exiting the cabin, they discovered a double row of the men standing along the decks, cutlasses in their hands, points down.

"Raise arms."

The men lifted their cutlasses at the call, holding them with blades pointed to the sky and crossing at their tips to form a long arch.

"Looks like we're getting the honor guard treatment," Farrel murmured. They made their way along the decks under the weapons. Passing the last pair, they turned to admire the formation. One by one, beginning at the great cabin end, the cutlasses lowered to their original positions. Farrel bowed and saluted before scooping Ravyn up into his arms. She gave a squeak of surprise.

"Your place, or mine?"

"Mine. 'Tis where my clothes are, ye foolish man."

"We're going to have to move some things around." He pushed the door open with his boot. Laughter and a few ribald catcalls followed them inside.

Ravyn discovered getting out of her finery much easier than resuming her breeches and shirt. Farrel had other, more interesting ideas.

She started to undo the tiny pearl buttons fastening the front of the dress. Farrel put her hands aside and took over the task with a mischievous smile. Pushing the sleeves from her shoulders, he let the gown rustle to the floor.

"Your turn." He stood still so she could slide his coat from his shoulders. It joined the dress at their feet. Farrel unfastened the tapes securing her petticoats, and the gauzy layers whispered to join their companions.

It continued, each divesting the other of garments, until both stood naked. Farrel swept Ravyn into his arms and set her on the bunk, following her down and easing his weight atop her.

"This is more like it." He claimed her mouth before she could form a witty response.

Farrel made love to her in a slow, leisurely way devoid of urgency. This time, it seemed even their spirits joined in a mystical union, and Ravyn's senses sang with the sweetness. They savored each other, delaying the moment of completion until Ravyn could hold it back no longer. A low cry escaped her at that paramount moment, her body quivering in total surrender. Farrel continued pleasuring her until at last spilling into her with a groan.

They lay quiet, Ravyn cradled in his arms as they drifted from the pinnacle.

Farrel pressed a kiss to her brow and caressed her hair. "You're like a fine wine I can't get enough of, no matter how drunk it makes me. I love you, angel."

"And I love ye," she returned on a sigh. "Ye make me feel...complete. Aye, whole, as I've ne'er felt afore."

He kissed her slowly, thoroughly. "I know I can't take away the bad memories, but I hope you see there's more to living than seeking vengeance. But if that's the closure you need, I won't deny you the right. Probably couldn't, with your stubborn disposition." He kissed her again, arresting the instant of protest that tensed her body. "We do this together. I serve your need as you serve mine. In every way."

Ravyn took his words into her heart, too moved to respond. Instead, she kissed him, pouring her gratitude into the caress.

They dozed for a time then Farrel woke her with wandering hands and lips, lifting her from quiescent fulfillment to tumultuous passion. She should be returning to duty but reminded herself she had another obligation, to please her life's partner. That was the easiest and most gratifying undertaking of all.

It neared dusk as they lay in each other's arms, thoroughly sated.

"I think we should turn my cabin into a sitting room." Farrel bent an arm over his head while he stroked her hair with his other hand. "A pretty settee, a coffee table and footstool. Maybe even a bookcase in place of the desk."

Ravyn laughed. "Next ye'll be wanting to install a fireplace and hearthrug."

Farrel reached around and tweaked her nose. "You're making fun of me. I'm serious." He gave a repining sigh, "But I guess we'd better keep our options open. Liam will need space of his own, and once we have little ones—"

"I would rather not think on that now." She closed her eyes, hoping he hadn't seen the sudden moisture filling them. Yet, rather than inspiring old pain, the notion of children with Farrel stirred longing that swelled into a wistful ache. She could almost hear the echoes of childish laughter from his cabin. But until the matter of Will Flemington was settled, she could not contemplate the happy picture Farrel painted.

"You might not have much choice, seeing we haven't been putting the sponge to good use," Farrel reminded her.

She sat up, struggling to hide the warring emotions that set her stomach churning. "I ought to be getting back on deck."

"Want company?" He ran his hand along her arm, eliciting a shiver and goose bumps in its wake.

"It seems to me your company would be more distraction than help." She rose and strode to the chair where she had left her ship's clothes.

He chuckled. "You might be right." He watched her dress but made no effort to rise.

Finished, she stared at him in the dimming cabin, rumpled covers around his waist, hair loose and tousled about his face, chest bare and oh, so tempting.

He yawned, jaw cracking. "Maybe I'll take a nap. Join you later?"

"Aye. I'd like that." She walked back to the bunk and bent to kiss him. "Just don't be taking my attention from duty."

"Tough call, but I'll try not to." Catching the edges of her waistcoat, he drew her down for another kiss. "Don't let the guys razz you too much."

She caught the meaning of the unfamiliar word and chuckled self-consciously. "Aye, well, they can't be saying much after our handfastin'. Some think it as binding as the church rites." She straightened and gave him a severe look, "And they'd best not be getting on the captain's bad side."

Farrel laughed. "As contented as you look right now, I don't think you have a bad side."

She sniffed. "Men are ruttin' beasts. E'en ye, Professor."

"Mmm. And doesn't ye love it, Cap'n."

She gave his cheek a playful swat, pivoted, and left.

Farrel hadn't given much thought to having a family of his own. He'd been alone for so long, too afraid of losing any more people he cared about to look beyond the superficial. He realized how unfair that had been, both to himself and the women with whom he'd been involved. They had wanted permanence, a depth of commitment he couldn't give, which explained the abrupt end to each relationship.

No more.

Ravyn was his love, his life. Though the fear of losing her still gripped him, he refused to let it rule. He would fight to keep her, no matter what it took.

Will Flemington had—or would—disappear without a trace. Did that mean they would succeed in defeating him? Farrel gripped the sheet in one fisted hand.

It must. He would see it end no other way.

Chapter 62

$\mathcal{F}$arrel squinted along the barrel of the Light Dragoon pistol, sighting the target bobbing in the wake of the *Retribution*'s stern. He held the weapon in both hands and pulled the trigger. His arms jumped with the recoil as a resounding bang split the morning air. The acrid puff of smoke nearly made him sneeze. A tiny geyser shot up from the ocean a foot or so clear of the wooden target with its tar-painted circles.

"Bloody hell, if ye keeps that aim, ye'll be shootin' fish enough to do us the winter." Mr. Poole's growl intensified Farrel's own aggravation.

"If the target didn't bounce around like a bloody porpoise, I might stand a chance of hitting it," he snarled, shaking out the tingling in his arms.

The weapons officer chuckled. "Aye, well, 'tis easy to see ye've ne'er shot a porpoise either. Let the Cap'n show how 'tis done."

Ravyn stepped up beside him. Casting Farrel a sidelong glance and a crooked grin, she held her pistol in one hand, taking aim. Her weapon spewed its ball shot at the spark of the gunpowder. The thwack of it hitting the center of the wood had her lowering the gun with a wider grin.

"Showoff." Farrel leaned over and kissed her.

"Ye can't be doin' that in the midst of battle," Mr. Poole shouted. "Focus, Mr. McQuaid. And nay on yer wee wife."

Ravyn shot the officer a reproachful look, but the smile still curled her lips.

Farrel had spent the morning learning how to use and maintain the pistol. Ropes tied to the stern rail pulled the target on a raft a distance comparable to the separation of two ships at broadsides.

"We has to be ready to shoot enemy boarders," Mr. Poole said. "Once they set foot on our decks, we'll be fightin' hand-to-hand. Felling 'em afore they gets here saves trouble and lives."

Farrel nodded grimly. The thought of taking a life held no appeal, but when he mulled over what could happen if they didn't fire first, his initial hesitation turned to rock-steady resolve. Kill or be killed, the first rule of survival.

Mr. Poole gestured to the loading materials laid out on a barrel top. "Now, reload like I showed ye."

He concentrated on performing each step with care. Done, he approached the rail once more, gripping the pistol in both hands. He took aim at the bobbing target, steeling himself for the recoil as he pulled the trigger. This time he was rewarded by a satisfying thunk as the ball connected with the edge of the target, spinning it in the mooring ropes.

"Yes!" He pumped a fist in the air.

"Ye just nicked 'im, lad. Won't stop 'im but fer a second or two." Mr. Poole stood with arms folded on his barrel chest. "Ye'll keep at it till ye hits the center mark. That's 'is heart."

"Aiming takes time, though, doesn't it?" Farrel returned to the barrel to reload.

"Aye. Ye won't be aimin' save in the general direction, but if ye can hit the center target now, ye tends to havin' more luck hittin' yer man rather than the hull behind 'im."

Once finished for the day, and after getting much closer to the center mark, Farrel sat down to clean the gun, a task Mr. Poole said needed doing after each session. Finishing the dismantling, wiping and oiling of each part, he polished the weapon until it gleamed, reassembled it, and set it down with a satisfied smile.

"Ye're improvin' nicely." Ravyn spoke from behind him. He glanced over his shoulder. "We'll make a proper soldier of ye yet."

"Gee, thanks." He rose to face her. "Do you think we'll have to go all the way to the Caribbean? I'm not looking forward to crossing the Bermuda Triangle."

"The...Bermuda Triangle?"

"Right. It hasn't been named yet." He leaned against the rail, staring out over the white-tipped, aqua-green waves. "It's the place where strange things happen. Ships, aircr...ah, flying machines disappear under mysterious circumstances."

"Oh, aye, I know where ye mean now. 'Tis said the devil rules that part of the ocean. And 'tis said the devil looks after his own, so Flemington may well be hiding there. Or he may have sailed north, or e'en toward the Continent." She frowned. "I loathe sailing with no directive. I want to find that vermin and get this done."

He slipped his hand over hers on the rail. "Ditto. If I can't dissuade you, I want it over with." Though, in truth, the uncertainty of the impending battle weighed heavy on his heart.

The capricious wind and prevailing currents sent them as far as Wilmington, North Carolina over the following days. No sighting of pirates, though when they crossed paths with a few American vessels. Ravyn ordered matching colors hoisted.

Farrel returned to teaching when he wasn't practicing pistol or blade training. The purpose of the journey was never far from their minds, keeping Ravyn on edge.

Every man remained on high alert. Tension tainted the air with the heaviness of the increasing heat and humidity. No one spoke of battle, yet she knew it rested at the forefront of every mind, in taut expressions and brooding eyes.

Even questioning the crews of vessels they deemed safe to approach yielded no new information, no recent encounters, only tales similar to their meeting with the burning ship.

Ready ammunition sat by the cannons, with sacks of sand situated along the decks to spread on the planking in the event of bloody battle. Cutlasses remained within easy reach, and baldrics with pistols already loaded.

She intended no enemy to catch them by surprise.

Two days later, they entered the waters of what Farrel had called the Bermuda Triangle. Though the morning dawned sunny, the orb rose a deep, fiery red. The omen bore out as clouds gathered along the southeastern horizon in the early afternoon, scudding across the sky to block the sun with angry metal-gray thunderheads.

A ship emerged on the darkening horizon. It plowed toward the *Retribution* with the unnatural speed of a phantom through heightening waves.

Ravyn studied the vessel, puzzled. How could it advance so rapidly, as though pushed by the storm, when the *Retribution* rode a tailwind toward it? The circularized currents made it possible that the ship rode the directional flow. Still, it closed the distance more quickly than it should.

Ravyn lifted the spyglass. "A Royal Navy sloop-of-war." She lowered the scope. "A Bermudian, one of the Navy's swiftest. She's sailing far from her regular course."

"Unless they be American privateers thinking to fool us," Mr. Hennessey suggested. "What're ye wanting to do, Cap'n?"

"I'm not changing the colors we're flyin'." Her brow furrowed. "There are tricksters aplenty besides the ones we seek. I doesn't like the clouds rolling in, though."

Behind the sloop, lightning arced between the black billows, casting pink-hued light rippling like eerie flames across her sails. The waves swelled, choppier ahead of the storm and foaming against the low-hanging clouds. Ravyn glanced toward the great cabin.

"Best be bringing the lads out. We may need to trim the sails. This looks like a nasty tempest."

"Ye be wanting the cannons manned, Cap'n?"

Ravyn thought for a moment. "Aye, as a precaution."

"Aye, aye." He saluted and strode away.

She headed for the great cabin. "Bad weather coming, along with a Navy sloop-of-war. All hands on deck."

The sailors set slates and chalk aside and grabbed weapons on the way out.

"Is there anything I can do?" Farrel asked.

"Remain here. I'll let ye know otherwise."

She ascended to the foredeck, watching the lighter vessel push closer. Ominous, with sails run out full, the lightning seemed to disgorge the sloop from the bowels of Hell and propel it onward. An irrepressible shiver rippled through her.

She called an order to reef the sails against the driving wind and roughening seas. The mysterious vessel skimmed up the swells and down into the troughs, with no regard to the wind's contrary direction.

Ravyn gripped the rail in whitened knuckles, trying to ignore the warning that churned in her belly. She did not want to unleash cannon fire until certain of the other crew's affiliations. She had no wish to contend her own countrymen.

Too soon, the sloop neared enough to see figures on the deck.

"Ahoy!" A man stood on the forecastle with a speaking trumpet at his mouth. He wore a Naval uniform, but something wasn't right. Over the years, Ravyn had learned to trust her gut when it came to approaching ships. Though this one gave every appearance of being a legitimate British vessel—

the visible men clad in regulation dress, the Navy Union Jack lashing and snapping in the squall—a knot of unease settled in the pit of her stomach. She lifted her hands to return the call.

"Ahoy! Who be ye?"

"H.M.S. *Castellion*. Prepare fer boardin'."

Ravyn considered identifying her allegiance. A few sailors scurried across the sloop's decks, battening down hatches, or so it appeared. "Nay. Stand down. 'Tis too choppy for boarding."

The man ran from the forecastle, shouting, "Cast the grapplin' irons. We're takin' 'er!"

How often had she uttered that same cry? She spun to descend from the quarterdeck.

Her men stood ready with cutlasses and pistols. No time to outrun the sloop or avoid the raid. Her mind whirled as she tried to discern the true nature of the other vessel.

The Ensign flag lowered from the mizzenmast, and in its place ran up a plain red standard.

No mercy.

"Pirates!" She pulled her cutlass from her sash.

One of the lads spread sand over the decks. It was too late to set the powder and load the cannons as grappling lines whizzed through the air. How had they narrowed the gap so swiftly?

The crack of metal on wood brought Ravyn spinning around. Men swarmed onto the decks of the *Retribution*—far more than had occupied the sloop decks only a moment afore. Some wore ill-fitting Royal Navy uniforms, others the ragged attire of common pirates.

She looked to the sloop and froze.

Will Flemington stood, rope in hand, ready to cross. His shaggy black hair whipped in the wind. A wide, wicked grin split his black beard. Even from where she stood, Ravyn saw the penetrating black of his eyes beneath bushy brows.

A spear of fury flared hot in her belly. The moment of reprisal had come.

He swung across, landing on his feet in front of her. An offensive stench rolled off him, caustic enough to curdle milk. Cutlass in hand, he eyed her up and down. His evil grin widened to reveal broken, rotting teeth.

"Found ye at last, me sweet wee puss."

The unwelcome, insulting endearment set fire to her rage. She lunged, weapon raised. He blocked her easily, pushing her sword arm back until the guards met. He leered into her eyes.

"Ye've lost none o' yer fire, girl. I'll be testin' that later."

His foul breath sickened her. Whether the lust lighting his eyes was for her blood or her body, Ravyn couldn't tell.

She shoved him, hard, but he barely budged. Bloody bastard. Forcing her breathing to slow, she twisted away, focusing on the devil incarnate confronting her.

The battle raged around them. Despite the intermittent crack of pistol fire, the clang of blades, or the cries of wounded men, she must not be distracted. Even the thud of falling bodies, whether dead or wounded, mattered not. She dared not take her eyes from this ruthless piece of filth.

Farrel. A stab of fear plunged into her heart. She prayed he would stay in the great cabin. If her crew lost this confrontation, not only would she be at the mercy of this treacherous snake, but Farrel's life would be forfeited. They had to win. There was no other choice.

She trained her thoughts, her skills, to the defense of her ship—and the life of the man she loved.

Pirates? Farrel dropped the slates he had gathered onto the table. Gunshots and the resounding clang of metal filled his ears.

Good God, what was happening out there?

He sprinted for the cabin door. At a glance, he saw all the cutlasses had been taken. A single baldric remained with a lone pistol. He grabbed the loaded gun.

On the deck, bedlam reigned. Lightning flickered, casting surreal light over the gory scene. The air crackled with static. The strong tang of ozone mingled with salt spray and the metallic reek of blood.

The *Retribution*'s crew fought men in Royal Navy uniforms. Confused, Farrel scanned the flashing cutlasses. Dark pools of blood oozed from unmoving bodies on the deck.

He found Fisher's hulking form at the stern, surrounded by opponents. They jabbed and swung at him with merciless precision. The big man held his own, fending them off with two cutlasses. But as quick as he cut one down, two more took their place.

He wasn't where he should be. Protecting the captain.

Farrel's heartbeat kicked into a panicked staccato.

Where was Ravyn?

He glimpsed her in a split-second flare of lightning, between the mainmast and their quarters. Her cutlass flew as she fought off a huge bear of a man. Compared to the black-haired monolith, she looked so tiny, so frail. But the way she wielded her weapon was neither. She slashed in broad sweeps, thrust and leapt back as her opponent blocked and countered her every move.

"Bloody hell." Farrel dashed across the deck, swooping to snatch up a blood-edged cutlass. Ignoring the still body beside it, he zeroed his focus on Ravyn.

Combatants obstructed the way. He swerved around adversaries and blocked weapons. Bodies fell in his path. Desperate, he lifted the pistol, aiming for the huge man.

Then he saw one of the uniform-clad pirates sneaking up behind Ravyn, his blade raised to strike. Farrel swung the pistol and jerked the trigger. A spray of blood burst from the man's head. He dropped to the deck.

Ravyn's head swiveled at the close blast.

The tip of her opponent's blade sliced through her vest and shirt. Blood spurted from her side. She cried out, her hand clapping over the wound as she sank onto the deck.

"Ravyn! No!" Farrel bounded forward, dropping the pistol. The brawny, black-clad man stepped toward him. A wide grin split his beard.

Farrel stopped, teetering on the balls of his feet. Go to Ravyn, or fight the behemoth eying him with predatory eagerness? Did he have a choice?

The barrel-chested man lunged, his cutlass arcing back. Farrel swept his blade up, barely in time to block the swing. The clanging vibration quivered up his arm.

Dear God, Ravyn was right. He didn't have the skills to fight this man.

Mr. Poole's words rang in his head.

'When ye're standin' with a blade at yer throat, ye won't be worryin' as to whether ye're ready or not. Sometimes men learn more in actual battle than by the practicin' of it.'

Right. And some men die.

Farrel's own words haunted him as he blocked another swing. Sweat ran down his face and body, competing with the first spatters of rain. He dared not take his eyes off this fiend even long enough to see if Ravyn lived. The thought that she could be dead ignited rage so powerful it sent a tingling charge through his body.

He knew without being told his opponent's identity.

The notorious "Madman" Will Flemington. Ravyn's rapist.

And now, his nemesis.

Chapter 63

Farrel leapt back, only just escaping Flemington's vicious lunge.

"Look aloft!"

"Sweet Jesus, we be cursed."

Farrel tore his gaze from Flemington, to glimpse combatants gaping up. On the tips of the masts hovered sparking balls of blue light. St. Elmo's fire.

A flicker of movement sent him scrambling back as Flemington came at him. But Farrel's sidelong attention returned to the glimmering spheres. The scintillating one on the mainmast expanded as it slid down, becoming translucent at its center.

Farrel's head whipped around as Flemington attacked again. The pirate tripped on a body that rolled between them on the tilting deck. Flemington fell like a tree, hitting the planking hard. Farrel looked toward Ravyn. She lay with her head lifted, eyes on the St. Elmo's fire.

Alive. Thank God.

A strange shiver rushed through him. It felt like the sting of static electricity, but stronger. He looked again at the ball of light, almost on the deck. Men cried out, shrinking away. Farrel's gaze fixated on it.

In the transparent center, a filmy image materialized of the beach where Ravyn had found him. The charged shimmer gripping him became an irresistible pull. It drew him steps closer to the image.

Was that his way back? Could he walk into the image and emerge on that same shore in his own time? Close enough to reach out and touch the flickering edge, a sizzle of current surged through him.

"Farrel!"

Ravyn's cry brought him swiveling back around.

Flemington had regained his feet and scooped up Ravyn. He held her upright, securing her with one arm. The other hand held his cutlass blade at her throat. Malice glittered in his eyes and manifested in his evil grin. Ravyn's wide gaze fixed on Farrel, her face ashen in the dreary light.

Farrel's chest clenched. No. He shouldn't have to make this choice.

He set his jaw. "Let her go. You have no claim on her."

"Doesn't I?" Flemington nuzzled his beard against Ravyn's cheek. She flinched away. A thin trickle of blood seeped along her neck from under the blade. "She's my woman. I owns 'er maidenhead."

"But not her heart." Farrel took a step forward. "That belongs to me."

Ravyn's lips parted, but she remained still. arms trapped in Flemington's hold. Her hands fisted at her sides. Blood from her wound dripped at her feet.

A glance past Flemington revealed Eli Fisher sneaking across the deck. If Farrel could keep Flemington distracted for a few more seconds...

"Come and get me, you rotten piece of shit. Quit hiding behind a woman and fight like a man."

Flemington let out a roar at the same instant Fisher sprang. He flung one burly arm around Flemington's neck, yanking him into a chokehold. His roar cut off to a strangled growl. He released Ravyn to claw at Fisher's arm. The two being of equal size, he could not free himself. Vicious hatred contorted Fisher's scarred face.

Ravyn stumbled away and collapsed onto the deck. She lay unmoving. Farrel tensed, ready to leap to her defense.

"Aarrggh!" The mangled snarl from Flemington brought some of his men running. They managed to rip Fisher away, calling to their comrades for backup. Fisher sidestepped out of their reach. With one sweep of his weapon, he cut down two men.

The pirates closed in, forcing them away from Flemington. Fisher put his back to Farrel's. "Allow 'em no quarter."

"Ravyn." Farrel tried to see her through the surrounding men.

"Ye'll ne'er 'ave 'er again." Flemington pushed his way into the group. He flicked a glower around the circle. "They's mine, lads. Same as the woman." He sneered, a malicious glare pinning Farrel and Fisher as he brandished his cutlass. "Ye's dead men."

The pirates backed off. Some returned to fighting the *Retribution*'s crew. The remainder flanked their captain.

"Bring it on." Farrel stepped away from Fisher, raising his own cutlass.

Flemington threw his head back and guffawed. "Ye think to cut me down, little man? Well then, let's 'ave at it."

Farrel steeled himself for the buccaneer's next move—a wide blow toward his shoulder. An easy block.

He ducked the next higher swing, aiming his blade toward Flemington's legs. The pirate pulled back, laughing. His cutlass arced through the air, too quick for Farrel to avoid. It ripped through his waistcoat and shirt, scraping across his skin as he flinched away.

Farrel gritted his teeth and dove at Flemington. The pirate retreated a step before raising his weapon for another sweeping arc. This time, he was too close. The razor-honed edge swung toward Farrel's throat.

Ravyn lifted her head but could see nothing beyond the pirates. On hearing Farrel's challenge to Flemington, her heart thudded in terror. She had to save him.

She pushed herself up. The wound sent a spear of pure agony through her. Staggering, she sank to her knees, gasping at the intense throbbing.

Her cutlass lay at the fringe of the largest ball of blue fire. Azure light glimmered over the blade. Gritting her teeth, she dragged herself toward it. Stretching out her hand, she grasped the hilt.

A blaze of sheer, raw energy tore through her, sending her springing upright. The pain of her wound ebbed. A tingle settled into it and sizzled over her body in prickling gooseflesh.

"Stand aside."

Her shout brought the pirates pivoting to her. She raised her still glowing cutlass, pointing the gleaming tip at them. Some of the men skittered away like frightened rats. The others stood immobilized, mouths agape, their eyes bulging.

"Witch!" A flash of lightning and the rumble of thunder echoed the rustling whispers. "Run, afore she bespells us."

"Aye, run like the vermin ye are." Ravyn raised her weapon higher, mouth widening into a rictus grin. The buccaneers scattered, tripping over one another.

Her cutlass felt alive in her hands. Surging forward, she threw her weight into a swing that blocked Flemington's blade shy of Farrel's neck.

Farrel jumped away. He stared at her cutlass, amazement and confusion evident in his expression. "How—?"

"She's my woman, wee man. Me pirate queen, witch or nay." A hungry light glittered in Flemington's eyes. Ravyn stepped in front of Farrel,

"She is mine." Farrel swerved around her and closer to Flemington.

"Farrel, this be my battle. My vengeance." A single step brought Ravyn to his side. She looked up at him, summoning command to her eyes. For an instant, Farrel scowled, then inched back. He dipped his head in an indication that he understood.

Flemington made a grab for Ravyn. Farrel sprang and swung his cutlass down two-handed across the pirate's extended arm below the elbow. Flemington howled as blood spewed from the deep wound. Farrel drew the blade through the gash to a grinding scrape against bone.

Flemington yanked his arm against his stomach. Pure madness blazed in his eyes as he stared them down.

"Ye're dead," he bellowed then glared at Ravyn. "And I'll ravish ye till ye screams fer mercy while yer man looks on. Then I'll slice 'im an inch at a time." He bared his teeth at Farrel. "Startin' with 'is wee cock an' balls."

"I'll see ye in hell first." Ravyn sent her blade's tip toward Flemington's chest. He thwarted her, grinning. She met his retaliating swing, blocking him, and danced out of range.

Flemington thrust at her, nearly sending his cutlass through her shoulder.

Farrel yelled, lifting his blade over his head. Flemington's eyes flicked to him.

Ravyn slid her cutlass into Flemington's chest like a hot knife into a block of lard. The brute roared, dropping his weapon and closing his hand around her blade. She shoved it in to the hilt, eyes mere inches from Flemington's. Blood poured from his fist.

She let go and jumped back. Flemington swayed and staggered for a span of ten seconds. Then he fell onto his back like an upended standing stone. The cutlass's tip stabbed into the planking. Even so, he didn't die, his wild eyes looking to the sky as rain pelted him.

Ravyn grabbed Farrel's cutlass. Shrieking, she plunged it into Flemington's groin.

The sound that ripped from his throat pierced the air like a banshee's wail. The keening sound endured for long seconds before it died away, along with the maniacal glitter in Flemington's eyes. He gave one last convulsive shudder, and lay still.

Ravyn stood panting, her heart thumping. It was finished. Will Flemington was dead.

Emotions swept through her, akin to the waves buffeting the ship— relief, triumph, vindication. She need never fear him again, either for herself or Farrel. Satisfaction washed over her at sight of the cutlasses spearing him. The last had been instinctive—clear retribution for the pain and anguish he had caused her.

She drew breath to shout her elation, but a sudden, piercing wrench at her side halted the effort. Instead, her yell of victory erupted as a strangled groan. The mysterious strength rushed from her, leaving her dizzy and weak. The ship spun around her, the rolling deck too unstable to keep her footing. She sank to the boards, her energy spent.

A moan and a thump brought Farrel's gaze to Ravyn. She lay crumpled on the deck, hands clutched over her wound.

Farrel gathered her into his arms and surged to his feet. Turning, he stepped toward the elongated ball of light. Or where it had been. The St. Elmo's fire had vanished, along with his inspiration of taking Ravyn with him to his own time. "Shit."

"Ye employ that word overmuch," Ravyn whispered.

Swallowing his frustration, Farrel lowered his gaze to her ashen face. "Only when warranted, sweetheart." He looked at the lifeless pirate and the cutlasses impaling him. "Remind me to never really piss you off."

Ravyn's attempted laugh ended on a gasp.

He carried her across the deck. The other sailors, both *Retribution*'s men and pirates, stood like statues. Then the men he recognized launched into action, cutting down those he didn't. He wondered how many of *Retribution*'s familiar faces were missing but didn't take time to see.

"Doc Page." He had seen the physician moments before, wielding a cutlass with as much expertise as his mates. "Get over here. Now!"

He set Ravyn on their bunk, careful to keep her wounded side from contacting the bed. She whimpered nonetheless.

"Shh. It'll be okay. Doc'll stitch you up and you'll be fine." He hoped.

He tried pulling her vest aside, then, aggravated, yanked the torn edges apart, He did the same with the shirt as the doctor's footsteps pounded across the floor.

"Get needle and thread. Whiskey too. Make sure everything's sterilized." He barked the instructions without looking up.

"Aye, aye." The doctor's footsteps retreated. Farrel fetched water from the wash basin. He dipped a cloth, cursing that the water wasn't properly boiled, and wiped the blood from the edges of the gash. It looked bad, but not as deep as he feared.

The instant he touched the wound itself, Ravyn did something he'd have sworn she never would. She moaned and passed out.

"Cook had water already boiled," Dr. Page entered with a bowl and his medical kit, a bottle of whiskey tucked under one arm. Farrel took it and poured a liberal amount along the gash, thankful Ravyn wasn't awake. If she hadn't fainted already, she probably would have then.

He stepped back and let Dr. Page take over. The surgeon stitched with a quick, sure hand.

"Do you know how many we lost?"

"A dozen dead. Many more wounded."

"The pirates?" Farrel clenched his jaw.

"All dead. We'll replace them aboard the sloop and set it afire once we've emptied her holds."

"And the St. Elmo's fire?" He couldn't repress a whisper of hope.

"Gone with the rain. The storm veered off to the northeast. Passed us by, thank the Lord. The corposant may have saved a good many of our lad's lives."

And could have taken Farrel home, with Ravyn, had things worked in their favor.

"Help me turn her so I can get her clothes up to bind her."

Farrel lifted her, allowing the doctor to pull up the remnants of her shirt and vest to wrap her in pristine bandages. Though he had closed the wound, spots of red bloomed on the white linen.

"How is the lass?" Fisher had come in without either the doctor or Farrel noticing.

"Stitched up. She's passed out, but mebbe 'tis best for now." Dr. Page stepped back. "'Tis a severe enough wound to put her life in peril."

Farrel turned in time to catch the concern etched on Fisher's craggy face.

"Infection is the greatest risk." He returned his attention to Ravyn. "I don't know how she managed to get up and fight. I thought we were all goners." He glanced back at the bo'sun.

Fisher favored him with one of his fearsome grins. "Ye did well, lad. Her da would be proud o' ye."

Farrel laughed, an explosive sound born of the adrenaline high still gripping him. "She killed Flemington. I just provided him with target practice."

Fisher gave one of his familiar snorting chuckles. "Aye, well, 'twas ye who kept him distrait. If ye hadn't..."

Farrel knew all too well what Ravyn's fate would have been in those callous hands.

He gazed at her as he stroked her hair, his heart almost bursting with love—and terror. It was just wait and hope nothing virulent settled into her wound.

He got Ravyn out of her bloodied clothes and into her oversized shirt, then changed himself. His injury, almost forgotten, was no more than a scratch.

Ravyn developed a fever during the night. Dr. Page and Fisher checked in periodically, but they had other wounded to care for. Farrel felt deep relief when Mr. Hennessey slipped in to apprise him of the casualties. The younger man had become a valued friend.

Farrel kept cool, damp cloths to Ravyn's heated forehead. She didn't wake but muttered and cried in her fevered sleep. Farrel wondered if she dreamed about the battle or the rape, or perhaps both. One time, she clutched her middle, drawing her legs up as though suffering a cramp. Farrel lay beside her and held her, speaking soothing words until she settled again.

So it continued for four days, Ravyn wracked with fever. Farrel cooled her down with frequent sponging, kept her wound clean, changed her bandages and comforted her when the nightmares, or hallucinations, set her thrashing and crying out. The longer she remained heated, the worse her chance of surviving became. He talked to her, cajoled and badgered her, when she sank so completely into herself that he feared for her life.

On the fifth day, Farrel woke from restless sleep to find Ravyn uncommonly still, her respirations dangerously shallow.

"Come back to me, dammit," he whispered, raining kisses on her burning face. "I can't stay here without you. If that portal was my last chance back, how will I survive if you die on me now? Should I have gone? Did my staying cost you your life?" He choked on a sob. "No, I won't believe that. I had to stay. That bastard would've killed you without me." He drew a slow, pain-filled breath. "I don't want that other time. You're all I need, my lifeline, my heart, my soul." He gripped her shoulders, aching to shake her back to consciousness. "I won't let you slip away. You're stronger than this."

Curling beside her, he enfolded her in his arms, aching to absorb the heat radiating from her supine body. Her rasping breaths fell further and further apart.

"Please, don't go. Stay, for me. For us." He stroked her hair, kissed her dry, cracked lips, tried to breathe his own life into her. "We've just found each other. I want a life with you, whatever that brings."

He began to cry, his tears falling onto her burning face.

A soft sound left her lips. "Farrel...love...ye... Good...bye..." Then nothing but her slowing breaths and the labored beat of her heart.

"No, no, no." Farrel hugged her closer, his own heart breaking. A sob burst from him as he buried his face in her hair. "Don't leave me, sweetheart. I need you."

Chapter 64

*R*avyn floated on the edge of Stygian darkness, pain lancing her with every throb of her heart. She wanted peace, stillness, an end to agony. Yet, as she yearned toward that final void, a voice reached through, gripping her heart, refusing to let her go.

Farrel.

His pleas and exhortations restrained her from that final plunge into oblivion. But with his voice came visions—battling Will Flemington, falling victim to his unethical tactics, her body, bloodied and violated, melding with the image of a stillborn babe. Curling into herself with the grief of loss, she cried out.

Heat—so much heat—her body, burning. Was she in Hell?

Coolness soothed her. A tender voice—Farrel's—telling her she was stronger than this. Determined, courageous, stubborn. His love, his lifeline.

Yet, darkness beckoned, promising an end to her suffering. She strained toward it, ready to let it take her.

Farrel's voice called her back, his lips on hers recalling shared pleasures. Warm, wet drops spattered onto her face.

She had to say good-bye, assure him of her love.

"Farrel...love...ye... Good...bye..."

"No, no, no. Don't leave me, sweetheart." His voice quivered, and a sob broke into the next words. "I need you."

With one foot hovering over the abyss, she hesitated.

Was this cowardice, seeking release from her pain? Did Farrel deserve to be left to face the past without her?

Nay, he had been left alone too often afore. No matter the cost, she could not desert him. She pulled her foot back and was yanked once more into agony.

But the greatest torment was hearing Farrel's weeping.

She fought to open her eyes, to reach out to him, but her body seemed frozen, her heart slowing, each breath a labor. Had she waited too long? Would death yet claim her?

Nay. She would not let it.

She swam against the tide, a relentless current threatening to pull her under. But she would not yield. Mayhap weak in body, her mind and her heart yearned toward that distant shore of consciousness.

Love waited for her, holding her fast.

She would not drown.

Her eyes fluttered open. She groaned, pain sharp as a sword piercing her side.

A sword, aye. Images flashed across her mind.

Flemington's blade sinking into her—Farrel, charging to her defense—the strange blue light glowing over her cutlass—plunging her blade into Flemington's chest. Snatching Farrel's to make a more meaningful thrust.

Moaning, she tried to sit up.

"Ravyn? Thank God." Farrel's beard-stubbled face appeared above her. He held her down, one arm across her chest. Dark circles stood out like bruises under his eyes, and deep lines bracketed his mouth.

"Farrel." His name rasped from her parched throat.

He leapt from the bed, returning with a tankard. Slipping an arm around her, he helped her sit up and put the cup to her cracked lips. Cool water trickled down her aching throat. She gasped, pain spearing her side again. Farrel laid her back with the care of delicate porcelain.

He took her face between his hands and kissed her lips, her nose, her eyelids, cheeks and even her ears, until she wanted to bat him away in spite of enjoying the attention.

"My men." Tears slipped from her eyes when he recounted the losses.

Sixteen had expired from their injuries. Farrel assured her their burial at sea two days before was touching. He also told of the captives freed from the pirate's seized ship, along with chests of money, gold bullion and jewels.

"One of the prisoners is a Navy chaplain. He performed the ceremony for our deceased. We put the pirates' bodies on the sloop before we set it on fire."

"Ye burned the *Castellion?*"

"Even the captives agreed to that. They'll say the rest of their crew went down with the ship. As far as history will be concerned, 'Madman' Will Flemington disappeared."

"Like the story in your time."

"True." Farrel chuckled. "I just contributed to my own research."

"Who's been givin' the orders in my stead?"

"Mr. Hennessey. He's quite good at it."

"Aye, well, the men respect him." She touched her side and hissed, then shifted her hand to her abdomen. "Did...did I bleed while I slept? I-I mean, my course...it was due..."

"I think Dr. Page or I would have noticed that. You did draw your legs up once or twice." He frowned. "But you didn't bleed. Not that way."

"I-I dreamed...about my lost babe."

Sympathy creased Farrel's face, and he stroked her hair. "Maybe it's because you lost so much blood with the wound. But still...it would be nice to think a baby might be possible." He looked away, but not before Ravyn saw the hope that flared in his eyes.

"Well, 'tis good to see ye's finally awake. An' what is this about a babe?"

Neither of them noticed Mr. Fisher entering the cabin. He hadn't bothered to knock. The lowering of his bushy brows and pulling of his scar gave him his usual fierce look.

"We're nay certain. It may be that I'm in the family way." Ravyn couldn't help wishing it were true. Surely not, as ill as she had been. A wistful sigh escaped her.

"Then ye'll be wantin' a proper churchin'." He turned. "I'll be fetchin' the padre—"

"No. Wait." Farrel rose. "Ravyn needs a day or two to get her strength back. What you should be fetching is some of Cook's chicken soup."

"Aye, ye has the right of it, I wager." Mr. Fisher's glance went from Farrel to Ravyn. "'Tis glad I am to see ye back with us, lass." He left them alone again.

Soup. Her stomach growled like a wild beast newly awakened. Farrel laughed as he sat down beside her again.

"We'll get you nourished and rested before having a wedding." Farrel's eyes shone as he gazed at her with more love than Ravyn thought she would see in her lifetime.

"Aye." She barely got the word out before he kissed her.

"We'll do it the same as the handfasting. On deck, before the crew—at least the ones we have left." Sorrow shadowed his face. "I think they deserve to see there's still something to look forward to in life."

"Aye." She reached for his hand. "We'll say our vows again before friends."

"No. Family." Farrel kissed her hand then turned to Mr. Fisher returning with a tray bearing a bowl and cup. "I wish I had a ring of my own for the bride."

"Why doesn't ye look in those chests we took? 'Tis sure 'Madman' won't be mindin'." Mr. Fisher grinned.

Ravyn couldn't repress a shudder at the memory of Flemington's evil visage. She wished she could have watched the *Castellion* burn with him on it.

Farrel fed her the soup in tiny spoonfuls. When she'd had enough, he took the tray to the desk.

"I'll go and have a look in those chests. Will you trust my choice?"

"Always. Find me something pretty."

"No ring could ever outshine my Ravyn." He bent and kissed her. "God, I love you, woman."

"And I love ye." She closed her eyes, basking in contentment.

Farrel opened the chest in the cargo hold and stared down at the contents glittering under lamplight. Gold and jewels. How much more stereotypical could a pirate's treasure be?

He dug into the coins, strands of pearls and precious stones, looking for the perfect ring. Then he saw it. Glistening gold and sparkling green. A square-cut emerald set on a gold band.

"I'll be damned." A low laugh escaped him. He hadn't lost Rowena's ring. It had merely gone back to where it was supposed to be in this time and place, just like Andrew's wooden horse. He turned it, squinting at the inside of the band. No date. No faded inscription. Well, by God, he'd fix that once they got to port.

The next day, Ravyn felt much improved. Farrel helped her into the blue muslin gown, minus the corset. He assured her she looked beautiful, though a critical inspection of herself in the mirror showed pinched lines around her mouth and eyes.

There wasn't a dry eye among crew or rescued navy men as she and Farrel said their vows. She sat in a chair from the great cabin, doing her best to ignore the throb in her side. Instead, she focused on the new life she might be carrying. Farrel's child. Though doubting it could be, a small part of her shared Farrel's hope.

"So where will ye set up housekeepin'?" Mr. Hennessey asked over a cup of grog.

"If Mrs. McQuaid agrees, we'll make a home on shore. Some nice little property in Nova Scotia, maybe. I think we need some alone time in lieu of a honeymoon." Farrel beamed at her, defying her to disagree. She didn't, though a small frown puckered her brow. "I won't expect you to give up sailing. We can return to sea when the war is over."

"Ye're a hard man, Farrel McQuaid," she muttered, and he laughed.

"Aye, that I am, Ravyn McQuaid." He bent and whispered in her ear, "Always hard for you, sweetheart." He kissed her amidst clapping and cheering from the crew.

She wondered if she could be content with life on land, away from the familiarity of tilting decks, billowing sails and command of her men. Should she even permit Farrel to choose that life for her? Nay. However, she would allow him his way for a time. Mayhap, after all that had happened, a period of privacy was the ideal curative. She could not resent quiet time with her new husband. But she would make him understand that they functioned as equals, as their handfast vows had stated.

She would not relinquish her tie to the sea. Let him think he had won. In due time, she would take the helm again.

In every way.

Farrel waited a couple of days to tell Ravyn about the vision he'd seen in the St. Elmo's fire and his conclusion that it could have been their gateway to 2013.

"I wanted to take you with me, but it was gone by the time Flemington died. You saw it, didn't you?"

She shook her head. "Nay. I saw the fireball lower to the deck, and my cutlass e'en touched the edge of it. It did seem bigger, but I saw no vision. No shore."

"Nothing?"

"Nay, and I was as close to it as yourself."

Farrel sank back in his chair, seized by sudden heartrending suspicion. If she hadn't been able to see the shore, then maybe she wouldn't have been able to pass through to it. He shuddered. He could have killed her in trying to save her.

"So, why did ye not go back to your old life?"

"And leave you to Flemington?" He leaned forward and took her hands to kiss her knuckles. "Not a chance, sweetheart. The only life I want is here, with you."

But that was all right. As long as Ravyn belonged in this world, so did he.

Chapter 65

*I*t took over a week to reach Norfolk. Storms delayed them, and Farrel and Ravyn chafed at the holdup. Since they couldn't simply sail into the Norfolk harbor, Ravyn chose a secluded cove. Some of the crew rowed them to landfall with the surviving Americans, while *Retribution* rested at anchor further out. The American colors on their flagstaff had saved them from harassment by military and coast guard vessels.

Though far from recovered, Ravyn maintained she could endure the trek. They came upon a village the first day out, where Farrel hired a coach.

The Markses' home stood at the outskirts of Norfolk. Situated on generous acreage, the house of classic red brick Georgian design featured a wide, white-columned portico and a gabled roof.

"The merchant business must be profitable," Farrel remarked as he handed Ravyn down from the coach. She wore one of Marianne's dresses as her breeches irritated her wound. The higher waistlines left her more comfortable. She insisted on wearing her boots, a disparity in appearance that brought a smile to Farrel's lips.

Her belly, formerly flat, had taken on a slight rounding. Bouts of morning sickness, which she detested, Farrel took as a sure sign a baby was on the way.

Marianne answered their knock. She stared at them in shock then threw her arms around Ravyn.

"You're safe. Thank the Lord." She stepped back. "Please, come in."

The bright vestibule opened onto a long hallway leading to French doors. Farrel and Ravyn gazed about in wonder. This was not the home of a man of modest means.

"Liam. How is he?" Ravyn's anxiety darkened her eyes. "Did Dr. Lorriman deliver him?"

"Oh, yes. He's in the back garden with Stuart and Jacynta." Marianne looked Ravyn over more closely. "That gown suits you, Captain."

"Aye, well." Ravyn glanced down at the butter-yellow cotton with its square neck and small puffed sleeves. "I was wounded in battle, and my breeches rub the stitches."

"We're having a baby, too," At Ravyn's reproachful look, Farrel added, "And we're married."

Marianne's hands flew to her mouth and her eyes widened. Then, once again, she hugged Ravyn.

"What is this I hear? Married? And a baby?"

Farrel looked up the curved stairway at one side of the vestibule. Andrew Marks stood halfway down, elegant in buff trousers, white shirt with sleeves rolled up to his elbows, the collar open at the throat, and a blue vest.

"Isn't it wonderful?" Marianne beamed his way before returning her gaze to Ravyn. "I thought she had a glow about her."

Andrew chuckled. "Well, if his lovely wife doesn't, Mr. McQuaid certainly does." He descended to join them. As he reached the bottom of the stairs, the French doors opened. Liam entered with Stuart, and Jacynta carrying Rachel.

"Cap'n! Mr. McQuaid! Ye came back." He dashed down the hall, prepared to throw himself into Ravyn's arms. Farrel stepped in his path and scooped him up.

"Whoa there, kiddo. Careful of the captain. She has a healing wound."

Liam stretched his arms to Ravyn, and she accepted his hug. Once Liam calmed down, Farrel set him on his feet. He hunkered down and laid his hands on the little boy's shoulders.

"We have news. The captain and I are married now. And," he added, giving Ravyn a sidelong look to see her nod, "we have a baby on the way, sometime next spring."

Liam's smile dwindled. "B-but if ye has a baby, what of me?" His eyes glistened with sudden tears as he looked from Farrel to Ravyn.

Farrel patted his shoulder and chuckled. "Let's see. I might have an answer for that." He drew out the moment, stroking his chin as if thinking the matter over. "How would you like it if we adopt you?"

Liam opened his mouth, his lower lip quivering. Then he gave a vigorous nod. "Oh, aye, I'd like that very much." He looked suddenly shy and unsure. "Truly?"

Ravyn ruffled his hair. "Ye'll be the eldest of our children."

Almost dancing with joy, Liam whirled to Marianne and Andrew. "'Tis the grandest thing. I has a family."

"Ye always did." Ravyn bent and pressed a kiss to his unruly curls.

Stuart took Liam by the hand, and the boys followed Jacynta up the stairs.

"Come into the drawing room." Marianne linked her arm with Ravyn's. "I'll have tea brought in." The two women strolled off to a room on the opposite side of the stairs.

Andrew faced Farrel. "You don't believe in wasting time, do you? It seems you've had quite the adventure."

"You don't know the half of it." Farrel shook his head, grimacing. "Between burning ships, storms and pirates, I'm ready for shore leave."

"I want to hear all about it. And we must celebrate your marriage." Andrew gestured the direction Marianne and Ravyn had gone. "Let's join the ladies for brandy."

"Not for Ravyn or your wife. Alcohol isn't good for the babies."

"Ah, yes. You have insights that I don't. Very well. I'm sure the ladies will be content with their tea."

When they entered the drawing room, Marianne and Ravyn sat on a brocaded sofa, a workbasket between them, their heads bent together over some of Marianne's needlework. Ravyn held a tiny bonnet and pair of booties.

"Well, there's a sight I never thought I'd see," Farrel murmured. "They look like old friends."

"I doesn't know how to knit." Ravyn examined the little garments. "'Tis a poor mother I'll be, lackin' such skills."

"I'll teach you, but it means you must stay for a time." Marianne turned wide eyes to Farrel. "Please say you will."

"Yes, you're welcome to stay for as long as you'd like." Andrew handed a snifter to Farrel. "Why not make the winter of it, until after the babies arrive? I'm sure Marianne would appreciate the company." He directed an indulgent smile at his wife.

"We couldn't presume on your generosity." Farrel sipped the liqueur.

"Nonsense. We owe you a great debt. Had we been captured by anyone else, we might have faced a long separation. And you saved our son's life." Andrew clapped a hand on Farrel's shoulder. "Consider it yet another way of saying thank you."

In the end, they decided to prolong their visit. Over the next weeks, the two women developed a kinship Farrel would never have foreseen on the ship. Marianne took Ravyn to her dressmaker, and she soon had a wardrobe befitting any mother-to-be.

Farrel insisted on finding employment to support their stay. Andrew suggested approaching local families seeking a tutor for their children.

Farrel found himself back in the schoolroom, a place welcome and familiar.

Mr. Hennessey and Mr. Fisher visited after *Retribution* went to dry dock for the winter. Along with the trunks of clothing, they delivered proceeds from the July auction and the portion of the take from Flemington's treasure due the captain and clerk. With no prize captures after the *Lady Annabelle*, Ravyn and Farrel felt under no pressure to return north.

"Did you ever tell Marianne about your journey through time?" Farrel asked after Christmas while the two men sat over drinks in Andrew's study.

"No, and I don't think I ever will." Andrew's lips twitched. "My wife wouldn't comprehend such a thing. It's truly a wonder yours accepted your story."

"Well, I did have the camera as proof. Actually, still do, and I keep it charged up." He chuckled. "Guess I can be thankful that solar charger works as long as there's sunshine. One of these days I'll get you to take a photo of us. For posterity." He lifted his glass in a toast. "To futures and pasts and having neither change."

Isaac Elijah McQuaid arrived on a sunny April day in 1814, with the trees in full leaf and flowers blooming in the Markses' garden.

Ravyn went into labor late the prior evening. Despite the midwife's huffing attempts to shoo him from the room, Farrel insisted on staying at Ravyn's side. After listening to her heap curses upon him for hours on end—some familiar, some not, and a colorful few in Gaelic—Farrel was relieved when Isaac rested in Ravyn's arms and she gifted father and son with a radiant smile.

"I shouldn't have said all those terrible things," she confessed as Farrel caressed the baby's silky cheek with one finger.

He looked up, unable to repress a rueful grin. "Oh, I probably deserved a few of them. Just wait till the next time. I'm sure I'll hear them again."

"The next time?" Some of the color drained from her face. "Ye want me to do this again?"

Farrel merely smiled, reaching to stroke her fingers, around which a coil of the baby's dark hair curled. Bending, he kissed her lips, cradling her face with his other hand.

"Ye're a cruel man, Farrel McQuaid." But the gaze she turned to him, along with a crooked smile, shone with love.

The *Retribution* returned for them late in May. Though Andrew and Marianne protested their departure, Farrel felt it best they leave before August, when the British would attack and burn Washington.

Though he wanted to land in Halifax and find a home for them, Ravyn's spirit remained bound to the sea. Few vessels were captured that summer, so Farrel let her have her way on condition that if the war turned ugly, they return to shore.

She was pregnant again before the ship went to dry dock that fall.

They purchased property on the outskirts of Halifax and took rented lodgings until their house was built in the spring. Farrel began tutoring children from the upper echelon of Halifax society, soon establishing himself as a teacher of fine repute.

Though Ravyn had much to learn about domesticity, with the help of an efficient housekeeper and biddable maid, she soon established an agreeable routine.

Their daughter arrived late in July, 1815.

"What shall we name her?" Ravyn gazed tenderly at the baby in her arms. "Would ye mayhap like Julia?"

Though touched by Ravyn's gesture, Farrel shook his head. "Let's call her Rowena." The look of repugnance that passed over Ravyn's face shocked him. "What? You don't like the name?"

"I loathe it. No daughter of mine will be bearin' that hideous name."

"But Ravyn... If it hadn't been for a lovely young woman named Rowena, I might never have met you." Over time, he had come to believe the ring played a crucial role in his journey.

She stared at him, disbelief replacing the revulsion. "When ye said my name sounded made up, ye had it aright. My true name is...Rowena."

Farrel gaped at her, the pieces falling into place.

"My God. She had your eyes, my hair, your husky voice." He laughed. "I think I met our... I don't know how many greats to throw in there, but I think she was—will be our granddaughter in a few generations." He lowered his gaze to the baby's tranquil face. "No, this is Rowena. Her name goes down through our family. Whether butterfly effect or time paradox, it has to be preserved. For us, sweetheart." He bent and kissed her.

Ravyn said no more. After all, who was she to question destiny? She lifted the hand bearing her wedding ring, thinking of the inscription Farrel had set into it when they arrived at Norfolk.

August 1813. Butterflies are carried on Ravyn's wing.

Epilogue

June 10, 2013

$\mathcal{R}$owena McQuaid stared at the emerald ring. A lovely thing, but she couldn't keep it.

Setting the band aside, she studied the trunk passed down through her family, its contents secret from outsiders. No one would believe the treasures it contained.

She opened the lid and picked up a stack of pictures she had printed off more than two years before. One showed a distinguished blond-haired man standing beside a striking black-haired woman, both in Regency-era dress. Her far removed grandparents. They smiled, their hands entwined as they gazed into the lens. Cameras had been unknown when the picture was snapped, but she had a suspicion who might have taken it.

The next one showed the man and woman with a newborn baby, Isaac McQuaid. Underneath it, a sepia photograph from the Victorian era depicted the complete family—mother, father, adopted son and their own four children. At least they had lived a long and surprisingly peril-free life after their ocean adventures.

Rowena picked up a stack of pencil sketches. The first showed a little boy with light curly hair, then another of him as a young man. Liam. A McQuaid, after the couple adopted him. In her efforts to learn more about her family's ancestry, she discovered Liam was Farrel's far removed grandfather— another of her own ancestors.

Liam married Rachel Marks, a fact she found beyond ironic. It boggled her mind to think that Andrew Marks lived in her present day, under another name, a child of five, his journey yet to come. She had given serious thought to trying to locate him, but not knowing his name in this time, had been persuaded by her father to let it go.

Had Farrel ever researched his family history, he would have discovered the connections but not their significance. Liam had never been told Farrel's story. Only the eldest son of each generation from Isaac on, until Rowena's birth, had been privy to the truth. Since Liam was Farrel's progenitor, and a different branch of the family, Farrel had no means of knowing his eventual fate. The secret had been too fantastic to share beyond those responsible for carrying it through the years to its fruition.

Rowena wondered why Farrel had never explored his genealogy. Perhaps the bitterness of his father's desertion had soured the appeal. It seemed the most likely probability, borne out in his writings. His mother had severed connections with the McQuaid family with the move to Ontario.

The last drawing depicted a young, light-haired woman, Julia McQuaid, Farrel's sister. Even knowing her heartbreaking story, Rowena had dared not attempt to change it.

At one time, the chest had held a digital camera, its solar charger, a cell phone and watch, along with a complete set of clothing. Each item had vanished at various times over the past few years. Rowena was glad she'd been able to print the pictures before the camera had gone. It had lain in the trunk for two centuries, the battery dead long before. By some miracle, the memory card survived. A techno-geek friend of hers had managed to download the contents, intact. Then, one day the camera had simply been gone. She could only assume the items disappeared when they came into Farrel's hands.

She set the pictures down and touched the leather-bound books filling the trunk. Carefully she lifted out and opened the final journal. The pages, yellowed and brittle, crumbled around the edges. She would transfer the contents to computer files before they disintegrated completely. Or disappeared.

The ring had been documented in one of the early journals. Even her name was mentioned. That had freaked her out—how could something that hadn't yet happened be documented as reality? After digging through volumes of metaphysical research, she at last came to the conclusion that a time paradox had no rationality.

She knew Farrel struggled with the same complexity. He gave a warning in the last journal, written before he passed the trunk to Isaac:

To those of my future generations;

Though, once knowing what has and will happen, the temptation may be strong to try to prevent or fix the tragedies to come, you must never interfere. Even the death of my beloved sister, one of the greatest sorrows of my life, must come to pass. To change one event, even the smallest, could alter our family's history to the point of erasing us all from existence. One cannot tamper with the butterfly effect without some radical result, whether in the past, present, or future. I have been happy with the life to which I was carried, in all likelihood far happier than I would have been had I never found my Ravyn.

There should be a Rowena in each generation, to keep the name alive until the one responsible for my journey is born. In that way, it can be assured that nothing will be changed or forgotten in the subsequent eras.

To the children still to come, I send my love and my hope that the life I have lived will give cause for celebration in the ensuing years.

Keeping his suggestion in mind, the eldest daughter of the eldest son had borne her name ever since.

Rowena closed the book and set it back in the trunk.

She had already started transcribing the entries. If, as she suspected, the other items returned to their place and time in the order of acquisition, the first of the chronicles would be gone the next night.

While living in Toronto for a year, she had audited some of Farrel's lectures. Watching him pace in long strides behind the podium, hands gesturing as he spoke with passion about history, particularly the War of 1812, it had been easy to imagine him in breeches, boots, a billowy shirt and waistcoat. He reminded her of her older brother, Michael, almost a mirror image of her sibling. If it were true, as the saying went, that everyone had a twin, perhaps it was the result of many far-reaching time paradoxes.

In a few days, he would be reported missing, his rental car abandoned on the bluff above the shore. Her father, a will and estate lawyer, had already looked into filing a familial claim to Farrel's assets and estate, even if it meant having to wait seven years for him to be declared legally dead. Dad would find any loopholes they might require.

She looked forward to visiting Farrel's home in Aurora, Ontario, to seeing his artifact collections and manuscripts. She shared his enthusiasm for history and would see everything preserved as he would have wished it.

She closed the trunk and rose. Maybe someday she could have the journals published. As fiction, of course. But she would be continuing his work in an ironic way.

Passing her bed, she picked up the newspaper with the article about Farrel. Then she gathered the manila envelope containing an early sketch of Ravyn. He would realize what she had given him when he did the drawing. She smiled, imagining his confusion.

With a determined set to her jaw, she picked up her copy of his book. Stuffing it into her tote bag with the envelope and the ring, she headed out for the book signing.

It was time to meet her ancestor and send him on his way.

Acknowledgements

Heartfelt appreciation to the fellow writers who have contributed to the development of this book. To my critique partners, Katie S., Luba H., Leslie G., and Austen (Sandy) L. And to Theresa D., whose critical thinking about character interactions assisted in developing a pivotal scene.

Also, to the many members of my writer's group, the Barrie Writers' Club, for catching and questioning plot development flaws and encouraging me to do as much research as possible on the time period of the story. Though I sometimes arrived home frustrated, under reconsideration, your suggestions often had merit. Thanks for prodding me even when I didn't want to be prodded.

Special thanks to Dan Conlin, maritime historian and museum curator in Halifax, Nova Scotia, whose suggested reading about privateering in the Atlantic during the War of 1812 proved not only helpful, but enlightening on less prominent coverage of an important era in Canadian history.

To my beta readers, Lorraine, Becki and Lauren, many thanks for taking the time to read the whole novel and answer the many questions I posed.

You're all the best!

About the Author

Mary-Lynn Cordero resides in Barrie, Ontario, Canada under a not-so-secret identity. A mother of two and grandmother to four+, she resides with her husband, Fred, and cat, Chloe, who has her owner well trained. (Who knew cats could have such regimented routines?)

Mary-Lynn enjoys a variety of crafts, and (apparently) watches way too much TV.

Contact Information

E-mail
Free.Spirit.Press@hotmail.com

Friend me on Facebook
https://www.facebook.com/Codero.Mary.Lynn

Follow me on Twitter
https://www.twitter.com/MaryLynnCorder1

Please leave a review on Amazon and/or Goodreads. Authors appreciate your support and comments.

www.ingramcontent.com/pod-product-compliance
Lightning Source LLC
Chambersburg PA
CBHW060218030726
47499CB00004B/1104